THE ALTAR

Borgo Press Books by JAMES ARTHUR ANDERSON

The Altar: A Novel of Horror
The Illustrated Ray Bradbury
*Out of the Shadows: A Structuralist Approach to Understanding
the Fiction of H. P. Lovecraft*

THE ALTAR

A NOVEL OF HORROR

JAMES ARTHUR ANDERSON

THE BORGO PRESS
MMXII

THE ALTAR

DEDICATION

For Lynn Llorye

CONTENTS

PROLOGUE
JULY, 2002

Bill Johnson let out the decelerator pedal, lowered the blade and rammed the dozer forward through the tangled grove of blackberry bushes and ragweed. The treads squealed in protest as the big blade crushed forward to gather its load of foliage and blackish earth. Johnson puffed contentedly on a Phillips cigar, a leftover from his daughter Marsha's wedding last weekend. The hot sun scorched his tanned arms, raising up beads of sweat on his forearms as he wrestled with the steering levers to keep his caterpillared beast moving ahead in a straight line.

It was funny, he thought, inhaling the cigar deeply and tasting its fragrance, how this open field of bushes and vines appeared out of nowhere in the middle of acres of thick oaks. It had come as a welcome relief to the construction crew who had spent the past seven weeks cutting and mulching the trees and uprooting the stubborn oak stumps.

Bill guessed that a house probably stood here once, long ago from the looks of it—maybe back as far as Roger Williams' time for all he knew. The dozer would uncover it, though, or at least what was left of its stone foundation. The dozer would uncover it all and by next summer a road would cut the forest in two. Brand new homes and maybe even a shopping plaza would crop up almost overnight, like maggots on a piece of meat. Who knows, he thought. Maybe it would even be a mall someday. He chuckled at the thought—the Chepachet Mall. The mall would be larger than the town. But why not? Once the road was finished, anything was possible. It would only be a half an hour to Route 95, and from there you could get to anywhere in the state in less than an hour.

He took another puff of his cigar, tilted his yellow hard hat over his graying forehead to stop the glare of the sun, then shifted the dozer into reverse for another run. He smiled as he felt the power of the dozer beneath him. To his friends and his family, he was just a small, quiet guy who liked to do paint-by-numbers and drink a beer or two while watching the Boston Red Sox game on TV. But Monday through Friday, eight in the morning until four-thirty in the afternoon, he was ten feet tall riding high on the seat of his twelve-ton black-and-yellow bulldozer. He could do anything.

Intoxicated by the smell of diesel fuel and exhaust fumes, he dropped the blade down again and edged the machine forward, bringing order and civilization to this tract of wasteland in western Rhode Island. It was weird how this, one of America's most densely-populated states (at least that's what they'd taught him at Aldrich Junior High School) still had so much open space that you could lose anything in it. He was thinking about that—and how for all that anybody knew Jimmy Hoffa might be buried right here in this field—when the dozer blade shuddered as it hit something hard. The tractor ground to a halt, the treads going round and round in the earth without moving the machine forward. He frowned as he thought of a turtle flipped over on its back.

"What the hell?"

The cigar popped out of his mouth and fell into the dirt, still only half smoked.

He backed the dozer up, then edged forward again, more carefully this time. He tried to peer into the furrowed earth in front of him as the blade jammed again.

"No old foundation's gonna stop this baby!" He bragged to no one in particular as he charged the dozer forward.

Still, it wouldn't budge.

"Shit!" he said as he put the machine in neutral and climbed down from his perch. Cursing fluently, he walked around the front of the blade to examine the problem. "Must be one hell of a boulder."

He scrambled around the front of the blade and over the wall of dirt he had plowed forward. He looked at the pile of heaped earth and examined the ground carefully, digging into the soft dirt with calloused hands.

It was a rock, all right. But it didn't seem that big. In fact, it stood straight up, like a tall tombstone with only the top edge poking through the dirt. The dozer should have knocked it over easily. As he felt around the edge of the stone, he realized that the thing was polished smooth. And despite the heat, it was cold, almost icy to the touch.

"I'll be dipped in shit," he said, yanking his hand away. It felt as if he had touched something from another world. If it hadn't been so cold, he would have thought he'd touched the very gates of hell. But everyone knew hell was hotter than...well, hotter than hell.

Hot, cold, or whatever, he had hit something very strange. It was a gravestone, he realized. It had to be. And this open place was—or at least once had been—a graveyard. It all made sense now, this clearing in the middle of the woods. A sudden draft chilled his bones. Though he was a practical man who made fun of ghosts and spooks and vampires, he hissed a final curse and turned back towards the bulldozer. The historical people would want to see this, he rationalized as he climbed up on the tread. Meanwhile, his gut feeling told him to just beat it the hell out of this place, beat it out of here before....

Without warning, the dozer's tread leaped to life, crawling backward through the mulch with a sudden life of its own. Johnson gasped once and swore in defiance before the tread pulled him down, down, and under....

He felt his legs go first—intense, flaming pain shot through his entire being as the bones broke and twisted like green tree limbs. Then coldness flooded him where the joint had been. A sticky fluid covered him from the waist down. Vaguely, he wondered if it were blood, then he knew it was much worse.

The sun blinded him as he tried to roll over and crawl. Then he saw a shadow moving forward, impossibly forward, as the blade lowed and aimed directly for him....

He heard a laugh that wasn't his own. In the few seconds he had left he remembered his fallen cigar and, with regret, wished he'd been able to finish it.

PART ONE:
PARADISE LOST

The glory of the One Who moves all things
Penetrates all the universe, reflecting
In one part more and in another part less.

—Dante

When night darkens the streets, then wander forth the sons
of Belial, flown with insolence and wine.

—John Milton

CHAPTER ONE

-1-

"That's the last of them," Erik Hunter said, dropping a cardboard box full of paperback books on the floor.

"Does that mean we're all moved in, Daddy"

Erik smiled easily at his ten-year-old son, then took a slow, deliberate look around the room—around his room. It didn't look like much now. The walls were bare, waiting for painting, wallpaper, and pictures. Boxes of books cluttered the floor. The furniture was all against one wall, waiting to be arranged. But in just a couple of days it would be his special place.

Finally, he had a place of his own, a house of his own and his own work space. He and Vickie had already designed the space—he'd call it the "Thoreau Suite" and would design it with a Walden Pond look reminiscent of his favorite author. Vickie had already created the Thoreau collage, which would cover one wall, and the rest would follow—authentic 1840's antiques, pictures of Walden Pond, and other interesting artifacts. He looked toward the large double window that dominated one wall with a perfect view of the green oak forest that stretched for miles in his backyard, broken only by the small brook that cut the tree line like a knife. Yes, old Henry David would have approved.

It certainly was a far cry from the tiny apartment they'd rented in Providence, and a long way from the gangs, drugs, and violence that plagued any city. Built to his exact specifications, this was his dream house, a perfect place to work and raise a family.

Just then Vickie walked up behind him and slipped her arm around his waist.

"Yeah, Todd, I guess we're all moved in," he replied to his son while holding his wife close.

She brushed a stray lock of brown hair from his face and kissed him gently on the lips. Erik stepped back and was once again astonished at her soft, unassuming beauty which was now blossoming with eight and a half months of pregnancy. He loved the sweet but sexy look of her green eyes and the color of her rosy cheeks, framed by the most gorgeous red hair. She reminded him so much of the redhead from the *X Files* he had lusted after for years before he'd met Vickie. Only, this redhead could quote any of the sixteenth-century poets by heart, if she wished. The fact that she wasn't pretentious about her learning made her even more attractive to him.

"Ok, hot shot," she teased, pushing a stray lock of hair from her own face. "Now that we're moved in, how about unpacking all of this stuff?"

"Unpacking? I thought that was your job."

"Fat chance," she said, patting her oversized belly.

"I would just love to unpack," he said. "But I can't work on an empty stomach."

"Oh, so I suppose you want a seven course meal?"

"Complete with three kinds of wine."

Todd, accustomed to his parents playful teasing, grinned at his Dad.

"That's going to be tough since the refrigerator's empty and everything in the kitchen is packed into boxes. Would you settle for Domino's pizza?"

"Pizza!" Todd squealed. "Yeah! With pepperoni."

"Domino's Pizza? Way out here?"

"There's one right up the road at the plaza? And they deliver."

"Oh boy!" Todd said, jumping up and down.

"So much for living out in the country," Erik said. Even the real Walden Pond now had a McDonald's nearby.

"I already called it in and I can't eat it all by myself. They'll be here any minute."

"Goodie," Todd said, smacking his lips. "I'll go downstairs and wait for the pizza guy to come."

Once his son had gone, Erik turned toward his wife and pulled her close.

"Alone at last," he breathed in her ear.

She giggled like a teenager and kissed him fully on the lips. "You haven't changed one bit."

He furrowed his brows and cocked his head to one side to look at her.

"What do you mean by that?"

"I mean that you're still crazy."

"You didn't expect me to change, did you?" he replied, admiring the way her eyes seemed to dilate when she looked at him. That always caused a shiver of joy to run up his spine.

She caught his look and lowered her eyes as her cheeks flushed.

"Erik...I'm so proud of you. Of all this."

She hugged him close.

"I'm glad," he said. "But don't expect miracles. Once they start filming there's no telling what they'll do to my story. The movie might not look anything like the book."

"I know that. But it's not just the film. The money's sure nice," she added quickly. "But that's not what I mean, either."

He put his hand under her chin and turned her face up so he could look into her eyes again. She met his eyes for a long, lingering moment. Then she turned serious.

"I don't really care about the money. I just want you to be happy. And writing makes you happy, whether you make money or not. I'm just so happy that you can do what you want now and not have to worry about the money. And I'll be able to stay home and take care of the baby."

"Well, *The Star Warrior* isn't exactly Pulitzer Prize material."

"Maybe not. But it was fun. And it'll be a fun movie."

Erik laughed. He'd spent years working on his graduate degree in English and working any menial job he could find while writing "serious" fiction that no publisher would accept. He'd been a steelworker, a book store clerk, a janitor, a private detective, and even a phlebotomist (he still remembered how they'd call him a vampire whenever he told a patient he was there to take blood). The best he'd done was to sell a short story to a tiny university press in Manitoba, Canada that paid him the kingly sum of two dollars and two contributor's copies. He'd taught public school and Vickie had taught part-time at the Community College, trying to make ends meet.

Then in a whirlwind three months he'd written a hack space opera that was published and was now about to be turned into a feature length film that was expected to gross millions. It didn't make any sense.

He shrugged. "I guess it was fun," he said. "At least some people liked it. But the important thing is that I now have the time and money—and space—to work on the kind of book I really want to write. And mostly the time to spend with you and Todd, and soon with Christine, too, when she's born."

Although Vickie admired his self-confidence, Erik knew his serious works were not good enough to be published. When he compared himself to "real" writers like Irving and Updike, he fell far short. His first book had made him plenty of money— but it was merely hack work and he knew it. But now he'd have the time and energy to write and not have to worry about publishing. More importantly, he'd be there for his family, and be able to take care of them.

"Mom!" Todd yelled from downstairs. "The pizza guy's here."

"Be right there," Vickie called back.

Arm in arm, like newlyweds, they walked down the stairs and into the kitchen.

Later, after they'd finished eating, Erik began unpacking the boxes in the living room while Vickie cleaned up the mess. Todd, ever watchful, wanted to help his father out.

"Here, put this empty box over by the door," Erik told him.

As Todd moved the box against the wall, a black cat slipped soundlessly into the room and jumped into it.

"Faith!" Todd squealed. "Where have you been hiding?"

"She's probably getting used to the new house," Erik said as his son stroked the cat's soft fur.

"Dad, I think she's hungry"

"I'd better unpack the cat food," Vickie said from the kitchen. She'd finished with the clean-up and was now unpacking kitchen things.

The doorbell interrupted their work. Vickie walked into the living room as Erik went towards the door.

"That could be Pastor Mark," she said. "He's supposed to stop by."

At first glance, Erik thought the man standing in the doorway was black. Then he recognized the dark features of a Narragansett Indian, whose ancestors occupied Rhode Island before the first white man set foot on the New England shore. Part of Erik's back yard, in fact, abutted Narragansett tribal land.

The stranger's wrinkled, leathery skin betrayed a long and weary life of hard work, as did his coarse, paint-stained Wrangler jeans. His eyes, deep and shiny as obsidian, met Erik's gaze boldly, while his calloused hands clenched a small package wrapped in brown paper.

"Can I help you?" Erik asked.

"Evenin'. My name's Johnny. Johnny Dovecrest. I live just over the brook. I guess that makes us neighbors."

Erik quickly noted that the brook was a good half mile away where it crossed the road. Although new houses and even a small strip mall had recently been built to the south, the reservation occupied land to the north, which made Dovecrest his nearest neighbor in that direction.

"Please come in."

Todd scampered to join his mother, who was drying her hands with a dishtowel.

"My name's Erik Hunter," he said, extending his hand. Dovecrest shook it with deceiving strength for what looked to be a frail old man. "And this is my wife Vickie and my son Todd."

The Indian nodded politely to them both.

"Nice to meet you," Vickie said.

"Pleasure," Dovecrest replied. "I'd like to welcome you to Cheponaug."

"Cheponaug?" Erik asked.

"That's what my ancestors called this place. The name isn't used anymore."

"How interesting," Vickie said. "Thank you very much for the welcome."

Erik felt a chill run down his spine as he looked at the stranger. He exchanged glances with his son and noticed that something about the man bothered Todd, too, as the boy stayed unusually close to Vickie.

"I've brought you a small gift, a token of welcome," he said, holding out a small package.

"Thank you," Erik said.

"It is our custom," Dovecrest said in a voice that left no room for argument. "Please accept it."

Erik self-consciously untied the simple white string and unwrapped the brown paper. Inside the package he found a string of broken quahog shells polished to a fine luster and set in a necklace.

"How beautiful!" Vickie said, stepping forward to admire the trinket. The shells contained intricate polished patterns of blue, violet, and white. Then she took it from Erik and held it up to her neck.

"You don't wear it," Dovecrest explained. "You hang it over your door for protection. It will keep your home free from evil."

Erik frowned and caught his wife's gaze. She obviously thought the old man had been smoking too many peace pipes. He took the trinket back from her.

"Would you like some coffee?" Vickie asked, nervously.

"No. No thank you. I must be going. But please, hang the talisman over your door, the door facing the forest. It will keep away evil spirits."

Then he turned and was gone before Erik could even say goodbye.

-3-

About an hour after Dovecrest had left, Pastor Mark Brian of the Chepachet Baptist Church paid a visit. Erik and Vicki had met Pastor Mark about a year earlier when he'd filled in for their regular pastor, who was on vacation. Having a good church in the neighborhood was just one more benefit of moving to the country, and Erik felt that it was a lucky coincidence that they'd now be attending Pastor Mark's church.

"We're so very happy to have you in the neighborhood," the pastor said.

"We're very happy to be here," Erik replied. "This sure is different from the city. You're the second member of the welcoming committee so far."

Mark laughed. "Things are much more personal in the country. I suspect your neighbors will be dropping by, one by one."

"Yeah," Erik said. "Johnny Dovecrest stopped by just a short time ago. Do you know him?"

"Old Dovecrest," Mark said. "Yes. Everyone knows him. Quite the character, that one. There are more rumors about him than you can shake a stick at."

"What kind of rumors?" Vickie asked.

"Mostly pretty harmless. It seems like he's lived here forever and never gets older."

"You've got to be kidding. The guy is ancient."

"That's what my father said, too. He's been ancient since I was a boy, and even the old-timers never remember him being young."

"He gave us this thing to ward away evil spirits," Vickie said, holding up the talisman. "It...kind of scared us. He said to put it near the back door, by the woods."

Pastor Mark looked at the object for a moment.

"This is just an old Indian superstition. You don't need this."

"Are the woods safe?" Vickie asked.

"Well, I wouldn't exactly say that. Those woods go on for miles. Part of the land is on the Narragansett reservation, and part of it is state land that's been put aside and not used. You could easily get lost out there if you didn't know your way around. I wouldn't go wandering around out there if I were you."

"So it *is* dangerous?" Vickie insisted.

"Yes and no. Like I said, you could get lost out there. You wouldn't want your boy wandering off there by himself. He could get lost very easily. There aren't any bears or lions or anything, but there is the occasional fox and lots of raccoons. A few years back a moose even wandered in from Maine and had to be tranquilized and brought back when it fell into someone's swimming pool. But you could get hurt there, just the same. It's never a good idea to go into the woods alone anyway, especially city folk like you.

"Dovecrest tries to scare people away because he doesn't want people in the woods—and, honestly, you don't belong on the reservation anyway. He tells people the place is possessed by evil spirits, and talks about the dogs and cats that disappear there. Most of that's just for show—even the Indians don't worship evil spirits anymore. They have their own church. These woods are just a large stretch of oak forest. No more and no less."

Vickie laughed. "I know it's silly, but the Indian scared me a little."

Mark laughed. "There are all kind of rumors in New England. Someone's pet runs off and gets lost in the woods and the next thing you know the place is overrun with vampires. These woods aren't any more evil than any other place on this earth."

"Lord knows, I've seen enough evil in the city," Erik said, but he could tell that all of this talk made Vickie nervous.

"Pastor, would you mind blessing our new home?" she asked. "I think we could all use as much of God's presence as possible."

"I'd be happy to."

The family bowed their heads and Pastor Mark led them in prayer.

CHAPTER TWO

-1-

After the darkness came the pain. A blinding, burning pain of fire and brimstone, straight from Dante's *Inferno*. The agonizing pain seared the nerves, choked the lungs, burned the tissues from the inside out. It tortured each and every cell—or the memory of each cell, for the actual, living cells had long ago ceased to carry on their biological functions of osmosis, respiration, and division.

His was the awful pain of remembrance, the terrible pain of awakening after three centuries of sleep—of death.

The first sacrifice, accidental, had awakened the pain and with it had come reluctant consciousness. Despite his resolve, he had questioned and protested. He had tried to close his nonexistent eyes and return to the emptiness of sleep, the nothingness of death.

But the pain had invaded his peace, his stillness, rolling over him like endless waves of fire. With shock, he realized that he *had* no nerves, no lungs, no tissues or cells. Without a body, he should feel no pain. Yet the pain tortured him with its vivid and impossible reality.

Time passed and he imagined himself in hell. Gradually, he became lucid and remembered, despite the pain. The agony never lessened; he merely grew accustomed to it, like a festering, cancerous growth that continued to burn and bloat.

Finally, after what seemed an eternity, he learned that he

could force the pain into the background while his thoughts flourished. Only then did the memories become more clear and his purpose more focused.

The flames. The rancid black smoke. The awful scent of burned flesh—his own flesh—roasting away as the blood boiled within his veins. The memories returned in vivid, wrenching detail as he relived the moment over and over again.

Then, like a film played in an endless loop, the pain and emotion of the memory faded somewhat, allowing him to recall his purpose.

The curse had emerged from the flames, bright and bold as the phoenix. He would exact vengeance upon them and upon those who came after them. He could see it all clearly now, not only up until the time of his own death, but beyond. He saw the world move on, while he slept. And now the curse had pulled him back, had reawakened his purpose.

Yes, the curse. They would pay with their own lives and their own pain, just as the first one had paid, restoring his power and bringing him back from beyond the very reaches of Hell. There would be more deaths, more suffering. Death and pain would restore him, make him whole, provide life and substance to his anger and hatred and hurt. It would quell his own agony as his consciousness reached out to claim what belonged to him. Fighting against the pain of remembrance, he flexed his power like a muscle and began to reach into this new and different world.

-2-

Todd had trouble sleeping that night, plagued by bad dreams of the old Indian man who had visited them earlier. Twice during the night he woke up crying and had to be comforted by his mother. He couldn't remember exactly what the dreams were about, but the old man played a part in them. His father tried to tell him it was nothing, just the unfamiliar sounds of the new house and the wind rustling through the trees in the woods out back. But by the time the morning sun had peeked through his window to awaken him, Todd was secretly convinced that the old Indian was some kind of mummy that had been dead for a thousand years.

Todd spent most of the day unpacking his things. He had his own room on the second floor and his happiness in not having to share space with the new baby made him forget his bad dreams as the day wore on. He took special pleasure in helping his father arrange his bedroom and in setting up his treasures and special things where he wanted them. He was happy despite his mother's constant nagging about how he'd have to keep his room picked up, and by suppertime he'd managed to convince himself that the dreams were silly after all, and that the Indian was just an old man, nothing more. He didn't have a chance to go outside and really explore the back yard until after suppertime. But he knew this huge and wonderful yard would become his own private playground.

Now, as the sun began to set, he sat on the cool, damp ground beside a small, newly-planted shrub, aimlessly digging the loose dirt of his mother's future garden with the point of the geologist's hammer his uncle Mike had given him for his birthday. It was a cool night and the dew had already begun forming on the short, neatly cut grass. Todd breathed deeply, drawing in the crisp, fresh air. He nodded in satisfaction.

But as he looked off into the dense woods behind the back yard, his thoughts returned to the Indian man who had visited them the night before, and the memory of the nightmares returned once again. He shivered, despite himself, as he tried to rid himself of the uneasiness he had felt at the man's appearance. His palms were sweaty and his mind whirled around like bathwater going down the drain.

Then the memory of the nightmare that had plagued him returned in vivid detail. In a terrible but realistic vision of pure imagination, he had seen the Indian laying spread-eagled on a huge stone slab, bleeding and twisting in agony from a hundred wounds that covered his entire body. Somehow, Todd knew that the man was ancient beyond belief as he lay on the slab like raw meat on a plate.

The vision had been so real, so intense that he'd bolted upright in bed, screaming in terror until his mother and father had come running into the room to comfort him. Just remembering the dream, it was all he could do to choke back a scream and bolt back inside the house and into his mother's arms.

But something stopped him. He was a big kid now, he reminded himself and he could even read adult books. He liked scary stories best, and had read some Stephen King books, though they were supposed to be too old for him. But he'd been reading them for almost a year now—his teacher said he was "advanced"—and if his mother thought he was frightened she'd blame it on the books and she'd take them away and make him read boring stuff instead.

With a shudder he remembered his father's words—it was only a dream and dreams can't hurt you. They're only make-believe, like in the books or movies, and when you put the book down or left the theater, or turned off the TV or woke up from the dream, it was gone. Just a memory. Of course he still wasn't convinced that the monsters on TV *weren't* real, despite the thing he'd seen at the Boston Museum of Science a few weeks ago where he learned about something they called "blue screen technique" to make imaginary things look real in the movies.

He quickly decided to put all these ideas about ghosts and monsters out of his mind as he looked out at the woods beyond his back yard. The thick forest grew on two sides of the square yard that he now called his own. To his left the irregular brush gradually blended into an oak forest that was cut by a brook a little way down the road. His Dad had told him that they'd never have any neighbors on that side because it was a wetland and part of the reservation, though it looked dry enough to Todd. They did have neighbors on the right, just beyond a row of trees that separated the yards. The house next door, like all of the houses on this road and the small shopping plaza, was brand new. Most of the families had moved in a couple weeks ago, his Dad told him.

Straight ahead, at the furthest end of the yard, the woods grew thickest and probably ran for miles before meeting a road or another house. These thick woods fascinated Todd, and he felt no fear, only wonder as he looked into their endless depths.

He heard the trees silently calling him, huge, grizzled oaks older than his grandfather, probably even older than Dovecrest. They beckoned him, luring him into their embrace with the sweet promises of adventure. Maybe they hid a secret treasure, he thought, or maybe a fossil of an animal or fish instead of the usual fossilized ferns he'd found when they were digging up Grandpa's sewer pipes. Maybe he could even find an arrowhead. After all, Dovecrest was an Indian, and he lived near here.

His mind filled with excitement as he thought about what the woods might hold. He doubted that anyone had ever been in these woods before. Todd immediately decided that *he* must be the first to explore this forest, which was, after all, part of his very own back yard. He must explore these woods before any of the other neighborhood kids had the chance.

Then he remembered his father's warning about wandering off in the woods. He looked at the sky and calculated that it was still light enough to explore for a little while, as long as he didn't go very far in. Besides, he was a big kid now, not a little baby anymore.

I'll just go in a little ways, he thought. And I won't go so far away that I can't see the house. That way I won't get lost.

He walked slowly to the edge of the grass and looked back at the house. Dad had turned on the light in his study and was probably working on his computer, while Mom, no doubt, was still fussing with the baby's room. A tinge of jealousy burned his cheeks when he thought about the new baby. Already his Mom was fussing over it and it hadn't even been born yet.

Well, at least they wouldn't notice he was gone, and he'd be back before dark. He'd just duck a little way into the woods, have an adventure, and come right back. They'd never miss him.

He turned away from the house and stepped through the underbrush and into the woods.

-3-

Erik spent most of the day unpacking and helping Vickie rearrange furniture. He couldn't quite understand the female preoccupation with designing rooms. It must be that nesting instinct.

Yet he was very pleased with the job she'd done on his office—the Thoreau Suite. Naming the room had started as a private joke between them. While on their honeymoon in Miami they had visited a mansion built by one of those turn of the century capitalists. The place had a gold name plate on the door of each room. They'd laughed at the pretentiousness of rich people.

"When we get a place of our own, we'll name the rooms, too," Vickie had said.

"What if we only have two rooms?"

"We'll still name them. They'd be our rooms, right?"

The new house wasn't a mansion by any stretch of the imagination, but it did have more than two rooms. And Vickie had promised him an office of his own, designed any way he wanted. She had delivered on her promise.

He sat back in his luxurious office chair—an elegant nut-brown leather—and looked at the result. With a simple natural look, including small plants, nature prints, and the Thoreau collage, the room had Walden Pond written all over it. Erik had done most of his work in tiny apartments on a kitchen table. Now, for the first time, he really felt at home.

As happy as he was with the new place, though, he couldn't stop thinking about the woods behind the house, and Johnny Dovecrest's visit. Pastor Mark hadn't done much to reassure him, either. He hadn't realized the woods were so deep. The first investment he'd make would be a good, sturdy fence to enclose the backyard.

The trees towered over Todd, reminding him of the time they'd gone to a museum in New York that had an old stone building right inside the place. The old building hadn't had walls, just these giant stone things that looked like tree trunks without any branches. Like that building, these trees formed a sort of roof over his head, and he could hear the chirping of thousands of birds that were settling down for the night. Somewhere an owl hooted and was answered by the angry caw of a crow. The damp air attracted swarms of mosquitoes, which he absently slapped away from his face. One lighted on his arm, where he smashed it onto a bloody smear.

He walked slowly, occasionally stumbling over a blueberry bush, or being picked by thorns, until he came to a narrow path which, while not overgrown, looked as if it hadn't been used in some time. He glanced back at the house and saw the light shining from Dad's room like a beacon from a lighthouse. Finding his way back would be no sweat, no sweat at all. He clutched his geologist's hammer tightly and moved on.

He remembered a movie he'd seen in first grade about Daniel Boone, and he imagined he was a great explorer as he pushed forward along the path, blazing new trails into the wilderness. The hammer was a tomahawk. His sneakers were moccasins and his Boston Red Sox hat became a coonskin cap as he turned it backwards on his head.

The path narrowed as it edged deeper into the woods, but he hardly noticed. And when the trail ended altogether, he still didn't notice, so intent was he on his role as a pioneer.

The silent voice drew him on, promising discovery just ahead, perhaps just beyond the next tree. The voice in his mind grew stronger as he moved deeper into the forest, and his excitement increased with the intensity of the voice.

Although the voice didn't speak in words, it uttered the poetry of a language understandable to the mind of an adventure-seeking boy. Todd eagerly listened and heard.

He came to an abrupt halt as the forest unexpectedly broke into a circular clearing of neatly cropped grass. The last rays of the setting sun bathed the clearing in sinister shadows that seemed to take on strange shapes as the light flickered through the surrounding trees.

But it wasn't the clearing that stopped Todd in his tracks. It was the huge rectangular black slab sitting exactly in the center of the circle. It was the same stone Todd had seen in his dream— the very same stone where he'd seen Dovecrest's tortured body.

His breath rushed from his lungs like a popped balloon as he stood paralyzed, unable to do anything except stare at the terrible rock and wonder if it were real, or still a left-over from last night's dream.

The rock was large enough to make a bed for a tall man, and stood shoulder-high to Todd. Blacker than any rock he had even seen, it reminded him of the coal-dark eyes of Dovecrest, eyes that looked as if they knew all of his innermost thoughts and secrets. He wondered if the blackness were real, or a trick of the shadows.

Then the voice in his mind grew stronger; the rock itself seemed to call him. Without even realizing that he was moving, Todd found himself crossing the open field, drawing closer to the slab. The birds had stopped their chatter and even the mosquitoes had disappeared, though Todd noticed none of this as he fixated on the huge rock. The air took on a sudden chill as his feet carried him forward with a power of his own.

He stopped at the base of the slab. His heart pounded madly and he had broken out in a cold sweat. Swallowing hard, he felt his body trembling with fear as he slowly turned away to look back at where he'd come from, hoping to see his house back through the trees.

The beacon from his father's study had long since been consumed by the trees, and the path had disappeared also, now hidden in the darkness.

Vaguely, he realized he was lost and it had become dark.

When he turned to look at the huge rock, though, he instinctively knew that being lost in the woods was the least of his troubles. As much as he wanted to run, *needed* to run, his feet remained glued to the ground, frozen in place by fear and some unknown, unseen, and unnatural power.

The slab was shiny and polished smoother than Grandma's dining room table. A groove resembling a rain gutter ran around the outer edge. Tentatively, Todd reached his hand out and rested it on the polished surface. It felt cold to the touch, colder than an ice pop right out of the freezer. He was overwhelmed with a feeling of intense loneliness, as if he were the only person left in the entire world. Then, for no apparent reason, the slab began to warm up. His fingers tingled and he jerked them away.

The image of Dovecrest again flooded his mind and last night's vision returned as he stared at this slab's nightmare surface. This time, though, he didn't see a vision of Dovecrest, but of a teenage girl lying upon the smooth, polished stone—a blonde girl. He flushed in embarrassment as he realized that she was naked, and she began to whimper softly as the moon poked its face over the tops of the trees.

Todd watched in fascination and terror as a shadowy figure appeared beside the girl and raised its arms high in the air. The moonlight glinted off a shiny steel surface as a knife blade hovered over the girl's body for just an instant before plunging down in a sweeping arc of silver death.

The girl screamed once and a fountain of blood spewed from her chest and flowed out and over the slab to fill the grooves on its edge.

Todd clamped his eyes shut. His knees buckled and he fell forward to sprawl against the stone. Slowly he opened his eyes again, willing the dream to be gone.

The vision evaporated in an instant and only the slab was left. This new dream, a daydream, had been the product of his imagination after all.

Yet somehow he sensed that it was more—perhaps a history of what was, or a taste of what was to be.

He suddenly felt sick and the contents of his stomach did a back flip. He looked at the slab with hatred as he choked back the bile.

Without fully realizing what he was doing or why, he swung his geologist's hammer over his head and brought it down with all the force he could muster. A loud clang echoed through the clearing as the hammer struck the rock; the shock of the impact vibrated up Todd's arm and into his shoulder as the hammer bounced back like a rubber ball hitting the street.

Todd had slammed his eyes shut with the effort of the blow. When he opened them again he stared at the rock for a full ten seconds before he began to scream. It took him that long to fully comprehend the vision before him.

The very stone itself was trickling blood from a tiny chip he had made on its otherwise perfectly smooth surface.

-5-

Johnny Dovecrest was dicing onions for a stew when he heard the scream coming from deep within the woods. He paused, his knife poised in mid-air, and listened intently. But there was only silence now.

He put the knife down, walked to the window and looked into the blackness of the forest. His experienced eyes bore into the darkness but saw nothing. It might have been his imagination. But the hair on the back of his neck tingled, telling him it might have been something else. Something he didn't want to think about.

He had tried to tell them not to build here, that it wasn't safe. But they had refused to listen. Just like they always refused to listen. Now he feared the worst.

Either way, he had to know. He took his old M1 Carbine from its case in the closet, stuck his .45 caliber Beretta Mini Cougar into the waistband of his jeans, and went outside, praying to God that it wasn't happening again.

CHAPTER THREE

-1-

A sound caught Erik's attention and he walked over to the window overlooking the back yard, thinking that Todd might have hurt himself. The sun had gone down and the yard was quite dark by now. He couldn't see any sign of his son as he pressed his face against the windowpane.

"Vickie?" he called, making his way downstairs to the kitchen where she was arranging the contents of her cabinets. "Vickie, is Todd down here with you?"

"No. He went outside to look for rocks."

"I didn't see him out there. I'd better check."

"Maybe he's in his room."

"Would you check for me? I'll look outside."

Erik stepped out into the crisp night air that had suddenly chilled now that the sun had set.

"Todd? Where are you?" he called

His voice echoed with hollowness in the woods.

"Todd?" he called again, louder. "Are you out there?"

He walked around to the front yard, saw nothing unusual, then returned to the back again. Vickie hurried outside to join him.

"Erik, he's not in the house. I've checked everywhere."

"And he's not out here, either."

"Oh my God," Vickie whispered. "You don't think...."

"He probably wandered off into the woods. I *told* him not to leave the yard! I just got through telling him not to go off into the woods by himself...."

"Let's find him first. Then you can lecture him. I'll go get the flashlight."

Erik nodded, then walked across the yard and stood at the edge of the woods.

"Todd!" he screamed, cupping his hands around his mouth to amplify his voice. He waited for the echoes to die down, and then called again.

The more he thought about it, the more he was convinced that the noise he'd heard earlier was a scream. Todd was probably out there frightened half to death in the darkness. At least he'll never wander off into the woods alone again, Erik thought grimly.

Vickie returned with the flashlight. Its beam bounced up and down over the dew-coated grass as she ran.

"Anything?" she asked hopefully.

Erik shook his head, then realized she couldn't see him.

"Nothing at all," he said, finally, and decided not to mention anything about the scream to her.

"He's all right, isn't he?"

Erik forced a nervous laugh. "Sure. He just went out into the woods and got lost. How far could he have gone?"

"Yeah," Vickie said in a trembling voice.

Erik knew she was thinking the same thing as he was. The pastor had told them these woods went for miles. Still, how far could a little boy go in such a short time.

Together they stepped tentatively into the woods, using the flashlight beam to guide them. The moon had come up, a yellow half moon lying low on the horizon, but its light couldn't penetrate through the treetops.

"Look," Erik said, sweeping the ground with his flashlight. "A path."

He knelt down and studied the dirt; though he was no Indian scout, it was quite obvious to him that someone had passed this way very recently.

"He's been here," he said, confidently, though he really had no way of knowing for sure if it had been Todd's sneakers that had disturbed the dirt.

"If he stayed on the path it should be easy to find him," Vickie said.

"Yeah. It's got to go somewhere, right," Erik replied. He laughed nervously.

The darkness hung heavy as a quilt by now, filling the forest with mystery and strangeness. Erik called his son's name as he walked, as much to bolster his own courage as anything else. Though he hated to admit it, something about being in the woods at night frightened the hell out of him. Despite his dream of living in the country, he remained a city boy at heart, and didn't know or understand very much about nature. Although a downtown street posed far more danger at night than a rural forest, he was much more at home there than he was here right now.

Growing up in the city had made him street smart. As one of the few academically talented kids in an inner city school, he'd quickly learned how to defend himself. He'd studied a bit of the martial arts, joined the high school wrestling team, and worked hard at building an image of toughness while earning high grades.

At least he knew what to fear from the city—and how to handle it. He knew that the scum who prowled the city streets preferred easy prey to someone who might fight back. As a result, he'd been left alone.

But here in the blackness of this strange forest, his fear was vague and undefined, somehow sinister and mysterious. Although he knew he could be no more than fifty yards from his back yard, he felt as if he had crossed the boundary into some ancient, primitive world where the rules he learned to play by didn't work.

His concern for his son increased with every step he took. Since the path was too narrow for two people to walk side by side, Vickie followed behind him, clinging to the back of his shirt like a child holding onto her father, while he led the way, holding the flashlight beam low over the path ahead of them while pretending to be totally in control of the situation.

The path gradually narrowed even more until it disappeared entirely. Erik found himself standing in the underbrush looking out at an endless forest that seemed like it went on to the ends of the earth. He remembered what Pastor Mark had told him, and vaguely remembered from the plot map that the real estate agent had shown him that these woods did continue all the way to the Connecticut border, several miles away.

"Todd!" he screamed. "Todd! Can you hear me? Are you out there, Todd?"

He was almost frantic now, and his voice betrayed his panic.

"Maybe we should go back and call the police," Vickie suggested. "Before we get lost, too."

She was the calm one, now, and her tone settled him down a bit.

"They don't have police out here," he reminded her. "They have a sheriff."

"Maybe we should call him. Or 911."

For once, Erik wished he owned a cell phone.

"Who knows," Vickie said. "Maybe he's back home right now wondering where *we* are."

Erik sighed deeply. "I told him not to go into the woods."

Part of him wanted to press on, while another part of him trembled in terror when he thought of going deeper into these woods. Another part wondered if Vickie were right, and Todd was home waiting for them. Wouldn't that be a kicker, he thought, imagining Todd home watching cartoons.

"You should have stayed home," he said to Vickie.

"It's too late now."

"Maybe you could go back," he said feebly.

"We've got to stick together now," she replied. "Besides, there's only one flashlight."

"Yeah. We should have brought two."

"We only own one," she reminded him. "And it's a good

thing we unpacked it last night or I never would have found it."

He shrugged, then realized she couldn't see him. His mind was a battle of confusion. Vickie might be right. Todd might be home, even now. But what if he wasn't? They couldn't just walk away and leave him out here. He'd heard somewhere that in missing persons cases, the first few hours—the first few minutes, even—were critical. He might not just be lost—he might be badly hurt. He couldn't turn back now.

Besides, there had been that scream.

I think we should go on," he said quietly.

She squeezed his hand and forced a smile. Without hesitation, she followed him. He wondered if he should tell her about the scream—if it were a scream. No. It wouldn't do any good. Although she didn't show it, she was already frightened enough without adding to her worries.

They trudged forward, Erik leading the way and Vickie following. Erik had no idea where they were going. He didn't think he could find his way back to the house even if he wanted to, now. He remembered hearing stories about people lost in the woods who wandered around in circles for hours within just a few feet of a road or trail, and for the first time he understood how this could happen.

As they pushed forward through the thickening underbrush, Erik began to feel an uncertain sense of loathing that guided his direction. It was nothing definite, just a gently prodding that turned him slightly to the north, almost as if it were turning him away from something.

-2-

Johnny Dovecrest knew exactly where he was going. Although he knew his gun was useless against what he expected to find, he carried the rifle and the semiautomatic pistol, just in case the scream turned out to be the result of an animal attack, or something equally mundane. While these woods might be just a few miles from the city as the crow flies, they might as well be a million miles away. Dovecrest knew for a fact that a couple of bears had claimed this area as their own, though if he told anyone they'd surely come and shoot the bears. And moose had been spotted here on more than one occasion. He was happy to leave the animals alone, since the land was rightfully theirs and man was the real intruder.

Deep in his heart, though, he knew it was happening again. He had waited for this moment for so many years, hoping against hope that it was over forever, but knowing for certain that it wasn't. No. It was only a matter of time. That was the way it was, and he had prepared himself for the time when it would happen again. This time he would be ready. Or at least he had thought he would be ready.

But now that it was beginning all over again, he doubted his own ability. How ready was he, really? Had he let himself go weak? The years were certainly beginning to tell on him. He didn't feel the confidence and invincibility he had when he was young. And this world, this modern world—it had changed so very much and would present problems of its own. He'd have trouble recruiting allies. No one believed any more. Not even the preachers. Even they discounted such things—regardless of the fact that their own holy book spoke about devils and demons.

This new world thought that science could explain everything, that it could fix anything that might happen, solve any problem, defeat any enemy. He laughed. Science couldn't even solve the problems that *it* had created, terrible problems like pollution, overpopulation, and extinctions. How could it be expected to deal with problems that were far beyond its comprehension.

These thoughts rolled around in Dovecrest's mind as he entered the woods. He immediately felt the influence of the stone exerting its force to try and turn him away. Its power turned people away from it. It created a vague, hazy feeling, something the scientists wouldn't have accepted or understood, but very, very real, all the same. It was a feeling of dread and gloom and disgust that spoke in a soft, innocuous voice that did not register on the conscious level. If it could have been translated into words, the feeling would be telling him to turn back.

"Not that way," it whispered to the unconscious mind, speaking softly in a soothing monotone that touched the nerves and emotions rather than the mind. "You don't want to go that way. There's nothing there for you."

And along with the voice came the sudden feeling—no, the certainty—that if you did go that way it would be most unpleasant. Not dangerous, really. Just unpleasant. Like falling into a vat of rotten tomatoes swarming with maggots and fruit flies. Or swimming in a pool of fresh, pungent vomit.

The feeling was extremely obtuse and subtle, and only the rare individual would recognize it. Most men would simply follow its directive, without further thought or question.

But to Dovecrest, it spoke with the brilliance of a neon billboard. It told a fearful, terrible tale, a tale that he had heard before, so very long ago, and had waited for once again. That which he had feared and for which he had been prepared, had returned.

-3-

Seth Dobson, the man known as Seti to his followers, pulled into the Seven-Eleven and parked next to the door. The weight of the 9mm Glock felt comforting tucked into the belt of his jeans, covered by a loose-fitting shirt. He fought back the urge to take the gun out and clear the chamber, like they did in the movies. But no. That was Hollywood stuff and would only waste a round and possibly leave evidence behind. Real criminals didn't do that, he thought, just like they didn't hold the gun sideways when they shot. Not unless you wanted to get a hot shell casing in the face. That was only for the movies. And he was for real.

He knew they were watching him, ever since he'd done that

stupid radio talk show. That probably hadn't been a very smart thing to do. And now they were watching him.

But he couldn't help himself. He hadn't tasted blood in almost two weeks now, and it was driving him crazy. The best he had done was bat around a couple of his women disciples, but that wasn't enough. He needed to kill again and he needed it now.

It was that dream, the one that had started last June, and had brought him here. He knew it was the Evil One talking; it had told him to go east, until he had come here to this place. But now that he was here, he was lost, without a purpose. If he killed again, and bathed in the blood, then he would know.

He stepped out of the old van and went inside the store. The clerk nodded at him as he walked in. He was a young man, probably a college student, and he deserved to die. In fact, he wanted to die and he, Seti, Satan's servant, would be happy to oblige.

He walked towards the counter and imagined the surprise on the clerk's face when he was shot. He'd shoot him in the guts first, so he wouldn't die too quickly. Then he could take his time with him.

"Can I help you?" the clerk asked.

Seti was about to draw the gun when he felt the presence. It was still far away, which surprised him. He thought it would be close now that he was in this place, the place where it had led him. Still, it was closer. He paused.

No. It wasn't time. The presence made it known to him that he must wait, must be patient a little longer. He couldn't draw attention to himself, not here and not now. His people were waiting for him back at the campsite, and they needed direction. They needed him. *It* needed him.

"Sir? Can I help you?"

Suddenly, Seth was aware of the clerk's presence once again.

"Ah.... Yeah. Give me a pack of Marlboros."

He didn't need cigarettes, but it was all he could think of at the time. He paid for the cigarettes and left disappointed. He could have had so much fun if the voice hadn't stopped him.

Erik was about to tell Vickie that they were hopelessly lost when the distant sound of crying saved him from his confession.

"Todd!" Vickie screamed, immediately recognizing her son's cry with a mother's instinct.

A man's deep, voice returned her call with a muffled "Over here!"

"Where?" Erik screamed.

"Just stay put," the voice replied. "I'll find you."

Sure enough, the crying grew louder.

"Todd, are you all right?" Vickie shouted.

"He's fine," the man answered. "Just a bit shaken up."

The owner of the voice suddenly appeared in the beam of Erik's flashlight. It was Dovecrest. He carried Todd in one arm, and held a rifle in the other. Todd hung on with both hands around the man's neck, sobbing like an infant.

"Oh, Todd!" Vickie cried and ran to him, oblivious to the briar bushes that snapped and picked at her.

Todd's arms were clenched so tightly around Dovecrest's neck that she had to pry the fingers apart.

"Oh my poor baby!" she soothed. "What happened? You're drenched with sweat!"

"Todd, what happened?" Erik asked. But his son couldn't stop crying long enough to answer.

"The rock...the rock...," was all he could manage, and Erik thought he was talking about the wrestler on TV by that name. Then Todd burst into tears again and couldn't talk.

"I thought I heard something," Dovecrest explained. "So I decided to come out and take a look."

Even though Erik stood in complete darkness, he was certain that Dovecrest could see him, could see not only his physical body, but right into his very soul. The man came out without a flashlight and found his way effortlessly through these woods.

Erik shivered at the thought.

"I found him running through the forest," Dovecrest said. "He ran straight into my arms."

The Narragansett paused for a moment.

"He was carrying this," he continued, pulling Todd's geologist's hammer from his belt and giving it to Erik.

Erik looked down at the tool as he accepted it from Dovecrest. The pointed end of the hammer had broken off neatly, a full inch away from the tip.

"I don't know how we can thank you," Vickie said, hugging Todd close to her. "I don't know what would have happened if you hadn't come along."

Dovecrest shrugged. "These woods are very deceptive. Not a good place to be, especially at night. It would be very easy to get lost. Would you mind if I walked you back to your home?"

"Not at all," Erik said with obvious relief.

The house wasn't really far away at all. Dovecrest didn't say anything until the lights finally came into view. Todd's sobbing had stilled under Vickie's hugs.

"You asked me how you could thank me," Dovecrest said. "There are two things you can do."

"Anything," Erik said, sensing that they owed Todd's life to this man.

"First of all, promise me that you won't go off exploring these woods by yourself. I don't think you'll have to worry about your son going back."

Erik met Vickie's eyes and the both nodded.

"Second. The gift I gave you. Hang it over your door. Your back door. Do it tonight."

"Consider it done," Erik said.

"Good. Don't forget. It's very important."

Then, just when Erik was about to ask the man to come in for a cold drink, he was gone, stepping out of the flashlight beam and vanishing like a creature of the night.

The pain had subsided a bit as he had called the small boy to him. But now it was back again, stronger than before and mixed with the frustration of failure.

He cursed his bad luck and his weakness. If he hadn't been distracted and had to reach out to stop the other one from killing the store clerk, he might have won.

But the boy had gotten away. Just when he had had his prey trapped like a fly in his web, he had let his guard down, and the tiny insect had suddenly turned on him, stinging his still-sensitive consciousness hard and escaping from his jaws. And as he'd reached out to punish the boy's transgressions, he had felt the familiar presence of his age-old enemy, the one who had put him down so long ago. Then the other one, the one he had called to him, was about to do something very stupid. Still hurting and suddenly shocked by his enemy's presence, he had been forced to pull back and deal with the other one, which enabled to boy to get away.

He was still weak and in pain, not yet ready to take on the boy—or any other human life form, for that matter. No. He needed more strength. He would start out smaller and build his power gradually, despite his continuing pain.

After all, he wasn't going anywhere. He had all the time in the world. All the time. The suffering would only make him meaner, more determined.

As the searing, burning pain gripped him once again, he allowed himself the luxury of hate.

He would have the boy before it was over. But not until he grew stronger. Not until he was ready. Not until his power was full. He had tried to move fast, but he'd take his time now. Then he would make the insect pay the price. And he'd destroy his age-old enemy once and for all and claim his rightful place in the world.

CHAPTER FOUR

-1-

The smell of freshly brewed coffee woke Erik from a sound sleep. Vickie was already up and had opened the curtains so that the sun shone fully on his face. Ever since they had been married, that had been his wife's way of waking him up without being cruel; he never had liked mornings.

He crawled out of bed, remembering the ordeal of the night before and silently thanking God that his son was all right. It could have been a real tragedy.

He came downstairs and saw that Todd and Vickie were already having breakfast. Todd was playing with his Corn Flakes instead of eating them, and Vickie nibbled on a piece of toast and watched him with a worried expression.

"Morning," Erik said.

"Morning," Vickie replied, while Todd looked up at his father and forced a smile.

"How you doing, Sport?" Erik asked, tousling his son's hair as he shared a nervous smile with Vickie.

Todd shrugged.

"I think he's got a fever," Vickie said.

Erik placed his hand over Todd's forehead. "He does feel warm. Maybe you'd better get some Tylenol into him."

"Already did."

He poured himself a large mug of coffee, dumped in two spoonfuls of powdered creamer and three spoons of sugar and then sat down at the table.

"Do you want any breakfast?"

"No, thanks. It's too early to eat."

"It's nine o'clock."

"That's right. It's too early. You know I never eat before noon."

"You writers," Vickie said, shaking her head.

They quickly ran out of small talk and watched Todd absently playing with his cereal.

"So, Todd," Erik said, trying to act nonchalant. "Want to talk about what happened last night?"

"No," the boy mumbled, looking down into his cereal bowl.

Erik looked helplessly at his wife. The boy had refused to talk last night, but they had hoped he'd say something this morning, in the light of day. The kid had been frightened terribly—they all had.

"It's all right, Todd, Erik said in a reassuring voice. "I'm not going to yell at you. I'm not even going to punish you. I don't think you'll be pulling that stunt again in a hurry. We just want to know what happened. What ever possessed you to go off into the woods like that anyway?"

Todd shivered as if an ice cube had slithered down his back.

"Nothin'," he said softly, still staring down.

"He doesn't want to talk, Erik. He doesn't feel well."

"I want to know what happened, Vic."

"He got lost in the woods, for God's sake. It was darker than pitch out there. That's enough to scare the hell out of anyone. Hey, I was scared. And so were you. Admit it."

"I was afraid for Todd," he said, telling only half the truth. He wanted to tell her about the scream he'd heard, and about his own terror of the woods. But he was embarrassed by his own weakness. And the scream—who knew what he had really heard.

"He'll tell us about it when he's ready," she said.

"All right. All right. I'll leave him alone, ok?"

Erik finished his coffee and poured himself a second mugful.

"How'd we do on getting the house in order?" he asked, deliberately changing the subject.

"Pretty good. The kitchen's in good shape, and so is the bedroom. The living room's a mess, though. But at least we can eat and sleep."

"Well, don't kill yourself. Wait until I get home before you do any heavy stuff."

"I will. You didn't think doing a radio talk show would get you out of doing work, did you?"

"Hey, I scheduled this appointment a month ago. How was I supposed to know we'd still be unpacking?"

"You had it planned all along," she teased. "I know your kind. You'll do anything to avoid an honest day's work. But I'm wise to your tricks."

"That's why I became a writer," he said, and laughed. Then he looked over at Todd who was still stone-faced.

"So what do you say, Sport? Are you going to listen to your Dad on the radio this afternoon?"

Todd suddenly looked up at him as if he'd just come back from another world. He looked into his father's eyes for a long moment, and Erik realized that his eyes looked like those of a man, not a little boy. Then he spoke in a soft, trembling voice.

"The stone bled."

"What?"

"The giant stone. In the woods. I hit it with my hammer and... it bled. The stone bled."

Then he broke out in a fit of sobbing and returned to being a 10-year-old boy again. Vickie rushed to his side to hug him. She spoke soothingly, trying to calm him down.

"Did you dream about a stone?" Erik asked.

"No!" he said, meeting his father's eyes. "It wasn't a dream. It was real! The stone bled and it was real!"

"It's ok," Vickie said. "Whatever happened, it's over now. Come on. Let's go to your room. I think you should get some rest."

Trembling with a dreadful nervousness of his own, Erik

watched them go up the stairs.

"Ever since he saw that damned Indian," Erik muttered to himself.

And as he remembered Dovecrest's piercing, black eyes, the hair on his own back tingled with the electricity of fear.

-2-

Erik arrived at the radio station at 11:30, a half hour before he was scheduled to go on the air. An attractive blond reception-ist ushered him into a small waiting room where he sat down and pretended to thumb through an old *Time* magazine.

He found that he couldn't concentrate on either the magazine or what he'd planned to say for the two-hour talk show. He was too worried about Todd.

As if the kid's terrifying experience hadn't been bad enough, he'd managed to pick up a nasty cold as well, helped along, no doubt, by last night's unseasonably cool and damp air. At least the boy had finally told Vickie what had happened—or what he *thought* had happened, because the story was too farfetched to be true. He'd claimed to have found a huge rock in the woods, right in the middle of an open field. The rock had "called out to him" somehow, and he'd hit it with his geologist's hammer. Then, the thing had begun to bleed.

Todd had screamed—which was what Erik had heard from the house—and had run off blindly into the darkness before the stone could get him. The kid was convinced that the thing was alive and was "after him," as he said it, and would do something terrible to him once it caught him. The next thing he'd known, he had run straight into Johnny Dovecrest.

The story had obviously been the product of his son's over-active imagination, coupled with the beginnings of the cold he was now suffering from. The darkness and the eerie atmosphere were enough to frighten anyone. Dovecrest's bizarre visit on the night they had moved in and his insistence that they hang up his magic talisman only added strangeness to the situation. And the tempered edge of the geologist's hammer *had* been neatly broken off, which made Erik wonder what had happened out there.

Still, the real problem wasn't what Todd *thought* he had seen. The problem was that the kid believed it, despite its impossibility, and the belief triggered the fear. When Erik looked into his son's eyes he had seen his terror, seen his belief in that horrible vision. Nothing either he or Vickie could say would change that belief or eliminate his irrational fear. No amount of explanations would satisfy him—according to Todd it *had* happened and that was all there was to it. And before he had left home, Erik noticed that Vickie had hung Dovecrest's charm on the back door.

Erik sighed. He doubted that his son had slept for even a single hour last night—and God only knew if he'd be able to sleep tonight.

Well, at least it happened during the summer and not in the middle of the school year, he thought. Still, if things didn't improve, his son would be a prime candidate for counseling.

The sound of an opening door interrupted his thoughts as Steve Harvey, the WKRI talk show host walked in. With his short curly brown hair, blue eyes and winning smile, Harvey would have been just at home on television as on the radio. Erik had met him in Boston during a science fiction convention where he'd been speaking. After he'd finished his presentation, Harvey had approached him about being on the show. They'd worked out the details over a couple of drinks and had set a date.

"How're you doing?" Steve said as they shook hands.

"Just fine. And yourself?"

"Oh, I can't complain. I hear they've started shooting the film. That must be exciting."

"They began last week."

"Wow. Imagine that. Have you visited the set?"

"No, I haven't. Not that I haven't been tempted. I think I want to be surprised when it's released.

"But wouldn't it be worth it to see Nicole Kidman in person?"

Erik laughed. "Yeah, and my wife is dying to meet Robert Downey Jr. Maybe that's why I haven't visited the set. I'd kind of like to stay married."

"They've assembled quite a cast, that's for sure. They will be a draw at the box office. And that'll help sales of the book."

Erik nodded.

"It's nice to see a native Rhode Islander make good," Steve said. "I'm so happy for you. I'm sure you'll do quite well."

"Thanks," Erik said, and was pleased that Steve's words were genuine.

"So, have you thought about what you'd like to talk about on the show?"

"Nothing specific. Any ideas?"

"Well, like I told you in Boston, I have some pretty strange people on this show, so just about anything goes. I've had psychics, witches, faith healers, UFO freaks, you name it. In fact, you're the first normal guest I've had in weeks."

"Me, normal?"

"Well, everything's relative," I guess," he teased. "Have you had a chance to listen to the show?"

"I heard the one a couple of days ago. You had on a guy who claimed to have been taken away by a UFO. I see what you mean about having assorted weirdos as guests."

"Oh, yeah. John Smallwood. Actually, he was quite tame. Last week I interviewed a devil worshipper."

"A what?"

"A devil worshipper. The guy really was weird. Gave me the shivers."

"I'll bet. Was he serious?"

"As a funeral. Claimed that he heard voices. And that the voices led him here. You could see something in his eyes—this guy's not normal. Not by any stretch of the imagination. And you want to hear the worst part?"

Erik nodded.

"I was talking with my friend in the A.G's office. The FBI is watching this character."

"For being a devil worshipper? I mean it's weird and all, but it's not illegal, is it? Isn't he protected by freedom of religion?"

"If all you're doing is worshipping, yeah. But it's more complicated than that. You can worship anything you want as long as you don't break the law. But some of these weirdos go beyond that. They've tracked this guy all the way from California. He left there about a year ago and has slowly been making his way across the country. He's the leader of a cult group and he and a few of his followers get together in the woods every so often and do their thing. Only no one knows for sure what exactly their thing is. The guy wouldn't talk about it much, except to hear him tell it they worship the birds and the breeze and little voices in his head. But according to the A.G.'s Office they're doing more than just reading the Lord's Prayer backwards and frolicking in the bushes."

"Orgies?"

"A lot worse than just sex. Kidnapping. Child molestation and abuse. Maybe even murder. The F.B.I. thinks they're performing human sacrifice. With children."

"My God!"

"Of course, nothing's been proven. The F.B.I.'s been following a string of missing teens that seem to follow the path of these weirdos. A couple of bodies have turned up. They were killed in some perverted form of Satanic ritual. They haven't been able to pin it on this group, but they are definitely suspects."

"That's worse than a Stephen King novel!"

"You know what they say about truth being stranger than fiction."

"What are they doing to stop these nuts?"

"There's not much they can do, except watch them, I guess. There's no hard evidence to connect the murders to this group. The F.B.I. has tried to get an undercover agent into the group, but it hasn't worked. You'd have to be really weird in order to fit in, I guess."

"Where is this guy now?"

"I'm not sure. He was in Rhode Island a week ago. Maybe they've moved on by now. They like to stick to the out-of-the-way wooded areas. My guess is that they're headed north. New Hampshire. Maybe Maine. They could really get lost there."

"I live out in the country. Chepachet. You don't think they'd be there, do you?"

"I doubt it. I suspect they've gone north. Rhode Island's too small. I wouldn't worry about it."

Erik shook his head in disgust.

"Well," Steve said. "It's just about showtime. Hey, listen, don't tell anyone what I told you about these devil worshippers, ok? It might screw up the investigation if word got out. I wouldn't share this with the usual weirdos I have on the show, but, like I said, you're the first normal guest I've had in a long time."

He could see why Steve Harvey made such a good talk show host. The man loved to talk, and could make other people talk as well. Erik suspected that he'd probably told half of Rhode Island about these devil worshippers that were supposed to be so secret. The whole thing was probably just an urban legend. If not, he guessed the talk would force the devil worshippers to move on.

"Don't worry," Erik said, wondering how the time had gone so fast.

"Thanks," Steve said. "Now, let's go do a show!"

CHAPTER FIVE

-1-

The two-hour talk show passed quickly as Erik easily fielded questions from local callers. In fact, he relished his new-found role of home town celebrity and promised Steve that he'd return and do another show when the film was released. As usual, most of the callers asked him about films rather than books. It was ironic, he thought, that he, a novelist, should be making his money from the movies. But it was the video age, after all, and he'd come to expect people to be interested in pictures instead of words. Besides, Nicole Kidman and Robert Downey Jr. could sell horror a lot better than he could. Having grown up a fan of horror and science fiction films, he'd had no trouble displaying his expertise to the local audience.

It wasn't until he was driving home that he thought about Steve's story of devil worshippers again, and related it to Todd's experience in the woods. With sudden panic he wondered if Todd might have stumbled into some bizarre Satanic ritual in the woods.

Then again, he suspected Steve Harvey was prone to exaggeration and fiction. But even the remote possibility was frightening enough. The thought of it unnerved him.

And what about Dovecrest? Could he be part of something? It seemed like quite a coincidence that he just happened to go out wandering into the woods last night. And that Todd had just "run into him." Something didn't add up. He was convinced that Dovecrest knew more than he was telling. Even that thing about hanging the talisman on the back door was strange.

This whole thing was just too scary. Here he'd moved out of the city to get away from all of the trouble and the violence, and what happens? His son gets the scare of his life on his first trip outside.

Devil worshippers, in this day and age. How weird was that.

Not that he believed in the devil—at least not with the red suit, the horns, and the pitchfork. That image was quite silly, really, something to scare children into doing the right thing. But he did believe in evil. And he'd read enough history to know that sick individuals had been torturing and maiming their fellow humans since the dawn of time—sometimes in the name of Satan, and sometimes even in the name of God.

But this was probably a fabrication, and exaggeration. And even if it wasn't, this wacko had probably moved on by now, as Steve suspected. He could really get lost in the thick forests of New Hampshire, Vermont, and Maine.

And he was probably jumping to conclusions about Todd. The boy had probably been frightened by the dark, and by his own imagination. Still, Dovecrest troubled him. Something about the Indian just wasn't right.

He decided to ask his son some specific questions as soon as the opportunity presented itself. He also decided to do a little research on his own about this devil worship crap. If nothing else, he could use it in one of his horror stories. And while he was at it, he intended to check out this Dovecrest character.

He intended to find out everything he could about the place where he now lived, just for his own piece of mind.

-2-

"Do you want to go out, Faith?"

The cat looked up at the woman-who-feeds and scratched again. The woman-who-feeds obediently opened the door and

Faith strolled out into the back yard as if she had all the time in the world—which, in fact, she did. The sunshine felt good, and she dropped to the warm cement of the patio and began to roll, both scratching her back and heating it at the same time. She opened her legs to let the hot afternoon sun beat on her belly before she ventured off to explore new territory. Finally, satisfied with the sun worship, she rolled back onto her feet and sniffed the strange air.

The smells here were different, very different from those of her previous territory. She'd spent yesterday growing accustomed to the new house, marking it with the scent of her fur as she rubbed against the walls and doors and exploring every closet and nook for possible rats, crickets, or other quick, scurrying creatures. To her immense disappointment, the house was completely empty, brand new, and sterile. Her previous house had provided plenty of crickets for her to play with, and even the occasional mouse, which she would torment until it died and then she'd offer it to The Woman Who Feeds as a gift of appreciation. Although the woman never accepted the gift, she always praised her lavishly and gave her special treats in return, so mice were especially prized.

Since this house had offered no challenge to her superior hunting skills, her instincts took her outside. Here, surely, she could find an interesting plaything. Besides, the time had come for her to mark off this new territory as her own.

The air was remarkably clear here, full of many different scents. The city had provided only a thick, dirty smell, which had masked all but the nearest competing scents. This place offered a kaleidoscope of ever changing smells, all waiting to be explored.

The sounds, also, were different. She distinguished the chirps and songs of a number of different kinds of birds, as well as the chorus of millions of insects, and even the sounds of small toads and other animals. She knew the toads and left them alone, just like you didn't mess with a skunk. But many of the sounds were new and demanded investigation. She licked her lips in anticipation as she moved her eyes quickly back and forth across her yard, seeking the slightest hint of motion. She'd stiffened her tail straight into the air to show the world that this place belonged to her, and when she saw nothing of particular interest scurrying though the grass, she began the methodical task of marking her territory.

She hadn't detected the scents of any competing cats, so the area, in essence, did belong to her already. Still, instinct declared that she must claim her own turf and she obediently followed that higher command.

She began with a small tree, first by rubbing the side of her head against the rough bark to leave her fur scent behind, then by clawing the trunk to show any potential intruders the fierceness of her claws. She went over to the next tree and repeated the process, then stalked a robin redbreast that had the audacity to land in her territory and pluck a fresh worm from the grass. The bird spotted her movement, however, and quickly flew into the woods with the worm hanging from its beak, leaving her still crouching in the grass, nervous and frustrated.

The short grass offered little camouflage, but the bushes and large trees just beyond promised not only plenty of hiding places, but unsuspecting prey as well. She took a quick look back at the house, flinched her long tail once, then with feline determination padded off into the woods.

Her instincts took complete control and, for a moment at least, she forgot she was an ordinary housecat used to being pampered and fed. In her own mind she became a wild animal of the jungle, the primeval cat, more fierce than the lion, more swift than the cheetah, more cunning than the tiger. She was a killing machine designed to deliver death to whatever stood in her path.

Then a new sound and a new scent attracted her attention. She sensed a presence, an alien presence that recognized her as one of its own. It called to her with the voice of the mother of all cats, beckoned her, coaxed her, enticed her with the promise of food.... Some small part of her brain flickered with the thought of home, of the Woman-Who-Feeds and The-Boy-Who-Strokes-Ears. Then the thought was gone, banished by this new presence, and she was feline again, attracted by the new and the strange. She cocked her radar ears forward toward the sound while lifting her nose to capture the scent.

That tiny portion of her brain that remained housecat flinched with fear at this alien, uncanny presence that beckoned her. A call from the Woman-Who-Feeds or The-Boy-Who-Strokes-Ears, or maybe even The-Man-Who-Gives-Milk would have been enough to send her bolting for the safety of home.

But there was no such call.

Her feline instincts recognized the smell of blood. Fresh blood. Unable to help herself, she rushed into the woods.

She ran with a purpose, ignoring everything around her: the birds, the insects, and even the forest itself. She buried her fear within her semi-domesticated brain as she cut a straight course through the woods, leaping over bushes and fallen branches, instinctively knowing the shortest route to her destination. The sound and the scent grew stronger the deeper she went into the forest, and she could not ignore the call.

She stopped when she came to an open field with a huge, flat stone in the center. The stone called to her. Even while her tail twitched in agitation and indecision, her four legs were already carrying her forward to the base of the stone. Sensing danger, she dropped into a crouch and hissed an angry snarl. She raised the fur on her back and bared her teeth, realizing that this was no Mother Cat, but something far more dangerous and inexplicable.

Could she have articulated her thoughts she would have wondered why the stone was so black—as black as her own ebony fur—and why it seemed to project such evil from itself. Perhaps she would have wondered how it had come to be and who controlled the powerful force she sensed within it. And, were she capable of the thought, she would have wondered how a thick, black shadow could grow out of nothing and advance towards her so quickly, despite the fact that the sun shone over her shoulders.

But, being merely a cat, she could not wonder. Instead, she bared her fangs, lifted her tail high in defiance, and prepared to do battle as she felt the shadow's coldness approach.

-3-

He mentally licked his lips in satisfaction. In reality, of course, he had no lips, no mouth, no substance. The blood had helped, though, and the pain had diminished somewhat. It was never really gone, but diminished. The feeding had helped take the edge off of his agony and give him at least a shadowy existence. Yes, it felt good, so very good to feed again, to taste the sweet, fragrant taste of fear, and death.

The feeding would restore his power, slowly at first, as he took whatever blood he could get. He'd sufficed with mice and squirrels until now. The cat had helped. It, at least, had experienced fear as it felt its own impending doom.

Taking advantage of the relatively pain-free moments after feeding, he reached his mind out in snake-like tendrils, projecting his feelers quickly before the pain could return and weaken him again. Tentatively, he made contact with the other presence, the one who sought him out. This one wasn't very smart, but his heart was dark enough, even if his mind was not right. He probed this one's mind. He was easily led and was very close now. Waiting and ready to do whatever was asked of him.

This creature—this mortal man—had already done his bidding as he traveled closer. He had done so without fully knowing what he was doing, or why. He had come very close to letting his emotions force him into making a grievous mistake, though, which would have resulted in beginning all over again.

He could control this man, this creature, and he would. First he must bring him even closer and bind him. Then he would use him and destroy him.

This other was much closer indeed, and responded eagerly to his call.

"Come, my son," he coaxed, assuming his ancient role once again. "Ease my pain and I will be your God. We will quench one another's thirst, feed one another's hunger."

The other one heard, but did not fully understand. He responded by instinct, the call of one evil soul to another.

Soon. Soon enough. He repeated the call, and the other heard and knew. Soon you will arrive and help to free me from this prison of pain. Then I will have the boy. And the others. All of those who did this to me, and all of their children. And one in particular who has haunted me through the ages. This one will suffer most of all, along with any who ally themselves with him.

Yes, I will have them all. Then the pain began its slow return, like the changing of the tide.

CHAPTER SIX

-1-

Todd lay in his bed, staring absently at the life-sized poster of his wrestling hero, The Rock, which hung on the wall beside his bed. The poster had always given him strength in the past. But now, looking at The Rock made him feel small and weak. He didn't think that his fear would go away even if his hero suddenly appeared before him in person.

He had tried to understand what had happened to him. He had rolled it all around in his head, every way that he could, but it still didn't make any sense. He had tried to believe his Mom and Dad, had tried so very hard to accept the horror as a dream, a product of his imagination, the darkness, and the moonlight.

But in his heart, he couldn't believe. He knew it had all been real. Hauntingly, terribly real. He hadn't imagined the polished stone. And he hadn't imagined the blood.

He could still see the terrible place whenever he closed his eyes. The sight of the awful black stone was permanently engraved into his mind. His fingers still tingled with the remembered cold, then heat of its touch. He shivered involuntarily at the thought and pulled the blankets up around his neck. Yet they did nothing to stop the cold, which chilled him to the very marrow of his bones.

He looked into the Rock's eyes, seeking an answer. But the poster stared past him as if he were not even there. It would offer no help.

No, he was alone on this one. And Mom and Dad would be no help. They still thought his imagination was running wild. He remembered how his Mom had taken his temperature and started feeding him pills, as if that would do any good.

It *had* been real. The blood had been real. And his geologist's hammer was broken—that was real. His Uncle Mike had taught him a lot about rocks and had told him that hammer wouldn't break. He'd been able to chip quartz with that hammer. And quartz was harder than almost anything, except diamond, he remembered. The hammer hadn't broken by itself.

Then he thought about the Indian, Dovecrest. Maybe he would understand.

Todd couldn't remember the Indian actually finding him in the woods, but he sensed that somehow, Dovecrest *knew*. Yet despite being rescued by the strange man, the thought of speaking to him was almost as frightening as the black rock itself.

Loneliness suddenly consumed him and he shivered harder. He wished Faith were here to console him. Scratching her ears and listening to her purr always made him feel better.

"Mom!" he shouted. "Mom!"

Having a fever definitely had its advantages. His mother immediately hurried up the stairs to tend to him. She entered his room and he noticed that she walked funny now. It was because of the baby growing inside of her, and he suddenly felt bad about making her hurry.

"What is it, Todd?"

"I'm cold. And I need Faith."

"Oh, I put Faith out about an hour ago. She was scratching at the door. She should be back soon, though."

"Oh," he said, disappointed. Then a sudden chill ran up his spine as he thought of what might be lurking outside.

"Can I bring you some chocolate milk?" his mother asked.

"I guess so. But I really wanted Faith to sleep with me."

"I'll bring her up as soon as she comes in."

"Thanks, Mom."

His mother leaned over and hugged him, and it was good. Even though he was a big boy now, too big for such things, he hugged her back as tightly as he could.

-2-

"Well, Erik said, placing the bag of groceries on the table. "How did I do on my world-wide radio debut?"

"Just great," she said, hugging him. "You did fine. I even missed my favorite soap opera for you," she teased.

"That was very nice of you. But, really? Did I sound ok?"

"You sure did. I taped the show so you can listen to it for yourself."

"Great. Than I can hear me embarrass myself on the radio. Now that everyone else has heard."

Vickie laughed. "But seriously. Even I didn't realize you know so much about old movies."

"Just bad ones," he replied. "I had a warped childhood."

"That explains a lot of things."

They both laughed.

"How is Todd? Is he any better?"

"He'll be all right. It's just a cold. And he had a scare. He'll be fine."

"What's he doing now?"

"He fell asleep."

"Not from listening to me on the radio, I hope."

"No. He listened to a little. I don't know how much he understood, because we don't let him watch horror movies," she teased.

He laughed. "The kid must have a bad cold. It's not like him to sleep during the day. We've got enough trouble getting him to sleep at night."

"He hasn't slept much since we moved in. But I've been giving him cold medicine. That makes you sleepy."

"I know. Let him sleep."

Vickie nodded. "Erik, you haven't seen Faith around, have you? Did she follow you in?"

"Ah...no. I don't think so. I haven't seen her since this morning. Why?"

"Well, I let her out this afternoon right after your show and I haven't seen her since. It's been at least an hour."

"She usually stays out all afternoon, Vic. I wouldn't worry. Did you call her?"

"Yeah. That's what bothered me. Todd wanted to sleep with her so I went outside and looked around and called her. It's not like her not to come when she's called. You always say she's like a dog that way. You don't think she's gotten lost, do you?"

"I don't think so. Cats are really good about finding their way home. I read an article once that a cat found its way home all the way across the country."

"You don't think she headed back to the old place, do you?"

"No. She's probably out exploring. Probably stalking a blue jay or something. Or maybe she's sleeping in the SUV. You left the windows open, you know."

"Oh, I forgot. Did you close them for me? You never know about those late afternoon showers this time of year."

"I did. But I didn't check to see if the cat was inside."

"Then she might be out there. I'll have to check. If she is, I don't want her taking a dump in the back seat."

"I'll go check," he said. "I wouldn't worry about her. She'll come in when it's time to eat. And that should be any minute now."

Still, as much as he tried to act nonchalant, he had a bad feeling about this.

-3-

The man known as Seti to his followers stepped out of his trailer and breathed the fragrant air of the forest. Soon the sun would be down, he thought, stubbing his cigarette into the ground with his boot. Then his favorite part of the day would begin—the night. Perhaps this would be the night when he'd locate the voice, the presence that had spoken to him, called him from so far away.

He scratched the smooth, shaved surface of his skull and smiled as, even now, he sensed the presence once again. Yes, he was close, now. Very close. Probably only a few miles away. Probably in these very woods. For the past week he had felt its power as it grew stronger every night.

The moon would not be full for another week. By then he would have found the presence and the ritual would be complete. He licked his lips in anticipation of the blood that would be shed.

But there was so much to be done between now and then. Everything must be carefully prepared. And a child must be found. No, an infant, he realized suddenly. That would be best. Rhonda, the dark-haired one, might have her baby before then, but there was no guarantee. Her baby—it was probably *his* baby, too. As if he gave a shit.

But tonight he felt good, felt confident. Tonight he would find the power that had drawn him across an entire continent to this desperate forest that hadn't changed much since the Pilgrims and the Indians.

He closed his eyes and breathed deeply, in and out, slowly and evenly. Yes. The power was still there. He reached his mind out to it, probing for direction.

For over a year now he'd sensed its presence, ever since that first dream in June. He shuddered at the memory. So full of pain. Yet so damned intriguing.

That dream had initiated a chain of events that had resulted in a path of bloodshed that ran through some 15 states and which had made him the High Priest of his very own church. He laughed out loud at the thought of it. "Church" was probably a misnomer for the ragtag collection of followers he had assembled. But they were *his* followers. All his, and they would follow him wherever he led, even to the death. Even with his eyes closed he could see the half-dozen trailers surrounding him in the campground, each containing one male and one female.

Yes, they were his. He had fucked them all, both men and women, singly and in groups. Yet deep down inside, *he* was incomplete, unfinished, and that was what had brought him here to these woods of ancient evil.

The power touched him again, stronger this time, and more insistent. He fed it images of tortured, bleeding teenage girls, images taken from his fondest memories, from places with strange names like Paradise Valley, Winnebago, and Zoar. And, of course, a place called Wonderland California, where it had all begun.

Yet the rituals, while gratifying for the moment, had not satisfied him. During each orgy of blood—and orgy of sex that followed—he had been fulfilled. But it hadn't lasted. The following morning, the emptiness always returned, stronger than ever, leaving him hollow, as if some vital part of him were missing.

Now, as he felt the presence deep within the forest of Chepachet, Rhode Island, he knew that he was about to discover his destiny. He sighed deeply and opened his eyes. Then, slowly, he walked out of the campground and into the forest.

-4-

Johnny Dovecrest looked up from the page he was reading and frowned. The gray hairs on his arms tingled as he gently closed the book and walked across the room to stare out the window into the darkness. He could see nothing, of course. Yet he could see everything. And he knew that unless he acted soon—within the next few days, at most—he would be powerless to prevent it from happening all over again.

It might already be too late, he thought, and chided himself for not acting sooner. He had grown too comfortable in his soft, easy life. He had forgotten the lessons he had been taught.

Rubbing his forehead, he turned away from the window and

wondered what to do next. He could feel the nebulous, indistinct forces of evil coming together. One force was powerful, so *very* powerful. The other was weak, a slave to be used, consumed, and then thrown away. But Dovecrest remembered and he knew just how much damage that slave could inflict before it was stopped.

Destroying the weaker one would be easy. But it would solve nothing. Now that the evil had been disturbed it wouldn't rest until it was destroyed again—and destroyed wasn't even the correct word. Imprisoned, sent back to hell, was probably more accurate, since the thing *couldn't* be destroyed. No, destroying the slave would only delay the inevitable. It would just find a replacement. And in the modern world, such hosts were more plentiful than ever.

It had been much easier in the olden times. He'd had the support and understanding of others, of the tribe and even of the white man. They had worked together. This time he was on his own. Even his own tribesmen no longer believed. It was entirely up to him. Unless he could get help from the new people, the ones whose boy had nearly fallen victim.

The boy would understand. But what help was a ten-year-old boy? And the parents? He didn't think so. They'd think he was crazy. Maybe he *was* after all these years. The boy would be the only one. And Dovecrest didn't expect him to be much help at all. Better to just leave it alone and do it himself.

Dovecrest sat back down and looked toward the window, trying to imagine what was happening out there. He knew better than to interfere. It would do no good. And, besides, he couldn't kill the weaker one, even if it would help. He'd just be arrested and thrown in jail, and that would be that. He would really be useless trying to work from a prison cell. The law was the law, and he'd be the one punished under this warped system of justice.

No. Better to let tonight happen. Then later, when the time was right, he would strike. He'd need a plan and a time of his own choosing. He was not ready to fight just yet.

Still, he knew he would get no sleep that night.

-5-

Erik searched the entire yard, the house, the SUV and the car, and even the basement, but Faith was nowhere to be found. He stood at the edge of the woods and looked into the pitch darkness towards the narrow trail that had lured Todd in. He called for the cat, but with no luck. Not even the smell of a freshly baked chicken could tempt her back.

He could almost hear a voice calling him, beckoning him into the darkness.

"Erik," Vickie called from the patio. "You're not going into the woods to look for that cat are you?"

"I guess not.... I just can't imagine where she might be."

"Well, you might as well come back inside. There isn't much we can do tonight. And I wouldn't even go into those woods alone in the daylight."

"Maybe I can get Johnny Dovecrest to help me look for her tomorrow," he said, turning back toward the house. "I sure hope she's all right."

"So do I," Vickie said.

-6-

Seti stood beside the huge stone altar and marveled that he could see, even in the dark. He didn't know how—and he didn't care—but he did know that this presence, perhaps it was even Satan himself, inhabited this ancient place of blood and sacrifice.

He had seen this place before in his dreams. And in his nightmares. It was a place of power. A place where miracles could happen.

Tentatively, he reached his hand out and touched the highly-polished stone. Its surface was ice-cold to the touch and he wondered how many souls had perished on its smooth surface. Then, with a smile, he thought of how he would be adding to its history.

"Master, I have come," he whispered. "I have answered your call and have traveled many miles to be with you."

And the presence, which had shared his mind all along, seemed to come awake and find him, as if opening its eyes for the first time.

"Yes, you have," it said in words that were not sounds, but patterns in his own mind. For a brief instant he wondered if he were going mad and carrying on an internal dialogue in his own brain. The outside world already considered him crazy. That idiot talk show host had actually called him a nut case on the air.

Then the presence began to show him things, things he could not possibly know, but which were true. He watched and he believed.

The mental slide show may have lasted for hours, or it may have flashed past in a matter of seconds. He had no way of knowing for sure.

But now he understood. For the first time in his miserable, tormented life, he truly understood. He accepted this presence as his god. If it were not Satan, it was the closest thing to him. And this master promised him rewards beyond his wildest dreams.

He dropped to his knees beside the magic stone altar and knew that this was real, that this was a god of power, a god that would take the world for its own, destroying the weak as if stepping on a worm. This god would give pleasure, not deny it. This god would take what it wanted, when it wanted, and he, Seti, would reap the rewards.

"I will serve you," he said, still touching the stone. "Show me how."

And, as the presence responded with unspoken instructions, Seti realized that his purpose in life was now fulfilled. He had found his home at last, had found meaning in his life. He would feed his next victim to his new god, to bring it strength, to help it resume its place in the world.

Now that he had met his god, the world would learn to fear his name.

CHAPTER SEVEN

-1-

The next morning, Faith had still not returned, though they had left the patio door open all night, which had let in a swarm of mosquitoes. The bowl of chicken they'd left outside had attracted a horde of ants, but the cat had completely disappeared.

Erik and Vickie stood on the patio looking into the woods.

"You remember what Dovecrest said," she reminded him. "Those woods go on forever."

Yeah, he thought. And for some reason he thought there were stranger things going on than either of them could imagine.

"What do you think happened?" she asked.

"I don't know," he replied. But deep down inside, he had a very bad feeling that the cat would never come back. He was probably jumping to conclusions, but he couldn't help thinking that Faith was dead.

"She's never stayed out all night before," Vickie said. "Not in all the years we've had her."

Erik nodded. "How's Todd taking it?"

"Not too well. He keeps saying that the stone got her."

"I guess I'll have to have a talk with him," Erik said, hoping he could finally get to the bottom of this whole thing, once and for all.

They stood silent, looking off into the woods.

"Faith will be all right, won't she? I mean, after all, she's a cat and cats can pretty much take care of themselves."

"From most things."

But the nervous edge to his voice betrayed his concern.

"What do you mean by that?"

He shrugged and debated about telling her about the devil worshiper that Steve Harvey had told him about. He was jumping to conclusions, though. What would devil worshippers be doing in Chepachet, anyway? It didn't make any sense.

"I mean, she can't protect herself from everything. She's a house cat, not a tiger. I just hope she hasn't been hit by a car. But, knowing Faith, she probably stopped at a neighbor's house for a hand out and decided to stick around."

Erik looked back towards the house to where Todd was watching from his bedroom window. The boy waved, almost sadly, and both Erik and his wife waved back.

"Poor kid," Vickie said. "He loves that cat. Do you really think someone might have found her and taken her in?"

"It's possible," Erik said, trying to remain positive, despite his bad feeling.

"Maybe we could make a 'lost cat' sign," she suggested. "We can hang it up in the neighborhood, and I can knock on a few doors with it. Todd's heartbroken about this. We've got to do something."

"Yeah, that's an idea," he said. "We can try the sign. I can scan a picture of Faith into the computer. And I can hang copies at the plaza down the road, too."

Vickie nodded.

"I really should search the woods," he said gravely.

"Maybe you could go see Dovecrest and he'll go with you. I really don't want you out there alone. You might get lost. I'm sure he'd go with you if you explained the situation."

Erik still wasn't sure how he felt about involving the Indian, but he nodded anyway.

"I suppose," he said. "But let me make one of those posters, first. Then we can copy it."

"Why don't you ask Todd to help you," his wife suggested. "I think his cold is better and it would do him good to feel useful."

"Sure."

Then he took one last look into the woods before returning to the house.

-2-

Just as Erik went inside, Johnny Dovecrest was going out. He'd been plagued by bad dreams all night, and even after waking up this morning he couldn't rid his mind of the terrible feeling of dread that permeated his very soul.

It was definitely beginning all over again. As if there had ever been a doubt. Only this time, he didn't know if he had the strength to win.

He stepped carefully into the woods, expertly making his own trail through the dense undergrowth. The woods hadn't changed much over the centuries, he thought, as a squirrel scurried up a huge oak tree and peered down at him. The birds chattered to themselves as the early morning sun filtered through the canopy of leaves. It was a peaceful scene of quiet beauty that might have graced a *National Geographic* cover. But he knew that this forest also held evil and death within its depths.

The woods grew thicker and darker as he picked his way forward, and before long he felt the unseen presence enter his mind and tentatively look around, like a child exploring an unfamiliar attic. Dovecrest felt the ominous, chill touch of the thing tickling his brain. Then he felt its sudden silent laughter reverberating through his mind, echoing throughout his skull like an ancient bell. It was not sound he experienced, but pure thought.

"Ah, my old friend," it said, its caustic thoughts eating into his mind like a powerful acid. "So, you, too have survived. We are two of a kind, you and I. Not really so much different at all."

The laughter echoed again.

"Only this time, you will not survive. You grow weaker, even as I grow stronger."

Dovecrest grimaced as he continued to walk forward, and the presence immediately sensed his thoughts and knew that the Indian was aware of his own weakness. It seized upon his fear and gripped him tightly until his breath came in spastic gasps. Then, just as suddenly, it let go again, and laughed.

"Come," the presence commanded, softly, but with much power. "I have something quite interesting to show you."

Dovecrest cleared his mind, breathed deeply and followed the silent command as it took him further into the woods. He tried not to think as he pressed forward, mechanically placing one foot after the other.

The open field appeared suddenly, virtually out of nowhere and Dovecrest blinked rapidly as he stepped into the brilliant morning sunshine. He stopped and saw the black stone altar waiting for him in the center of the open circle. It was just as he remembered it, formidable and indestructible.

"Come," the presence taunted. "See what I have for you."

Dovecrest sighed and walked towards the ominous black stone. Yes, something was splattered on the slab, a small figure that had once been alive. He silently prayed that it wasn't human.

With relief mixed with revulsion, he realized that the mutilated body belonged to an animal. The black fur was peeled back to expose the organs, which had been strewn out like spaghetti on the altar in a dried pool of blood. Dovecrest studied the body closely and saw that the animal's heart was missing entirely.

The Indian swallowed hard as he noticed a flea collar around the animal's neck. It was a cat. Somebody's pet. But now all that remained was a pile of moldering meat.

"A small token of things to come," the presence said. "You could join with me and save yourself. You would be richly rewarded. You would receive everything, to your heart's content."

Dovecrest refused to answer or show any emotion as he picked up the remains of the animal and cradled them in his arms. He suspected the cat had belonged to the new people, the ones whose boy had also wandered into the woods. He shuddered to think of the fate that had almost met the little boy.

"So be it," the presence said in his mind, almost regretfully. "Then we will meet in hell."

He did not realize how prophetic that statement would be at the time.

Dovecrest couldn't bring the cat back to life, but he couldn't leave it on the altar either. He'd best return the body to the owners and fabricate some explanation. He certainly didn't want them out there searching for their pet, and he knew that was exactly what would happen if the cat didn't return home soon.

Slowly, he trudged back to his house. The body of the cat stained his shirt and the laughter of the unseen presence slowly faded away in his brain.

-3-

The Patriot Plaza was just up the road a half mile or so from Erik's house where Farmington Road joined Route 102. He stopped several times along the way to post his "Lost Cat" posters to utility poles, and to stuff them into rural mailboxes. Then he pulled into the plaza, parking in front of Dockside Cleaners, his first stop.

The brand new plaza was cut from the forest like a frontier fort, and contained four small stores, each with large front windows. Just behind the plaza on the Farmington Road, he noticed a small cemetery, also cut out of the forest, with what appeared to be a brand new sign: Rhode Island Historical Cemetery #6613, Cheponaug.

He looked at the cemetery for a moment, then went into the dry cleaners where he hung up a poster. His next stop was the pizza shop. He decided to save the convenience store for last, since he needed a gallon of milk, so he went into Annie's Antiques store next.

The antique store looked out of place in the new plaza. A bell rigged to the door signaled his entrance. An old woman nodded to him from a rocking chair behind the counter as he quickly surveyed the assortment of collectibles that included everything from Victorian furniture to what claimed to be authentic Indian arrowheads.

"Can I help you?" the woman asked?

He looked around quickly and decided that he might like to browse around in the shop some day when he had more time. A large bookcase filled with old volumes caught his eye, and he wondered what treasures might be hidden there.

"Ah...yes," he said, still looking around the shop. "Could I please hang this poster in your window? I'm new in the area and our cat is missing."

The old woman got out of the rocking chair and hobbled over, leaning on a cane that looked even older than she was.

"You're welcome to hang it," she said. "But I suspect more people would see it in the Dairy Mart next door."

"Thank you," he said and taped it to the window. "I'd planned on hanging one there, too."

"Of course, I don't expect it'll do much good."

He looked at her curiously.

"Why not?"

She sighed. "Wouldn't be the first time someone's pet has disappeared into these woods. Strange things a-goin' on. Ever since that guy got run over by his bulldozer about a year or so ago."

"What?" Erik was beginning to think this old woman was senile.

She laughed. "I'm sorry. I didn't mean to spook you none. I'm just an old lady with too many memories and too many stories to tell. Name's Annie Jacques."

"Erik Hunter," he said, and shook her hand. It was cold, frail, and bony, but it radiated friendliness.

"Nice to meet you, Mr. Hunter."

"You live in the area?"

"Bout a mile up the road on route 102."

He nodded. "So, tell me this bulldozer story."

"Happened a little over a year ago," she said. "Last summer. When they was putting this road through. Farmington Road didn't exist last summer, you know."

"That's what the real estate guy said."

"Anyway, they was clearing the wood and the dozer ran into something. The driver got out to see what it was. Then, somehow, the dozer ran right over him. Squashed him like a pizza."

"He must have left it in gear."

Annie shrugged. "I don't know. But the darndest thing—the dozer'd hit a headstone—one of the ones just beyond the plaza," she said, pointing in the direction of the historical cemetery. "There was a whole graveyard buried there in the woods and nobody even knew about it."

"Hmm," Erik said. "That's interesting. How old is it?"

"Dates back to the 1700's. Roger Williams' time. The road was supposed to go right through here. But they had to change it because that was a historical site."

"I didn't know this area was settled that long ago."

She nodded. "No one did, I think. Or at least no one wanted to remember."

He frowned. This woman was definitely strange.

"But the darndest thing about the graves isn't how old they are," she continued.

"What is it, then?"

"It's the headstones themselves. One's made out of real weird stone. One of them professors from the University was here studying it and he said it's made out of a meteorite. A stone from outer space."

"That *is* interesting. A headstone made from a meteorite. I've never heard of such a thing."

"It's weird. But it ain't the only weird thing."

"What else is there?"

"The headstones. They all have strange markings. And some have weird sayings on them, too."

"Epitaphs," Erik said. "Some of those old headstones have

strange ones."

"And there were shells and Indian things all around the cemetery, too. The professors think the people in the graves might have been killed by the Indians."

"That's quite a story."

She nodded again. "And the Indians surrounded the place with charms and things, quahog shells and other unusual things. The bulldozer disturbed a lot of it when it ran into the stone. See, I have a few here."

She went behind the counter and brought out a necklace of polished shells, streaked with blue-violet and white. It had a striking resemblance to the charm Dovecrest had given them, the one Vickie had hung on their back door.

"Course the string was all rotted away," she explained. "But the shells were like new."

"Interesting," Erik said. "How did you wind up with it?"

"I own the land," she said. "Course I can't use half of it because it's a historical landmark. But I did pick up a few things that the professors and the historical guys missed."

"You've lived in the area for a long time?"

"Lived in this town all my life and I'll be 86 next month. When the road went in I built the plaza and opened my store. The store don't make no money, mind you, but the other tenants pay the bills and it gives me something to do. The Dairy Mart does quite a business. And the pizza place, too. That's where I'd hang my posters if I were you. 'Course, like I said, I don't suspect they'll do much good."

"So you say strange things have been happening ever since they found the graves?"

"That's right. Pets disappearing. People hearing voices. Weird noises in the middle of the night."

"What do you think it is?"

"There's a curse upon this place," she said in a firm voice. "And the dozer done disturbed those graves and woke up the curse."

Erik laughed nervously but she cut him off immediately.

"Don't you laugh until you know what you're laughing at, young man," she said. "You just go look at the graves for yourself before you make fun of an old woman, and then you tell me if you don't feel the hairs rise up on the back of your neck. You just go look, and then you tell me."

"I'm sorry," Erik said. "I didn't know if you were being serious or just joking with me."

"I'm not joking."

Erik nodded. "Thanks for letting me hang the poster, ma'am. And when I get a chance I will look at those graves."

"If I see your pet, I'll be sure and let you know, Mr. Hunter. Maybe she just wandered off."

"Thanks. I appreciate that."

The bell rang quietly as he closed the door behind him.

-4-

Melissa Jones frowned as the man hung the poster of the cat on the window of the Dairy Mart. He'd told her mother that the cat was lost, and that made her feel bad. She'd had a puppy once and it had run out into the road and had been hit by a dump truck. That was when she was just a little girl, but she still grieved.

But that seemed like such a long time ago. Since then her parents had divorced and she'd been living with her Dad in Miami for the last two years. But she'd fallen for a boy in her class and her Dad had sent her back to New England as punishment. Now she'd be staying with Mom in the store. She was afraid it was going to be a long summer. There weren't any kids her age in this hick town, let alone cute boys.

It wasn't even lunch time yet and she was already bored. She watched the man with the lost cat take a jug of milk out of the cooler. She felt bad about his cat. It looked really cute in the picture, like it was the kind that purred when you pet it. Maybe she could help and find the cat. That would be good. Anything would be better than staying here and waiting on customers.

"Mom, can I go outside? Maybe I can look for the man's cat."

"I don't think so," her mother said from her seat behind the cash register.

"But I'm bored. And it's a nice, sunny day outside."

"I'd rather you stayed here with me."

"Can't I just go for a walk?"

"Maybe later," he mother said.

Melissa knew what that meant. It meant it was going to be a long, boring summer spent inside the boring store and watching people buy bread and milk and ice. All of her friends in Miami would be outside now at the beach, or swimming in the pool.

"It's not fair," she mumbled as she watched the man with the lost cat pay for his bread and milk.

His eyes locked with hers for a moment, and, although he tried to smile, she saw that he looked scared, almost like the way her Mom had looked when her Dad had first left. She didn't like it when adults looked scared.

"That man must really miss his cat," she said quietly after he had left.

"What did you say?"

"Nothing," she replied.

But she really would like to help the man find his lost cat. Maybe she'd get a reward. Or at least she'd get to pet the cat. She looked over at her mother and yawned. All the while, the gearbox of her mind was hard at work.

CHAPTER EIGHT

-1-

Erik had lost just about all hope of finding Faith when he pulled back into his driveway. He'd left his computer-generated poster everywhere he could think of and, as expected, no one had seen any sign of his cat. He really didn't think the posters would do any good, but he felt like he should do something. And hanging the posters did keep his mind off of his real fears.

He supposed that Faith had wandered off into the woods in search of mice or birds—and after that, he didn't want to think of what might have happened. The cat could still be out there, of course. But he didn't believe that, not for a minute. Most likely, Faith had run into trouble of some sort. It had either become hopelessly lost—after all, she was a city cat—or had fallen victim to a larger predator in the woods. She might have been hit by a car, but he had been keeping an eye out on the side of the road in both directions, and hadn't seen a dead cat. Or, the other possibility—that some weird cult had gotten hold of her. It was just too unsettling to even consider.

He supposed he'd have to go and find Dovecrest and ask the man to go with him to search for the cat. He couldn't very well go off into the woods again on his own. The idea chilled him to the bone, even now, in the noontime heat of a summer day. That wasn't to say that Dovecrest didn't unnerve him nearly as much. But at least the Indian was a known quantity, while the woods were totally alien. The whole thing was probably a product of his own imagination. He had gotten after Todd for letting his imagination run wild, and now he, a grown man, was doing the same thing.

Slowly, he stepped out of the car, stalling for as long as he could as he walked towards the house. He wasn't looking forward to coming back home without any news about the cat. Todd and Vickie probably expected him to have found Faith at the plaza, or wandering by the side of the road, and he knew his returning without her would be disappointing.

Moving into the new house had not gone according to plan, he realized. First the incident with Todd, and now the cat. There were plenty of things to be unnerved about, as well. The radio talk show host and his story about the devil worshipper. Dovecrest. Then the lady at the antique store and her story about the graveyard. She had upset him more than he cared to admit.

He would explore that graveyard for himself as soon as he had the chance, and follow up by doing a bit of research of his own. Finding out the real story would put an end to the wild speculations that were whirling about in his mind—speculations that weren't doing him any good right now. Right now, he had an ominous feeling about that graveyard, without having even seen it. He could almost feel something wrong, now that he knew it was there across from the plaza.

"I've been watching too many horror movies," he mumbled.

Suddenly, a voice called his name, startling him and embarrassing him at the same time.

It was Dovecrest, who had appeared out of nowhere. Erik flushed, wondering if he had heard him talking to himself.

"Sorry to startle you, Mr. Hunter," the Indian said.

"No...it's nothing. You just sort of surprised me, that's all."

Dovecrest shrugged and Erik almost imagined that the man was telling him he had every reason to be frightened.

"I saw the posters about your missing cat. I think I might have found her."

"Oh, thank God. My son's been...."

But he could tell from Dovecrest's expression that something wasn't right.

"What's the matter?"

Dovecrest winced like a doctor about to deliver bad news to a patient, and Erik immediately knew that Faith was dead.

"I think it's your pet. You'll have to check it out for yourself. It is difficult for me to tell."

"What happened?"

Dovecrest shrugged. "I don't know," he said, and Erik knew he wasn't telling the truth. "It looked like an animal got ahold of her. Maybe a fox. Sometimes a wolf or even a bear wanders into these woods."

He held out his hand in a gesture of helplessness.

"Like I said the other night, these woods are dangerous. It might seem like you're just a few minutes away from the city, but it's a whole different world out there. Your little boy was lucky. Your cat wasn't."

"Where is she?" he asked.

He had no doubt now that the cat was his and he just wanted to get this over with now.

"I've got her at my place. I didn't want your boy to see."

Erik nodded. "Then let's go."

It only took a couple of minutes to walk to Dovecrest's place, a small log cabin that had existed long before the new road connected it to the rest of civilization. It was probably four rooms, Erik guessed, and a still-standing outhouse suggested that the place had only recently been connected to indoor plumbing, probably when the road was cut through.

The house looked out of place in the neighborhood of green manicured lawns. It stood right in the middle of a wooded area, as if it had been built within the forest. Then Erik realized that this house had stood here long before this new suburbia had intruded into these parts. The place had no driveway; and Dovecrest didn't seem to need an automobile. Erik guessed that, until the new road and the plaza, the man must have lived out here by himself, a hermit living off the land of the reservation.

Dovecrest led him around to the back of the house to where

a modern oak picnic table stood like an anachronism beside this frontier cabin, breaking the illusion that they had traveled back in time to the 1700s. Dovecrest further broke the illusion by opening a green plastic garbage bag and peeling it back to show its grisly contents.

"I found her in the woods," Dovecrest explained.

It was Faith all right. Erik knew immediately when he saw the red collar around the cat's twisted neck. His stomach churned as he looked at what remained of his pet. The head and neck had been bent backwards at an impossible angle and the animal's chest and belly had been opened up like that of a specimen in a sadistic lab experiment. Organs and entrails spilled out like spaghetti and the cat's eyes remained open—even in death the cat seemed to silently scream of unspeakable horror.

"It's her," Erik said. "God help me. How am I going to explain this to my kid?"

Dovecrest shrugged. "I would suggest you just bury her as quickly as you can and say a fox caught her."

Erik shook his head sadly. It was just a cat, but he felt like crying. Faith had been part of their family.

"Yeah," he said. "I can't let him see her like that. It's not right. How'd...her neck get twisted like that?"

"That's how a fox makes its kill. It goes for the throat and breaks its prey's neck. At least it's a quick death."

Erik nodded and wrapped the remains back up.

Only later, after he had buried the cat in the corner of the back yard did he stop to wonder why whatever had killed Faith hadn't bothered to eat its prey. But by then, Dovecrest was already gone.

-2-

Todd watched from his bedroom window as his father placed the plastic trash bag in the hole and covered it over with the freshly dug dirt. Todd knew he should cry about this. He'd cried over things that were far less important and much less sad. Like the time his Little League team had lost its first game. And the time his cousin had ripped one of his baseball cards by accident.

But when he thought about Faith being gone, the tears just wouldn't come, even though he wanted them to. He felt sad, all right. Terribly sad and lonely and let down, as if a part of him had been torn out and thrown into that garbage bag to be buried with his cat. Yes, there was an emptiness like he had never felt before since this was his first experience with death.

But another, stronger emotion drowned out his grief, engulfing him in a bottomless fear that choked away at his very breath. This terror lived with him always now, had, in fact, been his constant companion and bedfellow ever since that awful night in the woods.

His Dad had told him that Faith had been killed by a fox and he wouldn't let him see his cat because it would bother him even more. But Todd was already beyond being "upset" as his mother called it. Not because Faith was dead—that itself would have been terrible enough—but because he *knew* what had killed his beloved pet. It hadn't been a fox, or any other animal either. He knew what had happened to Faith and that was why he was almost paralyzed with a terror so complete and so devastating that he couldn't even cry now when he needed to the most.

It was that thing in the woods. That rock. That's what had gotten to Faith. That's what had killed her. He knew it without the slightest doubt.

And he knew the thing would kill again, would kill him, in fact, if it possibly could. The thing enjoyed killing. It fed off of making its victims suffer. The thing wanted to kill again, and it wanted to kill him.

He had escaped from it once and that had made it angry. That was why it had chosen his cat. He knew this. He also knew that the thing was growing stronger and more powerful with each day. Now it would wait for its victims to come to it. But soon enough it would be strong enough to come for them. Strong enough to come for him.

He turned away from the window and crawled onto his bed, remembering how Faith would curl up beside him on his pillow and allow him to scratch behind her ears, pretending to only tolerate his advances while betraying her pleasure by purring like a lawnmower.

Todd sighed. Somehow he'd have to get that thing in the woods before it got to him. He didn't know how, but he knew it was important, that his very life depended on it.

But he was only a little boy and this...this *thing* had all of the strength and experience of time.

Then, when he realized how small and insignificant he had suddenly become and how hopeless his situation was, only then did the tears begin to flow.

-3-

After burying the cat, Erik decided it was time to do a bit of research and find out a bit about the history of the place where he now lived. He began by logging into the *Providence Journal's* online service. Annie from the antique store was right about the bulldozer incident, which had happened just about a year ago.

The driver had been killed when the machine ran over him. It was ruled a freak accident. But it was rather odd that an experienced driver had made such a critical mistake, and questions had been asked, but never really answered.

The dozer had, indeed, unearthed the graveyard, and, in particular, a headstone made of some sort of meteoritic rock, according to a geologist from the University of Rhode Island. The cemetery contained thirteen graves of unidentified colonists from the early 1700's. It was believed to be a small colony of Europeans who had been massacred by the Narragansett Indians. A couple of URI professors were still researching the subject, but so far, there wasn't much specific information. Erik jotted down their names. Maybe he'd give them a call at some point.

The path of Farmington Road had, indeed, been moved after the discovery of the historical cemetery. The final construction of the plaza and the housing development had begun as soon as the road was finished. A look at the police log did show a number of pet disappearances, including that of a Rottweiler, but most of these disappearances had subsequently been explained as road kill.

It was a little bit weird, but there was no mention of anything out of the ordinary, or any reference to cults or devil worship. Erik breathed a mental sigh of relief. The old lady's imagination must have been as vivid as his. There was also no mention of the rock that his son had told him about, though the description did seem consistent with the rock that made up the meteoritic headstone. But the headstone was right out in plain view at the side of Farmington Road, not in the middle of the woods, so that made no sense.

Finally, he checked out Dovecrest's name on the *Journal's* search engine. There were sporadic references to a Johnny Dovecrest from all the way back to the late 1800's. Dovecrest and his father, Erik assumed, had held tribal offices with the Narragansetts until the 1960's, when Dovecrest seemed to retire even from tribal life. Some of Dovecrest's relatives were still heavily involved in tribal affairs, it seemed.

Erik wondered if it were unusual for Dovecrest to have the same name as his father—he didn't know if the Indians used "juniors." He decided it might be worthwhile to visit the small town library, and perhaps even the town hall to check out some of the vital records.

Still, there were some things that didn't add up. Like Todd's mention of the big rock, and his broken geologist's hammer. And how Dovecrest always seemed to be in the right place at the right time—first to find Todd, and then to find the remains of his cat. Then there was the question of his cat—why hadn't the predator eaten its prey?

Just on a hunch, he decided to do a search on Satanic cults. Even as he typed the keywords into the search engine, he felt a shiver run up his spine.

-4-

Melissa waited until her mother was busy with a customer ordering fifty "Powerball" tickets, and then she took the opportunity to slip out the back door unnoticed. The lottery jackpot was up to about a zillion dollars and there'd been more people buying tickets than buying food. It was just about supper time, the time when the store got really busy with people stopping on their way home from work, and Melissa knew her mother would be pretty busy for awhile. There was plenty of time for her to sneak out and look for the lost cat. And who knows? Maybe there were some cute boys in town.

She made her way around to the back of the plaza and around the side of the store. The cat wouldn't be wandering around in the parking lot—someone would have seen her by now—so she supposed it had either gone off into the woods or had been hit by a car.

She looked at the woods beside the plaza and decided that would be the best place to start. She wouldn't actually go deep into the woods—she was really a city girl at heart. But she sure was anxious to get out of the boring store where she'd been cooped up all day. She followed the edge of the parking lot, looking into the woods as far as she could. A blue jay regarded her with interest, and she wondered if it were true what they said about jays, that they'd peck at your head if you came too close to their nests. The bird looked harmless enough, but she wasn't about to find out first hand. She walked away.

The wood grew thick quickly, and before long she realized that her view was blocked by the heavy undergrowth and she found herself standing beside the iron railing that surrounded the cemetery. She'd seen this graveyard before, though she'd never been this close. The place gave her the creeps. Now, as she looked at the ancient, crusty headstones, she felt a sudden chill.

One headstone stood taller than the rest and seemed to stand over her like a statue, casting a long shadow across the ground. There was no doubt that the thing was old—older than she could imagine. Yet, unlike the other headstones, this one looked new and ageless. With a mixture of fear and fascination, she opened the iron gate and made her way inside the small graveyard. She walked around the edge of the cemetery, looking at the place as if it were another planet.

Unlike the cemetery where Grandpa was buried, this one didn't have green grass or planted flowers. In fact, nothing seemed to grow near this place, as if the very ground were poisoned.

Frowning, she looked back at the largest headstone, the one that was so old, yet looked so new. Unlike the others, this stone was black and shiny, as if it had been polished like the side of a brand new car. While the other stones had funny, blue-green stuff on them, this one was perfectly clean.

Slowly, she walked around the thing, attracted by its strangeness. It had weird lettering on the front. The letters were hard to read. Some were normal, though worn with age. Other letters were different, things she had never seen before.

"I am watching you," she read slowly

As soon as she read the words, she imagined the headstone actually *was* watching her, and she shivered violently. Sudden panic covered her like a blanket, blinding her with fear. She laughed nervously.

"This is like something out of a bad horror movie," she said out loud, and then laughed again.

Then she turned away from the graveyard and a sudden, mindless panic gripped her, squeezing her heart, it seemed. She felt a horrible tightness in her chest and an overwhelming urge to escape. Without thinking, she ran as fast as she could, tripping over the gate, and then stumbling over branches and undergrowth as thorns bit at her legs. She ran with her head down, mute with terror and totally unaware of her surroundings. She imagined the thing—a nameless, horrible thing—watching her, chasing her....

Only after it was too late did she realize she had run off into the woods. By then she was already hopelessly lost.

-5-

Erik was astounded that there were over 4,000 entries under "Satanic Cults" on the search engine. Some were reputed cases of ritual child abuse by cultists. Some appeared to be the lunatic ramblings of paranoids who claimed that either (a) the government was a Satanic plot, or (b) they were personally being tracked down, chased, and persecuted by Satan and his minions. There were some "official" Satanic church sites that claimed that Satanists were really just rugged individualists who worshipped a god that favored "unique individuals," a redundancy in Erik's mind, and that these people used harmless magic to advance themselves and their personal causes, like getting rich, having lots of sex without shame, and obtaining power and control over themselves and their environment.

Then there was the site that required you to be "registered." With some trepidation, Erik applied for a username and password, thinking that this would probably get him put on some sort of FBI hit list. He received the confirming e-mail, but still couldn't log on until he verified his existence twice, confirmed his e-mail address again, and submitted to an age verification. He was just about to give up and move on when the password finally worked and he was able to find his way onto the message board.

There were literally hundreds of posts onto the message board, ranging from satanic theology to a discussion of when a child might be old enough to choose his religion for himself (16 years old seemed to be the consensus). Most of the messages were rather silly, and Erik had the impression that most were written by adult children who were playacting rather than serious.

However, buried deep within the archives of one of the threads he found a disturbing message from a man with the username of "Seti the First" who claimed that the voice of the Master was calling him home, calling him to the east and that he needed 12 disciples to follow him. Erik followed the thread and replies as this Seti plotted his course through the south and through New York and Connecticut. The writer claimed to have been sanctified in the blood of the innocent, and that he was personally going to set the Master free. Some of the replies treated him like the nut case he seemed to be, but there were some who seemed to be cheering this guy on, acknowledging his ideas about the flesh and blood of the innocent, and claiming to also hear voices.

Erik might have dismissed the entire thing as irrelevant were it not for Seti's last post. He read it again.

"The voice is very close now," Seti wrote. "I will find him before the full moon and set him free using the flesh and blood of the innocent. All who follow Him will be rewarded. Those who oppose Him will suffer misery and death at the black stone."

The last entry was datelined Chepachet, Rhode Island.

-6-

Dovecrest turned off the six o'clock news and sat by the window, listening to the chirping of the crickets in the woods. He disliked the television news, and hadn't even had cable TV connected until a few months ago. Now that it had all started again, he watched out of a sense of duty. He especially disliked the news reporters, who made a drama out of everything, and tried to look grim as they reported tragedy, but were secretly hiding their delight in covering other people's misfortunes. This had been a particularly good news night, he thought, looking out into the woods and wistfully yearning for earlier, less complicated times.

He sighed and wondered how so many years could have passed so quickly, how he could have grown so old and so weak. He was tired of it all. Tired of the waiting and now tired of the responsibility. He felt like he had already lost the battle before it had even begun. If only he could just pack up and move and leave the worries to someone else. But as Medicine Man of the tribe, it was his responsibility, and had been for so, so many years. No one else would take over. No one else even believed. So he shouldered the burden alone.

He sat back in his chair and remembered that time so long ago when Running Deer lay dying in his hut, and how Dovecrest had sat beside his bed to obtain his wisdom. Running Deer had seemed older than the earth itself, then, and Dovecrest had wept to see him dying. But Running Deer smiled and welcomed death.

"It's all right, my friend," he said. "My time has come. I am old and worn out by time as the rock is worn away by the river. It is my time to go and I face my death with joy. It is your time to take over my burden. I give my medicine to you. You will be the watcher now, the guardian of the tribe and of the people."

And when his spirit passed on later that night, his face glowed with the joy of death, as if a great weight had been lifted from his shoulders.

Now Dovecrest understood how Running Deer had felt. He, too, would be happy to lie down and die, to let his spirit go to the Great Beyond in peace. It had been long overdue; the years had drained both his spirit and his will. And now, after his last trip to the terrible place of death, he felt even more drained, as if he had been poisoned by his enemy.

This was not good medicine. Not good at all. And worst of all, he could not give up, could not even die, for he had no one to come after him, no one who would take up his heavy yoke of responsibility.

Reluctantly, he flipped the television back on again and channeled to a different station. The news was just going off and the anchor recapped the day's top stories: a three car wreck on I-95 that left two people dead; a murder-suicide in Barrington; and an apartment fire in Cranston.

It had been a good day for the news—a busy day with plenty of human tragedy. The newscaster almost gloated in his good fortune. And already the first call had been put in about a single teenage girl missing from a Dairy Mart in Chepachet.

-7-

Seth was daydreaming when it happened, remembering a time that seemed like a lifetime ago. In the daydream, he was back in high school, a skinny, pimply-faced kid with thick glasses and no dates. This particular daydream had haunted him often, as he recalled just one of the painful incidents of his teen-age years.

He was in gym class, which was bad enough by itself, but this was worse—this was gymnastics and, his worst nightmare, the parallel bars. He stood beside the bars with a half-dozen kids, all of whom hated his guts. They were spotting for Jeff, the school jock and his most-hated enemy, who was showing off all the tricks he could do on the apparatus. The kid moved across the bars as effortlessly as a chimpanzee. And, Seth recalled, he had about the same I.Q. as well.

Seth was useless as a spotter, of course. If the kid did fall he had about as much chance of catching him as he would have had being inducted into the Baseball Hall of Fame in Cooperstown. At best he would get in the way just enough to break Jeff's fall, probably killing himself in the process. Not that Jeff was likely to fall. And not that he was likely to even try to catch him if he did.

He snuck a glance over to the girls' side of the gym and saw Jennifer, blonde, blue-eyed, the head cheerleader and every high school boy's wet dream, which meant that she was completely out of Seth's league. For that matter, all the girls in his school were out of his league, even the ugly ones. This, of course, had done nothing to stop him from falling hopelessly in love with Jennifer, lusting after her every waking hour and through much of his sleeping ones as well.

He had watched her from the corner of his eye as she took her turn on the balance beam. The firm muscles of her long, smooth legs tightened as she began her routine. He watched in growing excitement as she did a forward roll on the bar, exposing one of the cheeks of her deliciously firm ass for one short but incredible moment, a moment that Seth would remember forever....

Then he heard his name being called. He blinked and saw Mr. Russo, the gym teacher, glaring at him.

"Come on Seth, you still awake? You're next. Up on the bars."

Seth gave him one of those "what, who me?" grins and the other kids began to giggle, already anticipating the train wreck that was about to occur.

"Come on, Seth. Get up there," the teacher said, and before Seth even realized it, Jeff had come around behind him and hoisted him up and over the bars, one of which was now on either side of him.

He reached out and grabbed one with each hand, while Jeff lifted him up until his arms locked at the elbows.

"Just keep your arms stiff," Mr. Russo said. "Then, when Jeff lets go, swing your legs up over the bars."

Seth sensed the eyes of the entire gym class on him now, even those of Jennifer, watching with the other girls from across the gym.

"Ok, Seth. Are you ready?" Jeff said, his voice filled with contempt.

Seth wanted to scream out, to demand to be let down before he killed himself up here on this horrible torture machine, but everyone was watching, probably hoping that he would scream out in terror so they could use that as ammunition to torment him further, as if he didn't already have enough misery in his life.

No. He wouldn't cry out like a wimp. Not this time. He would do this. He *could* do this.

He nodded. Jeff let go.

For a split second he held himself up between the bars, looking out at the gym class and thinking that, yes, this wasn't so bad after all. Then his muscles betrayed him and his arms let go.

He felt it and he knew it was happening, but he couldn't stop it. Gravity pulled his body straight down, but his arms, locked at the elbows, flew out to the sides and the space between the bars wasn't large enough to accommodate the impossible angle of his elbows....

He heard the cracking of his bones before he actually felt the pain. But what he saw hurt much worse than the pain he felt, even though each of his arms were being broken in two places, literally ripped apart at the elbow joints. As he fell he saw Jennifer watching him. But not just watching. Laughing. All of them were laughing. But in his own mind, he knew that Jennifer was laughing the hardest.

Later that night, he'd receive a nasty beating from his father, just icing on the cake, so to speak, for being a "wuss" and not a "real man" like Daddy was.

Seth felt the tears running down his cheeks and suddenly realized that the daydream had passed. It wasn't the gym teacher calling his name after all, but someone else—make that some *thing* else.

He blinked rapidly, trying to clear the cobwebs from his brain. He wasn't Seth anymore. He was Seti, and he was the main man here. And his new God was summoning him.

"Don't you want to make them pay?" the voice chimed in his head. "Don't you, Seti?"

"Yes. Make them pay. I'll make them pay."

"Excellent." The voice filled his brain now, inhabiting every cell, every nerve of his being. "Let us begin."

PART TWO: PURGATORY

Now I shall sing of the second kingdom,
There where the soul of man is cleansed,
Made worthy to ascend to heaven

—Dante

Demonic frenzy, moping melancholy,
And moon-struck madness.

—John Milton

CHAPTER NINE

-1-

The sun had just gone down and Erik was reading the newspaper when the doorbell rang. He opened the door to find a uniformed man holding out a badge.

"I'm Sheriff Roy Collins," the man said. "We're looking for a teenage girl and I hoped you might have seen her. She went missing at about six o'clock."

"Come in, Sheriff,"

"Thank you. Call me Roy."

Erik motioned him into the living room, where Vickie and Todd were watching TV together, and he made the introductions.

"Can I get you some coffee?" Vickie asked.

"No thank you, Ma'am. I just wanted to ask a couple of questions."

The sheriff took a small photo from his shirt pocket and passed it to Erik. He recognized it as the young girl he'd seen earlier in the day at the Dairy Mart.

"I saw her this morning," he said. "At the Dairy Mart."

"Do you recall what time?"

"Well...it was this morning. Before lunch. I'd guess ten o'clock or so."

"She was at the store until about suppertime," the sheriff said. "You haven't seen her since then?"

"No," Erik said, handing the photo to Vickie. "I haven't been outside since then. We just had supper and then were relaxing."

Vickie looked at the photo and shook her head. "I'm sorry, Sheriff. Is there anything we can do?"

Collins shook his head sadly. "We may be organizing a search party. We think she may have wandered off into the woods."

Todd leaned over and looked at the photo.

"I know where she is," he said confidently.

"What? You've seen her?" Erik said.

"No. But I know where she is."

"Then tell me," Collins said, walking over to the boy. "Where is she, son?"

Todd looked at the sheriff for a long moment.

"The rock's got her."

"The...what?"

"The big rock in the woods. It's got her. It tried to get me, but I got away, so it took her instead."

-2-

Seti dragged the girl through the woods by the arm, ignoring the briar bushes and the undergrowth that pulled at them. It was pitch dark and he didn't have a flashlight, but he knew exactly where he was going. The voice guided him, and all he needed to do was follow. The voice had told him where to find her, had instructed him to bring a roll of duct tape to stick across her mouth and stifle her whimpering, and had told him what to do with her when he found her. A couple of hard smacks to the face had taken the fight out of her.

He had wanted to kill her right then and there in the woods and probably would have, if the voice hadn't stopped him.

"Not yet," the voice had instructed. "Bring her back with you and be patient. I will tell you when the time is right."

So now he dragged her back towards his car, an old Taurus which was parked on Route 102. He slapped her in the back of the head and tossed her in the passenger's seat, then quickly tied her hands behind her back with a short length of twine. Tears rolled down the girl's face as she whimpered, but the duct tape did its job and he didn't have to listen to her. Not that it would have mattered. When they cried it only stirred him up. He never felt sorry for them, no matter what they did. And this one was a slut anyway, he decided. A little cock-teasing slut. He locked the door, then went into the driver's side and climbed in.

The girl looked at him accusingly through a blackened eye, but he just grinned.

"I'm taking you home with me," he said to her. "And we're going to have some fun. You're gonna like it!"

Then, with anticipation, he pulled out onto Route 102 and headed down the road to his makeshift campground in the woods. The voice had told him to be patient. But it hadn't said he couldn't amuse himself with his new victim in the meantime.

-3-

For the second time in a week, Erik found himself tramping through the woods in the darkness with a flashlight. Only this time, at least, he wasn't alone. Several State Troopers from the Scituate barracks, Pastor Mark, and about a dozen volunteers from the village fanned out on either side of him, spaced 25 feet apart as they moved carefully forward through the thick forest. Each of them carried a portable walkie-talkie and a compass to keep them walking straight.

Erik felt about as comfortable in the woods as zebra would on a tight rope, but he really hadn't been able to refuse when the sheriff had asked for volunteers. It could have been his own kid out there—in fact, if Dovecrest hadn't found Todd when he wandered off, it *would* have been his kid.

He walked slowly forward, sweeping the ground with his flashlight beam. He still couldn't help thinking about what Todd had said—the rock got her. And he couldn't help remembering the last post he'd read on the Satanic web site—"those who oppose him will suffer misery and death at the black stone."

Then there was the graveyard with the headstone made out of a meteorite. Could that be the black stone? Was there a connection? He wanted to ask the sheriff these questions, but the man had looked at Todd as if he were crazy when he'd said that the rock had got the girl. He'd laughed it off and told the boy he'd been watching too many movies. Then he'd asked Erik to go to the shopping plaza and meet up with the other volunteers.

Pastor Mark had already been there when Erik arrived, but he had not had the opportunity to ask the preacher any questions. He wondered if the pastor would think he was crazy, too. It was funny, he thought, how the Bible dealt with Satan and demons and people believed, but such things weren't accepted in the modern world.

The forest was darker than everything he could imagine, and he looked to the right and the left and was comforted by the flashlight beams to either side of him. Whatever moonlight that shone was completely obliterated by the canopy of leaves overhead. There were no paths here, so the going was very slow as he pushed himself past and through bushes and around tree trunks. It looked as if no one had passed through this section of woods in decades.

Vaguely, he wondered what it was about these woods that attracted kids into them—first his son, and now this teenager. It didn't make sense. Then he reminded himself that the actions of kids seldom did. Like the time he, as a little boy, had stuck a bean in his ears so he couldn't hear the teacher, and then had been unable to get the thing out without a painful and embarrassing trip to the emergency room. That hadn't made sense either.

He pressed forward, not knowing exactly what he was looking for. Occasionally the searchers would call out the girl's name, but there was no response. He wondered how far into the woods she could possibly have gone. And that black stone—that still haunted him.

Then, just ahead, he caught sight of something white in his

flashlight beam. He charged through a rhododendron bush and there it was, right at the base of a large oak tree.

He recognized it immediately—it was a girl's white sneaker, and it probably belonged to the missing teen.

"Over here!" he called. "I've found something."

Everyone on the line stopped as the word was passed down. The State Trooper on his right edged over to take a look.

"I'd say it's probably hers," he said. "Don't touch anything. We may be looking at a crime scene."

-4-

Todd woke up sweating, his heart beating a mile a minute. It was just a nightmare, he thought with relief. But it had been so real.

He had been in the dark, huddled in a tiny space with his knees up to his chin and his hands tightly tied behind his back. The knots hurt his wrists and his feet hurt with pins and needles where they had fallen asleep, as his mother called it. A thick piece of tape held his mouth closed and it was hard to breathe through his nose. Something had hit him in the nose, he realized, and in the eye, which was swollen almost shut. He also hurt in his private places, but he couldn't even think about that because what had happened was just too scary and too disgusting.

He could sense the presence of the man who had done this to him—he was very close but he couldn't see him in the dark. He knew this man would kill him. It was only a matter of time. He sensed it and he knew it.

Then he had woke up and realized it was just a dream, a horrible, frighteningly real dream that still echoed throughout his entire being. Yet he also knew that it was not a dream. At some level, it was real and either was happening or would happen in the near future.

Then, with sudden shock, he realized that he was dreaming about Melissa, the missing girl, and that for her, it was not a dream at all, but a terrible, terrible reality.

Todd wanted to tell someone about his dream and tell them the girl was in trouble. But he knew they wouldn't listen. The sheriff had laughed at him when he'd mentioned the rock, and even Mom and Dad thought he was imagining things.

He rolled over and wished that Faith were here with him to curl up in his arms. He didn't expect to get much more sleep that night.

-5-

It didn't take long to positively identify the sneaker as belonging to Melissa. The searchers then converged on the spot, which was roped off with yellow tape. Erik joined the sheriff and one of the State Police investigators and they followed the girl's trail through the woods until it abruptly ended on Route 102.

The State Trooper spent a long time looking around near the side of the road, and made Erik stand back and away so as not to disturb anything.

"I think we may have a crime scene here," he said. "I'm calling in the detectives. It looks like the girl was put into a car."

"Could someone have stopped and picked her up?" the sheriff asked.

"Well, I'm not a crime scene expert," the trooper said. "But it looks to me like there was a struggle here. I'd say the girl was abducted. In fact, I think she was taken in the woods and brought back here."

Erik shook his head. "Is there anything we can do?"

"We'll put out a state-wide alert," the Trooper said. "We'll put her picture on the news and hope someone's seen her. And we'll follow the evidence and see what we can find."

Erik didn't like the sound of the man's voice. It didn't hold much hope.

"Come on," the Sheriff said. "I'll give you a lift home. There's not much else we can do tonight. We'll let the experts take over."

Erik nodded and got into the sheriff's car. It was almost midnight by now, and he was glad they were only a half mile from home.

"What was your boy talking about? The sheriff said. "A rock? Where'd he get that from?"

Erik sighed deeply. "He was lost in the woods a couple of night ago. I don't know what it is about woods that attract kids," he said.

"Happens all the time," the sheriff said.

"Yeah. Anyway, he was lost for about an hour. Johnny Dovecrest found him and brought him back."

"Now that one's a weird bird," the sheriff said.

"He does appear a little strange. But he found Todd in the woods. Todd wouldn't say anything at first, but later he told me there was a big black rock in the woods, and that the rock tried to get him. He claims he got away by hitting the thing with his geologist's hammer."

The sheriff was silent for a moment.

What do you think happened?"

"I really don't know. Todd's not the kind of kid to make up things like that. He's a pretty practical kid, usually. But it just sounded so farfetched. I mean, a rock trying to get him. I thought it was all in his imagination. Then I heard about that gravestone in the historical cemetery. I wonder if there's a connection. I don't think he could have wandered that far, but...."

His voice trailed off into silence. The sheriff pulled into Erik's driveway and parked the car.

"There have been some weird goings-on since they dug up that cemetery," the sheriff said.

"Like what?"

"Well, nothing I can really put my finger on. Just weird stuff. Like people reporting voices from the woods. Pets disappearing. And just...well...I don't know how to say this...."

"Just try."

"Well, it's a creepy feeling. Like I said, I can't put my finger on it. Just a creepy feeling. And now your boy going off into the woods and getting lost. And this teenager disappearing. I don't know. It just *feels* wrong."

"Yeah," Erik said. "I think I've felt it too. I thought it was because I just moved into the place and it wasn't familiar. But now I'm not so sure."

He stopped and waited a moment before he opened the car door.

"Sheriff, have you heard any reports of a Satanic cult in the area?"

"Hmmm. There's been rumors for as long as I can remember about things going on in the woods. Mostly the Indians get blamed. But it's just urban legends. There hasn't been a kidnapping or a murder in this town for fifty years, at least. I think every small town has rumors. I don't pay any attention to them."

"I heard there was a Satanic cult traveling east and they were in Rhode Island."

"I'll check into it. But my guess is that the devil hasn't got anything to do with this girl's disappearance. I suspect we might just have your run-of-the-mill pervert. Or it might even turn out to be a relative. I think the father ran off and left. Maybe he's come back."

Erik nodded. "You're probably right."

"Still, though, I'll check with the State Police on your cult. If there is one around, I want to know about it."

"Thanks," Erik said, and climbed out of the car.

-6-

Johnny Dovecrest hadn't answered the door when the police knocked. He'd pretended not to be home, and since the place was completely dark anyway, they had believed it, too.

Dovecrest didn't need the police to tell him what was going on. Another child had disappeared, this time a sixteen-year-old girl. He'd heard it on a news bulletin, and even if he hadn't, he would have known. He had *felt* the girl's fear this time. It had been strong and close. He wondered if he could have helped her. He felt guilty for not trying, but he was convinced there was nothing he could have done. The entity had a human helper now, someone who was strong and swift, and guided by a power beyond anything that could be imagined on earth.

Dovecrest knew that his power was limited. Very limited. The entity might play with him and let him live, at least for now. He could almost hear the thing taunting him in his brain, daring him to come out and try to stop things.

No, Dovecrest knew that he couldn't stop the nightmare by himself. But he didn't know where to turn to for help. His own people were useless. And the white man would just think he was crazy—and why wouldn't he? The story was certainly beyond anything in modern culture—the kind of things that bad movies were made about.

The boy was the only one who would believe him. The boy knew, and Dovecrest sensed it. But what good would one little boy be against this? Unless the boy could make others believe. Maybe his father. Maybe the preacher. Maybe even the sheriff.

Dovecrest was torn. Part of him felt that he should rush out into the woods right now and confront this thing before it became more powerful—and its power was increasing each and every day. And part of him felt that he needed to wait, recruit others and develop a plan.

He feared that by the time he could do that, though, it would be too late.

Whatever he decided, he needed to do something and do it fast. He felt his window of opportunity leaving him. It was already too late to help the girl, he realized. She was gone, taken away to some place where she would be dealt with later, at a time and place of the being's own choosing. He knew the place. The time was less certain.

Tomorrow would be the day when he would begin his recruitment efforts. He would go and see the boy and his father, and try to make the man understand the truth of what the boy had seen in the woods. He would make him understand what was happening—what had happened and how history was poised to repeat itself in a new and improved version. The man—Erik Hunter—had seemed intelligent. He could make him understand. He could make him believe.

Then he would at least have an ally. Together they could perhaps recruit others and make a plan.

Otherwise, Dovecrest feared that this sleepy little town would never be the same again.

CHAPTER TEN

-1-

The Chepachet Public Library was something right out of a Norman Rockwell painting. The small, stone building was well over 150 years old, with ivy crawling up the sides like ancient weeds. The place even smelled like an artifact, Erik thought, as he opened the heavy oak door and stepped inside.

The library itself was smaller than many executive offices Erik had seen, and as he looked at the two men standing behind the reference desk he wondered why it took two people to run the place. He'd met them both before on a previous trip, though, and had taken an immediate dislike to them. When he'd asked them to order his book for the library, they had given him a hard time. The acquisitions guy, it seemed, didn't read fiction and, therefore didn't order any.

"What do you read?" Erik had asked.

"Magazines," he had snapped, and walked away.

The director, a thin, fragile-looking man, always looked like he was going to cry, and when he wasn't crying he was constantly whining about something. He hadn't been much help either about ordering the book.

This time he avoided the two and went right to the reference shelves. They didn't even acknowledge him, and Erik understood why the library was always empty. Although the library in Foster was a good five miles further down the road, it was well worth the investment of time to deal with librarians who actually liked helping people.

But this time he knew the information he needed could only be found here, in the local village vaults. He found the section on local history and began his search.

Most of the published history books weren't much help, except for some pictures of the village from the past century. He found a couple of pictures of the old library—it really hadn't changed in the last hundred years, and Erik suspected that Jane Austen was still catalogued under "new fiction." He found some old pictures of the village, and even of some of the woods along Route 102, where the new road had been cut. He also found some pictures of the Narragansett Indian tribe, and one of Dovecrest. Although the picture was a hundred years old, Dovecrest looked exactly the same. It must be his father, Erik thought, but the name in the caption was clear enough. It had to be a misprint.

He rummaged through the ancient card catalogue—although the library system was on computers, no one had bothered to computerize the local records. Erik did ask the director about that.

"Oh, we haven't gotten to that yet. We're too busy cataloguing the video tape collection."

"Won't the videos be obsolete now that people have DVD players," he'd asked, but the director merely shrugged and went on to complain about the burning pain in his stomach, so Erik merely threw up his hands and went back to the musty card catalogue.

One entry referred to a vertical file on Chepachet history, which Erik couldn't find anywhere. With a sigh, he went back to the reference desk.

Both the director and his partner were glued to their computer screens and wouldn't acknowledge him, so he went around the desk and stood in front of them. He couldn't help noticing that the director was fooling around on E-Bay looking at lace curtains. Your tax dollars at work.

"Ah, you're not supposed to be back here," the director said. "It's employees only."

For emphasis, he pointed to a sign on the wall.

"I need to find the vertical files on local history," he said.

"Ah, those don't go out."

"I know they don't go out," Erik said, as if speaking to a child. "I don't want to take them out. I just want to look at them."

"What for?"

"What is this, twenty questions? Not that it's any of your business, but I'm doing research for a story I'm writing. I need to see the files. This is a library, isn't it?"

Erik made a silent vow to speak to someone on the town council about this idiot.

"Ah, yeah. It's just that no one ever looks at those files."

"Well I want to look at them."

The director looked at him for a moment, then decided Erik meant business and was likely to cause trouble if he didn't get what he wanted.

"Ted, could you show this guy the vertical files and open them? I'm kind of busy right now."

The dwarfish man scowled and walked off into the stacks of books at the rear of the library. Although both of these men were in their early thirties, they acted like old men—like trolls, Erik thought, guarding their little treasures under the bridge. God forbid that anyone would actually want to *use* any of the library materials. They must both have political connections, he thought, or else they'd never be able to keep their jobs.

The vertical file was exactly that—a tall, green metal filing cabinet filled with files—most of them misplaced. When the librarian opened the door, it kicked up a wad of dust that must have been fifty years old.

"Let me know when you're done so I can lock it back up," Ted said, then shuffled back to his computer.

The files seemed to be in random order, and most weren't even labeled. Erik pulled out a packet of old photographs of the World War I veterans' reunion filed with an old *Providence Journal* article about fly fishing in Western Rhode Island. None of it made any sense. It was almost as if no one wanted anything to be found.

After going through half of the top drawer, Erik was just about to give up when he came across a photograph and an article from the *Chepachet Call*, dated July, 1943.

"Ancient Altar Stone Found by Youth" the title of the article said. Underneath the title was a reprint of the photograph in the file.

The photo was of a huge black stone, an altar stone, set in the center of a clearing in the forest. Although the size was difficult to judge in the picture, the thing looked to be about eight feet long, three feet wide, and raised about three feet off the ground like a bed. What really troubled him, though, was that the thing was a deep, shiny black, like obsidian. It looked exactly like the rock that Todd had described.

The article went on to say that two boys had been playing in the woods and had found the rock. The boys had found George Fleming, the reporter and editor for the local newspaper, and he had accompanied them and had taken the photograph. Fleming speculated in the article that the stone might have been an ancient Viking stone—the Vikings had visited Newport and other areas along the East Coast, so why not here?

Behind the article, though, Erik found another one from the same writer and the same paper, proclaiming the whole thing a hoax. In the article, Fleming apologized for making up the story and involving the boys. The altar didn't exist and never had existed, he said.

Erik frowned and made photocopies of both the articles and the pictures. He'd have to show this to Todd—and maybe to Dovecrest and the Sheriff as well.

-2-

Erik stopped at Burger King on his way home and brought lunch for everyone. He found Todd in his room coloring on a loose leaf notebook.

"What ya doing, Sport?" he said.

"Nothin'," Todd replied.

"Well it looks like you're doing something."

"I'm just coloring a picture."

Todd looked over his son's shoulder at the drawing, and his heart chilled. It was a picture of the black rock in a field with a full yellow moon overhead.

"Is that the rock you saw?" he asked.

"Yeah. That's it. But nobody believes me."

"I believe you, Todd."

"No you don't. You're just saying that to make me feel good."

Erik took a deep breath, then pulled the pulled the photograph from his notebook and extended it towards his son. The boy's eyes went wide and his mouth dropped open.

"See, it is real," he said. "I told you it was."

"Yes, it is," Erik said. "Now, come on down and let's get some lunch. I brought you back a burger and fries."

"Ok," Todd said.

"Oh, and just one more thing. Don't tell your mother about this. At least not yet. Not until I figure out what to do about it."

"Ok, Dad. Just...just don't take too long."

-3-

Seti spent the afternoon playing with the teenage girl until he became bored with her. She was pretty and innocent, but he knew that she was a slut and must have enjoyed it. They all did, even when they cried and screamed and whimpered. They all wanted it, deep down inside. He'd done everything to her that he could imagine, and had let his followers have her as well, while he watched. But now the girl was little more than a zombie, staring at him glassy-eyed and without emotion, no longer conscious of him or of her surroundings. Like a rotten fruit, she'd spoiled much too soon, he thought.

He looked at her for a moment and almost felt sorry. She

looked like she'd been in a train wreck. Her hair was tangled and plastered with dirt, blood, and other bodily fluids. Her left eye was swollen shut and her nose was battered and broken. If he could have felt any emotions, he would have felt sorrow. But instead, he just felt empty. Besides, he knew she had loved every minute of it. They all did.

"Be patient," the voice cautioned. "Wait until the sun goes down. Then you will bring her to me and I will begin the process of becoming complete."

"Yes," Seti said. "When the sun goes down." He only had an hour or so to wait. And then his dreams would be fulfilled.

"I will go gather the others and prepare," he said, "for when the sun goes down."

Then he kicked the girl to the side of his small camper and went out to gather his followers.

-4-

Dovecrest had planned to go and see the boy and his father, but he'd seen Erik drive by in the morning, and he never did quite find the energy to stop by in the afternoon. Now that the sun had set, he knew he had waited too long and would have to act on his own. He'd forgotten how the voice could influence you—sometimes, the influence was just to do nothing. It seemed to tap one's strength, one's willpower and one's energy. Sometimes it caused people to do things; other times it caused people to just sit on the couch like a vegetable, and watch the world go by.

Yes, Dovecrest thought. It's been working on my mind.

He knew that tonight was something big, something important. For one thing, the entity had left him alone for the last hour or so—he no longer felt its presence like a heavy blanket over his face. That meant it was occupied with other things. Like the girl he had taken.

It had taken the cat, and that had made it stronger. The life of a teenage girl would be most prized and would bring its strength to a new level. The girl was still alive. It had waited until the time was right. Now that the search party had left the woods and the police were concentrating on Route 102, it had the chance it was waiting for. He might not be able to stop the monster, or even stop the pawn it was using tonight, but if he could snatch the girl away, he might at least buy a little more time—and a child's life.

This time he didn't take the rifle, but stuffed the Beretta into his waistband, just in case. It wouldn't have any effect on the entity, but a .45 caliper hollow-point could sure do some damage to its human helpers.

Dovecrest stiffened his shoulders and went out the back door. I am getting way too old for this, he thought, as he walked into the woods, relying only on his instincts to guide him. He knew where it would happen—he had always known that. And now he knew when it would happen as well, at least this first installment of horror, anyway. There would be more versions after this, new and improved versions, but he couldn't worry about that now. One thing at a time.

He picked his way through the woods as effortlessly as if he were crossing his own bedroom. He had lived here for more than a lifetime, and had made it his business to know this land. It, and the knowledge of what was about to happen, were his only advantages.

The altar stone wasn't very far away in terms of mileage—only about a half mile as the crow flies—but it was centuries away in terms of time. Dovecrest could almost feel himself traveling back in time as he walked. He felt the decades, the centuries peel away as he returned to a more primitive time, a time when good and evil were stripped of their trappings and laid bare for the world to see. A world where evil existed in its most pure, unadulterated form, not camouflaged by politics or culture or religion. This was a world where it dared to show itself as it was, without shame and without excuse, a world where it did not hide or justify its existence, but challenged good men to stare it in the eye.

As Dovecrest made his journey, he felt some of the old power returning to him, and even as he did he realized that he had made one critical mistake. He had failed to purify himself properly and make peace with God. How could one do battle against evil without seeking the protection of its counterpart? It had been easier in the old times, when worship was part of the daily life. Now, not even his own people believed anymore. And the white man was not much better. Sure, he made his weekly pilgrimage to whatever church he attended. He worshipped faithfully and then returned to his everyday life of lying, cheating, stealing....

But it was too late for such thoughts now, and he felt himself weakening beneath his own doubt, even as he felt the strength of the entity growing near. He was close to the altar now, and he could feel its presence radiating throughout this place. The white man was strange, he thought—he equated graveyards with supernatural power. That wasn't to say there was no power in those places of death. But the truly powerful, once they were set free, preferred to infest and infect places of life and power, places where they felt strong and secure. This was such a place, and now it was cursed with this awful and awesome power, which would only grow stronger with each new death.

Dovecrest heard the sound of voices ahead and he knew he was near. He stopped and moved forward slowly to the edge of the clearing. He slipped behind the trunk of an ancient, withered oak tree and watched.

There were thirteen of them, as he had expected, carrying torches and dancing naked around the ancient stone. It would have almost looked comical if he didn't know what was happening. It was the kind of thing they would make documentaries about, and show them on cable TV, and people would laugh and say, "look at those idiots, can you imagine!" Only this was not funny, and although much of it was little more than a silly ritual to entertain the thirteen, who, of course, needed carnal pleasures for their own fulfillment, the essence of it all was very real and very serious.

The realness of it all became very clear when he saw the naked body of the teenage girl being laid out on the altar stone. Dovecrest hunkered down behind the tree and waited for his chance. If it came, the opportunity would be swift and fleeting.

-5-

After dinner, Erik used the excuse that he was going out to the plaza to check on news of the missing girl, and then he went to see Dovecrest. He actually did stop at the plaza, which was now a makeshift command post, of sorts. But they told him what he already knew—there were no new leads in the case. He looked for Sheriff Roy and couldn't find him—he was going to show him the pictures of the altar stone and ask him about them. But he did find Pastor Mark, who had been offering some comfort to the missing girl's mother earlier.

"Erik, I wanted to thank you for your help last night," Mark said.

"Oh, it's nothing. It could be my kid out there."

"These are very sad times. Very sad times."

Erik made some small talk as he tried to figure out how to ask the pastor about the altar stone. Finally, he decided to just jump in.

"Pastor, do you have a minute? There's something important that I'd like to share with you?"

"Why sure, Erik. What is it?"

Erik led him over to his car and took the folder containing the picture and the article from the front seat.

"Pastor, I've been doing some research and I think something very strange and unsettling is going on here. I'm not sure what to do."

"What do you mean?"

"Well, these woods.... Here. Look at this stuff I found in the library."

Pastor Mark looked at the picture and read the article, then the retraction that followed later.

"What are you saying, Erik? That this stuff is real?"

Erik went on to explain what had happened to Todd, and what the boy had told him. Then he told him about Steve Harvey, the radio talk show host, and his story.

"I don't know if any of these things are connected or not, or how it all adds up, but even the sheriff thinks there have been some weird goings on here. And now we have a missing girl."

Mark rubbed his forehead for a long moment. "So you think this...thing, this rock is out there in the woods somewhere? Why hasn't anyone found it?"

"Because I don't think it *wants* us to find it. Look, I know this stuff all sounds crazy and I'm probably being paranoid because my son got lost in the woods a couple nights ago and now this teenage girl has disappeared. But I had to share this with someone. If I'm wrong you'd at least be the guy to help me out."

"Well, I am from the old school, the conservative school...."

"And what I'm saying is 'New Age', right?"

"On the contrary. The Bible teaches that Satan exists and that there are demons. That was true in ancient times. Why wouldn't it be true today?"

"So you think this is possible?"

"Possible, yes. I'll admit that I'm not convinced yet, but that doesn't mean it doesn't exist. It just means I haven't been convinced yet."

"So what should we do?"

"I think we should begin by seeing if this altar stone really does exist."

"If it does, I know one man who could lead us to it. Johnny Dovecrest. I'm sure he knows something about all this."

Mark nodded. "Then let's go pay him a visit."

Seti watched his followers dance naked around the altar. There was Rhonda, the dark-haired one, so pregnant that she might burst open at any second. She disgusted him now, but the brat might have a use. And there was Marion and Monique, the twins. Fine young bodies and great in bed—especially together. Crissy, the blonde, with the perky, upturned breasts and the expert tongue. Shanika, the black one with the hard body. And Rosea, the brunette, plump and juicy.

And the men. Seti wasn't as interested in the men, though he had gone both ways. Frank, the electrician, a little rough around the edges but very easy to control. And Jack, the schoolteacher, so gay that it hurt to watch him walk. Bud, the ex-cop who had been drummed out of the force for messing with children. Tony, the ex-stripper whose life was one drama after another. That one was going to be replaced, Seti vowed—he'd had enough of his emotional outbursts and pouting. The others were easy to control, but this one was emotional and unstable. He wouldn't last much longer. Then there was Pete, just 16 and a runaway. Seti imagined this life of sex and scandal was a fantasy come true for this cast-off teen. And finally, Ryan, the cold, quiet one. Sometimes Seti worried about what might be going on in that dark mind.

They were finishing the dance now, and it was almost time. Seti felt the ceremonial knife in his hand and licked his lips in anticipation. He felt the entity quivering in his mind, almost orgasmic with anticipation.

Guided by the voice, he walked closer to the altar, past the ring of dancers, and looked at the girl. She looked back at him through one good eye with a gaze that showed no fear, only resignation. Just get it over with, she seemed to say, though her lips did not move. Ah, Little Girl, he thought. If only it were that easy. A quick, painless death would be so easy. But it was not about to happen. He had something more for her in mind. Her suffering was like food, her pain like nectar to this unseen god. And he so very much needed to feast.

Seti lifted his arms up over his head, pointing the knife up towards the moon. The dancers stopped, on cue. The time had come.

"Master," he said. "I give you this child's suffering as my gift to you. May you feast and grow strong."

He lowered the knife to her heart—merely a tease, since he wouldn't cut deep enough to kill, but just deep enough to begin a cut that would open her up for all to see. Then he and the dancers could feed on her still-living entrails while the demon fed on her pain. He felt the knife pierce the tender skin, and the first drops of blood spill forth. He pulled a drop of blood up with his finger and licked it off.

Then he felt a sudden impact in his side, just below his shoulder. He felt the impact before he felt the pain or heard the loud crack of the gun. The sudden jolt sent the knife deep into the girl's flesh, much deeper than he intended and straight into her heart. She jolted upright, her body almost pulling the blade into her, and her eyes bubbled up in her head. Seti dropped the knife and reeled to face his attacker as another bullet flew past his left ear. A madman was dashing across the open field, shooting a semi-automatic pistol as he ran.

"Stop him!" Seti shouted, as the voice in his brain suddenly shrieked.

His followers immediately surrounded him, and he saw Tony go down, holding his chest. Good riddance, Seti thought, as he knelt down on the ground, holding his own side. His wound wasn't fatal, he knew, but it would need treatment.

He saw his followers flee; only Ryan turned to face his attacker. Even the ex-cop ran away from the onslaught.

Then, as if by magic, the attacker stopped cold and threw up his arms. The gun fired uselessly into the air until it clicked on an empty chamber. Then the attacker looked directly at Seti, horror filling his eyes. He turned and ran back the way he had come like a whipped dog.

Then the voice filled Seti's brain with a force that he could never have imagined.

"You idiot!" it screamed throughout his being. "It's been spoiled! She didn't suffer enough!"

Just the same, the voice had increased in power by tenfold. In fact, it was no longer just a voice now, but an actual, physical presence. Seti could feel it at the base of his neck, and when he reached around he felt a solid growth, like a tumor that had run amok. The thing was the size of a small melon, and squishy to the touch.

"That's right," it said. "I am part of you now. And I will remain part of you until you can bring me back in my own, true form!"

Seti felt the blood running down his side and over his legs. He looked up at the moon one more time before passing out beside the altar stone.

CHAPTER ELEVEN

-1-

Erik and Mark knocked on Dovecrest's door, but there was no answer.

"Maybe he's around back," the pastor said.

The back of Dovecrest's place butted directly against the deepest woods, and with only the light from inside his living room shining out, it was as dark as pitch. Mark took a small flashlight from his pocket and guided them around to the back.

The back door was open and swinging gently on its hinges in the breeze.

"That seems strange," Erik said, and poked his head inside. "Why would he leave the door open?"

They called Dovecrest's name and were debating whether or not to go inside when they heard the first gunshot. It was quickly followed by a second, a third, and more. The two men looked at each other and then towards the woods.

"This is probably the only place in the state where a cell phone won't work," Mark said. "We'd better take a look ourselves."

Erik hoped that the pastor knew his way through the woods better than he did. Mark hurried to the edge of the woods and located a path leading in.

"I used to be a Boy Scout," Mark said.

Tentatively, Erik followed.

The pastor's flashlight was small but very powerful, lighting up the woods just enough so that they could follow the path.

There were more gunshots, quick and in rapid succession, but it seemed that the pastor had already locked in on the sound and was heading towards it. They struggled forward through the woods for several minutes, then Mark stopped.

"Wait, I hear something."

Erik pulled up beside him and listened. Someone was heading towards them.

"Who's there?" Erik said.

Suddenly, Dovecrest crashed through the bushes, nearly knocking them both down. The pastor's flashlight shone full in his face. His eyes were wider than saucers, and his brow was contorted with a look of outright terror. Erik didn't think he had ever seen such a look of panic on a face before.

He locked his arms around Dovecrest and the two of them fell to the ground in a heap. Dovecrest struggled to get up, but Erik, with Mark's help, held him down.

"Relax," Mark said in his best soothing preacher's voice. "What's going on."

Dovecrest struggled for a moment more, then looked at the two men as if seeing them for the first time.

"It's...it's gone now," he said, finally. "It was so...awful, but it's gone."

"What's gone?" Erik asked, and Dovecrest looked at him as if he were a complete idiot.

"Come on," Pastor Mark said. "Let's get you back home and then you can explain everything."

Dovecrest nodded slowly. "I have to tell someone," he said. "Even if you don't believe me."

-2-

Dovecrest allowed the two men to lead him back to his cabin. Nothing had gone according to plan, he thought, but at least he had saved the girl undue suffering. If only his aim had been a little better and he could have killed the leader. But he knew even that wouldn't have mattered in the end. It would have just found another leader, and the girl still would have been sacrificed.

He trudged through the wood between the two men and wondered how he was going to explain it to them. They wouldn't believe. Surely they wouldn't believe. And when he tried to take them back to show them, all of the evidence would be gone. Or else they would think *he* was the one who killed the girl.

Still, he had to try, though. He couldn't win any other way. The demon was too powerful for him, even now, and it wasn't even fully transformed yet. It would only become stronger with each new sacrifice, and he would be powerless to do anything to stop it.

The few hundred yards back seemed endless. His mind was still reeling from the shock he'd experienced when the thing had entered his mind. It had felt like a sharp, red-hot needle being thrust directly into his brain. The thing had taken him over completely, making him shoot the pistol harmlessly into the air while he watched the girl bleed to death on the slab. Then, when all of his ammo was gone and his mind was virtually writhing in agony, it had turned him loose, just as suddenly as it had taken him over. The thing had left one thought in his mind—that it was as easy as that for it to take control of him at any time. The message had been clear—you can go free for now, but I can have you back whenever I want you. And I can make every moment of your life a living hell.

Finally, he saw the lights of his cabin come into view and he knew he was home free, at least for now. Tomorrow would be another story. But he didn't want to think that far ahead. All he could think of was a hot cup of steaming black coffee and sitting down at the table to unburden his soul to these two men, who probably thought he was either lying or insane, either a criminal or a maniac. But he no longer cared what they thought. The time had come to tell his story.

The first thing Dovecrest wanted to do was make coffee.

"That's really not necessary," Erik said. "We'll be fine."

But the Indian insisted, saying that he needed a strong cup of black coffee, so Erik tried to be patient as he sat at the kitchen table, exchanging worried looks with the pastor. Finally, Doverest placed a cup of coffee before each of them. Erik added cream and sugar, and waited for Dovecrest to sit down. Once he had, Erik slid the file with pictures of the altar stone and the accompanying story across the table to him.

Dovecrest looked at the pictures without showing any surprise, then nodded as he looked over the newspaper clipping.

"I think you know what this all means," Erik said. "And I'd like to hear about it."

Pastor Mark nodded. "I'm interested, too."

Dovecrest looked back and forth from one to another, and Erik could tell from his expression that the man was having an internal struggle about what to say next.

"I don't think you'll believe me," Dovecrest said.

"Just tell us what you know," Erik replied. "At this point I think I'm ready to believe anything."

"OK. First of all, let me begin by saying that I'm an old man."

Mark nodded. "We're all getting older."

"No," Dovecrest corrected. "I'm an *old* man. But I'm not getting any older. I was born just about 350 years ago, right here in this forest."

"That's impossible...," Erik said, and Dovecrest held up his hand.

"See, I knew you wouldn't believe me."

"OK, ok. I'm sorry. Go on with your story."

"I was born about 350 years ago in this forest, and I became the medicine man for the tribe. Mostly I'd heal cuts and bruises, and give out herbs to women trying to have babies. There wasn't much too it, really, until the Evil Ones came."

"The evil ones?" Mark asked.

"Yes. The evil ones. You see, the founder of this place, Roger Williams, said that anyone could live here and worship whatever god they chose in whatever way they chose. So people from all beliefs and all faiths were drawn to this place. That's why the Evil Ones came. So they could worship their evil god and his demons.

"Only worshipping the devil wasn't exactly what Roger Williams had in mind. His idea of religious freedom didn't go that far, so he drove the Evil Ones away from the city and into the forest. They came here, to this place."

"So you're saying that a group of devil worshippers lived here in the late 1600's?" Erik asked.

"Yes. But their ways of worship were evil and included death and suffering. This stone in the picture is real—very real. They built it from a rock that fell from the sky, and they would sacrifice living men, women, and children upon it.

"The tribe didn't like what was going on. We worship a good god, a god of life who cares for his people, not a god of pain and suffering. Even so, we might not have interfered if our own children did not start to disappear.

"So we sent a messenger to the city to Roger Williams. We did not want war with the city or with the white man, but we could no longer tolerate the Evil Ones. Roger Williams agreed that these Evil Ones must be stopped. Some white men came and helped us. We rounded up the evil ones and put them to death. There were twelve of them and their leader. The twelve were killed swiftly. But the leader was infested with a powerful demon that had to be killed by fire.

"The men from the city told us we would have to build a huge fire and tie the leader to a stake in the center where he would be burned alive. So that is what we did. As he burned, we could hear the demon within him screaming. And the demon promised us that it would be back, and be more powerful than ever before. The burning didn't kill the demon; it only drove it back into the pits of hell. And it has been waiting for a chance to return ever since.

"As the medicine man, I was given charge to watch over this place and make sure the demon did not return. And since that time I have watched. God has entrusted me with this duty, and after I reached my 60th birthday, he granted me the gift of never growing older."

The Indian stopped for a moment and smiled. "I only wish I could have been granted that gift at the age of 30."

Erik and Mark forced a small laugh.

"And so now the demon is coming back?"

"I am afraid so, my friend."

"These Evil Ones," Erik said. "What happened to their bodies?"

"They were buried along with the ashes of their leader, and markers were put in place to keep them dead."

"The historical graveyard," Erik said.

"Yes."

"The graveyard was disturbed by a bulldozer when the new road was put through. That's what started all of this."

"Yes," Dovecrest said. "I feared that is what happened. Now I know it for sure."

"The altar stone," Erik said. "Why wasn't it destroyed?"

"It cannot be destroyed. It was formed with powerful magic from beyond the earth itself. We have tried to destroy it, but it cannot be destroyed."

"So what, exactly, is happening now?" Mark asked.

"The demon is trying to come back. It feeds off of the pain and suffering of others. It demands a sacrifice, and grows stronger with each one. After it has grown strong enough, it will appear on earth in the flesh, where it will kill and destroy."

"The missing girl—was she...."

"She was sacrificed tonight. The demon has a new group of followers and they took her to the altar. I thought I could stop them, but I failed. She was killed."

"We're going to have to call the sheriff," Mark said.

"It won't do any good," Dovecrest said. "The law won't help

us now. The girl is dead and they won't find her—unless it wants her to be found. I wounded the leader and I may have killed one of the others. But it will find replacements easily enough. No. We're going to have to handle this ourselves."

"But how?" Erik asked. "Do we burn the leader at the stake again?"

"That won't destroy it. That only sends it back to where it comes from. Then it will come back again. I think the only way to destroy it is to go to where it comes from."

"In other words, you need to go to hell," Erik said, and then realized that what he said might sound flippant.

"Yes," Dovecrest said. "I think that's exactly what has to be done."

"Ok," the pastor said. "Suppose you're right. Suppose the only way to destroy this thing it to go where it lives, even if that place is hell. How do you get there?"

Dovecrest swallowed the last of his coffee and thought for a moment. "I don't know," he said finally. "I just don't know."

-4-

Vickie was waiting for him when Erik got home. "Where have you been?" she asked. "I was so worried. "It's almost ten o'clock."

"I ran into Pastor Mark and we went for coffee," he explained. "I'm sorry, Vic. I should have called."

"It's all right," she said. "But with all that's been going on, I was worried about you."

"Thanks," he said, giving her a hug. "It's nice to be worried about. But I didn't mean to upset you."

She smiled at him. "Todd was worried too, for a little while. Then he said it was ok, that you were all right. It's like he knew."

"Is he sleeping?"

"He's in bed. Sleeping? I don't know about that."

"I'll go check on him."

Erik found that his son was still awake, but at least he was quiet and in bed with just a nightlight on. He wouldn't go to bed without it any more.

"You doing ok, Sport?"

"I'm ok, Dad. But that missing girl's dead."

"How do you know that?"

"I don't know how. But I know. I could just feel it. But I knew you were ok."

Erik nodded. Even though it didn't make sense, it made sense. "I talked with Johnny Dovecrest and Pastor Mark about that rock," he said. "And we're going to put a stop to what's going on."

"I'm not sure you can do that, Dad."

"I'm not sure I can do that either. But with the pastor's help, and Dovecrest, I think we can."

Todd didn't look too convinced as Erik studied his face by the dim light of the nightlight. And Erik admitted to himself that he wasn't very convinced either. But they had to do something.

"It'll all work out fine," he said, and he kissed his son goodnight. "Just don't tell your mother about any of this yet. It would only upset her."

"I won't, Dad. There isn't anything she could do anyway."

Erik nodded. It was really quite funny how quickly his whole world had turned upside down, he thought. He'd woke up this morning living in a normal, mundane world, and now, just a few hours later, he was having no trouble at all believing in demons and magic. Some small part of his brain still wanted to be skeptical. That would make it easy—he'd be able to just bury his head in the sand and ignore it, and it would all go away, would never have existed.

But in his soul, he knew the truth, and his son knew it too. His son felt it. Todd had almost become the thing's first victim. He's experienced it, and that made him somehow closer to it.

"Good night," Erik said, and wandered back downstairs to spend some time with his wife. He thought he'd better take advantage of a few quiet moments while he could, because he had the feeling that things were going to get extremely wild in the days to come.

CHAPTER TWELVE

-1-

The thing on Seti's back was driving him crazy. It hurt worse than his bullet wound, which, fortunately, had turned out less severe that he'd originally thought. The bullet had passed right through him, and had miraculously missed any vital organs. Monique, who had been a nurse before she and her twin sister joined him, had been able to patch him up and stop the bleeding. But she couldn't do anything about the monstrous growth that had appeared on the back of his neck.

The thing itched constantly with a stabbing pain that was worse than knives being driven into his flesh.

"It's your own fault," the thing had informed him. "Since you took the girl away too quick, I have to feed on *your* suffering."

Seti vowed that he'd find a new victim immediately to placate the demon. If it didn't drive him insane first. He'd also need to replace Tony to make up the twelve he needed to follow him. Tony's death had been fortunate, he thought. He'd wanted to get rid of him anyway, so it couldn't have worked out better. The demon had instructed him what to do; they'd carefully moved the big man's body and left it beside the road on Route 102 where an early morning commuter would be sure to find it.

"The bullets will match those in the Indian's gun," the demon had said. "And he'll be arrested and out of our way. Until we want him, that is."

Seti had to admit, it couldn't have worked out better. Now, if only he could get something decent to eat. Rhonda, the pregnant one, was supposed to be bringing him food. Where the hell was she?

He got up and looked out the window of his small camper. There she was, talking with Ryan. It looked as if they were up to no good. He didn't trust Ryan anyway.

The pain in his neck flared up like a volcano, burning and hot and sharp all at the same time. He tried to rub the thing with his hand, but it was hot to the touch. The pain only made him angry. That bitch! Why isn't she here with my food!

The pain died down just enough to fuel his fit of rage further. He stormed out the door and over toward her. Both Rhonda and Ryan looked suddenly very guilty, as if they'd been caught stealing from the cookie jar.

"Damn you!" Seti fumed. "Where's my food? I'm hungry, damn it!"

"I...I have some soup here for you," she said, nervously, holding up a small pot.

"Soup! It's July and hotter than hell. I don't want soup! I want real food."

He lashed out and sent the pot flying. The hot liquid scalded Rhonda's bare arms, causing her to scream. This only infuriated him further.

"Stop whining, you ugly bitch!" he screamed. Then in a moment of pure hatred, he forgot everything: who he was, where he was, and what he was supposed to do. He rolled his fist into a ball, wound up and punched the woman so hard in the stomach that he dislocated his wrist. The pain shot up his arm and into his shoulder blade.

Too late, he realized that he'd hit something else, too. He felt something pop inside the woman, felt her hard, pregnant belly suddenly go flaccid. She staggered backwards, holding herself and gasping for breath. Then her water broke, unleashing a putrid stream down her legs, a stream of blood-soaked liquid that suddenly reminded him of the child, and the reason he was here.

"No!" he heard himself scream, and then realized it wasn't him screaming at all, but the thing inside him, the thing that was living in the growth on his neck.

He had killed the unborn child, all right. He'd felt it and known it as soon as it had happened. And the thing living inside him was not pleased. It had had plans for that baby. And for the second time in one night, its plans had been spoiled.

-2-

Erik had a restless night filled with bad dreams, then his wife woke him up early.

"Wake up, Honey," she said. "Sheriff Collins is downstairs. He wants to speak with you."

"Ok. Tell him I'll be right down. Maybe you can offer him some coffee."

"I already have, and I'll fix you a cup too."

"Thanks, Vic."

He threw on a pair of jeans and a T shirt and went downstairs. It was a little after nine o'clock and Collins was sitting at the kitchen table waiting for him.

"Hey, Sheriff," Erik said. "What brings you out so early?"

Collins stood up and shook Erik's hand.

"I just wanted to ask you a few questions."

"Ok. About what? Did you find the missing girl?"

The sheriff looked down at his feet for a moment. "I'm afraid we did. We found her stabbed to death by the side of the road. Route 102. She'd been tortured and abused."

"Oh, God. I am so sorry."

"Yeah. We all are. We also found a man's body a few feet away. He'd been shot."

"Was he the killer?"

"I don't think so. But I need to ask you something."

"Go ahead."

"Did you see Johnny Dovecrest last night?"

"Dovecrest? What does he have to do with this?"

"We think he may be the involved. The bullet taken from the man's body was shot from the type of gun that he owns. We'll have to do ballistic tests to be sure. There aren't many .45 caliber Beretta's around here. And I know Johnny Dovecrest has one. I've seen him with it at the range."

Erik swallowed hard. He didn't know what to say. He supposed the truth was best—at least as much of it as the sheriff would believe.

"Well, actually Pastor Mark and I saw him at about nine o'clock, I'd guess. Where is Dovecrest? Have you spoken with him?"

"We can't find him," the sheriff said. "Tell me about last night."

"Well, I was talking to Pastor Mark about some photos I'd found in the library. About an altar stone in the woods. A stone where they used to do human sacrifices, so it is claimed, anyway. We decided to go see Dovecrest and ask him if he knew anything about it."

"Go on."

"When we got to his house, he was gone. We heard gunshots in the woods, so we went to find him. He was coming back to his cabin when we found him. But I don't think he killed the girl, sheriff. He may have shot that man, but if he did I'd say he was trying to help the girl. I think something is going on in those woods, something you should investigate."

"Something is going on in those woods, Mr. Hunter. A teenage girl was tortured stabbed to death and a man was shot in the head with Dovecrest's gun. And we definitely plan to investigate. We're looking for Dovecrest right now. I know he knows something he's not telling us. And I want to find out what it is. Do you have any idea where he might be?"

"No, Sheriff. I don't. But I'd like you to look at something. Just wait here a second."

Erik went into his study and retrieved the pictures of the altar stone. He passed them across the table to Roy Collins.

The sheriff looked at them and snorted.

"I've heard about this kind of thing before, Mr. Hunter. I even believed it for awhile. But I'm telling you there's no such thing as an altar stone in these woods. I've looked myself. And so haven't the people from the university. This is just an urban legend. It doesn't exist."

"So you're saying that there couldn't be a cult group out there in those woods?"

"I didn't say that. I have no proof one way or another about a cult group. I'm just saying there isn't an altar stone. If it were there, I would have found it. Now as for a cult group—anything's possible in this crazy world."

"The pastor and I saw Dovecrest last night and he claims a cult group had the missing girl and killed her. He shot one of the members. They must have moved the bodies later."

The sheriff made some hasty notes on a notepad. "Then why isn't Dovecrest around? Why didn't he call the police?"

"Because he knew no one would believe him. Sheriff, my son saw something in those woods a few nights ago. And my friend at the radio station told me there may be a Satanic cult in the area, a cult that's been killing people. I think that needs to be checked out."

"Thanks, Mr. Hunter. I will check it out. I'm on my way to see Pastor Mark right now. Then I may go back out into those woods one more time in daylight and see what I can find."

"Thank you, Sheriff. If there's anything I can do...."

"Just one thing. If you see Dovecrest, ask him to turn himself in."

-3-

After he had spoken with Erik and Mark, Johnny Dovecrest had gone deep into the woods, to a small cave on the western edge of the reservation. He'd taken his guns, plenty of ammunition, and a week's supply of canned food. If he had to, he could live off the land.

He knew the law wouldn't understand what happened. They would assume that he was behind the killings. The demon would have no problem setting it up to look like he'd killed the girl. And the bullet from his gun would be linked to the cult member he had killed.

Besides, he would be the easy suspect. He was the Indian, the outsider. He knew how it worked. When in doubt, blame the outsider. He'd seen the same pattern over and over again for more than three centuries.

In some ways, it would be easy to let them catch him. He'd be put in a clean jail cell, given three meals a day and cable TV. What more could he ask for?

But for him a life sentence would be eternity. Besides, he couldn't do anything to stop the madness from a jail cell.

He knew what had to be done. He had lacked the courage to do it the first time around, and had been content to merely imprison the demon. He thought the spells would hold it down forever, or at least until he could find someone to replace him as the guardian. But he had been wrong. The spells were temporary. And while they might have held for centuries, it took only a small disturbance to bring the demon back. And this time it had learned from its past mistakes. It would be much more difficult to defeat this time.

Furthermore, he didn't have the support of the tribe, or of the colonists. They had believed back then. They had been able to see the truth and to band together to take action. The world had moved on now, though, and people no longer saw the truth. They were blinded by modern science and technology, and could no longer see the primitive struggle between good and evil.

Dovecrest found the old spells in their hiding place in the cave. He knew what he had to do. But he couldn't act alone. He would need help, and he didn't have much to go on.

Erik and the preacher seemed to believe his story, but even they were not sure. They would probably go searching for the altar themselves, hoping to find proof. That was the tune that the modern man sang. Show me. Give me proof. Nothing could be taken on faith alone. Everything had to have evidence and proof. And that was the demon's strength. Dovecrest shook his head. If they only knew.

Of course, they wouldn't find the altar—unless it *wanted* to be found. It had remained a secret for all of these centuries, and had ways of keeping people from finding it. No, they would look for it and come up empty, then they would discredit him entirely. Unless he could bring them to it and show them....

He moved to the back of the cave, sat down and began to meditate. He needed to gather his thoughts and formulate a plan.

-4-

Erik called Pastor Mark and they compared notes. They agreed that something weird was happening in the woods, and the Pastor had also urged the sheriff to check into it.

"Sheriff Collins is trying to trace the identity of the dead man," Mark said. "I'd be willing to bet that he's a member of some cult."

"What do you think of the altar stone," Erik asked.

"I don't think the stone's the issue," Mark replied. "Maybe we should go and look for it, just the same, but even the sheriff said that the stone doesn't have to exist in order for there to be a cult. As long as someone thinks it exists, they might be drawn to this place. And the legends of this stone have existed for years, according to the sheriff."

"So what do we do now, Pastor?"

"For right now I think we need to wait—and pray."

"That's as sound advice as any I've heard," Erik replied. "Let me know if you learn anything new."

"I will. I'll see you at services tomorrow?"

"You bet."

Erik hung up the phone just as Todd walked into his office.

"Hey Dad. The girl is dead, isn't she?"

"Yeah. They found her today."

"They think the Indian did it, don't they?"

"He's a suspect. They're not sure though."

"It was the rock. The rock killed her."

"It may be more than the rock, Todd. I think there's a group of bad men running around in the woods."

"Maybe there is, Dad. But it's the rock that tells them what to do."

"How do you know that, Todd?"

"Because it tried to tell me what to do. Only I wouldn't listen. I fought back."

"Todd, could you find that rock again in the woods? If, say, the sheriff and I went with you?"

Todd thought for a moment. "It depends."

"What does it depend on?"

"It depends on if it wants me to find it or not. You can only find it if it lets you."

-5-

Seti wore a loose shirt that only half-covered the nasty growth that was throbbing and bubbling on the back of his neck. He felt like Quasimodo as he drove through the small town. The place was Hicksville, he thought, with its tiny one-room library, a miniature post office, and a small greasy spoon restaurant lining what they thought of as "main street." What a joke, he thought. The new plaza up the road was larger than this downtown. At least it had a convenience store and a dry cleaners.

He drove through main street and out onto Route 102, which would lead him to Route 6 and into Providence, less than 20 miles away. He had to recruit a twelfth follower, now that Tony was gone. But the voice in his mind—which now came from the growth on his neck, it seemed, had warned him not to take anyone from the town. Another disappearance would be noticed, and it wasn't quite strong enough yet to have too many questions asked. Later, it wouldn't be a problem—Seti was given a quick preview of what was going to happen to this town, and the sight wasn't very pretty—but for now they needed to be discreet. There would be lots of fun later, but not until the time was right.

The thing had also told him to begin looking for another pregnant woman. It had chastised him severely for killing Rhonda's unborn child. She herself had almost bled to death, and probably would have died if Monique hadn't been able to stop the hemorrhaging. The monster had tortured him for hours after he'd done that, making the growth on his neck burn as if it had been set on fire with gasoline. The next time he disobeyed, it would be worse, it had warned him.

He followed Route 6 until it turned into Hartford Avenue, certainly not the best part of town. This was what he was looking for. Anyone missing from here would probably not even be missed. He passed the section 8 housing projects, which looked like they had seen better years when Federal Funding had been available, and then passed an intersection where several hookers stood half-naked and revealing their wares. A man would have to be quite desperate to stop, he thought, and continued past, despite their best efforts to flag him down. Perhaps if he needed a woman, he thought. But he needed a sixth man to replace Tony. The numbers had to be correct. He didn't exactly know why, but he wasn't about to disobey the thing again.

He went through a section of town with a few boarded up stores and a closed down textile mill, and then he saw what he was looking for. Standing beside the on ramp to Interstate 195 stood a homeless man with a sign—"will work for food."

Oh, I'll feed you all right, Seti thought, slowing down. You'll eat better than you've ever eaten in your life. I just hope you like your meat rare.

The man was dirty, hadn't shaven in weeks, and smelled like a sewer, but he would do. Seti would clean him up and he would serve his purpose. Then, when he was no longer needed, he'd be gotten rid of.

Seti rolled down his window.

"Hop in," he said. "And I'll get you a hot meal."

"Are you a religious nut?" the guy asked. "If you're gonna preach to me I'd rather stay hungry."

Seti laughed. "I promise I won't preach to you. Hop in. I'm going to take you somewhere where you'll be happy—and welcomed."

The man appeared skeptical until Seti held out a bottle of wine. Then he grinned and crawled into the car.

CHAPTER THIRTEEN

-1-

The Sunday sermon was about evil and the reality of Satan, and Pastor Mark was in rare form. In true Baptist style his sermon was long and emotional. After the recent events in his new home, Erik found himself really listening to what the pastor had to say, and agreeing with him. Just a month ago he would have listened politely and thought that demons and devils were really just fairy tales to keep people in line. Either that or convenient villains to blame for all of the bad things that happen in the world. But now he was beginning to think that demons really were real—or at least evil people who worshipped them were.

He still had not fully digested everything that Dovecrest had told him. The Indian claimed to be hundreds of years old. He had trouble believing that—yet he had seen the picture of Dovecrest in the old newspaper looking the same age as he was now.

The part about the Satanic cult was the most believable. But he still wasn't fully convinced that the demons really existed. Perhaps if he could see the altar stone for himself. But, as the pastor had said, the existence of the stone itself didn't matter. A Satanic cult didn't need such a stone to justify its existence.

After the service, Erik saw Sheriff Collins in the fellowship hall drinking coffee. He excused himself from Vickie and Todd and walked over to the sheriff.

"Do you have any news?" he asked.

Collins nodded. "We traced the dead man to California. He was a drifter and has a criminal record. He disappeared about a year ago."

"So he might be part of a cult?"

"Anything's possible."

"Sheriff, would you talk to Steve Harvey at the radio station? He was telling me about this Satanist he had on his show. This guy was in Rhode Island a week or so ago and might still be here. He's from California, too."

"I know the one you're talking about. The F.B.I. was following them for awhile, but lost the trail."

"Do they know everyone in the group?"

"I don't think so," Collins said. "But I'll run this victim past them and see if he shows up as part of it."

Erik nodded. "I just have a bad feeling about this."

"So do I. I really don't think your Indian friend had anything to do with the death of the girl. But he knows something. I wish he'd come in so I could get to the bottom of this."

"He claims there's a cult out there in the woods and that he killed one of them," Erik said. "And I believe him. He'd have no reason to kill the girl."

"Well the State Police think he did it. But I think there's more to the story. I sure wish I could talk to him myself."

"I don't know if he'll contact me or not," Erik said. "But if he does, I'll pass on what you've said."

"I'd appreciate it."

-2-

The new man, Bob, accepted Seti's leadership without question. He was a Vietnam vet who'd become addicted to drugs and alcohol, and had developed a hatred for just about everything. Following the dark side was almost second nature to him.

Seti had fed him, cleaned him up, and introduced him to the group. Crissy had taken him in and given him sex. By morning, he would follow Seti and the group anywhere and do anything.

Looking as inconspicuous as possible, Seti stopped in the Dairy Mart for cigarettes and snack food, mostly Twinkies and hot dogs. An older man worked the counter. Seti sized him up and realized that he wouldn't be much value, either as a victim or as a follower. Just another forgettable member of the human herd.

But then, just as he was leaving, he saw her. She had gorgeous red hair—not the carrot red kind, which he loathed, but the flaming red of an autumn sunset, and emerald green eyes that were just to die for. He felt his loins twitch as she entered the convenience store, and he tried hard not to stare. What was even better, she was pregnant and it looked like her due date was very soon.

He felt the growth on his neck burn him, and he winced in pain, trying to hide the contortions that the thing induced in his face.

"This one," the monster said. "She'll do just nicely. Her child can replace the one you killed."

Yes, Seti thought. It would be two for the price of one. He licked his lips at the thought of the fun he could have with her.

He took his shopping bags and walked slowly to his car, hoping she would leave soon so he could follow her and see where she lived. He slid into the driver's seat and lit a cigarette while he waited. He turned on the engine and played with the radio to make himself look inconspicuous. Moments later, his efforts were rewarded and she left the store.

She was wearing an attractive blue maternity dress and he guessed that she had just come from church. How quaint. He watched as she climbed into the passenger's seat of a white SUV. A man was driving and a boy sat in the back seat. The boy gave him a piercing look as the SUV backed up and then drove off onto Farmington Road.

Again he felt the monster speaking to him, yet not really speaking. The boy was the one that got away, it explained. How perfect it would be to take his mother, and then later, to take him.

Seti thought it would be fun to take the whole family, then the demon reminded him that it was planning on taking the whole town. Seti was anxious to move this to the next level and get rid of the thing growing from his body, but the monster seemed more patient now that it had a foothold on the physical world. Still, Seti felt that he needed another victim soon, just to take out his own frustrations.

He followed the SUV at a respectable distance and noted when it turned left into the driveway of one of the raised ranch houses that had just been built. Yes, how perfect, he thought. Their back yard borders the woods. This one would be easy pickings.

"But not until the time is right," the voice said sternly, punctuated with another red-hot pain that almost made Seti lose control of his car.

"Not when I'm driving!" he screamed. "You'll kill us both."

"No," the voice said. "I'll only kill you. I can't be killed, remember."

And Seti wondered, for the first time, if the thing would destroy him once it was finished with him, or if he really would earn great rewards.

-3-

After dinner, Erik mowed the lawn and then sat out on the patio to relax and think. He was just starting to doze off when Vickie came out.

"There's someone on the phone for you, Hon."

"Who is it?"

"I don't know."

Erik figured it was a telemarketer and was about to have at them for bothering him on Sunday. But it was Johnny Dovecrest.

"Mr. Hunter, can you meet me at my cabin in twenty minutes?" Dovecrest said.

"Yeah. Sure. Where are you now?"

"Never mind. Just meet me there. I have to show you some things."

"Ok," he said, and the line went dead.

Vickie gave him a puzzled look.

"That was Dovecrest," he said. "He wants me to meet him."

"You don't think he killed that girl, do you?" Vickie asked.

"No. I'm sure he didn't. Maybe he wants to explain, or to turn himself in. I'd better meet him."

"Should I call Sheriff Collins?"

"No. He trusts me. I can't betray that."

Vickie nodded. "You be careful."

"I will," he said, and kissed her.

Dovecrest's cabin was empty when he reached it, but the door was still open so he let himself in. He sat down in Dovecrest's rocking chair and waited. Although the cabin had electricity, new appliances, and cable TV, the place still made him feel as if he were living in the past. It smelled old. Not unpleasant. It was the kind of smell and experience he'd had when visiting historical houses, like the House of the Seven Gables in Salem. It was almost comforting in a way to know that this structure had stood here for so long.

He wondered whether Dovecrest would even show up, and then he heard a creak on the wooden step outside the back door. Dovecrest snuck in, holding a finger to his lips to keep Erik from talking. Then he motioned for Erik to follow.

"Hold on to my back," Dovecrest whispered, "and just follow."

Erik grabbed into a fold of Dovecrest's cotton shirt, and allowed himself to be led into the woods. Amazingly, the Indian didn't use a flashlight, but walked effortlessly through the deep, dense woods as if he were strolling through his living room.

They walked for what seemed fifty yards or so, though Erik had no real way of knowing, and then stopped. Dovecrest turned his head all around and seemed to sniff the air. He held up a finger to gauge the wind, then peered upward, even though nothing was visible though the canopy of trees.

"Do you want to see the altar stone for yourself?" he asked.

Erik swallowed hard. He'd thought he did. But now he wasn't so sure.

"Yes," he said, finally.

"Then I will help you find it. You will need to know how to find it if I'm not here. So pay attention."

"Ok."

"Good. First, you must understand that the stone not only exists here, but it also exists beyond."

"Beyond?"

"Yes. Beyond. Beyond what, I'm not sure. But while it is of this earth, it is also *not* of this earth. It leads to a different place. A different time, maybe, or a place where there is no time. In your religion it might be the Hell that you speak of. I do not know for sure."

"I'm not sure I understand, but...."

"I am not sure I understand either. I am only telling you what I have learned and believe to be true. The thing that we are fighting comes from that other world. The closest word for it in your language would be a demon, but I'm not sure even that exactly fits."

Dovecrest paused and sniffed the air again.

"In ancient times we stopped the demon by sending it back to where it came from and sealing it off. We did this by purging the host of the evil through fire. It was successful in keeping it away for over 300 years. But now it is back again, and this time it will be more difficult.

"I have examined the old scrolls and the ancient legends of my people. The secret is buried away in our songs and our dances. The only way to destroy the demon is to destroy it in its own world, not this one."

"So you're saying that we have to go...go to Hell to kill this thing?"

Erik almost laughed at how ridiculous it sounded. How many times in his life had he told someone to "go to hell?"

But Dovecrest did not seem amused by the idea.

"Yes. One of us must go into the other world and kill the demon before it fully appears in this world. Or, if we fail and it does enter our world, then we must once again send it back to its domain. Only this time we must go in with it and finish the job by destroying it where it lives."

"How do we do that?" Erik asked.

"That is not for you to know yet," Dovecrest replied. "Let us take things one step at a time. I will be the one to go into the other world. But I will need the help of others here in this world."

Erik nodded. "I'll share this with Pastor Mark. And the sheriff."

"Any help we get would be needed. But we need people we can trust. People who will believe. That is why I must show you how to find the stone. Are you ready?'

"Yes."

"Good. Close your eyes and relax your body completely."

The dark was so complete that closing his eyes made no difference to Erik, but he complied. The night air suddenly felt cool. He could feel the soft breeze and hear the sound of the crickets.

"Just relax," Dovecrest said. "Relax and feel all that the forest shows you. Reach out your mind and your heart."

Erik felt almost embarrassed to be out here alone with this Indian. It was actually quite creepy. But the complete darkness also made him feel invisible.

"Relax," Dovecrest said again, in a soothing, hypnotic voice. "Just experience your surroundings."

It took a few moments, but Erik could experience the forest without seeing it. He felt the canopy of leaves overhead. He heard the breeze and the movement of insects. He felt the strong, earthy attraction of the ancient oaks, huge living creatures themselves, an primeval part of the very earth.

And then, quite suddenly, he felt something else. He snapped his eyes open and flinched.

"You found it," Dovecrest said."

"What...."

"You found it. You sense it. I could tell."

"It was...it is...unnatural. Not of this place. It doesn't belong."

"No. It does not belong. Now, take me to it."

"Can't you...just draw a map or something? Put up signs?"

Dovecrest laughed softly. "No. You do not understand. The stone is of this world, but *not* of this world. It's location—here—is not always the same."

"You mean it...moves?"

"Yes. It moves. But if you use your senses, your instinct, it cannot hide. You will find it."

Erik did sense it and began moving forward. It wasn't very far away now, and he would find it.

-4-

Erik had taken just two steps forward when a huge spotlight burned into his eyes. He held his arms up over his face and instinctively dropped to one knee.

"F.B.I.! Put your hands up!"

Erik could feel rather than see Dovecrest launch into a run, and then a gunshot cracked in the air.

"Stop and put your hands up!" the voice shouted.

Erik squinted through his fingers and saw that Dovecrest had complied. The shot had been a warning. Then he saw that a half-dozen camouflaged men were surrounding them, with M-16 rifles trained on him and the Indian. He very carefully put his hands up over his head and wondered what he had gotten himself into.

He felt his hands lowered behind his back and a pair of hand-cuffs being placed on his wrists. The leader of the men turned him around and looked at him by the light of the flashlight.

"Am I under arrest?" Erik asked.

"You are being taken in for questioning."

"Then why do we need these," he said motioning to the cuffs.

"Those are for your own protection," the agent said.

"Don't forget what you learned tonight," Dovecrest said. "You are going to need it."

"Right now, I think I'm going to need my lawyer," he replied.

"You can call him as soon as we reach town," the agent replied.

-5-

The Demon had been fairly content once it has gotten over the shock of the first botched sacrifice. Being a parasite on this other one wasn't as bad as it had thought. It was like having a foothold into this other world, at least, and once the foot was in the door the rest could squeeze through rather easily.

The man himself, this Seti, had quickly become an annoyance, though. Unlike the first body it had used so long ago, this one didn't understand the big picture, and was not able to control his own urges and emotions. All this creature thought about was pleasure—food, sex, drugs, alcohol, and punishing others. Not that there was intrinsically anything wrong with these things, but they must be used and controlled in order to achieve the large objective. Pleasure had to be measured with patience, or else it lost all meaning.

And now that it was so close to the influence of this new one, this unrefined creature who didn't know how to act, it found itself losing patience. It felt its own cravings taking over. It began lusting for another victim now, and just about any victim would do. It needed to climb through that gate and closer into this world. It wanted to free itself from the world of fire and live in the world of air. It wanted to feast on pain, punishment, and suffering, and it sensed that there was plenty of that to go around in this world. There were victims everywhere, just waiting to be taken—wanting to be taken, even.

He would give them what they wanted, and much, much

more. This world fed on violence and suffering, just like he did. He was their reflection. He would be their mirror and show them what they were really like.

CHAPTER FOURTEEN

-1-

It was almost ten o'clock by the time they arrived at the State Police barracks, which had become a makeshift headquarters for the F.B.I. investigation.

"Can I call my wife?" Erik asked. "She'll be worried sick."

The agent motioned him to a phone and then left.

Erik tried to remain calm as he explained the situation to Vickie, and told her that they were just asking questions and that he'd be home soon. He wasn't sure if she bought the story or not, but he told her that since he was the one who found the missing girl's sneaker, they were trying to get as many details out of him as possible in their search for the killer. He also told her that Dovecrest had been arrested.

"Should I call the attorney?" she asked.

"I think you should alert him, just in case," Erik replied. "If I'm not out of here in an hour I'd like him to come by."

"Erik, are you going to be ok? They don't think you're involved in this, do they?"

"No. I think they're looking at Dovecrest. They probably want to know what I know about him."

"I'll call the lawyer anyway and tell him what's happening," she said. "Just in case."

"Ok," Erik said. "Thanks, Vic. Love ya."

He hung up the phone and waited. Although he wasn't technically under arrest, the whole situation had been designed to put him ill at ease. He sat on a hard chair at a table. The room was small and rectangular, with three drab white walls and a mirror on the third. Erik had watched enough crime drama to know the mirror was a window on the other side and that people were probably watching him. He fidgeted in his chair and tried to look inconspicuous. He wondered how long they would make him wait.

After about five minutes, the door opened and a man wearing a blue suit entered. Erik stood up as the man extended his hand.

"I'm so sorry to inconvenience you, Mr. Hunter. I'm special agent Thralls. I've been put in charge of this case."

Erik nodded and took a good look at the man. He seemed vaguely familiar. He had short, close-cropped hair, a light complexion reddened by the sun, and piercing blue eyes.

"Would you like some coffee?" he offered.

"Ah, no. Thanks."

Erik sat down and Thralls took a seat across from him.

"Could I speak to Sheriff Collins?" Erik asked.

"Sheriff Collins isn't available tonight," the agent said. "This case has involved a kidnapping and crosses state lines, so the F.B.I. is handling the investigation now."

"I see. So how do I fit into this investigation?"

Thralls laughed. "Well I can tell you that you are not a suspect. However, your friend Johnny Dovecrest is. That means that if you are withholding any information, you could be charged as an accessory."

"Is that a threat?"

"No, Mr. Hunter. It is simply a legal fact."

Erik looked at the agent for a long moment. "Ok. What is it you want to know?"

Thralls sat back in his chair and folded his hands on the table. "Good. I'm glad that you're willing to cooperate. As you know, this has been a very serious case. The stakes are always much higher whenever children are involved."

"I understand. I have a child of my own and I'm very worried."

"Then let me ask you about Johnny Dovecrest. How well do

you know him?"

Erik told the agent that he'd met Dovecrest just a few nights ago when he'd warned him about the woods and asked him to hang the amulet at his door.

"Do you believe he could be involved in supernatural rituals?"

"Frankly, I don't know what the man believes in, or how he worships," Erik replied. "But I know he isn't involved in murdering children."

"How do you know that?"

Erik told him about how Todd had become lost and how Dovecrest had found him.

"Mr. Thralls," he said. "I'm going to tell you something that may be difficult to believe, but I don't know who else to tell."

"Go for it."

"I think there's a Satanic cult living in those woods and I think they have killed the missing girl."

"That's not so hard to believe, Mr. Hunter. We also believe a cult is behind the murders. We've been following them for some time now. And we think Johnny Dovecrest is part of that cult."

-2-

When Erik got home, he explained what had happened to Vickie, then took a sleeping pill to try to relax. The next thing he knew, the sun was shining in on his face through the bedroom window.

"Hey, Sleepyhead," Vickie said.

"What time is it?"

"It's almost noon."

"I guess those pills were more powerful than I thought."

Vickie smiled. "You want something to eat?"

"No. Just coffee."

"It's already made," she said. "Sheriff Collins called about a half hour ago. He said it was very important."

"That's one person I really have to talk to," Erik said. "Let me call him back."

Erik grabbed the cordless phone from its cradle and dialed as he made his way to the kitchen. Collins picked it up on the first ring.

"I need to see you," Erik said. "Can you stop by the house?"

"I'll be right there," the sheriff replied.

Collins was ringing the doorbell before Erik had even finished his first cup of coffee. Erik poured the sheriff a cup and explained what had happened the night before.

"Dovecrest showed me how to find the thing," he said. "I think I can take you there, if you'd come with me."

The sheriff thought for a moment. "What the hell," he said. "Let's go."

Erik told Vickie he was going out with Collins and two men went out.

"Let's start at Dovecrest's place," Erik said. "That's my landmark."

-3-

Seti was having sex with Shanika when the thing on his neck sent a lightening bolt of fire through his body. He screamed and rolled off, holding onto his neck and writing in pain.

"Woah, where'd that come from? Don't tell me you've come already! I'm not near ready yet."

"Shut up, you bitch," Seti gasped, and gave her a backhanded slap across the face.

"What's the matter with you?" she said.

"Get out!" he screamed. "Get out and leave me alone."

She scurried off the bed and ran naked from his trailer as he swatted at her again.

Seti lay back down and wailed. "What now! What the hell do you want now! Can't you just leave me alone?"

The pain slowly fell away, and Seti relaxed. Then the thing made itself known.

"I had to get your attention," it said, its very presence vibrating throughout his body.

"Couldn't you have just called?" Seti asked.

The thing sent him another quick jolt of pain for his insolence.

"You do not question me," it said. "You serve me."

Another jolt of pain racked Seti, and he doubled up in agony.

"I am hungry," the thing said. "And we have visitors in the woods. It is time for a snack."

Seti rode out the wave of pain, then sat up.

"Whatever your wishes, Master."

-4-

Tentatively, Erik led the sheriff into the woods behind Dovecrest's cabin. It had been pitch dark when he'd been here last night, so he had nothing to go on but his instincts. He decided to just charge forward a ways into the woods, and then let his instinct take over.

"I've been out here dozens of times and haven't found anything," Collins said. "How do you know where to find this... this stone of yours?"

"I'm not even positive I can," Erik said. "But it doesn't involve looking. It involves feeling."

Collins shrugged. "I don't get it."

"Neither do I," Erik said. "Ok. I need to stop and get my bearings. Just be patient and let me...feel."

Erik found a relatively clear spot and stopped. He closed his eyes, folded his arms across his chest, and began to breathe slowly and deeply. He felt the hot midday sun beating down on him from the breaks in the treetops. There was no breeze, and he heard the buzzing of mosquitoes and the chirping of birds. A crow cawed a warning from above, then flew away. Nothing but the mundane sounds of the forest. He waited and opened up his mind and his soul to whatever might come in. Still nothing but the ordinary sounds of the forest.

He was about to give up and go home when he felt it. It wasn't a sound, or even a sensation, but a *feeling*, not of the body but of the soul. It was like weak push, the feeling one gets when putting two magnets together and feeling them repel one another. It was a feeling of avoidance. Don't go there, it seemed to say. There's nothing for you in that direction. He suddenly remembered the Star Wars movies and how "the force" could make people do things. In this case this force was trying to make him *not* do something.

"I have it," he whispered, and slowly moved in the direction he was being pushed away from.

The feeling grew stronger, the force in his head more insistent. Now that he could recognize it, it was abundantly clear, as obvious as a street sign pointing the way.

"This way," he said, and opened his eyes. Once he recognized the feeling, he found himself navigating easily through the dense forest, making his way around trees and bushes and still following the unspoken command.

Dovecrest had said that the thing could only be found if it wanted to be, and Erik had the sudden frightening thought that maybe this time it did want to be found. How else could the feeling have grown so strong so quickly?

But whether or not it wanted to be found didn't really matter, because it must be found, and what better time than now, in the heat of the day and with the sheriff beside him. This was definitely his best chance, no matter how he looked at it.

Then, suddenly he stepped into a clearing in the middle of the forest. The sun shone down from overhead, and the grass was trimmed, as if it had recently been mowed. He felt it before he saw it—the altar stone stood in the very center of the clearing.

"I'll be damned!" Collins said. "This just can't be!"

Erik stopped at the edge of the clearing, but the sheriff kept on walking, almost as if he were drawn towards the stone. Erik called out to him but he didn't seem to hear. Then he saw a man enter the clearing from the other side of the altar stone. He shouted a warning. Still, Collins did not hear. If anything, he walked faster.

Erik took one step forward, and then stopped. That same inner feeling that had shown him the way here now spoke to him again. Only this time the stone called him towards it.

On an instinctual level, Erik knew better than to respond to the call. Although his feet yearned to pull him forward, he resisted. Again, he called out to Collins, but the man would not respond. In fact, he was now heading across the field at a full run. Erik couldn't have caught him now if he'd tried.

Collins pulled his gun from his holster, and Erik thought he was going to shoot the man heading towards him, but he merely held the gun out in front of him. The man was too far away to clearly distinguish his features. He walked slowly, almost robotically, as if he, too, were under some sort of spell. The man had short hair, Erik noticed, and held his head at an odd sort of angle. As he came closer, Erik noticed an odd-looking growth on the side and back of his neck.

The sheriff ran up to the altar stone and waited until the stranger reached the other side of the stone. The two of them stared into each other's eyes like two cats sizing one another up before a fight.

Collins pointed his gun at the man, and then began to scream. Slowly, he turned the gun back towards himself and pressed the muzzle against his abdomen.

"No!" Erik screamed. Without thinking, he rushed out into the field and towards Collins. Before he had even taken two strides, though, he heard the muffled pop of the gun. Collins doubled forward, then fired again into his stomach.

As Erik came closer, the sheriff turned and faced him. Erik could see the excruciating horror on his face as blood flowed from his abdomen, staining his shirt red. Whimpering softly, he climbed onto the altar and collapsed onto the polished black stone. Then he put the gun to his own left shoulder and fired again.

Erik stopped and looked at the stranger, the man with the

growth on his shoulder. The man was grinning, licking his lips in pleasure as he watched the sight. And Erik swore the thing on his neck was getting larger.

Finally, Collins put the gun to his head and pulled the trigger one last time. Only then did the man turn and look at Erik. Power and hatred clouded his eyes, and Erik felt himself shrivel under the terrible gaze.

-5-

Todd sat by the side of his bed and cried. He didn't know how or why, but he knew his father was in trouble. The stone was trying to get him, too. It had already gotten one man and now his Dad was on the list.

If only he could stop it. He had somehow stopped it from getting him. Why couldn't he stop it from getting Dad?

He balled his mind up like a fist, imagined the terrible black rock, and struck out at it with all of his will.

"I'll kill you!" he screamed out loud. Then he sent out another mental attack.

It felt like hitting a basketball with a fly swatter. The thing stopped for a moment and realized he was there. But his mental blow bounced off as if it were nothing. He tried again, and felt the thing laughing at him, taunting him, and he knew he could never win this way. The thing had become too strong, or else he was too far away. It was Dad that needed help....

Then, without even realizing what he was doing, he imagined his father standing beside the rock, and he sent out another burst of mental energy. Only this time it wasn't sent towards the rock, but directly at his father. He felt the demon thing's puzzlement and then he felt his father's reaction. He felt his father's strength, and in the demon's moment of confusion, he knew his Dad was safe. For a brief moment the thing had toyed with the son and forgot about the father. By the time it turned its attention back, Todd knew that his father had broken the spell and was already on his way back through the woods.

Todd dropped to the floor, just as his mother came rushing in to see what was wrong.

CHAPTER FIFTEEN

-1-

Johnny Dovecrest sat on his filthy cot and wondered how he had gotten himself into this mess. Now he was in jail and of no earthly good to anyone. What was worse, he knew something was happening in the woods; he could sense it. He hoped and prayed that Erik hadn't done anything stupid. He wasn't ready to take the demon on yet, even if he were able to find the stone. Dovecrest feared that he had acted rashly though. If so, he suspected he was already dead.

They'd arrested him for the murder of the cult member and for involvement in the death of the girl. They had interrogated him for hours, but he had refused to say anything. He knew they had matched the bullet taken from the dead man to his gun. He didn't know if they had any evidence linking him to the girl or not. But it didn't really matter. No one would believe his story. Besides, once they convicted him of the one crime, the other was simply overkill. He almost laughed at his own unintentional pun.

He put his head in his hands and tried to think this through. How had he gotten himself into this mess? Everything he'd tried to do had gone wrong. He hadn't saved the girl and he hadn't stopped the demon. He'd killed the wrong cult leader—he knew that the real leader hadn't been hurt badly and was already up to no good. He had lured Erik into a dangerous situation and probably had him killed—or worse. And now he was in jail where he couldn't do anything about anything. At least they had left him in the local jail, he thought, and not taken him to the Adult Correctional Institute yet. He was due to be arraigned tomorrow, though, and then they'd move him on.

They told him a Public Defender would be coming by to see him this afternoon, but he really wasn't interested in talking to someone he didn't even know. He would rather meditate and try to come up with a plan—any sort of plan.

He was just about to doze off when the guard came and tapped on the bars.

"You've got a visitor."

Dovecrest nodded. He expected it was the lawyer and was rather surprised to see Pastor Mark.

"They won't let me come in," Mark said shyly. "But I wanted to speak with you."

"I appreciate it," Dovecrest said.

The guard watched for a moment, then left. "I'll be right outside when you're done," he said to the Pastor. "Just bang on the door."

Mark nodded. "Johnny, I've been praying for you and for this community. There is something very wicked going on here. The devil's work. I feel it."

Dovecrest sat back down on his cot and nodded. "The devil," he said softly. "He exists in every land, in every culture, and in every time."

"Indeed," Mark said. "Though some might claim he is not real, he walks among us. Johnny. Tell me what happened. Tell me what I can do to help."

"I told you about what happened in ancient times. When your ancestors and mine banished this demon from the world and locked him away. That was true. All of it."

The pastor nodded. "I wasn't sure I believed you the other night. But I believe you now."

"Now it is coming back, stronger than ever. It feeds off pain, suffering, and destruction, and there is no telling how far it will go before it stops."

"That is the nature of sin and evil. It leads men to their own pain and destruction."

Dovecrest sat back and rested his head against the stone wall. This man seemed to understand. But what would he be able to do?

"Ok," he said, finally. "Last night I met with Erik Hunter. I wanted to show him how to find the sacrificial stone."

"Show him?"

"That's right. The stone is not of this world. It is not always in the same place. It must be found by feeling not by seeing."

"Ok."

"So I took him and I showed him. He's a quick learner. He headed right for the stone."

"So he's found it?"

"No. At least not then. The police followed us. They took us back. I was arrested."

"And Erik?"

"They let him go. But I'm afraid he went back looking for the stone today. If so, he's in serious trouble."

Pastor Mark paced in front of Dovecrest's cell. "I should let someone know."

"The State Police and the F.B.I. won't believe you. The sheriff might. But even he's skeptical. You might tell him Erik went off into the woods and you're worried about him."

"Hmmm. That would work. Now what about you?"

"Don't worry about me."

"How can you say that? Didn't you say we need to destroy this thing? You're the only one who knows how to do that."

"When the time comes, it will work out the way it needs to. How do you say it, Pastor? God will provide."

"Yes. God will provide. But God also helps those who help themselves. Does the Narragansett Tribe have an attorney?"

"Yes. But he's arrogant and doesn't believe in the old ways."

"Johnny, that's exactly what we need right now. Call him right away. We need someone else on our side, even if they don't believe us."

"He will make it a war between the white man and the tribe," Dovecrest said. "He will claim I was arrested because of my heritage. I do not want this."

"Maybe not. But it would be best for your case right now. If nothing else, he may be able to get you out on bond. Then we could worry about the real fight."

Dovecrest nodded. "I will take your advice, then."

-2-

Erik had no idea how he found his way home, but it was with intense relief and thankfulness that he stumbled out of the woods and into his back yard. He looked up and saw Todd waiting for him at the back door. As soon as the boy saw him he raced across the yard and hugged him so hard he almost knocked him down.

"Dad! You made it! I called and called for you."

"You led me home," Erik whispered.

"I guess so. I tried to stop the rock from getting you."

"How did.... Never mind."

Vickie hurried over and hugged him as well.

"What happened to you? You look like you've been in a fight."

"I have, Vic," he said. "I have."

"Where's Sheriff Collins?"

Erik raised his hands in a pathetic gesture. "He's...he's dead."

"The rock got him," Todd said matter-of-factly. "Just like it got the girl."

"Erik, what is going on around here! Has this place gone crazy?"

"I'm afraid it has, Vic. But before I explain I need to call the police. Maybe now they'll understand what's going on."

He found the number of Special Agent Thralls.

"Do you really think that is such a good idea? They'll think you had something to do with it. Look what they've done to

Johnny Dovecrest."

Erik put the phone down and thought for a moment. Just then, Pastor Mark's car pulled into the driveway and he rushed to the front door. Vickie let him in.

"Erik, thank God you're all right! Dovecrest told me something was wrong. The sheriff found you? I tried to call him but...."

"Collins is dead," Erik said.

"He's...."

"The rock got him," Todd said.

"Oh my Lord. Tell me what happened."

Erik sat both the Pastor and Vickie down and explained.

"You mean to tell me there's a demon running around in the woods? Really, Hon, you don't believe that, do you?"

"I know what I saw, Vic."

"It's true, Mom. It tried to get me, too."

"I'm sorry," she said. "But this is all happening way too fast for me."

"I understand," Erik said. "That's why I didn't want to tell you. I didn't want to upset you."

"Upset me? Erik, this goes way beyond upset."

Pastor Mark put his hand on her shoulder. "Vickie, maybe it would be best if you and the boy went somewhere safe for a couple of days. Back to the city. Just until this thing blows over."

She shook her head. "I don't think this will 'blow over', Pastor. It's not going away by itself, is it. And, mind you, I'm still not sure I believe all of this is happening."

She suddenly began to sob, and Erik went over and held her. "It's ok," he said. "We'll fix this thing."

"How?" she sobbed.

"I don't know yet. But we'll fix it."

"God will provide," Pastor Mark said. "We must place our trust in him."

Seti staggered back to his campground feeling worse than ever. He felt tired, weak, and old. The monster on his neck had grown larger now and was taking on a grotesque form. It was so bad he dared not even look at it. He no longer felt in control of his own body, but was merely a puppet of the other.

"Please, Master. Let me rest," he pleaded.

But the monster only responded with a shock wave of pain that jolted his entire system, from his hair to his toes.

"Stop whining!" it commanded. "Keep moving."

It was obvious that the monster was taking over his body. But at this point he was powerless to stop it. The thing could control him completely now, even as it had controlled that stupid pig-like sheriff, forcing him to shoot himself full of holes until he look like moldy Swiss cheese. That had been amusing. It had also showed him just how much power the thing had already. Better to do what the Master commanded.

Seti's brain felt as if it were filled with fluid, as if he had submerged his head inside a huge bowl of pudding. He could no longer think clearly. He wasn't sure of who he was anymore, or of what he even wanted. Vaguely, he remembered the promise of a good life, of treasures beyond his wildest dreams. He tried to focus on the image—of beautiful girls and orgies and fast cars and drugs and pleasure beyond all expectations.

"Master," he said out loud, though it came out as barely a whisper. "Will I be rewarded?"

The Monster eased the pain and answered with a silky smooth feeling that radiated throughout his soul.

"Yes, my son. You will be rewarded," it promised. "Be patient. Your pain will soon be over and only pleasure will remain."

Seti kept walking; they were almost back at the camp now. The monster's words sounded good—felt good. But he was no longer sure if he could believe them.

Erik comforted Vickie as best as he could, then he and Pastor Mark went out onto the patio.

"I think we should call the F.B.I.," the Pastor said. "They need to know that Collins is missing."

Erik handed him the card with Thralls' number.

"You call him. They already think I'm involved."

"What should I tell him? That Collins shot himself full of holes?"

"This thing is just too weird to be believed. I don't know what to say anymore, Pastor. I hate to lie, but no one will believe the truth."

"I'll tell them you went into the woods together to look for this altar stone and you were separated. We don't know where Collins is. They can take it from there."

Erik nodded. Mark pulled out his cell phone to make the call but Erik was too nervous to listen. He paced to the edge of the back yard and looked into the woods. He could still feel the repulsion of the awful stone, even from here. The thing did have a terrible power. Dovecrest claimed it was a gateway to hell, and he believed him now. It was channeling its power through the cult's leader—obviously the man Erik had seen in the woods— but the power definitely came from the stone. Erik suspected that the demon on the other side of the gateway was already making its way into this world. That probably explained the growth on the leader's neck.

He looked back and saw that Mark had finished his phone call. He took his time walking back to the patio.

"They're sending out a couple of State Troopers," Mark said. "They'll pick up the trail from Dovecrest's place. Thralls is coming here to talk to you."

"Did he buy it?"

"He thinks something's fishy. He just doesn't know what."

"I guess I should just tell him the truth," Erik said. "What's the worst he could do? He already thinks I'm a nut case."

"I'll wait around with you until he gets here," Mark said. "I already told him what Dovecrest told us, so he thinks I'm crazy too for believing it."

Erik laughed. Misery loves company.

-5-

Todd put his ear to the wall and tried to listen to what his Dad was saying to the man in the blue suit, but he could only make out parts of it. He heard something about Dad finding the stone in the woods, and he felt good about that. He'd been worried that Dad had thought he was either making the whole thing up, or that he'd imagined it. Now he knew his Dad believed him because he'd seen it too. At least that part had been cleared up.

He also heard something about the sheriff being shot. It sounded like Dad had said he'd shot himself, and he mentioned some strange man in the woods, too. Then he said a whole lot of things Todd either couldn't hear or couldn't understand. The man in the suit then talked for awhile, but Todd couldn't make out what he said either. It was frustrating. He decided to go into the living room and pretend he was looking for something.

Just as he walked in, the man in the blue suit began to raise his voice.

"So, Mr. Hunter, you're trying to tell me that we have demons lurking in the woods, and they're making veteran police officers just shoot themselves for no reason. And, oh, yeah, I forgot. There's this big black stone in the middle of the woods masterminding all of this. Only the stone doesn't stay in one place. It moves."

"There is a stone in the woods, Mister!" Todd said. "It tried to get me only I got away. But it got that girl."

The man's jaw dropped and everyone turned to look at Todd. No one said anything, and then Dad came and took him by the hand.

"Thanks, son," he said, leading him up the stairs to his room. "Everything's going to be ok."

CHAPTER SIXTEEN

-1-

When Erik returned to the living room, Thralls, Mark, and Vickie were sitting in a circle with their heads down. A Rhode Island State Trooper stood by the door.

"They've found Collins," Thralls said.

"Where...where was he?"

"In Dovecrest's cabin. He'd been shot nine times with his own gun. And his throat was slit for good measure."

"In the cabin...how'd he get there?"

Thralls shrugged. "Look, I'm not buying your demon story. But I do believe there's a cult running loose in the western part of the state. We've tracked them from California and recently lost them. We'd assumed they went north, to Maine or Vermont."

"You must know Steve Harvey. The radio talk show host."

"Yeah. Good friend of mine."

"I was on his show about a week ago. He told me about these nuts. I bet this guy is the same one who was on his talk show."

Thralls nodded. "The body of the man found with the missing girl was one of them. And I still think Dovecrest is involved somehow."

"He is," Erik said. "He caught them in the middle of their little ritual."

"That may or may not be true. But our job now is to find and stop these nutcases before they kill anyone else."

"That's the first thing anyone's said that makes any sense

whatsoever," Vickie said.

"Ok," Thralls said. "Erik, I'm going to ask you to do two things."

"Whatever you need."

"First, I need you to give me a detailed description of the guy you saw in the woods. We might have a sketch artist sit with you later."

"I'll do my best."

"And, second, I want you to try and draw a map to where that altar stone was. If it does exist, the cult will be drawn back to it. We can stake it out and be waiting for them."

"That's going to be a little difficult," Erik said. "Like I said, the thing moves."

Thralls let out a deep sigh. "All right. Would you be able to take us there?"

Erik thought for a moment. Dovecrest said the thing could only be found if it wanted to be found. Yet Dovecrest had no trouble finding it. He guessed it could be found, once you knew how.

"I can't promise anything," he said. "But I'll try."

"Good. I'll assemble a stakeout force. I won't call in the sketch artist just yet. We'll try the stakeout first. If we either can't find the stone, or if they don't show, then I'll have this cult leader's picture posted on every news channel in the world. I'll have you look at some photos, too, and see if you can identify him."

"I don't know if this is going to work or not. You should speak with Dovecrest again."

"You're assuming this is supernatural, Mr. Hunter. I'm assuming it's a group of killers that justify what they do by calling it a religion."

"For all of our sakes," Pastor Mark said. "I hope that you're right."

The guards allowed Dovecrest to call the attorney from the reservation, a man who went by the name of "Slender Fox" to the tribe, and Frank Barnett in court. Barnett was, indeed, a fox, Dovecrest thought and did live in both worlds, spending half of his time with insurance cases and the occasional criminal trial, and the other half lobbying for the Narragansett Indian casino that the state of Rhode Island so vehemently opposed. Dovecrest knew that if the casino ever succeeded, "Slender Fox" would become very fat off of the project.

Dovecrest was surprised when an hour later the attorney arrived dressed in his ceremonial regalia. He was about thirty years old, and, true to his name, slim and fit. The guards led them both to a private conference room in the State Police barracks. This one didn't have a two-way mirror.

After brief introductions, Slender Fox asked what had happened.

"I'll try to make this as simple as I can," he replied. "I discovered a Satanic cult in the woods. They had kidnapped a teenage girl and were about to kill her. I tried to stop them. In the process I killed one of them and wounded another. They killed the girl anyway and planted her body and the body of the other man I killed by the side of the road where they would be found."

"Why didn't you go to the police immediately."

"They wouldn't have believed me."

"Why not? Your story sounds believable to me."

"Well, there's more to it. This cult is worshipping a demon that's real. And it's coming back. It has supernatural powers and could move the bodies before the police ever found the site. In fact, I'm not even sure we could find the site if it didn't want us to."

"Ok, slow down. Now this is beginning to sound rather incredible."

"All right," Dovecrest said. "I'll start from the beginning."

The old Indian told the entire story from it's beginnings in the distant past, while Slender Fox hastily scribbled notes. When he was finished, the two men looked at one another for a long time without a word.

"If you don't believe me, look at the old tribal records. Read the songs and the myths. It's all there. And it's happening again."

Slender Fox shifted uncomfortably in the hard chair.

"Mr. Dovecrest, I know you and your family have been tribal leaders for many, many years. But this is the twenty-first century. You're talking mythology. This stuff doesn't exist. And it'll never fly in a court of law."

"I really don't care if it flies in a court of law or not. You've got to get me out of here so I can do something to stop this before it gets really crazy."

The lawyer shook his head. "I respect the old ways and our heritage," he said. "But this, I cannot accept or understand."

"I guess I can live with that," Dovecrest said. "The young generation wants all of the ceremony and trappings of the old ways, but not the truths."

"I...."

Dovecrest held up his hand to stop him.

"It's all right. I don't ask that you believe me in anything except this one thing. I did not kill that girl. I killed the man, yes, but I was trying to save the girl."

"That is something I can believe."

"Good. Can you get me out of here?"

"I don't know. I have two courses of action. First, as a member of the Narragansett Tribe I can try to have you brought back to the reservation and tried under our laws. Since the crimes they say you committed were not on the reservation, though, I don't think that will work. Our best bet would be to claim it was self defense and you were trying to stop a felony. If we go that way I can probably have you released on bail. Then we'll do some investigation. The F.B.I. will probably break the case open on this cult group before you ever go to trial. If worse comes to worse, we can plead insanity."

Dovecrest shot him a piercing look. "I am not crazy."

"I didn't say you were. But it's a defense. And the story of the cult is still plausible."

"So you believe in the demon worshippers?"

"Sure. Why not? People worship all sorts of strange things. I just don't believe in the demons."

Slender Fox left and the guard walked Dovecrest back to his cell.

Even if he were to be released on bail tomorrow, Dovecrest thought it would probably be too late. He could already feel the tension in the air, the power that was slowly growing, and the forces that were gathering. It was going to get ugly and it was going to happen fast.

-3-

Thralls made a few phone calls and before he knew it Erik's house resembled a military base. Swarms of SWAT team officers were getting into position dressed in camouflage uniforms and carrying automatic assault weapons. Thralls gave Erik some photos to look at.

"They're not very good. They were taken with surveillance cameras."

Erik looked at them carefully. "I think it's him. He doesn't have the growth on his neck, though."

"Ok," Thralls said. "It's almost six o'clock. We need to get out there and in position well before dark, just in case they happen to show tonight."

Erik nodded. "I'm ready whenever you guys are. I hope we can put an end to this thing tonight."

"When they show, we'll get them."

Erik joined Thralls and they walked to the edge of the forest. "Should we start from here or from Dovecrest's place?" the agent asked.

"I think I can find it from here, now. If I can find it at all. I don't think it matters where I start from now."

Tentatively, Erik stepped into the woods, following the small trail that Todd had followed just a few days earlier. Thralls and the SWAT team stayed close behind. Erik was amazed at how silently they traveled. He walked for about 50 feet, then paused.

"Why are we stopping? Are you lost?"

Erik took a deep breath and closed his eyes. "Look, Agent Thralls," he said. "I know you don't buy this supernatural stuff. And I'm ok with that, at least for now. But I told you, I can't draw you a map. I can't just lead you there by sight. I have to find it by feel. So just bear with me and be patient. I don't even know if it'll work."

"Ok," Thralls said.

Once again, Erik let his mind go blank and allowed his senses to take over. He heard the sounds of the birds, felt the whisper of the breeze. He could even sense the insects in the ground and on the trees.

And, in the distance, he could feel the sacrificial stone, like a magnetic pole repulsing and attracting at the same time. It felt stronger this time, and he didn't know whether to be relieved or to be terrified.

"I have it," he whispered. "Follow me."

Slowly, he made his way through the forest, walking as silently as the experienced SWAT officers. His eyes were closed tightly, but he was still able to sense the trees, the bushes, and the rise and fall of the ground beneath him. It was a powerful feeling, a talent he never knew he had. Then again, it was probably something everyone had, if only they knew how to use it. Dovecrest had opened his eyes to this, figuratively speaking, and now it had become a part of him.

He felt the sun dropping lower on the horizon, but he knew there was plenty of time until darkness set in, so he took his time, moving slowly and carefully. Some part of him wondered if the thing had orchestrated all of this, and that he was part of some master plan. He couldn't worry about that now, though. He had to do something, and this was the only thing he knew of right now.

He thought of Vickie and Todd and hoped they would be all right. Pastor Mark had agreed to stay with them until this was over, and that made Erik feel more secure.

He felt the field open up before him, and only then did he open his eyes. Sure enough, the altar stone was positioned exactly in the middle of a field of neatly cut grass.

"There's your stone," Erik said.

Thralls rubbed his hand across his brow, rubbing away beads of sweat.

"Why can't we see this from the air?" he asked no one in particular. "We've had helicopters out this way and no one's seen anything like this."

"Like I told you," Erik said. "It moves."

Thralls shook his head, then looked back at the dozen officers who had come up behind them.

"Ok, you men. Take positions equidistant around the stone. Stay back in the woods and remain concealed. We don't want to tip them off."

Erik watched as the officers literally disappeared into the woods. He watched as the one closest to him scaled up the trunk of a tree and disappeared into the foliage. Within minutes, they were completely invisible in the forest.

"Ok," Thralls said. "Now you and I need to disappear. Unless you'd rather go back home."

"Not on your life," Erik replied. "I need to see this through. I don't care how long it takes or how many nights I'm out here."

But something inside him told him that tonight he'd see some real fireworks.

-4-

The growth on his neck was becoming so obvious that it was becoming difficult for Seti to go out in public. At the same time, the monster was becoming more demanding. Killing the cop had only wet its appetite and made it furious that the other one had escaped.

"The time has come!" it demanded. "I've waited long enough. Tonight is the night I become whole!"

Seti knew that meant he had to find a new sacrifice. The younger and the more innocent, the better. It also meant that a turning point had come for him. After tonight, he would either be free of the monster and receive the reward he had been promised, or else it would destroy him completely. His life had become so unbearable now that he didn't particularly care which outcome happened. Anything was better than what he was already enduring.

He decided to take Crissy with him tonight. She, at least, could be seen in public without people throwing up. The thing on his neck had become so grotesque that he could no longer even look in the mirror, and efforts to cover it up just weren't working. So he tucked his Glock under his shirt and into his belt, grabbed Crissy by the hand, and tossed her into the van.

"Where are we going?" she whined.

It was obvious that even his own followers didn't want to be around him now. The girls, especially, were repulsed and avoided him. Hell, he repulsed himself—what did he expect?

"Never mind," he said. "We're going to get some fresh meat. Unless you'd rather be on the menu tonight."

The blonde wrinkled her nose, but got into the van.

"We don't have much time," he said. "I want to get back before dark. The thing's hungry tonight. Real hungry."

"*That's right,*" the monster said. "*You don't want to keep me waiting.*"

Seti started the van and slowly backed up, then turned around. They'd made camp in the forest at the end of a narrow dirt trail that exited to a dirt road that, eventually, led to Route 102. Seti never would have found the place if the voice hadn't led him to it. He wasn't even sure anyone else could find it, which was probably the only reason the cops hadn't caught them by now.

He drove for awhile, then turned down Farmington Road. If

only he could get that pregnant woman. That would be a two for one. He drove slowly by the house, but noticed several vehicles parked in front and in the driveway. Cops, he thought. He could smell them a mile away.

"We'll save her for later," the thing said. *"After tonight, nothing will be able to stop me."*

"When are you going to do something about that thing on your neck?" Crissy said. "You should have it looked at. It's gross."

"I'm taking care of it tonight," Seti replied. "Now shut the fuck up."

"Hey, I'm just trying to help."

Seti turned around and headed back to the plaza on Route 102. He had avoided the area in the past. You don't shit where you eat, he'd always been told. But after tonight none of that would matter. The thing would be too powerful to stop. He pulled in at the Dairy Mart and parked the van.

"You want to help? Then shut up and do what I tell you."

Seti hunched down in the seat a little and waited. It was just 6:30, a busy time for the convenience store. He watched as a middle-aged man came out. Then a fat lady. A car pulled up and a younger man in a business suit got out and hurried into the store. Probably one of those investment assholes, Seti thought, picking up a frozen dinner or something. A few minutes later, he came back out with a small bag and drove away. Then finally, he saw what he was looking for.

He could tell by the car, a luxury SUV, that its occupant was a young mother—one of those soccer Moms who's husband probably worked three jobs in order to be able to buy expensive shit they had and left her to cart the kids around to baseball practice, dance recitals, and whatever it was that spoiled yuppie kids did these days. Yeah, this one would be perfect.

His suspicions were confirmed when the slightly overweight and dowdy Mom got out of the car with a spoiled teenage girl in tow—probably about 16 years old or so. Actually, the woman wouldn't be so bad looking if she cleaned herself up a bit and didn't try so hard to look like supermom with the me-ma long dress and sensible shoes. Hey, lady, how about some makeup and a trip to the hair stylist, he thought. The daughter was much better looking though, dressed like a slut in a short denim skirt that rode up the back of her soft, white ass.

"She's the one," he said to Crissy.

"What do you want me to do?"

"When she comes out of the store you go up to her and ask for help. You're a college student and you're having car trouble. Get her over to the van. I'll take care of the rest."

He patted the gun in his belt for emphasis.

"Now get out and look pathetic until she comes back out of the store."

Crissy was, if nothing else, good at looking stupid and help-less, and her act worked like a charm. Seti hunched down in the back of the van and watched the woman and her slutty daughter come over.

"Maybe you could help me," Crissy was saying. "I've got some jumper cables inside...."

Seti waited until Crissy opened the door, and then he timed his move, grabbing the kid first, covering her mouth with one hand and putting the gun to her head.

"Lady, get inside or I blow the kid's brains out."

The woman's mouth dropped open. She looked like she wanted to scream, but she couldn't find her voice, and by then Crissy was pushing her inside. Seti motioned her to sit on the floor.

"You drive," he said to Crissy, who shut the back door.

It was as simple as taking candy from a baby.

-5-

Erik had no idea how difficult it was to sit still. Thralls had found a relatively comfortable spot for them behind some trees, and had wrapped them both up in camouflage materials so they'd fit in. But as the minutes turned to hours, his back had begin to hurt, then he'd started to itch everywhere. His legs fell asleep, his feet cramped up and he constantly fought back the urge to sneeze. It was a miserable experience, especially when the sun went down and the mosquitoes showed up in battalions. He couldn't talk, couldn't speak, couldn't even imagine what was going to go down tonight. The waiting was almost unbearable. The suspense and the anticipation were driving him crazy. And the worst part, he felt like he always had to go to the bathroom. He didn't know how the SWAT teams did it. They must have been specially trained just to hold their bladders.

He flipped the switch on his digital watch to see the time. It was 11:35 at night, just ten minutes since he'd checked last. Jay Leno would just be starting his monologue, and the news of the day would be over. He'd been here for hours but it seemed like days. And who knew if anything even was going to happen. The demon had already killed once today. Why would it strike again so soon? Still, something warned him that it would happen tonight.

He thought he heard a scuffling in the trees and wondered if it were the breeze, or maybe one of these elite officers was as restless as he was. He would have found the thought somehow comforting. He relaxed for a moment and then realized that something was moving through the field ahead of him. It was a line of people wearing white robes and carrying torches. It reminded him of the Ku Klux Klan rally he'd seen years ago in Washington when a dozen or so clan members marched and the government had to close down the entire city to protect them from protesters. This group looked almost as pathetic.

He looked more closely, trying to make out details through the flickering of the torch flames. He recognized the leader—the thing on his head was almost the size of a basketball now, and it flopped unceremoniously from side to side as he walked. It was almost comical, because he tried to walk slowly and dignified, like a professor at commencement exercises, but the thing on his neck made it look all the more ridiculous. Erik almost laughed. Perhaps he had given these idiots more credit than they deserved. Maybe Collins had just lost his marbles for the moment, and these fools had no more power than a defrocked priest.

Then he noticed a naked woman and teenage girl, being led along by the group. The two looked as if they had been beaten and perhaps drugged. They seemed to have no mind of their own as they walked along, flanked on either side by tall men in white robes.

Erik looked around quickly to see what the reaction of the police would be. So far, though, they did nothing.

Erik counted twelve others in white robes in addition to the leader. They slowly circled the altar stone with the leader taking his place at the stone's head. He nodded and the woman and girl were placed on the stone. They huddled together, holding one another for warmth and comfort. Only now did they seem to be aware of their surroundings. He heard the girl begin to whimper.

"Please let her go," the woman said. "She's just a child."

Erik heard a click, followed by a bird call, the signal that the troops were about to move into action. Thank God, he thought. The last thing he needed was to witness another killing today, particularly that of an innocent woman and her child. He held his breath and waited.

The leader raised his hands up over his head and shouted a brief chant. Erik could feel the troops moving, inching forward. But he could also feel something else, something sinister. A mist appeared out of nowhere just as the SWAT Team moved forward. The cult leader turned to look at the advancing troops, then closed his eyes. His head slumped to the side on his shoulders, and the growth on his neck seemed to straighten up and come to life.

"Halt!" Thralls shouted. "No one move! We have you surrounded."

The leader held his hands over his head for a moment, as if obeying the command. Then he took a step forward into the sacrificial stone. At first, Erik thought it was a trick of the light, or the mist, or of his own fatigue or nerves. The growth on the leader's neck was forming into a definite shape now, and the leader took another step into the stone. The entire lower half of his body, from the waist down, absorbed itself *into* the stone.

The woman and girl began to scream in agony as the thing came toward them, rippling through the stone like a tidal wave. Someone opened fire on the leader, but if the shot hit, it had no effect. Other shots rang out, and the twelve followers in white robes began to scream and scatter. One of them jerked backward and dropped; a smear of blood appeared on his back. Another was shot in the head and dropped. But still the leader advanced across the terrible stone like a ripple through a still pond.

The scene was a war zone now. The victims on the slab screamed in agony as they, too, were literally absorbed by this thing that had turned into a monster. It was growing larger and was glowing a bright red, like a hot piece of coal in a camp-fire. The original leader's head had all but disappeared into the molten mass the creature had become. Erik could just see the tiny face contorted in the worst kind of agony imaginable. The SWAT team peppered the thing with gunfire, but the bullets seemed to pass straight through, or were absorbed into the stone itself, which had also become like molten lava.

The woman and her daughter burst into sudden flames, and the demon rose up like a rearing cobra, spitting flame like poison. Erik watched in horror as the flame hit an officer, imme-diately transforming him into a red-hot inferno. He felt another shot of flame pass just to his right where it caught a fleeing officer and incinerated him on the spot. The heat from the blast singed the hair on Erik's right arm as he'd held it over his face.

He snuck a quick look back at the altar stone. It resembled a huge funeral pyre now as the stone, the sacrificial victims, and the demon all burned with an intense fury, lighting up the night sky. The SWAT team had given up the fight now, and were either dead, dying, or running for their lives. Erik had no idea what happened to Thralls, and didn't wait around to find out. Dovecrest was right. This was no ordinary battle. His only chance was to escape, regroup, and determine how to destroy this thing before it really was too late.

He looked back once as he ran and saw what looked like the entire forest engulfed in flames. Then again, maybe it already was too late, he thought grimly.

CHAPTER SEVENTEEN

-1-

Erik had no idea how he found his way through the woods and back home. His survival was strictly due to luck and not based on any special skills or abilities of his own. As far as he could tell, the entire SWAT team had been destroyed in a horrible attack of flame, molten lava and brimstone. It was as if the gates of hell themselves had opened and exploded like a volcano into the woods. The demon was definitely ready now, having absorbed the power from the stone as well as two new victims and the body of the cult leader.

He found the path leading to his backyard, and only when he saw the lights from the house did he realize where he was. He had suffered burns on his right arm, and had scratched himself badly on his flight through the woods. His clothes were covered with a coating of black ash, and his pants had been ripped in several places. In short, he looked like he'd survived a fierce battle. In point of fact, he had.

Vickie saw him first, as she looked through the glass sliding doors in the kitchen. Though he couldn't hear her, he saw her throw her hands up in the air and come running out. Pastor Mark followed. Todd, he guessed, was already in bed.

She ran through the haze of the backyard flood lights and wrapped her arms around him.

"Oh my God!" she exclaimed, looking at him. "Erik, what happened!"

"It's a long story," he said. "The...the demon. It is real. It destroyed the SWAT team. I don't know how I got away."

"Erik, what are you talking about?"

"Vickie, this thing is much worse that just a cult. I should have told you sooner...."

"There will be time to explain all of that later," Pastor Mark said. "Right now we need to look to our own safety."

Erik struggled to find the right words. "It...came to life. Took form. It was...fire and brimstone. I think they're all dead. All of the police."

"Did it follow you?"

"No. I don't think so. But I don't know what it will do next."

"Ok," Mark said. "I'm going to call the State Police and put them on alert. Vickie, you go and get Todd ready."

"Where are we going?"

"For right now at least, I think we'd be safer at the church."

Vickie nodded. "Erik, go clean up as best you could and put something on those burns. Just do it quickly."

"Ok. But Mark are the State Police actually going to believe us?"

"They will when they can't raise their SWAT team on the radio. And when they don't come back out of the woods."

"Right. Let's go, then. I'm afraid we're too close to the action here."

-2-

Dovecrest was awakened early the next morning by a guard clanging on the bars of his cell with a nightstick.

"Come on, get up! We're taking you out of here."

Dovecrest rubbed his eyes and sat up on the cot.

"Hurry up!" the guard said. "We've got to go."

"Don't I have time to clean up?"

"No time for that. I have orders to get you out of here now."

"I'd like to clean up a bit for court."

"You're not going to court."

"Then where the hell am I going?"

"Protective custody. The call just came in. Now move."

"I think I need to call my attorney," Dovecrest said, as the guard opened the cell and led him out. He noticed on the office clock that it was only six a.m.

"Look, you can call whoever you want when we're where we're supposed to be. But right now we've got to get out of here."

Dovecrest noticed that the guard didn't even put handcuffs on him, but just led him directly through the building towards the back door.

"Can you give me any idea of what's going on?"

"I couldn't tell you if I knew, but that's irrelevant 'cause I don't know. All I do know is that there's been an incident in the woods and a lot of cops were killed. Whoever did it may be after you next. That's more than I should have told you but it's all I know."

Things had escalated to the next level, then. Just as he had thought. Now everyone was in grave danger.

The guard led him outside, where a car was waiting with two armed officers inside. They opened the door and he climbed into the back.

Dovecrest sensed the commotion before anyone was aware of it. He felt the hairs on his neck tingle, and could sense a flow of energy, as if a lightening bold had struck nearby.

"Hurry up," he said to the officers.

The driver put the car in gear and rushed backward, then turned around. Dovecrest felt the energy come closer. Then, as the car turned out of the back parking lot, he saw it, in the driveway right in front of them. The driver screeched on the brakes and screamed.

The thing had already transformed. Dovecrest saw it for only a moment before the fireball hit the car, but the vision was engraved upon his brain like an epitaph on a tombstone. It wasn't that large as monsters go—maybe six feet or so, though he expected it would grow if it wanted to. But what it lacked in size, it made up for in ferocity. The thing still had a human shape, of sorts. But its flesh was molten and dripping, like red-hot lava. It's eyes were black coals, and the thing literally dripped fire. Its open mouth was a black, yawning pit that seemed to open into hell itself.

Most horrible of all, though, was the human head growing from the side of its molten neck. It was the cult leader—Dovecrest had only seen his face for a moment, but he recognized him just the same. The leader had been absorbed, transformed by the demon. The human face writhed and screamed in unabashed agony. Dovecrest almost felt pity for the leader who had once been human.

Then he saw a fireball fly from the demon and, within an instant, engulf the patrol car. Dovecrest ducked behind the seat as the flames blazed around him. He felt the car turning over. The engine blew, smashing into the front seat. The doors blew off, and Dovecrest felt himself thrown out and across the parking lot.

The demon was seeking him—he knew that—but its fury was out of control. State Troopers were swarming from the barracks like bees defending their nest, but their weapons had no more impact on the thing than if they were bees stinging a campfire. Bullets were either absorbed into the lava or just passed through. The thing was walking fire and brimstone, straight from the depths of hell.

Dovecrest found himself watching the debacle from behind a tree where the explosion had thrown him into the woods next to the driveway. He was sore and had twisted his arm badly, and he had a few minor burns, but he'd been fortunate enough to have been in the back seat, protected by the heavy barrier that separated prisoners from the police. He tried to get up and run away, but his breath had completely left him.

The demon caught one fleeing officer by the neck and pulled him back into its embrace. The man seemed to stand still in time for a single moment, and then erupted into a raging inferno, as if he had been dipped in lighter fluid and held to a hot flame. His screams pierced the early morning stillness of the tiny community. Others took cover inside the barracks, but the monster followed them inside.

The thing literally walked *through* the door, turning it into flaming kindling wood in a mere second. Dovecrest heard the sound of explosions from inside. A trooper may have tossed a grenade at the monster, but it only added fuel to the fire. A few more small explosions followed; then tongues of fire blew out the windows and licked at the morning air. Several officers, burning like flares, swarmed from the building and dropped to the ground in a desperate attempt to put themselves out.

Dovecrest felt his breath returning to him slowly and he knew the time had come to get away. It was now or never. If the thing found him, his suffering would be especially prized, since he was the one that had imprisoned the monster for so long. Slowly, he backed away from the road and into the woods, keeping his eye on the burning barracks.

With one final Fourth of July explosion, the entire thing seemed to boil and then blow, sending the roof of the building high into the air and collapsing everything inside in hot, red flames and acrid smoke. The thing went up like a fireball. Dovecrest knew nothing human could survive the explosion. Moments, later, the demon emerged, larger than ever, molten and dripping with coal black eyes and a mouth of black pitch. The thing walked easily from the fire and shook itself off, like a dog that had fallen in a lake.

Dovecrest didn't wait around for the sequel. He fled into the ancient woods that he knew so well.

-3-

Erik and his family had hastily packed some clothes and supplies and followed Pastor Mark to the church.

"This place may offer some sanctuary," Mark said. "A demon

would be uncomfortable here, in a holy place, I think."

Erik nodded but he wasn't sure how much good holiness would do right now. He didn't think he could stop this thing just by waving a crucifix at it. Perhaps if they could conjure up an army of angels of their own....

The church was fairly large for a small town, and had several classrooms, and a fellowship hall with a kitchen in the basement. The place was very secure and doubled as a shelter in case of an emergency. Erik guessed that this situation qualified.

The pastor's residence was attached to the back, a small, one bedroom unit with a garage.

"I think we should all stay here for now," Mark said.

Erik turned on the television in one of the classrooms to catch a glimpse of the morning news. What he saw shocked and horrified him. The news footage was showing what was left of the State Police barracks, which had been incinerated early this morning. The authorities were claiming it was a possible terrorist attack, and had mobilized the National Guard. There was also mention of an attack in the woods during the night where, they claimed, the F.B.I. had first encountered the terrorist group and had been outgunned.

"How else would they explain it?" Mark said. "Nobody'd buy it if they called it what it was."

"People will believe anything except the truth," Erik said. "Do you think it was after Dovecrest?"

"Definitely. And by the looks of it, I'd say it got him. We're on our own, my friend."

-4-

What was left of Seti could no longer be called human, yet it had human thoughts and feelings. The pain was so intense that he could barely think, barely remember, and not even hope to fight back. The thing had taken him over completely—no, not completely. That would be merciful. There was just enough of him left to suffer and to regret.

This thing had not turned out the way he had hoped. No life of luxury and pleasure for him now—just eternal suffering and damnation. For the first time in his life he could understand the meaning of hell. He was probably dead. His body was gone. That much was obvious. All that remained was his head and face and brain perched atop this demon's neck like a demonic version of a Siamese twin. He felt nothing below the neck and only the agony of burning above it. Yet, by some perverse miracle, his flesh did not burn. It only felt as if it were constantly on fire. He was probably immortal now, he suspected. Be careful what you wish for....

Even his screams of agony were dwarfed by the sounds of the demon's internal furnace, which never seemed to run out of hellish fuel. He could feel his screams vibrating in his throat, but couldn't hear them. It was as if he shrieked into a vacuum.

The demon itself no longer paid any attention to him. He could experience its thoughts, such as they were. Mostly the thing emanated raw hatred and raw evil beyond anything that Seti could ever have imagined. He was experienced in the art of evil and violence. But his feeble hatred was nothing compared to the all-consuming evil of this mind, where it was built into the very fabric of its existence. Seti no longer tried to communicate with the beast. His suffering was all that it required of him now.

He had seen the destruction of the SWAT team in the woods, but his suddenly being engulfed in the flames and lava of the monster made the memory very sketchy. He couldn't really see, but could only experience what occurred around him, all through a very thick layer of pain. He'd seen the Police Barracks go up in flames, and that had almost pleased him, if it were possible to be pleased in this condition. And he'd seen the Indian, the one the demon hated, as he'd escaped into the woods. He hadn't bothered to tell his tormenter about that. It was his one small victory—and his one miniscule hope.

By noontime, the tiny town of Chepachet Rhode Island was on every news station in the country. From what Erik and Mark could tell, the demon had disappeared, at least for the moment. Or, at any rate, the authorities couldn't find it.

"Maybe it's gone back to where it came from," Erik said.

"No. I don't think so. It's probably back at its altar stone gaining strength. As if it needs to."

"Maybe it needs sleep, like we do."

"Either that or it's moving on to someplace bigger, where it can do more damage. It's hard to say. All we can do is pray at this point."

Erik nodded. But he didn't think prayer alone would bring an end to this. After all, God helps those who help themselves.

"Dovecrest knew more about this thing than anyone. Do you think we could find anything at his place?"

The pastor shrugged. "It's worth a try. Do you think the thing will go there?"

Erik thought for a moment. "Not if it already killed Dovecrest. What would it want at his cabin? We could make it over there in just a couple of minutes, check it out, and be back within the hour."

"What about Vickie and Todd?" the pastor asked.

"I think they'll be ok here. They're as safe here as anywhere, I guess. And the church staff is around. They won't be alone."

The pastor nodded. "All right, then. Let's make this quick."

Todd was in the secretary's office playing with her computer. Erik told Vickie where he was going and that he'd be right back.

"I'd rather you didn't leave," she said.

"I'm not doing any good here. I feel like I've got to do something."

"You men are all alike," she said. "Just hurry back. We need you here, too."

He kissed her and then he and Mark got into the pastor's car and headed down route 102. Dovecrest's place was only a half a mile away and the roads were deserted. They pulled up at the Indian's cabin minutes later.

Nothing had been disturbed since the last time he'd been here, Erik noted. It was obvious that Dovecrest hadn't been back since his arrest, and even the police had left the place alone. It was as quiet, as if nothing had happened.

"All right, where do we start?" Mark said.

"I'd say with the file cabinet and the bookshelf. He mentioned something about old manuscripts."

"Who's to say they're in English?" Mark replied.

"Good point. But we have to try. I'll start with the files."

Erik opened the large metal file cabinet while Mark started looking through the book shelves. The files were in completely random order, mostly things about tribal laws and legal documents. None of it made any sense to him. Then he found some things on the history of the tribe, with minutes from previous tribal councils. Maybe there would be a clue in one of these documents. He spilled the file folders out onto the floor and sat down, surrounding himself with the material.

"I've got a couple of old books on local history," Mark said. "Maybe some of this will help."

"There might be something here, but there's just so much of it."

"Maybe we should put it all together in a big trash bag and take it back to the church."

Someone suddenly stepped out of the shadows and into the room. His approach was as silent as a cat walking on foam.

"You won't find anything useful in there," he said.

Erik and Mark both jumped back, startled. It was Dovecrest.

The Indian laughed, and after an embarrassed moment, the two men rushed to embrace him.

"We thought sure you'd been killed," Erik said.

"I figured the same about you. So we're even."

"So," Pastor Mark said. "What are we dealing with? And how do we stop it?"

"We're dealing with a real live demon," Dovecrest said. "Not something from the fairy tale books. Not something out of someone's imagination. This thing's real. And it's going to make life around here very unpleasant."

"How far will it go?" Erik asked.

"As far as we let it. As far as it can."

"Then we need to go to the authorities and tell them what it is so they can stop it."

Dovecrest shook his head. "It wouldn't do any good, even if they did believe us. Conventional means just won't work. Guns and explosives are just a joke."

"The thing ate up the SWAT team for lunch," Erik said.

"It was the same way at the police barracks. I don't think even an atomic bomb would hurt this thing. It's not from our world, remember?"

"So we need to go to its world, right?"

"That's right," Dovecrest said. "The portal's in the altar stone."

"You've done this before?" Mark asked.

"No. The first time we caught the leader before the demon emerged. So we trapped it behind in its own world. This time it's already made it through."

"And you know how to do this?"

"The information is hidden in a cave in the woods. I have to do some study and some translation."

"Why don't I come with you?" Mark said. "And Erik can go back to the church to be with his family."

Dovecrest nodded. "Then let's go."

CHAPTER EIGHTEEN

-1-

The monster had returned to the altar and rested after wiping out the police barracks. Not that it had to rest, but it enjoyed relaxation just the same. These rest periods allowed it to gather strength, and to relive and savor the suffering it had inflicted. It also allowed it to slow down and plan the next step. And, of course, going into hiding just made the game more fun, as the mortals tried to explain away the happenings due to natural causes. Although it didn't really mind if the world knew there was a demon on the loose, the larger purpose told it to remain more secretive. If people actually were to believe in demons, then they might realize the other end of the equation and begin believing in God as well. That wouldn't be good. So it had to show at least a little discretion, especially in this modern world that already belonged to the dark side.

Already it was anxious to leave its lair, so to speak, and go back out into the world of men. It would begin by destroying any information that might be found that might expose its weakness, or show how it could be captured or destroyed. Although, being immortal, it couldn't exactly be destroyed, but it might be permanently confined to the other world.

The altar stone was a comfortable resting spot, but the time had come to leave. It stood up, cool now and stone-like. As it swung its legs over the side of the huge stone, the fires began to burn once again, hotter and more fiercely than ever. The lump on its neck that had been Seti opened his eyes and looked at it, pleading to be set free.

"You have the ultimate reward," it replied to him. "Immortality, my friend. Enjoy!"

Then the fires once again consumed the being that had been human. Seti screamed in agony again, and the demon laughed. The devil's work was very much fun indeed.

It walked through the woods, leaving a line of burned cut destruction in its wake. It reached a deserted Route 102 and followed the road into town. It knew where information was kept, and it would make sure that nothing about its past survived. It saw the library just ahead.

Unfortunately, the library was quiet when the monster burned and smashed its way through the doors and crashed inside like a molten meteor. It had hoped to find some innocents—children were most prized—but was disappointed. The public section was deserted—it seemed that no one wanted the musty old books today. Two men had been sitting behind the desk when it entered. They had backed up and were looking at the demon with bug eyes. The monster probed Seti's brain for a moment and filed away everything the once-human had ever known about libraries and librarians. None of it was very flattering.

He'd give his once human follower a moment of fun, he thought, and probed Seti's mind again.

"What shall I do to them? This can be your revenge."

He'd picked up thoughts from Seti about how the man had been disciplined by a librarian in junior high school, how the man had sodomized him and threatened to kill him if he told. He then probed the minds of these two librarians. They were disgusting creatures, even to him, rolling about in perversion like a pig rolls in mud. They were evil little men with no imagination beyond their day to day existence. But he would give them something to think about. There are more things in heaven and earth than are dreamt of in your philosophy, Hortatio, he quoted into their collective minds.

The demon probed their minds again, just for fun. The

dwarfish man thought of himself as the macho type. He drove a macho car, read sports magazines, and thought he was attractive to women. The tall, skinny guy wouldn't get his hands dirty, didn't like to sweat, and enjoyed whining and complaining as his favorite pastime. He was sneaky and unable to take responsibility. This was fun, the demon thought. Human minds were so amusing.

Ironically enough, the macho, dwarfish man turned out to be the bigger coward. He tried hiding behind his friend, then pushed the taller man away so he could flee to the back door, all the time crying and weeping like a baby. The skinny man just dropped to his knees, shocked into silence by the sight of the molten demon standing before him.

The demon hurled a fireball at the dwarfish man's knees, bursting his legs into flames and bringing him down just a few feet short of the back door. It would be fun to watch him burn, so it turned its attention to the other man.

"No. No. Please...."

The skinny man spoke in a pleading whisper, not even expecting to be heard, but feeling the need to beg just the same. Maybe he'd save him for later, too. It paralyzed his legs with a thought, then turned to look at the books and information.

There was something here about him and about the past. He could feel it. But there was no need to be selective. He chose a shelf of books at random and incinerated it. He was surprised by how fast the flames spread. Two centuries of human knowledge, poof, gone like that. But what was two centuries to him, who was immortal? These men thought they were so clever, but they knew nothing.

He turned to a file cabinet and heated it until it turned cherry red. The contents exploded. The magazines went next. Then he melted the computers until they dripped onto the shelves like microwaved ice cream. The flames from the different fires were joining now, consuming the entire building.

Finally, with relish, the demon turned its attention back to the librarians. The dwarf-like one was huddled in a ball now. The flames on his legs had gone out, but not before his limbs had been charred through like charcoal—they would never work again, no matter what happened. But the demon wasn't leaving that to chance. It grabbed him by the ankle and pulled. The limb snapped off like a broken twig. The pain broke through the shock, making the librarian scream again. The demon grabbed him by the neck and threw him across the room where he landed on a red hot file cabinet, where he slowly baked like a potato.

The remaining librarian continued to whimper and plead as the demon ripped off his arms, then his legs, then left the torso and head to writhe and blister in the flames.

-2-

As Erik drove back towards the church, he heard the sound of explosions in the distance, coming from the direction of the town. Apparently, the thing was on the loose again. He needed to get back to Todd and Vickie. Though he didn't really know what he could do to save them if the thing showed up at the church.

Vickie and Todd were anxiously waiting for him.

"Where's Mark" Vickie asked.

"He's with Dovecrest. He's ok. They're both ok."

"What a relief. It's destroyed the library," Vickie said, softly, so Todd couldn't hear. "It's all over the news."

"How are they explaining it?"

"It depends. Some stations are still using the terrorist thing. Others are claiming a gas leak."

"Daddy, are we gonna be ok?" Todd said. "Is that thing in the woods gonna get us?"

"We're gonna be ok," Erik said. "Dovecrest is going to help us."

"We've gotta kill the rock," Todd said.

"Yeah. We'll do that."

Todd nodded. "I'm gonna go back and check out the computer

again."

Erik watched him go, then turned to his wife.

"Erik, I'm scared," he said.

"Yeah. I know."

"I started having contractions today."

"Is it...near time?"

"I don't know. They're not regular."

"I need to get you and Todd to the city."

"No," she said. "I think it's too risky. We'd have to go through town. I think we're safer here."

He nodded. She was right, at least for now. If the thing was, indeed, at the library, he'd have to go right past it to reach the main road. For now, they would be better to stay put.

-3-

Johnny Dovecrest lit a small lantern and led the Pastor into the cave. He knew the demon was nearby. He could feel it, could sense the presence. It was stronger than ever, and not the least bit shy about being seen. It was funny, he thought. In the old times it needed to stay hidden because people believed. No one believed in demons nowadays, even if they saw one with their own eyes.

He slid a rock out of the way and took a metal box from a recess in the stones.

"These are the ancient manuscripts of my people," Dovecrest said. "They were written before the white man came to this land, and have been handed down through the generations."

"Are they in manuscript form?" Mark asked.

"They have only been written down in the last 200 years. In the past my people believed in evil spirits. Today it is not so fashionable."

"That's something our cultures have in common."

"Let's bring this back to the church," Dovecrest said. "Then we can try to make a plan."

"The Bible says that Jesus cast out demons. And we can cast them out in his name."

Dovecrest nodded and led him out of the cave. "That might drive out a demon. But it won't kill it. Only the Great Spirit can do that. Besides, this is not just an ordinary demon. It is a creature of very great evil. A resident of hell."

"Won't driving it out send it back?"

"Sending it back is one thing. Keeping it back is another."

As they approached Dovecrest's cabin they heard an explosion. A fireball erupted from ahead, and flames erupted from the windows.

"Hide!" Dovecrest said.

They dove behind a boulder and watched as the demon emerged from what had been the back door of the cabin. It carried a man's body in its left hand, holding him upright by the hair of his head. Dovecrest couldn't recognize the poor wretch through the flames, but it was obvious that the man was in agony, literally burning up from the inside. The demon turned its victim and held him up to his face. Then, it spoke, in a raging, steaming voice that was almost human, but definitely not from this world.

"My name is Wrath!" it said. "Look at me and feel my flames. Feel the fury of hell!"

The man screamed and his head literally exploded in the demon's hand, blowing apart like a firework in a blaze of red, yellow, and orange. Splinters of burned flesh, bone, and brain fell like shrapnel, and the now headless body fell to the ground. The demon stood holding a handful of hair and laughing.

The growth on its neck—what was left of the cult leader—was not laughing. His clouded eyes were contorted in pain as he endured his torture. Once again, Dovecrest locked eyes with the being that had once been human, and once again he saw the man begging, pleading to be set free. The man seemed to see hope in Dovecrest, and the Indian realized how important his task was—not just for lives but for souls.

The demon—Wrath, it had called itself—seemed to sense

that something was happening with it's deformed twin, and stopped laughing. It stood tall and looked out into the woods. Dovecrest and Mark remained still as the demon seemed to search into the trees, looking for a sign of life. Dovecrest could feel his heart beating hard within his chest. He was sure the demon could hear it if it tried. He counted the seconds. The monster was silent. Only the sound of cracking flames from his cabin broke the silence.

He looked at Mark and saw the internal battle going on within the pastor. He knew that Mark wanted to confront the thing with his God and, with a word, banish it back to where it had come from. He shook his head back and forth, very slowly, and mouthed the words "no, not yet. Not now."

He could almost see the gears turning in the pastor's mind. He felt the man's faith, but he also knew that the time wasn't right. It would be suicide.

He shook his head again. Mark looked at him for a long moment. Then he nodded, bowed his head and his lips began to move in silent prayer.

Still, the demon did not stir. If the thing came any closer, or discovered them, the decision would be made for them. Dovecrest held his breath and waited, expecting to die at any moment.

Then, without any apparent reason, the demon made a deep, throaty noise and turned away. Dovecrest peeked around the boulder and saw it walking away. Its flames seemed to be cooling, from cherry red to orange, to yellow. The thing on its shoulder appeared to be just a ball of flesh from the back. It flopped up and down on the monster's shoulders as if it were sleeping or dead.

Dovecrest tapped Mark on the shoulder and motioned for him to wait as the demon turned right and down Farmington Road. He motioned Mark to follow him as he kept the boulder between them and the monster, hoping against hope that it didn't stop and look back.

"He answered my prayer," Mark said. "And he would have

defended me."

Dovecrest didn't say anything for a moment.

"Perhaps," he said finally. "But it's heading towards the church. Does your cell phone work?"

Mark nodded.

"Then call them and warn them. Tell Erik to meet us back at his house."

"We should have fought."

"Doesn't your Bible teach that there is a time for everything?"

"Yes."

"Then now is the time for us to join forces and gather strength. The white man and the Indian. The old and the new. We must join our spirits as one. Only then can the fight begin."

"We have joined forces."

"But we have not yet joined spirits. Your God and mine. Come. We'll gather our strength. Then we will know. He will tell us. But in His own time."

CHAPTER NINETEEN

-1-

Erik didn't know what to do. He sat in the fellowship hall of the church and watched the television, hoping for an update on what was going on. There was nothing new, though, and the newscasters were resorting to old footage and old reports. Apparently, the authorities weren't letting the news people get too close and the government wasn't saying anything. It seemed apparent that they weren't letting anyone into town, and were encouraging people to get out.

Erik knew the truth, but who would listen? And if they did, what good would it do? He knew the demon had been on the outer edges of town earlier. Now he might be anywhere. He felt like he needed to get Vickie and Todd to a safe place in the city; he also felt like he had to stay and help destroy this thing, or else no one would be safe anywhere.

Vickie hurried in, pulling Todd in tow. Her face was pasty white.

"We've gotta go, Hon," she said.

"Is it...time.... The baby?"

"No, no," Mark called. "The thing just ruined Dovecrest's place. It's headed this way."

"Does the staff know?"

"They're on their way out. Come on. We've gotta run. They want us to meet at our house."

"Let's go out the back. It's closer."

He led them up the back stairs and out to the parking lot. He could hear screams from the front of the church, and knew that the thing was in sight..

"Hurry," he said. "And don't scream or yell, no matter what you see. It'll only attract it."

Erik was glad they lived in a small town where you didn't have to lock your car doors. He jumped into the car and started it up as Vickie slid in beside him and Todd hopped into the back seat. He was hoping the thing wasn't in the driveway or the road—he'd just have to assume it wasn't and hope for the best. He gunned the engine, peeled out of the parking lot and around the front of the church.

Sure enough, it was waiting in the street right outside the church's front door. It looked different now, though, no longer hot and fiery. Now it was cold and black, the exact color and texture of the altar stone, in fact. It was as if the demon's lava flow had cooled and turned into volcanic rock. Even the once-human twin head on its neck seemed petrified. In fact, for a moment he thought he was looking at a statue. Then the thing moved.

With amazing quickness, the thing charged forward. That's when Erik saw where the scream had come from. It was Vera, the church secretary, an elderly woman, who was standing frozen on the front steps to the church. The demon reached out and grabbed the woman by the throat, stifling her screams immediately. The woman flailed her arms and legs like a wind-mill, and her eyes bulged out in their sockets.

The demon shook her like a rag doll. Erik pulled the car to the far side of the driveway, hoping he could make it around the monster. He debated whether to help old Vera—but he had no idea what he could do.

Suddenly Vickie gasped and clenched her belly.

"Contractions," she said between gasps. "Oh, dear God, not now."

The dilemma regarding Vera resolved itself quickly; the monster stepped forward and hurled her like a major league fastball against the stone foundation of the church, where she hit head first. Erik could hear the cracking of her skull even through the closed windows of the car. He took a quick look and saw a dark patch of blood flowing down the wall and pooling up on the ground. Vera's twisted body lie contorted and lifeless on the ground.

"Todd, get down on the floor," Todd said, as he gunned the engine in a desperate attempt to race past the demon before it noticed him. "Hold on!"

He targeted the right part of the driveway where it joined the road, punched the gas pedal to the floor, and prayed with all of his heart. The car rushed forward, throwing him back against the seat. He tried not to look at the demon, but he couldn't help it. It was like trying to drive by a car wreck on the highway without looking—you knew it was wrong, that it wouldn't be good to see, and that it would just hold up traffic even more. But you looked anyway.

He had hoped the demon would be more interested in what was inside the church than what was outside. His hope was only partially fulfilled. The thing smashed its head through the front door, but then turned around when it heard the car racing towards it. It looked almost comical, like something out of a cartoon—this huge, fierce, rock-solid demon, now complete with horns and quartz-like fangs, standing there with a smashed door around its neck like a broken picture frame. If the effect had been done in a horror movie, Erik would have laughed. Instead, he just gritted his teeth and pressed as hard as he could on the gas pedal, gripping the steering wheel so hard that his knuckles turned white.

He wouldn't have believed that anything so large and so solid could move so quickly. The effect was even stranger now that the demon had transformed itself into a solid shape. It was like watching a rock run. Erik instinctively knew that he wouldn't make it. The demon would catch him just as he reached the road.

Without even thinking, he turned the steering wheel hard

right at the last instant. The car jumped the curbstone and went up onto the grass and directly for a tree. He yanked the wheel left, scraped the side of the tree with the passenger door, then tugged it to the right. He could feel the demon close now as its solid presence cast a shadow over the car. Vickie was still gasping in timed rhythm next to him. Todd, thankfully, was quiet and on the floor. Erik hoped he had his eyes closed and his head buried in his hands.

He felt the car slam into the landscaping, taking out a layout of flowers and running over and through a small stone wall. Sparks flied as the chassis scraped cement. The right front wheel rode up the stone wall and Erik thought the car would flip. Then it jolted back down, almost knocking him against the roof.

He saw the demon's hand shoot out towards the car and just miss grabbing the roof, and the car righted itself. He felt the stone fingers scrape along the back of the vehicle like nails on a blackboard, searching for a grip. The car slowed and he gunned the engine again. It leaped forward, eluding the grip for a moment. Then he felt the car slow and stop as the demonic hand wrapped around the rear bumper.

He pressed the accelerator down so hard he felt like his foot would go through the floorboards. The wheels spun as Erik engaged the demon in a terrible tug-of-war. He felt the car being pulled backwards. Then, as if it were suddenly being launched from a slingshot, the car lurched forward. Erik looked in the rear view mirror and saw the demon holding the bumper in his hands. It twisted the metal into a pretzel and threw it to the ground as Erik maneuvered the car onto the road and sped down Route 102 towards Farmington Road and his home.

-2-

The demon knew it had missed a major opportunity as it watched the car speed off into the distance. It half-thought of catching it, then decided it wasn't worth the effort. At least not yet. There would be time for that later.

It twisted up the mangled bumper like a paper clip and threw it on the ground. It hadn't realized that the woman was in labor until it was too late. Those were the best kind—a two for one. And what could be more innocent than a mother and her newborn. That would have been very good.

But the brat wasn't born yet, so it had time. That's one thing it did have—plenty of time. It had eternity.

It looked back at the church, the home of its enemy, the home of those who would destroy it. Something would have to be done about this church. It would send a clear message.

It stepped through the shattered doorway and stopped. The place was empty. That was disappointing. Especially since it'd killed the woman too quickly. It would destroy this place though, so no one could ever return to it.

It stepped forward down the aisle leading to the altar, and it recognized the hated sign, the sign of the cross. It had memories of that sign, when it had last walked the earth. Many of those who had sent it back had carried that sign. It felt wrath and rage burn from within it like a furnace. There was an alcove in the back of the church, with an open door leading to the altar, and glass windows making up the top section of the way on each side. It strode forward and smashed his fist through the middle section of windows. Glass flew everywhere, splintering and shredding into a billion pieces that embedded themselves on the floor, on the walls, and even in the ceiling. The sound was like music to it. The thing that had been its human contact woke up on his neck and looked at it in puzzlement, wondering why the endless burning had ceased. But now the demon Wrath wanted to make it more personal, more hands on, at least for now.

It walked through the glass wall, shattering the waist-high wood and plaster wall and walking right through several rows of pews. It looked at the cross at the back of the altar. That was its prize.

But as the demon stepped forward to pluck its prize, it felt a sudden barrier, weak at first, but definitely there. It stopped and probed ahead with its mind and its powers. There was no life. But power. Definitely power. It let out a deep, throaty grunt that sounded like fires churning from deep inside a volcano.

It stepped forward again, ruining another row of pews. The force was stronger now. It pushed back harder.

The demon growled once again. From deep inside, it relit the fire within itself. Time to put this place to the torch. The fire grew slowly, and the demon's fires ignited. Its solid, black form turned orange, and became fluid. The human twin on its neck began to scream once again, and the demon laughed. Its body turned into a living volcano of superheated lava. It looked at the cross on the church's altar and shot its hand forward. A piece of fire flew forward, like a meteor.

It all happened so quickly that an ordinary human eye wouldn't have seen what happened. But the demon saw. Before it had traveled the fifty feet or so to the altar, the fireball had cooled, become solid, and turned into a rock-solid cube of black ice. The crystal stopped just inches from the cross, stopped dead in its tracks. It hung suspended in the air for several seconds, then dropped to the floor and shattered into a thousand harmless pieces each no larger than a grain of salt.

The demon stood in stunned silence. Even its human attachment stopped screaming, though the fires still burned at him. It felt its rage and wrath burn within itself, heating to a crescendo. Then, the tiny ice crystals reassembled themselves, magically, into a rock solid shape, the ice cold shape of a cross. The demon roared but could not find the strength to move forward. The cross then shot across the room and fastened onto what would have been the demon's chest. The cherry-red fire turned white in the shape of the cross, and went out, cooling the area around it. Within seconds the demon had returned back to the black volcanic rock it had come in with. Only this time the transition wasn't of its own choosing.

The cross burned it with the ironic fire of ice, an upside down cross that melted into its very chest like the cross of an ancient crusader, and a poet's words lingered in its mind. "Some say the world will end in fire, and some say of ice." The demon had courted fire. This new scenario had caught it by surprise.

It snarled in anger and found that it could not break any more pews. Its body had become cold and lethargic. Its will was even going.

"No!" it screamed. "Hellfire and brimstone will win. But for now the ice will suffice."

Furious, it walked out of the church. This place was too strong. At least for now. And he had other things to attend to. But he would come back and mess this place up when he became stronger. And each new life made him strong. So now he would go and kill some more. He'd kill children. And he'd take that baby that was just about to be born.

-3-

Once he had left the church behind, Erik did not look back. He knew that the thing could be just inches behind him, waiting to destroy him and his family in some steaming wreckage. He wasn't going to let that happen, though. He was going to go home, meet the others, and figure out what to do.

Vickie's contractions were becoming worrisome now. Though her due date was a couple of weeks away, Erik knew that nature was very unpredictable. He also believed in all of Murphy's Laws and their corollaries that basically said that things went wrong and usually at the worst possible time.

His breathing and heartbeat didn't even begin to slow down until they were turning onto Farmington Road.

"Is everyone all right?" he finally asked.

Vickie nodded rapidly, fighting off a contraction.

"Yeah, Dad," Todd said softly. "We're fine."

Erik passed the shopping center and noticed a few National Guard soldiers in the parking lot. He sped past before they could flag him down. He noticed a smoldering ruin where Dovecrest's cabin had been. He could only assume that Mark had called after the place had been destroyed and that they hadn't been already killed.

Finally, he saw the comforting sight of his home ahead on the left. Though this new home hadn't been much comfort, he thought. The tiny place where they'd lived in the city was looking better and better now.

He pulled his car into the driveway behind Vickie's SUV, then just sat back in the front seat for a long moment to catch his breath. He looked up and saw Mark and Dovecrest running over to meet them.

"Thank God you're all right!" Mark said.

"It was headed for the church. Did everyone get out in time?"

Erik shook his head. "It got Vera. I don't know what happened after that."

The two men were silent. "Poor Vera. She was a good woman," Mark said, finally.

"So what do we do now?" Erik asked. "I'm sure this thing's rampage isn't over. It's not going to just go away, is it?"

Dovecrest shook his head. "It gains power with each life it takes."

"I still say it cannot stand up to God!" Mark said. "We must stand and fight it."

"You are right, Pastor. It cannot stand up to God. But it can stand up to men. We cannot fight it alone. We need to have God on our side."

"He is on our side," Mark insisted. "God will not allow evil to rule over the earth. We must cast it out in his son's name."

"Perhaps we can cast it out. But then we must destroy it. To do that we must first arm ourselves."

"How do we do that?" Erik asked.

"We arm ourselves with God's wisdom and power. We ask his guidance and his help. And we join together, the three of us, through Him and his strength. If our faith is not strong enough, the demon will prevail. Like all evil, it will find the smallest chink in our armor and invade."

"Then let us arm ourselves in His name," Mark said.

Erik led them back into the house so they could prepare.

CHAPTER TWENTY

-1-

The icy upside-down image of the cross had burned itself into the demon like a fossil embedded into hard rock. At first the cross had burned like frostbite, sinking deep into its rock-like body. Then it had become accustomed to the pain—after all, its entire existence had consisted of pain, the all-consuming agony of anger and wrath that could never be cooled. The pain was always there, whether the demon was imprisoned and unable to reek vengeance, or whether it was in the process of inflicting pain and suffering of its own. It was an addiction, a curse, a disease that had been inflicted upon it by the evil one himself. The suffering of others gave it meaning, existence, and life itself.

As it left the church it decided to remain in solid form rather than revert back to the flames. The cross had hurt it more than it cared to admit, and its pain was easier to bear in solid form. The flames wouldn't burn where it was embedded—it knew that—and this would cause more pain and expose its weakness. Instead, it grew a set of leathery bat-like wings on its back, gargoyle style. It knew that humans feared demons with horns and wings, so why not look the part. The remnants of Seti were also getting tiresome. He'd handle that as well, very soon.

With a single flap of the wings it propelled itself into the air, like a medieval dragon, of sorts, only this one made of stone. The effect completely defied physics, but that made it all the more interesting for the monster.

The ground shrunk beneath it as it flapped again and drifted higher. It could see the church in the distance—it was not finished with that yet—and in the other direction a small shopping plaza. It recalled it from earlier when it had been part of the human, instead of the other way around. The shopping center—the woman with the unborn child had been there. And that was where its previous coven had been interred. It had a special curse for this place.

It swooped down closer and buzzed by the place. About two dozen soldiers were lined up in the parking lot, herding people into a yellow bus. They thought they were going to safety. This was perfect. The soldiers pointed up at the monster and shouldered their weapons, while people hurried into the bus. This was even better than it had hoped for.

It felt the telltale "pling" of bullets flying past it. A couple hit it on the chest and ricocheted off. Another went through its wing, which immediately patched itself, as if nothing had happened. The soldiers were tenacious; apparently they felt that if they peppered it with enough bullets it would have to die. They obviously didn't know what they were in for. But they would find out.

The demon swooped down and landed just in front of the soldiers. It stood tall for a moment, letting them shoot it at point blank range. It watched in amused fascination as their eyes widened in surprise and terror as they saw that their attack had no effect. One man threw down his rifle and ran in terror. Another stood frozen, as if turned to stone. Another charged forward and tried to stick a bayonet into the demon.

The winged monster watched in amusement as the bayonet snapped in half. Then it grabbed the soldier by the arm, ripping the appendage from its socket and twisting it off at the shoulder. The man stepped back and stared at the bleeding stump as if it belonged to someone else, than passed out on the pavement.

As if on cue, the skirmish line scattered and ran for their lives. The demon was in no hurry to pursue them. There were plenty to go around. It lowered its head and skewered a pair of retreating soldiers, one on each of its obsidian horns. It ripped out another man's throat with its onyx teeth and spit the windpipe on the ground. Blood splattered into Seti's eyes, blinding what was left of the cult leader. Seti wailed in pain and the demon sent a jolt of agony into the remnants of the human's brain. This burden would be removed very soon.

The soldiers had given up trying to fight. One called desperately for help on his radio until the demon crushed the man's hand and the walkie-talkie, turning them both into pulp. As the soldier tried desperately to pull away, the mangled hand snapped off at the wrist. Blood shot out as if from a faucet. Then the demon raked its stone claws down the man's back splitting him open from shoulder to rump.

The monster heard the bus gunning its engine. But there was no hurry. With its new wings, it could outrun the bus. It flapped its wings and took off after another soldier who was running back inside the shopping center. It caught him just outside the door of the convenience store and they both crashed through the thick glass. The soldier's face was a bloody mess—the demon raked his eyes out of the sockets and left him there, where he dropped to his knees and sobbed like a baby.

Then it crashed through the adjacent wall and into the antique shop. The air from its wings spread antiques and merchandise everywhere. It spotted the old lady who ran the place huddling in a corner; apparently, she hadn't had a chance to get on the bus. It leaped across the store and grabbed her by the hair. A huge clump of gray hair and scalp ripped off in the demon's claw as the woman pulled away. She crawfished away, holding her hands out in front of her to ward off the monster.

"I banish you in the name of God!" the woman sneered, holding her hands out to make the sign of the cross.

The demon felt a moment of fear, but just a moment. This cross held no power. The woman lacked strength and faith. She didn't believe in what she was doing.

"Your God can't help you," the demon roared in a voice that was only barely comprehensible. Then he smashed his claws into her chest and pulled out her still pulsating heart.

-2-

After they were safely inside the house, Erik grabbed the remote and motioned to put on the television.

"No," Dovecrest said. "That won't help. Where it is now and what it's doing doesn't matter. We've got to think ahead."

Erik nodded and put the remote down. Vickie sat back on the couch with Todd next to her. Her contractions, for the moment, had stopped.

"I need to get my family out of here," Erik said. "This thing could be here any minute."

Dovecrest nodded. "I know," he said. "But we need you here. We need the three. Six would be better, or twelve even better still. But three is enough."

"Let me take them to the city and then come back...."

"There isn't time."

"I'd rather stay here," Vickie said.

"No. You can't. It isn't safe here anymore. Think about Todd. And the baby."

Vickie looked at him for a long moment.

"Ok," she said finally. "But I can drive myself."

"Hon, you're about to go into labor—if you aren't already there.... You can't drive."

"I'm going to have to. Either that or I'm staying here."

"Listen," Erik said. "The National Guard was at the plaza. Suppose I take you and Todd there and have them drive you out?"

"Erik, we really don't have time," Dovecrest said.

"I can at least drive myself a half mile up the road," Vickie said.

Erik shook his head. "I don't like it. I hate it. I need to be with my family."

"The best way you can protect your family is by hitting this thing where it lives," Dovecrest said. "And we need you here for that."

Erik looked at Mark. "Pastor, what do you think?"

"I think that no matter what we do, it's in God's hands," he said. "But I think God—and we—could work better knowing that your family was safe. I'll bet they'd send in a chopper for a woman in labor."

Erik thought for a moment. He hated the idea of separating from Vickie and Todd. The idea frightened him. But he couldn't bring them with him to do what had to be done. He'd be too worried about them to play his role.

This just wasn't right, he thought. He wasn't supposed to be a hero. He was a teacher and a writer. He wrote about characters that did heroic things. He didn't actually *do* them. More than anything he just wanted to get in the car with his family and drive to safety, where he could let the people who were supposed to protect them take care of this thing. This was a job for the police and the army—and maybe even the pastor, he thought. But it wasn't a job for a schoolteacher who wrote science fiction stories. He didn't want any part of this hero stuff.

Yet what choice did he have? If he didn't do it, who would? Maybe Mark could call some clergy together, but how long would it take? And Dovecrest was the only one who really knew what to do. What if the demon killed him?

"All right," he said finally. "I don't like it, but I don't have a better idea."

Vickie nodded. "Then I'd better get moving while things are still quiet."

Erik was silent. He didn't know what he'd do if anything happened to her. In the background, he heard Dovecrest asking the Pastor to come help him bring in something from outside. He knew they were giving him some time alone with his wife and son.

He knelt down and looked into Todd's eyes.

"You're going to go with your Mom and help her, ok, Sport?"

"Why can't you come, Dad?"

"Because I've got to help kill this thing that's gotten loose. Before it hurts anyone else."

"I could help kill it, too. It tried to get me but I wouldn't let it."

"I know. That's why I need you to go with your Mom. You need to take care of her."

He hugged his son hard. Then Todd broke away from the embrace.

"Ok, Dad. But I've got to get my geologist's hammer. Just in case I need it again."

"Ok, Todd. You do that. Then come right back down, you hear."

The boy nodded and ran off to his room.

Erik took his wife in his arms and hugged her tight, then kissed her deeply. "Vic, I don't want to be away from you," he said.

"I don't want to be away from you either," she said. Tears streaked down her face. "I'd rather stay here with you. Or go together."

"I know. But we can't."

She nodded. "Do me a favor," she said.

"Anything."

"You kill this thing that's been causing us so much pain. You kill it. And then you come back to me."

"You've got it," he replied.

-3-

The demon let the bus get about fifty feet down the road, just to make things interesting. Then it pounced on it like a cat on a toy mouse. It flew above the bus, then landed on the roof with a thud that jolted the vehicle, almost sending it off the road. It knelt down on the bus, then stuck a jagged, rock-like claw through the metal roof, peeling it back as easily as if it were opening a sardine can. The people inside began to scream, which was music to its ears.

The bus swerved back and forth—apparently the driver was trying to shake the demon off. It reached inside and grabbed a teenage boy by the shoulders, pulling him through the opening in the roof. It held him up and looked into his eyes for a moment, savoring his terror. Then it took his face into its mouth and clamped its solid jaws shut, literally ripping the boy's face off with its indestructible teeth. The boy gagged on his own blood, then slumped back. The monster tossed him off the bus and onto the road.

The bus driver, having realized the futility of trying to throw the demon off the bus by swerving, hit the brakes. The monster merely lowered itself through the hole in the roof and into the bus as the vehicle screeched to a stop. The passengers were flung forward by the momentum. Those in the front seats were flung through the windshield, while those further backwards were tossed around like numbered balls in a lottery machine. The demon reached out and grabbed a little boy as he flew passed; it crushed the boy's chest in a terrible bear hug, then threw the boy down, where his corpse crashed into an old man, knocking him senseless. The demon mashed the boy's mother against the side, smashing her head through the small window, where she hung like clothes put outside to dry.

The bus skidded to a stop and the passengers stampeded towards the exit, trampling those who had fallen or who were injured. The demon watched the carnage with satisfaction as its victims did its own dirty work for it. The exit doors became hopelessly jammed with bodies, both living and dead, and the windows were too small to fit through. The demon slowly walked to the front of the bus, crushing, ripping, and mutilating as it went. It killed most, but left a few maimed for life, blind or disfigured or crippled beyond repair.

After the carnage was over, it flew back to the shopping center. Now it was time to get rid of this piece of flesh that had once been Seti, the cult leader.

After Vickie had left, Erik walked out to the patio, where Dovecrest and Mark waited.

"That was the most difficult thing I've ever done in my life," he said.

Dovecrest nodded. "I'm afraid we have something even more difficult ahead. But first we must prepare. We must renew our strength and our faith. Pastor, we must rely on you to help with this."

"What do you want me to do?"

"You must lead us in meditation and prayer. I will prepare the ancient rituals and we will renew our strength."

"And if that thing comes here before we're ready?" Erik said.

"We must trust God to guide and protect us," Mark said.

Dovecrest opened the box containing the old manuscripts and instructed them to sit on the floor in a small circle. The Indian lit some incense and prepared a strong brew of herbal tea.

"This will help us to relax and open our minds," he explained. "I will begin with some ancient prayers of my people. You won't understand them, but that doesn't matter. Just listen to the rhythm and relax your mind."

Erik sipped the hot tea and immediately felt the sweat begin to bead up on his forehead. It tasted sweet, but pungent at the same time, as if it had a tint of mushroom,

"What's in this stuff?" Mark said.

Dovecrest laughed. "Don't worry. It's nothing illegal. Just a mixture of herbs."

After they had finished their tea, Dovecrest instructed them to close their eyes.

"The brotherhood of the red and the white man can be strong in faith and understanding," he said. Then he began to chant in a deep, melodic voice. Erik felt his muscles relax for the first time in weeks as he listened to the sound, not understanding the words, yet understanding the meaning just the same.

Dovecrest's voice was as smooth as honey, rich and resonant. It filled the room, and Erik felt all of the barriers of his mind being lifted, opening himself up to truth and meaning. The tension in his shoulders and neck evaporated. His worries and troubles melted away. Though he sat here on a hard wooden floor in the face of unspeakable danger, he felt peace and comfort take over his body and soul.

He had felt small and weak—now he began to feel strong and powerful. He felt his isolation disappear. He felt an acute kinship with these men, a Baptist pastor and an ancient Indian medicine man. He felt the bond between them grow strong. The three of them were drawn together in faith and in goodness, in the need and desire to do the right thing. He felt himself as part of the larger world, felt the three of them as a strong force that drew from the power of heaven and earth. He was no longer just a man, but an instrument of God Himself....

Erik did not know how long the ritual lasted. It could have been minutes or hours. Then the Indian stopped, and the trance was momentarily broken. Silence hung in the air.

Pastor Mark's voice broke the spell.

"Lord, we feel your presence with us today and we thank you for your strength and comfort," he said.

Erik experienced the sensation of ultimate peace filling his soul with a determination and fortitude that he didn't know was possible as the pastor continued his prayer. He felt empowered to deal with anything that came his way. Confidence replaced his fear. Brotherhood replaced his isolation.

The pastor ended his prayer with a final appeal for protection and strength against the ancient enemy, and the three men sat in silence with their heads bowed. Finally, Dovecrest spoke.

"We're ready. We know what we have to do."

And even though they had not planned, had not thought this through, Erik was aware of the fact that he did know what had to be done. He and the Indian would travel the most difficult journey, into the very reaches of hell itself. Pastor Mark would banish the demon from this world, and they would battle it in the other. He could see the plan clearly in his mind. He did not know if they would survive. But he felt more sure that they would prevail.

CHAPTER TWENTY-ONE

-1-

The demon left the bus smoldering and in ruins and headed back to the shopping plaza. It was time to get rid of its last vestige of humanity, the growth that had once been Seti, the cult leader.

It circled over the shopping plaza, now littered with dead, dying, and wounded, and saw what it had been looking for—the cemetery where its predecessor had been buried. The demon's first effort to come to life on earth had been stopped before it had ever begun. This previous leader had started a colony cut here in the woods, and though his worship and ritual sacrifice, had gained the demon's attention. A final sacrifice had been planned that would have brought the demon to life where the coven would serve it and it would prey on both the colonials and the Indians.

But the primitive people of that time had been more understanding than those of the modern world. They had learned of the plot, destroyed the coven, and burned the leader at the stake just as the demon had appeared to take over his body. The demon was granted the briefest glimpse through the doorway from hell, and then flung back into the flames just as quickly. This time, things had gone better. And it wasn't finished yet.

It landed beside the largest headstone. The ancient spells still held some power—it could feel their force surrounding the gravesite in an attempt to contain the spirits within. Once this site had been disturbed again, the demon had been aroused, had been given the power to reach out from beyond once again. The curse had been set off and the demon had been able to kill. This had given it the power it needed to search for a human conduit. Seti had served that role. But the human had outlived his usefulness now. The demon had granted him immortality, of sorts. Then again, everyone in hell was immortal.

The demon grabbed the huge, extraterrestrial headstone and pulled it from the earth as if it were a mere popsicle stick used to mark a flowerbed. This was a place of death. There was the ancient death of the coven. And the modern death that had started it all over again. The demon pushed back the earth to reveal the shattered coffin and bones of the one who had originally given him life.

The demon merged his mind into what was left of Seti's. The man was completely insane now, with no conscious thoughts or desires. The proximity of the demon coupled with the eternal pain had rendered Seti's mind nothing more than random nerve impulses.

It felt no regret as it reached over and plucked the deformed head from its own shoulders, then tossed it like trash into the newly-opened grave. The lump of flesh died without a whimper as the soul of Seti went from one hell to another.

"May you rest in pieces," the demon said.

Then, from behind, it heard the sound of a vehicle. It turned just as the SUV stopped, noticing the carnage at the shopping plaza. It was the woman who was with child. And her son. This was just too perfect. They would come back to the altar with him.

-2-

After the prayer circle, Erik and Dovecrest headed off towards the altar while Mark went into town where he was more likely to confront the demon. It would probably head there next. They hoped to drive it back to the altar before dark.

"I'm worried about Vickie, though," Erik said as he and Dovecrest walked through the woods.

"She'll be fine," the Indian said. "We need to finish this up quickly so you can get back to her."

"Yeah."

They walked in silence for a few minutes. The position of the altar was so obvious to Erik now that he wondered how he ever could have not known about it. The thing resonated evil.

"I'm just not sure about one thing," Erik said.

"What's that?"

"How did this...thing...get here in the first place?"

Dovecrest didn't say anything for a few moments, and Erik thought he wasn't going to answer him. Then he replied.

"Demons are really nothing more than human sins in the flesh," he said finally. "This one calls itself 'Wrath.' It has always existed, as long as there has been sin. These demon worshippers from early times merely woke the thing up by worshipping it. They woke it up and brought it here in the flesh, instead of just in the spirit."

"So this thing is the personification of wrath?"

"Pretty much. We burned the devil worshippers at the stake. That was the colonists' idea. That's how they dealt with witchcraft. So when the cult leader was killed, he placed a curse on the land so this demon would get brought back again the first time someone disturbed his spirit.

"It's been my job to keep watch all of these years. I'm surprised it took so long, actually. I'd just about given up and thought the demon was trapped permanently on the other side. I should have been more prepared."

"It's easy to get complacent," Erik said. "My son tried to warn me. I wouldn't listen. It's just that, this is the modern world. You just don't think about things like this as being real."

They were almost at the altar now. The thing seemed much closer than it was before.

"I told you it moves," Dovecrest said, as if reading his mind.

"So what exactly do we do at the altar?"

"We wait. When it comes back and goes through the portal, we follow it in."

"That's if it doesn't kill us first."

"Don't worry. If Mark does his job, we will be the least of its concerns. It won't pay any attention to us. You do realize that the Great Spirit is more powerful than the devil."

"Of course. But that's not to say that the 'Great Spirit' won't lose a few troops along the way."

Then they broke through the trees and into the field where the altar stood at the center. It was the same field, but Erik knew it was in a different place.

"We need to stay out of the way, but as close to this thing as we can get," Dovecrest said.

He skirted the edges of the field and found a secluded spot behind a large oak tree.

"This looks good," he said. "We might as well get comfortable."

Erik sat down on the ground and tried not to think about the last time he'd been here, and the carnage that had ensued.

-3-

Todd had seen the demon first. His mother had slowed down when they saw a wounded soldier staggering in the street, his eyes ripped out and blood pouring down his face. Todd had tried not to look, and when he'd looked away he'd seen the monster across the street, holding a headstone made of that black rock in its hands.

"Mom!" he'd screamed, and pointed.

His mother slammed on the brakes. The car screeched to a halt and the demon turned to look at them. Todd swore that the thing was grinning at them.

"We've got to get past it and into town," Vickie said.

She turned the wheel hard right and into the shopping center parking lot, narrowly missing the blinded soldier. Todd got a good look at his face and thought he might have been better off if his Mom had hit him. She swerved around an army truck, ran over a couple of dead bodies, and jumped a curbing to land on Route 102 heading into town.

Todd looked out the back window and saw the demon still grinning. The thing opened up a set of leathery wings and hunched low for a take off.

"It's gonna follow us!" he screamed.

Vickie gunned the engine of the SUV while Todd watched the thing take to the air. Its flight was easy and light. He thought it looked weird to see a rock floating on wings. But his idea of what was normal and weird had changed a lot in the past few days. The things he read about in his books looked pretty tame compared to what he'd seen lately.

Once the demon took to the air, it began gaining ground. Todd suspected that the thing could catch them easily if it wanted to. It was kind of like when he played hide and seek with other kids—sometimes you knew where they were but you wouldn't find them right away, just to make it more fun.

The trees were whizzing by him on either side. Todd had never seen his mother drive so fast. It would have been fun if they weren't being chased by something out of a bad horror movie.

Todd knew it wasn't too far into town, but he didn't know if they'd make it. The demon was almost over them now, and its shadow was falling over the car.

"Mom, he's gonna get us!" he screamed as the thing's face appeared just above the back window.

His mother hit the brakes and the demon flew past, then as the monster tried to stop she gunned the engine and roared by it. The thing was fast, but wasn't so good at stopping and turning. The thing took a few seconds to get back up to speed and by then they were entering the edge of town.

"He's still coming," Todd said, looking back. He gripped his geologist's hammer so tight that his knuckled turned white.

They entered the town and drove by the library, which was now nothing more than a smoking ruin. The place looked like buildings Todd had seen on the Discovery Channel that had been bombed in World War Two. The brick walls had collapsed into rubble, and what was left was black and still smoking. They passed the ruins and turned onto Main Street.

The place was deserted. The gas station was empty and shut down. The bank was closed. The tiny post office looked empty. Everyone had run away, Todd guessed. They all knew the demon was coming.

The thing had caught up with them again and was hovering over the car like a helicopter. His Mom swerved and lost it for a moment, but then it was back. A claw scraped on the roof, almost knocking the SUV off the road. Vickie swerved again. This time the thing's leg crashed through the back window.

Todd and his mother saw the soldiers at the same time, standing in front of the town hall. The SUV turned hard right and towards the parking lot.

"We're going to make a run for it here," his Mom said. "This is the safest building in town. As soon as I stop the car, run for the front door."

"Ok," Todd said. His mouth was tight and dry and his heart raced so fast he thought it would pop out of his chest. He'd never been so scared in his life—not even the night the rock had tried to get him.

His Mom pulled the car into the parking lot and up on the grass, stopping just in front of the door. The two soldiers were firing their guns at the demon, but it didn't seem to have any effect on the thing. The bullets just bounced off like they were hitting a brick wall.

"Now!" his mother screamed, reached over to undo his seat belt, and flung open her door. Todd opened his door and jumped out.

Once outside he was overcome by the awful stench of the demon. It was an awful collection of odors, a combination of something that had been burned far too long, something that had died and rotted for days, and old cabbage. The stench was like a thick cloud, and Todd thought he was going to throw up. He gagged once, and then put his head down and ran towards the front doors of the town hall.

The soldiers had moved forward and were trying to hold the demon back with their machine guns. Todd saw his mother out of the corner of his eye; she had circled around the car and was running for the door too.

Todd ran past the soldiers and could feel the air from the demon's wings beating down against his head. The smell was making him sick and the fear made his head ache. But his legs had taken on a life of their own and he was running faster than he had ever run in his life. If only he could do this in gym class he thought, and he suddenly realized how weird it was to be thinking about school while running away from a demon that smelled like a garbage dump. He almost laughed at the idea—in fact, he might have laughed if he hadn't seen the demon grab the soldier in its claws and lift into the air with him.

Todd couldn't help but look up at the mess. He didn't want to, but for some reason his eyes were drawn up, and he looked into the soldier's terrified face as the demon pulled him up. The man had blue eyes and they were wide with fear. He dropped his rifle and it narrowly missed Todd as it felt to the ground and bounced on the concrete stairs on the town hall just in front of him. It made a loud clatter and the hair-trigger went off, firing a bullet randomly into the air. The demon rose high with the soldier and Todd found himself stopping to look up. His mother was right behind him; he felt her arms wrap around him as she picked him up and ran to the cement stairs of the town hall. She stumbled on the first step; Todd was still trying to look up. Then he saw the soldier heading back down. The demon had dropped him.

"Look out, Mom," he yelled, pulling her to the side.

They half ran and half fell out of the way of the falling man. The demon had taken him quite a way up, so it took some time for him to fall. But the demon's aim was true—he would have hit them if they hadn't scrambled out of the way.

The soldier crashed to the steps with an audible plop, like an over-large water balloon. Blood squirted from the man, splashing Erik's legs and staining his new sneakers. The blood was all over his Mom, too. This time he couldn't stop his stomach from churning and he threw up hard on the steps of the town hall.

"Come on! We've got to hurry!" his mother screamed, and yanked him by the arm. He stumbled to his feet and saw the door there just ahead of them. The second soldier was beside them now, helping them along and then through the doorway. Todd was surprised to find that he was still clutching his geologist's hammer and hadn't dropped it in the commotion. He and his mother hid behind the soldier as he took another shot at the demon and then slammed the door shut behind them. Todd took a huge, deep breath, and smiled sheepishly at his mother. Then he felt his head go light and his knees buckle beneath him as he dropped to the floor in exhaustion.

-4-

The sun set and it was beginning to grow dark as Erik and Dovecrest settled in near the altar to wait for the demon's return.

"If Mark finds the thing and banishes it, it should be back here pretty soon."

"I think it'll be pretty easy to find, don't you?"

"Finding it will be the easy part. Standing up to it will take faith and courage."

"And if Mark fails?"

Dovecrest was silent for a moment. "It will come back here, eventually. To recharge its batteries. I don't know when, though. And it probably won't need to actually travel back to the other side."

"How will we know if Mark drove it back or if it came back on its own, then?" Erik asked.

"Oh, we'll know. If it's driven out it will definitely be on the run. It'll be afraid. Just imaging the fear you'd feel meeting God face to face on your worst day. I suspect it'll also be angry. It won't like being sent back, even if it's only temporary."

"Temporary?"

"Mark can drive it back. But it'll gather strength again and come back. That's why we have to follow it and destroy it once and for all."

"That's the part I'm really worried about."

"Me too," Dovecrest admitted.

Darkness was quickly covering the area. Though they each had flashlights, they didn't need them. Erik was surprised by how acute his night vision had become, and the stars did illuminate the open field in front of them. Knowing that they'd need to stay quiet and out of sight, they settled down with their thoughts.

Erik wondered what might be going through his friend's mind. The Indian had been alive for almost 300 years. He had seen so much—had seen the world go from the stone age into the space age. Erik couldn't imagine what might be locked in that ancient man's brain.

Then his thoughts turned to his wife and his son. He wished he knew that Vickie was safe. He had no idea if his baby had been born yet. He had no idea if it were a boy or a girl. The doctors knew—but Erik and Vickie were old fashioned and had asked them not to tell. The temptation had been strong. But they had held out.

Erik wanted a girl. A little girl to spoil. He had a son to toss the ball around with and play games with. Now he wanted a daughter to spoil with pretty clothes and with love. He might already have a daughter, right now. They would name her Christine. And he would spoil her with toys.

He remembered when Todd had been born. He'd bought the kid a tiny baseball outfit with a little cap and everything. He remembered how big the kid's eyes had been, how he'd looked right at him, as if he recognized him as his Dad. Todd had been a good baby, though very active. He had hardly ever cried, though. Hardly ever got sick. And smart. He'd been reading in kindergarten. One day he knew the letters and the sounds they made and the next day he was reading his picture books. Erik thought he'd memorized them. But then when he wrote down words for the kid on a piece of paper, he'd read them too, just by sounding them out. The teacher didn't know what to do with him, so she had him help her teach the other kids to read.

God, how he prayed that they were all right. They *had* to be all right. They were everything to him. So many times he had wished for things and prayed for things that weren't really important. He'd wanted so badly to sell his book. Then he'd wanted it to be successful. And then if only he could have more money, if only they'd option his book for a movie....

Now, none of it seemed important. He'd trade in everything just for the knowledge that his family was all right. If only he had a cell phone and could call. He swore that if he ever got out of this mess ok that he'd break down and get a cell phone. And he'd get Vickie one, too. If only he had one and could call her right now.

Then he remembered where he was. He looked out into the open field and saw the altar looming out there, a terrible relic from another world and another time. No, a cell phone wouldn't work out here anyway, not near this awful thing.

"Dear God," he prayed silently, "Please, please let them be all right. Please stay with them and protect them."

CHAPTER TWENTY-TWO

-1-

The old town hall was built like a fortress. It had, in fact, served as a fort during the Revolutionary War, and as an armory during the 1800s. Once Todd and his mother were inside, the soldier slammed shut the heavy, steel-reinforced door and dropped the iron bars to seal the place off. All of the windows and doors were barred and the walls were made of heavy granite. It was, without a doubt, the strongest building within 20 miles.

Although Todd didn't know the history of the building, he did sense its strength and security. The demon smashed against the door once and it did not open. Perhaps they might be safe in here after all, he thought.

The soldier was on his radio calling for reinforcements. Todd rushed to the window to look outside. His mother tried to stop him, but he was too fast for her. The sun had just set, but there was plenty of light to see by, with the streetlights and the spotlights from the Town Hall.

Sure enough, reinforcements were on the way. He saw a small convoy of men and equipment turning onto Main Street, and he heard a helicopter overhead. It looked like a lot of men—maybe fifty, he thought, and a couple of tanks and army trucks too. This wasn't just the police anymore. Surely the army would be able to stop this thing. The army could stop anything. And he wanted to make sure he saw it all.

"Todd, get away from that window," his mother scolded, tugging at him. He noticed that her face was white and she was having trouble breathing. She'd called it "labor pains" and that meant she was going to have the baby soon.

"I wanna see, Mom! Somebody has to know what's going on out there."

His mother was too distressed to argue. She sat cross-legged on the floor and breathed the way she was supposed to when she was having labor pains. Todd looked back out the window to see what was going on. He wanted to see the army destroy this thing once and for all, and then he could get on with his life again without being afraid all the time.

He watched as the demon turned away from the main door of the building and faced its attackers. Rather than wait for them to come to it, the monster went to them. Its first target was the helicopter. Todd couldn't actually see the helicopter, but he could hear it above the building. The demon looked up at it, then launched into the air—Todd knew that's what it was after.

He heard machine gun fire above him and the helicopter sound became louder, then drew away. More machine gun fire followed. Then there was an awful, screeching noise, as if gears were being ground up and turned backwards. Todd strained to see but the battle was going on above him and just out of his sight. He heard a popping sound, like the sound his uncle's car had made the time they'd driven to Putnam and the engine broke because Uncle Matt hadn't put any oil in it. Sure enough, he saw bluish-black smoke trailing over the top of the Town Hall. Maybe the helicopter guys hadn't put any oil into their engine, either, he thought.

That's when pieces of the copter began to fall. First there was what appeared to be a piece of the big propeller, and it was broken clean in half. The soldiers on the ground were close now, and firing up into the air. The propeller piece came spinning down to the ground, cutting through the soldiers like a lawn-mower blade. Todd screamed as he saw a head fly off, and an arm. Several others went down like bowling pins as the blade sliced through them.

The remaining soldiers took cover, dropping to the ground or ducking behind the building, and the two tanks rolled forward. The rest of the helicopter blade fell straight down, like a spear, and neatly speared a soldier through the back as he lay on the grass, sticking through him and into the ground below. The effect looked like a science exhibit he'd seen where they pinned a beetle to a corkboard. The man squirmed for several seconds before collapsing.

"Todd, you need to get away from that window," his mother was saying. It looked like her labor pains were over, so she was a threat now. He didn't really want to look out the window, but he couldn't help himself. He just couldn't wait inside this building without knowing what was going on. Even if it were bad.

"It's ok, Mom. The soldiers are gonna kill it."

But now his confidence level in the soldiers had fallen. Another piece of the helicopter crashed to earth—this looked like the tail, and burned up in a small fireball. This one, at least, didn't hit any soldiers. Then the rest of the copter crashed down across the street, right through the roof of the bank. A couple of soldiers caught fire and rolled around on the ground, frantically trying to put themselves out. Then a body dropped out of the sky to splatter in the road. Probably one of the guys in the helicopter, Todd thought.

Todd had never seen a dead body in his life, and now he was seeing them by the dozens—not only just bodies, but people being killed in horrible ways. Part of him felt sick and disgusted. The other part was just numb, as if he were playing a video game or watching a horror movie. But this wasn't the Hollywood blood and gore like he saw in *Fangoria* when he sneaked a peek in the magazine at the drug store when his mother wasn't looking. This was the real thing. The movies could come pretty close, but they couldn't get the real thing. They especially couldn't get the sounds. And the smells—the sickening smell of that demon, and the smell of people on fire—the smells were beyond anything he could possibly have imagined.

He thought for a moment that he might throw up again, so he turned away from the window for a moment and looked at his Mom. She looked as if she had been through a battle of her own. Actually, she had, he thought. They both had. And so far they had survived. His mother's hair was all tangled, and her eyes looked tired and old. Her face was sheet-white. Still, though, she managed a small smile.

"I wish Dad was here," Todd said. "He'd be able to get us out of here."

"We'll be fine," his Mom said. "We're safe here."

Todd looked past her at the soldier guarding the door. Maybe, he thought. But that one soldier wasn't going to stop this thing. He'd put more faith in the tanks. He looked back out the window and saw the two tanks taking up a position across the street.

The demon dropped into view, just in front of the town hall. For a moment, it blocked Todd's vision, then it half-flew and half ran towards one of the tanks. The tank's machine gun blazed, and bullets ricocheted off the demon and off the walls of the building. Todd instinctively ducked down and away from the window in case a stray bullet came thorough.

When he peeked back up, the demon was standing in front of the tank, holding a soldier above his head. The big gun of the tank fired at point blank range. The sound was deafening, and smoke filled the air, clouding over the area and engulfing the monster in black soot. Surely, that was enough to kill it, Todd thought. He watched and waited for the smoke to clear.

Everything was silent, shrouded in smoke and falling debris. Todd waited in anticipation.

"I think they got him," he said softly. He glanced quickly at his mother. She looked like she was praying.

Then, as the smoke and dust finally settled, he saw it still standing there in front of the tank. The soldier it had been holding over its head was now nothing more than a piece of meat, torn and charred and ripped into pieces. But the demon was whole. It had taken a step or two backward, but still stood tall. The thing looked down at itself and picked a small, fist-sized piece of rock off its chest, where the tank shell had hit. That was all that had come off. The demon seemed to laugh, then threw the small piece of itself at the man on the tank with the machine gun, where it crushed through his helmet and instantly brained him.

Todd couldn't watch the rest. He knew they were done for now, no matter what they did. The last thing he saw was the demon flipping the tank on its side. Then he ran over to sit by his mother, feeling the comfort of her arms around him. Although he wasn't very good at it, and didn't really feel like it would do any good, he joined her in silent prayer and tried hard not to pay attention to the screams and shrieks that were coming from outside the Town Hall.

-2-

The darkness was complete now; the last of the setting sun had disappeared, and the moon was low on the eastern horizon. But Erik didn't need any light to see. He could feel the presence of the altar stone standing across the field. In fact, it called to him, attracted him now.

"Come," it seemed to say. "Join with us. There's no need to fight. You can be on the winning side."

Erik shook his head in an attempt to clear it. He wondered if the thing was calling to Dovecrest, too, or if this piece of fun was just for his benefit.

He thought about Vickie again and this time he had a sudden bad feeling. They hadn't made it safely to the hospital. He didn't know how he knew, but he was sure of it.

"Join us and your family will be safe," the voice seemed to say in his head. "They will be taken care of. You won't have to worry anymore."

It was almost tempting. How many times had he seen evil rewarded during his lifetime? It seemed that those with the least amount of good in them were often the most successful. Some of these people just seemed to have a knack for getting ahead.

He, on the other hand, had to work for whatever he got. It hadn't come easy. Even now, though he certainly had achieved success, there were those whose work was half as good and who earned ten times what he made....

Stop it, he told himself. You're listening to this thing. You're letting it get to you. You have a good home and a decent living and a great family. Stop being jealous and enjoy what you have.

"You won't have that family for long," the voice said. Then it sent him an image of the demon clutching Vickie and Todd by the hair, dragging them along Main Street.

"Stop it!" he said, and only when Dovecrest turned to look at him did he realize he had spoken out loud.

"Sorry," he mumbled.

"Don't let it turn you," Dovecrest said. "It'll try to show you things...."

"It already has," Erik said softly. "The things it shows me— are they real? Will they happen?"

"Maybe. Maybe not."

"How will I know?"

"You won't know."

"Vickie and Todd are in trouble. I know it. I feel it. It's not just that thing getting to me."

"We are all in trouble, my friend. If you really want to save your family, we have to finish our work here."

"I know. It's just that...waiting is so hard."

"Waiting is harder than doing," Dovecrest said. "But that's what we have to do right now. We have to wait."

"How much longer?"

Dovecrest laughed. "I don't know. But if that thing is trying to get to you, that's a good sign."

"What makes you say that?"

"Because if it didn't fear you, it wouldn't be trying to convert you."

"So now it's afraid of us, right?"

"Maybe fear isn't the right word," Dovecrest agreed. "But we have its attention and it's worried."

"Then why doesn't it just come here and destroy us before we have a chance to act?"

"I don't know," Dovecrest said. "But I never said it wouldn't try."

Erik just shook his head. "That's what I've grown to love about you," he said.

"What's that?"

"The way you can be so comforting in times of stress."

Dovecrest laughed. "Hey, at least I got you to stop worrying about your family, didn't I?"

"Yeah," Erik said. "Only now I'm worried again."

-3-

The demon had enjoyed tearing up the town and killing the soldiers. The helicopter had come apart a little too easy, and the tanks hadn't even been a challenge. But the looks on their faces when the thing had fired at it and not damaged it had been worth it all. It had heard the collective groan of despair when they'd seen it still standing. Their collective hope had evaporated into dust. They had turned and run away without a fight. It had killed a few as they fled, but for the most part it had let them go. Just its presence had damaged them enough. None of them would ever be the same. Yes, it had enjoyed the killing spree. But it was time to get back to business now. The woman and the unborn child—ultimate innocence. That's what it wanted. To destroy it at the moment of birth.

It turned back towards the building where the woman and the boy had gone. They thought they could hide inside. But it would go inside and get them. Nothing would stop it now. It was invincible.

It could reignite itself and resume its fiery flaming shape and burn its way through the door. But it was enjoying the physical thrill of crushing and maiming in this form—hands-on, it thought. It leaped into the air once again and flew to the door of the building. The door was strong. But not strong enough. It reached out and grabbed the heavy iron handles and pulled. It resisted for just a few seconds, then popped off with a thud and a clang as it fell to the ground. The door swung back easily on its hinges now.

It could smell the fear of the woman and the child inside. It could also sense the unborn, which had no fear, only innocence. It would break, corrupt, destroy that innocence at that perfect moment of birth, just as an insult into the face of all that was good. It would do this because it could and because it must.

The last soldier made a feeble attempt at resistance. He shot the demon and tried to stab him with a bayonet. The demon grabbed his gun and twisted it into an obscene shape around the man's neck. Then it smashed his nasal cavity up into his brain. The soldier dropped to the ground, senseless and dying, blood flowing from his nose and mouth like a river.

The woman and the boy tried to run. But there was no place to go. They retreated further into the main hallway, then tried to run up a staircase. The demon took to the air and was halfway up before they made it to the top step.

It stared at the woman with its hypnotic gaze. She paused and looked back. Her eyes grew wider as she stared into the endless depths of its eyes. It could feel her mind, could feel the infant inside her. It was not ready to be born, not just yet, but it was close. It would happen very soon, and he would be waiting. He could take it out himself with a single swipe of a claw, but it wouldn't be the same. It wanted the baby to be born into its embrace, to know pure evil as the first, and last, moments of its human existence.

It would take this woman with him and keep her until the time was right. Now the boy was another matter.

It turned to stare at the boy. This was the one that had defied it earlier, had tried to swipe at it through the very portal back when it was on the other side and calling to the child. The boy still held that feeble hammer in his hands, and was lifting it over his head as if to strike. The thing had hurt him before, but that was before he'd gained strength and substance. That had been when it was trying to enter this world of men. Now it was here, in the flesh so to speak, and this hammer would be useless. It would show this boy a thing or two before it killed him. But first, the prize.

It reached around to its own wing and tore a strip of the leathery appendage off. Then it leaped towards the mesmerized woman, grabbed her by the arm and pulled her towards it. The boy whacked at it with his hammer, but it only glanced off its rock-hard skin. It then took to the air, holding the woman tightly and binding her limbs into a ball as it flew, much like a spider might tie up its victim with silk.

It watched in amusement as the boy raved and screamed down below. It'd take care of this one soon, and make him pay for his insolence. It might take its time with this one and let the mother watch. That would make things even more interesting.

Carrying the mother in one arm, he leaped forward and dove down at the boy, grabbing him in the other arm and flying directly out the front door of the building. The boy screamed and flailed but the mother was still in shock. It felt her labor contractions beginning again and knew the birth would happen soon. It'd kill the boy that had caused him so many problems and then enjoy the rest. It landed on the grass in front of the town hall and looked over its handiwork. The bank was in flames, a helicopter was ruined, and two tanks were overturned and helpless, like turtles on their backs. It had been so simple it was almost funny.

It put the woman down on the ground and turned back to the town hall. Still holding the boy under its left arm, the demon strode up to the building and kicked a hole in the front wall. It moved over and kicked another one. The walls began to collapse around it, until the entire front wall was nothing but rubble. The boy was still struggling, trying to hit it with his hammer. It grabbed the weapon from the boy and crushed it into a glob of steel on a stick, then tossed it away. Then, just as it was about to finish the boy off, a new distraction entered the picture.

A car had pulled up to the front of the building and a man

got out and walked purposefully towards the demon. It stopped what it was doing and looked at him. This was different. The man didn't have any weapons and didn't seem the slightest bit afraid.

Instinctively, the demon picked up the woman—it wasn't taking any chances that this man would take its prize away, or that she would be killed in a fight.

The man walked up to within six feet of the demon, walking with an intensity and confidence that the monster wasn't used to. Mortals were supposed to be afraid of it. The fact that this one wasn't made it angry, but also a little nervous. Did this human know something that the others didn't?

It would kill the man quickly and be done with it. But before it could take the first step to launch itself forward towards the man, he had pulled a small cross from his pocket and held it out in front of him. The demon stopped. It remembered this symbol from the church and detested it. In fact, it still felt the pain of the upside down cross that had been branded onto its chest. No, this man would have to die right now.

But the cross held him back for just a moment, and that moment was enough.

"I drive you out of this place in the name of Jesus Christ, our true Lord and the Son of God!" the man said. "In the name of Jesus I banish you from this place!"

The demon stopped, immobilized by the words and by the sign of the cross. It felt the upside down cross on its chest ignite in pain, burning deeply into it, scorching it again with the fires of hell. The demon doubled forward in agony and suddenly it no longer burned with wrath but with pain. It forgot about the pregnant woman and the boy, forgot about death and destruction and making the world dread and fear its presence. All it could think about was escape.

It took a step backward and the man stepped forward towards it.

"In the name of Jesus Christ our Lord, I command you to be gone from this place, to return to the depths of hell from where you came!"

The demon Wrath was no longer in control of its own body. It felt its wings begin to flap of their own accord and its knees bend to take off in flight. It willed its body to stay and fight, to destroy this weakling of a mortal who had the audacity to stand up to it. It wanted to smash this man with every ounce of strength and power that it had. But instead of fighting, the demon felt itself being lifted into the air. Only by fleeing would the pain diminish. Only by returning to the altar and going back through the portal to where it had come from. It didn't want to go back, but it must. There was no other way. The altar called for it now, needed it.

Then the demon realized that, somehow, it had managed to hang on to the boy and the pregnant woman. It still held them tightly, one under each arm. So, maybe it couldn't stay here—at least right now. But it could take these two back to hell with it. It would bring them back and destroy them. But not until the baby was born. That would be the ultimate victory over that cross-thing. To have the innocent baby born into the bowels of hell.

CHAPTER TWENTY-THREE

-1-

Pastor Mark watched in shock as the monster took to the air, carrying Todd and Vickie, one under each arm. He held his cross up over his head, and followed the path of the demon with it as it disappeared into the night sky. He could see the brand of the cross upside down on the thing's chest. The brand glowed like hot coals as the thing disappeared into the night. He watched with his mouth open, then looked down at the destruction around him.

The soldiers had either fled or been killed or wounded. Several maimed men lie scattered about, moaning in agony from various wounds. Some appeared burned. Others were bleeding from hideous wounds. Several appeared to be missing limbs.

If only he had arrived a little sooner. He might have prevented all of this. But tracking the demon had not been an easy task. The rumors of its whereabouts had outrun its actual presence. Finally, he had followed the trail of destruction, which led him to the town hall.

Now that it was done, he didn't know what to do next. He dropped down to his knees on the ground and tried to pray. His hands were shaking as if he were having some sort of fit, and he realized that he could no longer find any words to say, not a single word. His mouth was dry and he felt tears streaking down his cheeks. His legs collapsed beneath him and he lay down on the grass and wept openly, without shame.

Despite his faith, he hadn't really been sure this plan would work. He knew in his heart that God had dominion over all things, and that He had given man strength and power over evil. He knew it in his heart. Yet his mind had questioned, and he had been forced to make his mind be quiet. He had listened to his heart. Now his mind stood by in bewilderment of what he had done.

As he had banished the demon, he had really felt God's power within him. It hadn't just been the Sunday sermon designed to sound good for the congregation. This had been the real deal here. The power of the Lord had filled him to the brim, giving him a faith and confidence and strength that he could never have imagined.

"Thank you, Lord," he said at last, struggling to say even those simple words. His body felt as if it had been used to fight a war. In some ways, he guessed it had been.

But the war was not over. This was just the first battle. And the thing had escaped with Erik's wife and son—and the unborn baby. If he had only been here sooner, he could have prevented that, he thought once again. He could have saved Erik's family and prevented this death and destruction around him. How many lives had been lost because of his hesitation?

But that was his mind speaking. And once again, his heart took control, soothing and calming him. This was not his fault, it told him. God knows all and allows everything to happen, all in its own time. His heart knew this. Now his mind would have to accept it.

"Thank you, Lord," he said again. "Now help us to finish the job we have just begun."

Then, slowly, he stood up and returned to his car. He'd follow the thing back to the altar. Perhaps there he could be of some help to his friends.

Erik was now fully convinced that Todd and Vickie were in serious trouble. He couldn't think, couldn't concentrate, couldn't keep still in his hiding place in the brush.

"This is driving me crazy," he said. "I can't just sit here any longer. I have to do something."

"You'll get your chance soon enough," Dovecrest said. "I have the feeling the demon is heading our way."

"And I have a feeling that my family is in trouble! I've got to help them! I can't just hang around here waiting for something that might happen. I never should have left Vickie."

Erik stood up from his hiding place in the brush and Dovecrest was beside him, holding him back.

"No, you can't leave."

"Why not?"

"First of all, where are you planning to go?"

"I'll find a phone and call the hospital. Then I'll know if Vickie made it there or not."

"And if she's not there? Then what do you do?"

"I'll...I'll go find her. I'll retrace her steps."

Dovecrest shook his head. "You don't know which way she went. She could have gotten turned around and gone anywhere. The military might have evacuated her. She might have even gone to a different hospital. You wouldn't know where to begin and you wouldn't be doing her or Todd or yourself any good."

"You just don't understand," Erik said. "You don't have a family...."

"That's where you're wrong. I did have a family." The Indian dropped his head and looked at the ground. "But that was a long time ago."

"I...I didn't realize...."

"Well what did you think? Of course I don't have a family now. I'm over 200 years old, for God sakes."

"Don't you have...grandchildren? Some connection to them?"

Dovecrest sat down on the ground and was silent for awhile.

"I had a wife and a daughter," he said. My wife was beautiful. Running Moon. Long, dark hair. Big eyes. Slender and trim. A wonderful cook. We loved each other like no one else. And my daughter, Little Dove. So small and timid. And very smart."

Dovecrest was silent again. Erik thought the story was over, and then he spoke again.

"My daughter was just six years old when she and her mother were killed."

"What happened?" Erik asked, sitting beside him.

"I haven't told this story in over a hundred years. No one would believe it. Although maybe now they would.

"It happened when the devil worshippers tried to call to the demon the first time, and tried to bring it here. They didn't really know what they were doing, thank God. But they had learned some rituals that would attract spirits in the underworld.

"It was the beginning of August. My wife and daughter were out gathering blueberries. The blueberries here used to be as big as cherries, and Running Moon would mix them up with white corn flour to make journey cakes. They were out in the forest when they were taken.

"The tribe formed a search party, but we could not find them. There were no traces. That night I went out again—many of the men did. That's when I first saw the altar. The devil worshippers were around it. They had my wife and my daughter. I tried to save them, but I was caught. They forced me to watch while they were sacrificed. They planned to kill me, too, but I later escaped. That's when I spoke to the chief and he spoke to Roger Williams and his men. The colonists had lost women and children too.

"So we joined forces and put a stop to it. The colonists had laws that they could use. And we had our own set of laws. We killed them and the colonists burned the leader at the stake. When he cursed the land, my people made me the watcher. It was my job to wait and watch in case the demon should try to reappear."

"And you've been waiting for over 300 years."

"That's right. I did not know I would live so long. I thought I would pass the job on to someone else, but it seems I outlived all of my apprentices. And so here I am."

"So that thing got your family."

"Yes. That's why it's personal. That's why I have to get rid of it for good. I cannot move on as long as this thing can come back. I'm trapped here in this old body, and I can't join my family."

Erik nodded. For the first time, this was beginning to make sense, in a weird sort of way.

"Thanks," Erik said. "Then I need to wait with you and help you destroy it."

-3-

Todd thought he was going to die. In fact, he wished he would just die. The smell alone was enough to kill him. Let alone the fear. The demon was crushing him under its arm, holding him tightly on one side, and his mother on the other. It seemed to know just how much to squeeze to create unbearable agony without actually cutting off his breath. He couldn't see his mother's face, but he could hear her breathing. She was having those labor pains again.

When Pastor Mark had arrived, Todd thought he was out of his mind. He couldn't believe how the pastor had walked right up to the demon and had driven it away. He didn't think the pastor expected it to take him and his mother with it, though. Judging from the look on the pastor's face, Todd didn't think he'd expected anything to happen, except maybe that the monster would kill him. The pastor had been as surprised as Todd had been. The demon, too, had been surprised.

Todd knew where it was taking them. It was going to the altar where it would sacrifice them and kill them as part of some demonic thing. He knew where they were going even before the monster had taken flight. And, sure enough, the street lights below were gone and they were flying over the woods. He couldn't actually see anything in the darkness, but he knew. He could sense the altar's presence, even from here.

Sure enough, the demon turned around and began to circle. Todd could imagine the open field below them, with the altar in the center. He'd been there before and it had tried to get him. Now it looked like it was going to get him—and his mother, too.

For some reason the demon seemed cautious now as it circled lower. The pastor had frightened it, all right, with his cross and his demand in God's name. Todd wondered if he could banish the demon like the pastor did. Then he decided that even if he could, it would just make the monster drop him and he'd just crash to the earth. He remembered what the soldier had looked like after he had been dropped, and he decided he didn't want any of that. He'd take his chances right where he was for now.

He tried to call for his mother, but she didn't seem to hear. He wanted to ask her if she'd seen what the pastor did. Maybe if they both did the same thing after they landed, then the demon would let them go. But his mother didn't respond. She either couldn't hear him, or was in too much pain of her own to reply. Besides, he dared not give away his plans until the thing was back on solid ground.

The demon slowed its descent and came down towards the ground. Todd could vaguely see the clearing in the woods by the moonlight. His guess had been right. Once they landed he was determined to begin the fight on his own. His geologist hammer hadn't worked this time. But he'd seen what the pastor could do and he wasn't about to give up. He just wished he could get his mother's attention. Otherwise, he didn't know how he'd get her out of the thing's grip.

He felt the demon put on the brakes—they were about to land. Todd prepared himself for the showdown that would follow.

Erik felt it coming before he actually saw it. Dovecrest must have felt it too, because he heard the man stiffen up and get into a position of readiness. Then, after the feeling, he saw it cross in front of the moon.

Silhouetted against the moon, the thing looked like a medieval gargoyle, with thick, leathery wings. It seemed to be carrying something under either arm. It was carrying something—no, someone. Erik suddenly knew who it was. The thing had Todd and Vickie.

He would have leaped out of his hiding place and into the field if Dovecrest hadn't grabbed his shoulder and held him back. He stopped himself. The Indian was right. Taking off half cocked would only get him and his family killed. At least now there was a chance. The demon was doing him a favor. It was bringing his loved ones to him. Now he was glad he hadn't gone off looking for them.

Still, he had no idea how to get the demon to drop them. Perhaps it was planning to kill them on the altar, like it had Dovecrest's family. He couldn't let that happen. There had to be something he could do.

He knelt down beside Dovecrest as the demon landed, just to the right of the altar. He wasn't sure if Pastor Mark had driven it off, or if it had come here of its own accord. Either way, they needed to drive the thing through the portal and into the other world. But not until he'd made it set his wife and son free. That would have to come first. Then Dovecrest would go in after it. If his family were free, he'd have to stay behind and be with them. He knew he couldn't leave his wife behind again

"You take care of your family," Dovecrest whispered. "I can handle the other side."

It was as if the Indian had read his mind. Erik wondered how confident Dovecrest really felt about going in alone. But his family came first. Leaving them now was no longer an option.

But he'd have to free them from the demon first.

The monster crouched low and looked around as if looking for something. It seemed wary, as if it knew they were out there waiting for it. As if it feared them.

It placed Vickie down on the altar. She wasn't moving. Erik thought she might be tied up or restrained somehow. Todd was a different matter. As soon as the monster landed, Todd had begun to squirm. The demon didn't seem to pay any attention to him, though.

Erik didn't know what to do. He was torn by the need to run across the field and rescue his wife, and fear that his presence would cause the thing to act, killing them all. For some reason, it had kept Vickie and Todd alive.

He was still torn by indecision when his son made the decision for him. Todd suddenly began to shout at the demon. His words echoed across the field.

"I drive you out in the name of Jesus!" the boy screamed. "I command you to put me down and leave this place. Go back to where you belong!"

As soon as Todd began screaming, Erik jumped out and ran towards his son, no longer caring what happened. Dovecrest followed closely at his heels.

Amazingly, the monster dropped the boy to the ground as if he had just turned into poison. The thing turned and faced Erik. He noticed an upside down cross had been burned into the monster's chest. It glowed hot-white now against the obsidian stone of the demon and illuminated the field like a lantern. Apparently, Todd's words had set the thing off.

The boy staggered to his feet and looked at his mother, who was still lying motionless on the altar. With sudden terror, Erik wondered if she were still alive.

"Come on, Mom, say the words!" Todd screamed. "Tell it to go away!"

The monster backed away towards the altar, putting itself between Erik and his wife. Realizing he couldn't help his mother, Todd turned and ran. That's when he saw Erik heading straight towards him.

"Dad!" he screamed. "Tell it to go away!"

Erik reached his son in the middle of the open field and grabbed him, picking him up off the ground. Dovecrest ran past and towards the demon, which really seemed to be in pain now.

"It hurts it, Dad. When you tell it to go away it hurts it. I saw Pastor Mark do it and it worked."

Erik put his son down, then stepped forward towards the demon. If he could grab Vickie while the demon was still preoccupied....

Dovecrest began to chant in his native language and the demon backed up right to the altar. Erik charged forward but before he'd covered half the distance the thing had picked Vickie up in its arms again and stood on top of the altar stone.

"No!" he screamed. "Let her go!"

But the demon only looked up and grinned at him. Defiantly, it tucked Vickie under its left arm. It looked at Dovecrest with rage; it was obvious that the Indian's chants were doing something to the monster. The upside down cross was burning and smoking now, lighting up the entire field like an incandescent light.

"Let her go!" Erik screamed again.

He heard a helicopter overhead. Apparently the authorities had tracked the monster here as well. If they started shooting, though, they'd hit Vickie.

He rushed forward, no longer caring about his own life or his own situation. He ran right up to the demon, grabbed Vickie by the arm, and pulled. She wouldn't budge. His move was so quick that the demon didn't react; it just stood there looking down at him as if it couldn't believe what it was seeing. Dovecrest moved closer and continued his chants, louder now and with authority. Erik couldn't understand the words, but he knew the meaning just the same. Dovecrest, in his own way, was banishing the demon, driving it out from the world of men.

Then the demon slowly knelt down on the altar as if in prayer. A sudden, vicious thought assaulted Erik like a fist to the pit of the stomach.

"She and the unborn are mine!" it said. "When I have finished with them, I will be back on this earth. You will not be able to stop me."

Then the demon erupted in a black cloud of pungent smoke that choked Erik all the way to his lungs. He felt Vickie's arm slipping away from him and he desperately tried to hold on. No, not slipping away, really. Melting away. Evaporating as if it were never there.

Then both she and the demon were gone, leaving Erik crouching next to the altar, looking totally bewildered.

"I've lost her," Erik said.

Just then Todd rushed out from behind him and leaped onto the altar.

"No!" Erik screamed, but it was too late. He could see the boy's form silhouetted against the spotlight of the helicopter, which was landing just on the other side of the altar. The boy was there. Then his shape shimmered and became translucent. Then, within an instant, he was gone.

CHAPTER TWENTY-FOUR

-1-

Pastor Mark waited for the soldier to open the helicopter door, and then he jumped out and ran to his friends who were huddled near the altar. Spotlights flooded the area. The demon was gone. It'd taken Vickie with it and, as far as Mark could see, Todd had leaped in after his mother and was gone as well.

Erik was banging his fist against the stone; his hands were bleeding and raw almost to the bone. Dovecrest stood next to the altar with his head in his hands.

"What happened?" Mark asked. "Did the boy go in?"

"Yeah," Dovecrest said. "Only now we can't get in. He's locked us out."

"How?"

"It's complicated. But once someone follows the demon, the doorway closes. If we could have gone in at the same time...."

"So what do we do now?"

Dovecrest shook his head. "I need to look at the manuscripts. I'm sure there's a way to unlock the door. I just have to find it."

Mark nodded. "Then we'd better get working on it."

He walked over to Erik and put his arm around his shoulders. Even after all these years of being a preacher, of going to funerals and being with people during their most troubled times, even after all these years he still never knew what to say. He'd memorized all of the catch phrases, and may have even believed in them. But the words never seemed enough, could never offer the comfort that was needed.

"We'll get them back," he said. But in his heart, he didn't know how.

"I...I had her in my hands. I just...I just couldn't hold on. She just evaporated right there in front of me. And then Todd...."

"It's going to be ok," Mark said. "We'll figure out something. We'll get them back. We need to have faith. Now more than ever."

Dovecrest came over to stand by them.

"We've got work to do," the Indian said. "I think I can get us back into that portal to go after them. Are you coming?"

-2-

Erik looked up at Dovecrest but couldn't even hear his words. His system had suffered such a shock that even listening had become a task. He just wanted to bury his face in his hands and die. He didn't want to think. He didn't want to remember. But all he was left with was the memory of holding onto his wife's arm with all of his strength and then feeling it just dissolve right there before him. It was as if she had just evaporated into thin air. No, he didn't want to think, didn't want to remember. He just wanted to go to sleep forever. But this voice was shouting at him, insistent.

"Erik, come on. We have to move fast or we'll be too late. Come on. I think we can do this thing."

"What...thing?" he asked.

"We can get them back. Come on. I think I have a way."

"What do you want me do to?"

"We're going to go through that portal and bring them back out. And we're going to destroy that thing once and for all while we're at it."

"Go to hell!" Erik said. He felt the tears running down his cheeks, tickling a little as they flowed over his cheeks and burning his eyes. "I don't want to do anything. I just want to die."

"We are going to go to hell. But no one's going to die to get there."

He felt the two men pulling him along by the arms, the pastor on one side and the Indian on the other. His legs moved by themselves, and slowly he became aware of his surroundings. There were soldiers here now, and a helicopter. He had no idea where they had come from. There were flashlights everywhere, and the spotlight from the helicopter burned his eyes. His friends brought him over to the edge of the clearing and sat him down in the grass. One of the soldiers came over, shined a flashlight into his eyes, and opened a medical kit. The man started wrapping some bandages around his hands.

That was when he realized that his hands were cut open and bleeding from where he had pounded on the altar stone. He also realized that they hurt quite badly. He looked into the eyes of his two friends and saw their concern, not only for his family, but for him.

"Mark and I can go in," Dovecrest said. "And you can stay here. We need someone on this side in case it comes back. But I thought you might want to come and find your wife and son."

Erik hadn't realized how dry his mouth felt until the soldier offered him a drink from his canteen. He took a long swallow, then another. The water was cold and helped to clear his brain.

"You think you can get me in there?"

Dovecrest nodded. "I think I know how to open the portal. But just for a moment."

"Then I have to go. My wife's in there. And my son. And my baby."

"All right then. It's you and I. Pastor, you're going to stay here and if that thing tries to get back out, you're going to seal this end and keep it in."

Todd hadn't thought about anything when he leaped onto the altar and fell through the doorway leading to another world, another dimension, another existence. He'd seen his mother going away and he had just reacted. He didn't know if it were right or wrong, good or bad. His body had simply taken over his mind, and had acted on its own.

Only now, as he fell in what seemed like an endless thrill ride, did he have the time to consider what he had done. Except now he was too terrified to even think.

He felt as if he were falling from an airplane—only he was so far up that he couldn't see the ground. Everything was so black that he couldn't even see his fingers when he held them up in front of his eyes. He was falling fast and hard, and straight down—to what, he had no idea. If there had been a ground below, he would have smashed into it by now, and the horrible picture of the soldier smashing to the pavement haunted his memory once again.

He knew he was falling because he could feel the air rushing past him, like when you put your hand out the window of the car on a long trip on the highway. Only this felt even faster than what the car would go. His stomach also knew he was falling. He felt that it was at least a ten story building behind him already, and loosing ground with each second.

He felt like he should be screaming—that's what people did in the movies when they fell—but he couldn't. For one thing, he was falling too fast to even catch his breath long enough to scream. And for another, he knew no one would hear and it would be a waste of energy. In fact, he wasn't even sure if he could even dent this soundless vacuum with a scream. It would be like putting a drop of red paint into the ocean and expecting it to change color.

He wondered how much longer he would fall. After all, he couldn't fall forever, could he? That was impossible. Then again, so were demons that turned from molten lava into winged obsidian and that could overturn a tank and disappear into an ancient stone. Or at least he thought they were impossible until now. No, the rules of the universe, as he knew them, had definitely changed. And not for the better.

After what seemed like an eternity, he thought his fall might be slowing down, and he sensed that he was now falling forward and not just down. It was like he was flying. Not flying, exactly, because he couldn't go back up. Gliding, maybe. Gliding downward.

As he fell, he also felt it getting hotter. He'd overheard his Dad and the Indian talking about following this demon into hell. Apparently, that's where he was falling. Into hell. He wondered if he'd meet up with the devil. He supposed even Satan couldn't be much worse than this demon he'd already run into.

Finally, he felt the fall slowing, but the intensity of the fires was increasing. He felt sweat pouring from his forehead, and in the distance he could see a red-hot glow, like the top of an active, flowing volcano. Only this volcano didn't seem to reach upward. Instead, it was reversed, pointing downward, like it had been turned upside down and he was entering it from its base and heading towards the volcanic cone.

Before he got to the center, though, he slowed almost to a stop, and then felt solid ground beneath his feet. He dropped to his knees and reached down. The ground was made of the very same rock as the altar stone was made of. He wondered if this was another place or another planet. But the first thing he had to do was find his mother.

-4-

Erik and Dovecrest joined hands and stood beside the altar, while Mark and the soldiers stood back and out of the way, just in case the portal tried to draw them in.

"Are you ready?" Dovecrest asked.

"Yes," Erik said. He didn't want to wait another minute. He needed to do something and do it now. He'd already done too much waiting for one day.

"All right," the Indian said. "It may take a few minutes to prepare the way. But when it happens, we'll know. We jump onto the altar together and go through."

"I'm ready."

Dovecrest began a low, melodic chant in his native language. At first the chant was so subtle that Erik thought the man was humming, and thought it odd. But gradually the pitch and volume increased and it turned from a hum into a song. Erik couldn't understand the words, or even the meaning, but he found the cadence and rhythm comforting, somehow, as if this were a familiar song he had heard since he was a child. He closed his eyes and tried to relax. If this worked, he'd need all of his strength and all of his wits. He still wasn't sure how they'd destroy the demon when they found it, and Dovecrest had done his best to avoid all mention of that subject. It was as if he himself didn't know.

But Erik knew they couldn't do anything until they passed this first test and actually crossed over into the demon's realm. He wondered if it were really hell, or just a different world, or a different reality. He'd never quite thought of hell as having a portal connecting it with this world. Apparently, though, those devil worshippers from colonial times had created just such a portal, a gate. A gateway to hell.

He felt the Indian's voice growing stronger, more confident, and he felt the real world beginning to dissolve around him. Once it began, it happened quickly. He opened his eyes and saw the altar clouding over with a smooth, gray mist.

Dovecrest squeezed his hand.

"Now," he said, reverting to English as he stopped his chant.

The two men jumped onto the altar. Erik felt its solid, rocky surface beneath his feet, but only for a moment. Then the very rock itself began to transform. First it turned rubbery, as if he were standing on the surface of a jogging track that had been covered with that cork-like rubbery substance designed to absorb shock. Then it became even more spongy; he felt his feet sink in more deeply. He had his eyes open but couldn't see anything through the haze.

It seemed that sound had not become nonexistent also. It felt like he was inside a hollow chamber and insulated from all noise. Even if he tried to talk he suspected his voice would just not exist here. It was if he were entering some gigantic vacuum.

He looked over at Dovecrest but could not see the man, even though their hands were still tightly locked. Then the very rock beneath them disappeared. The solid bottom dropped away and the very ground beneath his feet was gone and he began to fall.

PART THREE: INFERNO

Abandon hope all ye who enter here.

—Dante

To bottomless perdition, there to dwell
In adamantine chains and penal fire.

—John Milton

CHAPTER TWENTY-FIVE

-1-

Todd could not believe the emptiness of this place. It was as if he were the only living thing in the universe. He thought he'd wind up next to his Mom and that the demon would be waiting for him. But there was no one, nothing in sight. Only that awful rock—the same stuff the altar was made of—and it went on forever.

It was hot—but this was not the broiling hot fiery place he'd been taught about in Sunday school. There weren't any people running around on fire, and there were no red devils poking people with pitchforks. It felt more like he was on the moon than in hell. He'd thought this place would be full of people, but it looked like he was the only one here.

"Hello?" He called, hoping to hear his mother's voice. Even the sight of the demon would have been welcome at this point, he thought. He could speak, but it was like yelling into a vacuum. The sound just didn't carry very far.

He decided that he'd better move somewhere. He'd never find his mother standing here on the rocks wondering what to do next. There really was just one way to go, and that was down. The whole thing reminded him of a program he'd seen on television about ant lions, which were bugs that made a big funnel-shaped trap in the sand. When an ant came by it would fall into the tunnel and the ant lion would eat it.

He wondered if this place was like that—a giant trap to catch you when you went down to the center. He supposed if that were the case it was already too late. He couldn't see any other way to go but down.

There was no path, but it was easy to navigate. The only landmark was the cherry-red mouth-like opening at the bottom, and that lit up everything with just enough light to see by. The slope definitely headed downward, but not so steep that he'd have to worry about falling. His mother was down there somewhere with that awful demon. Todd wasn't sure what he'd do when he found them, but he'd already committed to this by jumping through the gate, so he guessed he'd figure it out as he went along.

He slowly made his way down the rocky surface. Actually, as he went lower the thing did get steeper, and the volcanic rock was shinny, sleek and slippery. Its jagged edges did give him plenty of footholds, but they also cut into his hands and feet.

As he approached the large center opening, Todd became away of two things. First there was the overwhelming sense of loneliness and aloneness. He had never, ever been this alone in his life. His parents or an adult was always nearby. Even if he were alone in his room, he knew his mother or father were in the house, usually in the room next door. Any cry of help would be immediately heard and they would come to him. He'd almost felt this way when he was lost in the woods. But that had been different, too, because there had been sounds. Birds, crickets, and even the sound of the wind. And he'd felt that awful voice calling for him. No, he hadn't really been alone that night. At least the thing hadn't gotten back into his head.

The second thing he became aware of was the smell. It was a weird smell, and not altogether unpleasant—it wasn't anything like the smell of burning flesh that he'd smelled lately, and it didn't come close to that awful reek that the demon gave off. Just the thought of it made him want to throw up again. This was different. It was a little sickening, like the small of moldy fruit. But it was also a little sweet and pleasant, like a ripe coconut that had just been cut open. It wasn't either of those things, really, but it was close. He just thought it odd that hell would smell like a tropical fruit. Whatever it was didn't really matter, he thought. And if it did—well, he'd figure that out later, when he got to where he was supposed to be.

-2-

It seemed like he fell forever. Somewhere on the way down, he lost his grip with Johnny Dovecrest and the two men were separated, but he knew his friend was beside him, falling down as well. He felt like he was dropping like a bullet, with no end to the fall in sight. Everything around him was a piercing black that no light could penetrate, and he felt the wind rushing past him. He never had minded heights, but falling terrified him; he tried to close his eyes and pretend he was floating, but his stomach had different ideas. It was all he could do to keep from vomiting, and his head whirled around as if he'd been in a centrifuge.

At last the speed of the fall seemed to slow, and he began gliding, or so it seemed. Tentatively, he opened his eyes. In the distance far below him he saw a black opening, surrounded by a cherry-red circle of what appeared to be hot coals. He wasn't sure if that was where he came from or where he was going to, but the opening seemed to be getting larger. He could now vaguely see Dovecrest's shape beside him. The Indian flashed him the thumbs up sign to indicate he was all right. Though Erik didn't feel all right himself, he flashed the sign back.

He tried to speak and, even though he was shouting, no sound escaped his lips. It just seemed swallowed up in this endless, vast expanse of nothingness. There was no sound and no light other than the cherry-red glow of the coals below.

Finally, they landed on solid rocky ground. It was, in fact, the same kind of black, polished obsidian that the altar was made of. Only this was a virtual sea of volcanic rock. It went on for as far as the eye could see, downwards towards the black hole surrounded by hot coals. It was as if they were standing on the rim of a giant funnel leading downwards with a fire-ringed opening at the center. The center looked miles away, and it didn't appear that there was anything here except that endless black rock.

Erik wasn't sure what he imagined hell would be like, but it wasn't anything like this. Hundreds of millions of tortured souls, perhaps. Sinners being cut or burned or ripped apart by monsters. Endless pain and suffering. Fire and brimstone. Whatever vision he had of hell contained people, people who had sinned. He had imagined hell contained people like Adolf Hitler, Caligula, and Vlad the Impaler. Rapists, murderers, serial killers. He'd imagined there would be millions of sinners, from the most notorious criminals to those who simply did not believe.

But this place was empty, barren, devoid of any life whatso-ever. This version of hell was an aching void of emptiness and loneliness. It was silence and it was aloneness, the ultimate form of solitary confinement with miles and miles of hard, barren landscape and no where to lie your head. It was like being on the moon, but with no spaceship and no way back. And it would be like this for an eternity. He would have preferred the fire and brimstone. At least it would have been something.

For the first time he understood what it meant to be eternally separated from God—not only God, but all of his creations.

He looked at Dovecrest and saw the same thoughts reflected on the Indian's face.

"It's worse than you could possibly imagine," he said, and realized that his voice could now be heard after all. "I was expecting Dante and his circles of suffering. Not this. Where is everyone?"

"Oh, I suspect they're here," Dovecrest said. "Probably by the millions. But this place is so vast, so infinite, that they won't ever find one another."

"Then how will we ever find my wife and son. And that awful thing that took them?"

"Your wife and son are alive. They don't belong here. They're not damned souls, remember? And for that matter, neither is that demon. At least not damned in the way we know it. We'll be able to find them. They will stand out."

"How do you know that?"

"Simple," the Indian said. "You can see me, can't you?"

"Yeah. So what?"

"If I were a condemned soul, we'd never be able to find one another and communicate. Not even if we were standing just three feet apart. That's the punishment, don't you see? Eternal banishment—from everything."

Erik nodded. In a weird way, it made sense.

"All right," he said. "Where do we begin?"

-3-

The demon Wrath didn't need to climb down the portal that entered hell. It flew straight down the center and through the red-hot fiery gates, carrying the pregnant woman with it.

It was not pleased with the fact that it had been driven away and forced to come back to this wretched place. It had looked forward to spending some quality time with the people of earth, just getting to know them and their suffering. It had enjoyed the time spent there and was looking forward to a very extended vacation, so to speak. It hadn't grown tired of inflicting pain and suffering—after all, that's what Wrath was all about.

It believed it was one of the most formidable of the demons and, in fact, was not really a demon at all, in the true sense of the word. It was more a personification of sin itself. Compared to other demons—lust, envy, spite, and a host of others—Wrath felt very terrible indeed. It almost laughed to itself. It just couldn't see lust biting a man in half and chewing on both parts at the same time.

Things had been working out exactly according to plan until that meddling preacher had shown up and sent him back down to hell again. Not that it was the end of the world. It felt more like a child that had been disciplined and sent to its room without supper. The demon's pride was hurt as much as anything, that this little, meek, half-baked pastor had gotten the better of it

Not that it liked being in hell. No, by all means, hell was... well, hell was hell, even to those who ran the place. There was a reason people did not want to go here. It wasn't all fun and games and good times. It had looked into some human minds during its time on earth, and it had been amazed at the things it had seen. There were some who actually thought hell was where you were able to do all of the forbidden things that you couldn't do when you were alive because they were wrong. These people thought hell was just a huge orgy of sex, drugs, and good times. If that were so, they'd be dying to get here, the demon thought.

On the contrary, hell was not a happy place. It wasn't like the way it was pictured, though, that was for sure. There were no devils with pitchforks or scalding hot oil or perpetual burning. What kind of God would torture His creations that way? No, but the reality of hell was much worse. Sometimes it wondered at God's sense of humor.

The reality of hell wasn't burning and fires, at least not in the traditional sense. When people came here they got exactly what they had wanted, and what they deserved. People who came here did not want to know God, had, in fact, turned away from Him, and did not want to be bothered with Him or his rules. So that's what God gave them. Eternal separation. He showed them the light, dangled it before them like food to a starving man, and told them what they could have had, if they had chosen it. But they chose the alternative, so He took it away, just as they realized how absolutely wonderful it would have been....

Wrath knew all about hell. Because the demon too, was eternally cursed and could never be redeemed. It had chosen the dark side, never realizing the absolute radiance of the light until it had seen for itself, and then had been taken away. And now, to have to live for the rest of eternity with its sin burning up inside it like horrific brimstone, burning and eating away from the inside out forever and ever. And to have seen what could have been, and then given this instead, this miserable existence that could never know love or comfort, or freedom from the burning sin within.... That, indeed, was hell, and it was worse than anything that could ever be imagined.

Sure, it had escaped for a short time, and had been able to indulge in the sin that burned within it. But the story was the same. It was forced back into its room, and the wrath inside it would continue to burn and blaze and smolder. It was the personification of a sin that it could not indulge in while it was here, not without a trip back to earth. And now that was over, at least for now.

But this time would be different. This time it had brought a plaything back with it. It felt the woman writhing in his grip. Apparently she was having another contraction. They were coming closer together now. That meant the baby would come soon, all young and new and innocent. Its terror would be extreme as it died, and its delivery and birth in hell would cause quite a stir. Its death would be even more interesting.

The demon flew easily through the inner portal and into the main chamber of hell itself. This was its home, of sorts, such as it was. A deep funnel leading to the bowels of an entirely different dimension.

It thought for a moment about the human scientists who tried to explain things. This place defied their physics in so many ways. It wished it'd brought one of them with it, just to hear how they'd explain this world. They'd probably try to bring in rotating black holes, quasars, and quarks to make sense of it all. But this was so very far beyond their comprehension as to be laughable. The mortals thought they knew how things worked and what the universe was like. But their science was so very, very far off the mark.

It passed through the gates to another entirely different world, a world like a chocolate layer cake leading endlessly downward. This world was populated by billions of people, more people than what currently lived on the earth. Only they weren't people anymore. They were disembodied souls. Still alive—yet not alive. Dead, but not dead. And each one very much aware of its own misery. The demon Wrath could see each and every one of these souls. But the irony of it was that, although there were billions of them, they couldn't see each other. They existed in the same place of existence, often flowing through one another. But each one was as unaware of the next as they endlessly searched for others that they would never, ever be able to find. It was a doomed, damned solitary existence that would last for eternity.

The demon passed through the portals and came to a soft landing on the barren plains inside. This was an endless world of black sand and volcanic rock that went on for as far as the eye could see, and stopped just on the edges of infinity. No single being could ever search every corner of this world, not even in eternity. But they were each doomed to try in the ill-conceived hope that they would find someone, anyone, they could be with. At first they would search for specific loved ones from their past. But soon enough they would search for anyone, just anyone that could fill the void that was endless separation from God and all that was good.

The demon gently eased Vickie onto a patch of soft, black sand. It didn't want to hurt her or the unborn child—not yet. It untied her bonds. She wasn't going anywhere anytime soon.

As she sat up, the trance she had been in seemed to wear off some, though shock and horror kept her from becoming completely alert and aware.

"Where am I?" she said. "Where have you taken me?"

The demon looked at her for a moment and almost felt sorry for her. But it had lost all emotions millennia ago when it had become so consumed by rage that it had actually become the sin of wrath, in the flesh, so to speak. It no longer knew or felt anything except the pleasure it derived from inflicting pain and suffering upon others.

The demon folded its wings onto its back and sat down next to her.

"I am afraid that you and your unborn daughter are in hell," it said with a sneer.

The woman recoiled and moved back. "And who—or what—are you?"

The monster decided it was time to relax a bit and lose the demon persona. It pulled its wings back out and folded them around itself, covering itself completely, as if in a leathery shroud. It waited for a moment and allowed the transformation to take place. Then it unveiled itself to reveal a human form, a human male, naked and perfectly formed.

The woman was already so shocked that Wrath didn't think anything could shock her more. She looked at it for several moments before speaking.

"You're...human...," she said.

"I am whatever I choose to be," the demon corrected, now in a smooth and deep male voice. "Right now I choose to be human. At least in my form."

The woman seemed to relax a bit. Then another contraction came and she lay back on the sand and breathed in short, powerful spurts. It watched as the shade of an old man walked completely through her solid form, calling for the shade of his dearly departed wife. The cursed soul was as unaware of the pregnant woman as she was of him, both completely oblivious to each other.

"The grave's a fine, private place, and none I think, do there embrace," the demon said.

The woman's contraction ended and she looked at him for a long moment. "You quoted Andrew Marvell," she said. "How do you know about poetry? Who are you? What are you and what do you want with me?"

She seemed more surprised by the fact that it knew this mortal poet than by the fact that she was now sitting in the middle of hell holding a conversation with a demon that was sin in the flesh.

The monster smiled. Yes, that human poet had been so close to the truth, at least for those who ended up here. His soul was down here somewhere, with the billions of others, searching for his own lost love.

"I know about a lot of things," it said. "But mostly I know about suffering. And you and your daughter will know about suffering too before your time with me is done."

CHAPTER TWENTY-SIX

-1-

"Well, let's head downward," Erik said. He had to almost shout to be heard. It was like talking into a vacuum. "There's nowhere else to go."

The Indian nodded.

They made their way down the rocky slope as quickly as they could. It was steep enough to be treacherous if they were not careful, but not steep enough to slow them down very much.

"This is going to be difficult when we come back up," Erik said.

Dovecrest forced a laugh. "Somehow I doubt that we'll be coming back this way again."

Erik wished Pastor Mark was here right now. The preacher might be able to give him some insights into what he was seeing and experiencing. To him this was nothing but a vast wasteland, completely devoid of life, love, and hope. The pastor might understand all this better. But for now he had just one goal—to find his wife and son and get them out of this place and back home where they belonged.

The heat increased as they approached the portal. It was like the opening in the bottom of a funnel, with red, glowing embers all around it that lit up the entire world, or whatever it was, Erik thought. He wondered if they'd get burned going through the opening. It was large enough to drive a tank thorough, at least.

As they approached the opening the ground beneath them

curved upward to form a tunnel, or sorts, which led through the opening.

"So these are the gates of hell," Erik said.

"Abandon hope...," Dovecrest said.

"If I didn't have hope, I wouldn't be here," Erik replied.

Dovecrest nodded. "We must remember that whatever this place is, we are just visitors. If there is hell, there is also heaven. We are not of this place. We belong with the other. He has given us strength and power to come here and do what must be done. Then we return to our own place."

With trepidation, they went through the opening and stepped into another vast wasteland, this one even larger than the first. An endless plain of black sand and volcanic outcroppings stretched out into the distance for as far as the eye could see. It was empty, completely empty. Erik couldn't believe the vastness and the emptiness of this place. How would he ever find them, he thought. This went on forever. How could he even be sure they came this way, though this opening. For all he knew there could be hundreds more like it.

Dovecrest knelt down and examined the sand. Erik wondered what he was up to.

"Someone passed this way," the Indian said. "It looks like the demon stopped here. See the marks. They're deep into the sand. It may have landed here and then flew on."

"Was this recent? Or is it a thousand years old?"

Dovecrest took his hand and placed it on the sand. "Feel," he said. "It's hot."

"Right."

Then he placed his hand over the mark he had indicated.

"It's cool," Erik said.

"That's right. This was made very recently. And look here."

He moved ahead a little and pointed to the ground. "This looks like the footprint of your little boy."

Todd had scampered down the side of the giant funnel, through the opening and out onto the huge plain that spread out before him. He stopped and took a deep breath. The emptiness went on forever. But his mother was out here somewhere and he was determined to find her. He knew she was still alive. If the demon had intended to kill her, he would have done so. He would have killed them both. So it must have something in mind for her.

He had looked out ahead at the hundreds of rock outcroppings. His mother could be behind any one of them. Without thinking, he had set off across the plains in a dead run.

Now he stood up against one of the rocks and listened. He could hear a voice in the distance. It was far away and he couldn't make out what it said. It was strong and resonant, a man's voice, and it sounded like it was talking to someone else that he couldn't hear. Todd had the very strong feeling—a certainty, in fact—that this voice belonged to the demon and that it was talking to his mother.

He scuttled around the boulder and crept forward. The next one was about a football field away. It sounded like the voice was on the other side of it. He wasn't sure what he was going to do when he found his mother, but first he had to know if it were her. He caught his breath, then hurried across the open space towards the boulder.

The place felt weird, whatever it was. Todd felt alone and abandoned, yet he also felt the presence of others around him. He couldn't actually see or hear them, but he felt like they were there, just under the surface. It was almost as if he could touch them, yet there was nothing there to touch.

He slowed down when he approached the rock and crept closer, hiding just behind it. He listened intently, but couldn't hear anything. Then he thought he heard the sounds of rapid breathing. It was his mother.

He peaked around the rock and, sure enough, saw his mother lying in the sand with her head thrown back. She was breathing rapidly, having another one of those labor pains. In front of her, though, Todd saw a naked man. The man's back was towards him, but he saw the man's dark hair and very muscular body. He looked to be about his mother's age, maybe a little younger. He knelt down in front of his mother, as if he were concerned. Todd wondered if this man was a doctor.

He ducked back behind the boulder and wondered what to do. Should he make himself known and try to help his mother escape? Or should he just hide here and wait? Was this man a friend or an enemy?

He peeked around again in the hope that his mother would see him. Then, if things were safe, she'd call to him. And if not, she'd find a way to let him know. She didn't look his way, though, but merely stared upwards at what looked like a pitch black, starless sky that enveloped this entire world.

Finally, he couldn't stand it any longer. The aloneness was too much. The emptiness. The vastness of this place. His heart filled with sudden emotion and he could contain himself no more; he rushed out from behind his hiding place.

"Mom!" he called.

She sat up as soon as she heard his voice, and the look of horror on her face told him he had made a mistake. Her look said it all—grateful to see him but terrified for his life.

By now, what was done was done and he rushed into his mother's arms, where she held him tight.

"Oh, Todd, Todd. What are you doing here?"

"I came to get you, Mom. I came to bring you back."

"Oh, my dear boy, my love. You shouldn't have come. Oh dear God, you shouldn't have come."

Then she began to weep so hard that she shook all over. She squeezed him so tight he thought he would break.

"Oh, dear God, oh why did you come here?"

"I had to, Mom," he said. "I just had to."

She patted him on the back of the head.

"It's ok," she said. "We're going to be ok."

Then he felt the man grabbing him by the back of the neck and pulling him away.

"So what have we here?" he said. "Another moth just flying into the fire?"

The man swung Todd around to look at him. He had dark black hair, black eyes, and tanned, almost leathery skin. He looked like any ordinary man.

"Who are you?" Todd asked.

"Your worst nightmare," the man said, and then Todd saw him for who he was as he looked deeply into his eyes.

"You're that awful thing that took my Mom!" Todd said. "And you tried to get me back at the rock but I got away."

"Yes," the demon said. "I'm that awful thing that tried to get you. But guess what? Now I've got you."

-3-

Todd's trail was easy enough to follow in the loose sand. It appeared to be the only thing that had disturbed the ground in ages.

"Looks like he's running," Dovecrest said, looking down at the footprints.

"Hmmm. Is he running towards something..... Or away from it?"

"I guess we'll know when we find him."

The two men quickened their pace as they made their way across the large plains.

"So, do you think this place is really hell?" Erik asked.

Dovecrest paused. "It's hard to say. But from what I've read of the Bible, hell doesn't exist."

"What do you mean?"

"Hell is where all of the damned souls go after Christ's second coming, isn't that correct?"

"Yeah. I guess so. You'd probably have to talk to Pastor Mark about that."

"Well, that's what the Bible says. But Jesus hasn't returned yet, has he?"

"No. Not yet."

"Then I suspect this is a holding place for all of those souls who are destined to go to hell."

Dovecrest laughed. "I've read your Bible. A number of times. I've had a lot of time on my hands, remember?"

Erik smiled.

"And do you believe it?"

"That's a tough question," the Indian said. "I believe many different things. There is truth in many things. The old Indian ways show truth. Your religion shows truth. The ultimate truth is that there is a creator that is all powerful. That is without doubt.

"I do believe in a heaven and a hell. I believe with all my heart that my family is in heaven. Even though they were never able to know your Jesus, they believed in the Great Spirit and they worshipped him with love."

"And you, do you believe in Jesus?"

Erik realized that he was sounding like the pastor. He found it odd that here, in the very pits of hell—or maybe the holding cell for hell—he was trying to convert this man to his faith. He had never been one to convert people, and had always felt very uncomfortable with the idea. But now, for some reason, he thought it important to know where Dovecrest stood.

The Indian stopped walking and turned to face him. Erik looked into his eyes for what seemed like a long time.

"I believe in God," he said at last. "I was able to see His power in action through your pastor. I do believe."

Erik felt a chill run up his spine. All of his doubts disappeared. He knew that, no matter what happened, it would be ok. He loved his wife and child more than life itself, but he felt that they were safe in God's care. This world no longer mattered to him. It was the next world that counted now. Though they all might die here and now in the very sands of hell, God would not forsaken them. They might all die here in hell, but Dovecrest was right. They would not remain here. They were visitors to this place, not residents. They belonged with God.

Charged with new vitality, they continued forward. It looked like Todd had been dodging from one rock outcropping to another as they followed his path. Finally, after about two hundred yards, they stopped behind a large obsidian boulder.

"It looks like he stopped here for a bit," Dovecrest said. "He knelt down. See?"

Erik could see where the sand had been disturbed.

"He's trying to find his mother," Erik said. "We don't even know if she's still alive."

"I think she's alive. And when we find her, we find the demon. Remember what we've come here for. Above all else, we must destroy that thing."

They moved forward again. The next rock outcropping was about a hundred yards away. This one was larger than the ones they'd passed so far and Erik had the strong feeling that they would encounter the demon there.

"I'm assuming you have a plan once we find this thing," Erik said.

"You take care of your family. I'll take care of the demon."

Erik nodded. "I think we'll find what we're looking for up ahead."

Dovecrest nodded agreement.

They moved quickly but carefully as they approached the next rock outcropping.

-4-

The demon couldn't believe its good fortune. The boy had come straight to him, like a lamb to the slaughter. It was so perfect it couldn't have been planned better. Now it had a choice. It could kill the newborn and take over the mother, which had been his original plan. Or it could take over the boy, which might be even better. It'd thought about taking over the newborn itself, but that would leave it too helpless, unable to fend for itself for too long. But the boy offered different, more interesting opportunities. It'd have to destroy the mother, too, of course. But that wouldn't bother it a bit. Now that it had them all here, it could do whatever it wanted.

"You, boy, sit down over there and mind your business," it said.

The boy looked at it in defiance. "Why should I? You don't look so scary now."

The demon laughed. Then in a quick leap it was next to the boy, catching him entirely by surprise and grabbing him hard by the arm. It squeezed until the bone threatened to break, and the boy screamed.

"I can look any way I want!" the demon said. "And no matter what I look like, I can hurt you. And I will hurt you. So you do as I say or I can break both of your legs and you'll have to stay put! Understand?"

The boy was in too much pain to say anything.

"Do as he says, Todd," the mother said. "Please!"

The boy continued to scream until it eased up on the pressure. It didn't want to actually damage the boy's body, not if it planned on taking it over. But it would if it had too. It had suffered far worse pain than just a broken bone or two.

"Do you understand?" it said again.

The boy nodded.

"Good. Then you sit quietly and don't make any trouble or I'll have to hurt you again. Only this time it will be worse. I promise you."

Todd sat back on his haunches and rubbed his arm. The demon watched him until it was satisfied, then it looked at the woman.

"I trust you won't be trying anything stupid," it said.

"Please just don't hurt my boy. Or my baby," she said.

The demon didn't say anything. It backed away and sat down. Then it closed its eyes and began to chant, very softly, calling upon the name of Satan and cursing the name of God. The ritual wasn't very complicated. But it had to be exact. There were rules that governed even the supernatural. The creator himself was the only one that didn't operate by rules—he merely set them for others, and even the beings of the underworld had to follow them.

Someday, it hoped that Satan would overthrow this other one, and then things would be different. Then the tables would be turned and there would be no rules. But for now, things had to be done a certain way if they were to work.

It would have been better if there had been a dozen followers to help out. But the fact that it was taking place here, in its domain, more than made up for the lack of human followers. Its power was supreme here. Even in a human form it was more powerful than anything that could oppose it. The Creator Himself wouldn't even come into this domain, so rampant with sin and distress. Spending the night here would be worse than diving into an infested sewer.

No, it knew it was perfectly safe here. These mortals weren't going anywhere—after all, where could they go in this place? And no one could stop what was about to happen. Not even the Creator Himself.

CHAPTER TWENTY-SEVEN

-1-

As they closed in on the outcropping, they had heard a voice shouting, and then a scream.

"That's Todd," Erik had said, trying to remain calm.

"Shhh! Let's not let anyone know where we are. Come on. Stay low."

Dovecrest had scampered to the base of the rocky outcropping and Erik had followed. Now the screaming had stopped and they listened as a voice was chanting in some type of rhythm. Dovecrest held a finger over his lips and peeked around the rock. He watched for a second, then slipped back. Erik was almost insane with worry now, and it took every effort of his will to keep from jumping out from behind the rock and seeing what was going on.

Dovecrest crept close and whispered in his ear. "Your wife and son are there. They don't seem to be injured. Your wife is still in labor. The demon has taken on human form. Now would probably be our best chance of taking it."

"I'm ready."

Dovecrest nodded. "You come from one side. I'll take the other. On my word."

Each of the men took a position on each side of the outcropping. Erik quickly peeked around to get his bearings. Todd was in front of him, rubbing his arm gingerly and looking down into the sand. The kid looked scared, but not hurt. Most of all he looked angry and defiant. That's my boy, Erik thought.

Vickie was a few feet to the right of him. She looked weak and haggard. The stress and the labor pains were definitely taking their toll. She needed to be in a hospital, not out here. His heart melted at the sight of her looking so helpless and weak. He wanted to just run out there and take her in his arms and forget about this whole thing. She had no reason to be caught up in this mess, and he just wanted to get her out of here as quickly as possible. She, too, looked afraid, but mostly she looked like she was in shock.

The demon faced the two of them with its back towards the rocky outcropping. It would be just to Erik's right as he moved around the rock. Dovecrest would come at it from the other side. They hoped to wedge it between them and then kill it. He wasn't sure how you killed something like this. But at least it looked human now, so maybe some of the traditional ways would work. He looked around in the sand and found a loose rock about the size of a grapefruit. The thing even had a jagged edge. That, at least, was something.

He waited and tried to be patient, as he watched the demon. It was in a trance, with its eyes closed, and it was carrying on some incomprehensible chant. Erik couldn't understand the words, but even as he knew Dovecrest's chant had been virtuous, he knew this one was evil and corrupt. The words sounded like rottenness and decay. The atmosphere felt putrid. If it weren't for the fact that his wife and child were here, he would have run away in disgust.

It seemed like Dovecrest was never going to make a move. Then, when Erik didn't think he could stand it for another moment, he heard the Indian whistle.

Erik charged around the rock with the stone raised above his head. He found himself yelling at the top of his lungs, without even realizing he was doing it.

In a split second, he was aware of everything around him and saw it all in perspective for the first time. Dovecrest had charged out from the other side of the rock. Somehow, the Indian was in full battle regalia, with war paint, a headdress, and a tomahawk with an obsidian head. Erik had no idea how the man had transformed himself, but then again nothing else made much sense lately, so why should this? Dovecrest was also whooping, and came at the demon with a demonic fury of his own.

From the corner of his eyes Erik saw Todd jump back and then scramble to his feet. Vickie, too, crawled backward, away from the fight. Neither of them seemed to recognize either him or Dovecrest.

The demon jumped up with a curse; it had obviously been taken by surprise. It moved away from Dovecrest and towards Erik, who wound up with his stone and prepared to brain the thing.

It turned and faced him with hate in its black eyes as he leveled the sharp stone at its head. He plunged his arm forward with every ounce of his strength, aiming for a point on the thing's forehead just above the midpoint of its eyes. Erik had never felt so much hatred, so much passion, so much fury before in his life, and he channeled every bit of his emotions into that one single strike.

The stone hit with a force that would have smashed a ripe coconut in two. He felt it hit, dead center, bulls-eye. The shock of the blow traveled up his arm, into his shoulder and down his back. It felt good. It felt very good. In fact, he wasn't sure if he had ever felt anything quite so good, quite so satisfying.

The force of the blow drove him back a step, and he lost his grip on the stone. He looked up to see his handiwork.

The demon stood there with the obsidian stone embedded completely in its forehead, and sticking in a good inch and a half. Erik just watched as the monster-turned-man just stood there and grinned at him stupidly, as if having a rock embedded in its head was the most natural thing in the world. Dovecrest then hit it from behind, burying his hatchet deep into the top of its skull. The demon stepped back and looked from one of them to the other, then grinned. It reached back, took the tomahawk from the top of its head and held it in its left hand. Then it took the sharp stone in its right hand and pulled it free. The thing's skull was dented and cracked like a deflated ball as it looked at its attackers with disdain.

"Welcome to *my* home," the thing said.

-2-

Todd couldn't believe his eyes when he'd seen two warriors jump out from behind the rock outcropping and brain the demon with their stone weapons. One of the men was dressed like an Indian war chief, complete with war paint, the feathered head-dress, and a nasty-looking tomahawk, which he had smashed into the demon's head. The other guy looked like something out of a pirate movie, with a rag rolled up on top of his head, his face darkened with soot, and with a sharp rock in his hand, which he lodged right in the demon's forehead. These warriors attacked with the ferocity of barbarians and were completely without fear.

But even though the demon now looked and acted like a man, it was still a monster. Neither of the death blows had the slightest effect on it. It took the tomahawk from its head, then the stone from between its eyes, and it looked at its attackers with a grin and taunted them.

Only then did Todd realize that the warriors weren't warriors at all. Suddenly the war paint disappeared. The pirate was just a regular man. They weren't warriors: just his dad and the Indian. They, too, had managed to come through the portal.

All of Todd's hope vanished when the demon tossed the hatchet down to the ground with utter contempt. Then he threw the stone off into the sand.

"Dad!" Todd said. "It's the demon."

His father looked over at him with utter despair and Todd knew he had known, but that they thought they could somehow defeat the thing if it were in human form.

The demon laughed. "I only look human," it said. Then it

grabbed the Indian by the throat and tossed him to the ground like a rag doll.

Todd's father backed up slowly, shifting his weight back and forth in case he needed to move. The demon looked at him and laughed again, while the Indian rolled backwards, clutching at his throat.

"So now you have the family reunion you wanted so badly," it said. "Are you happy now? One big happy family."

The demon pointed to Todd's mom. "And about to get bigger."

"Vickie, are you ok?"

"Yeah, Hon. But it's getting close. Real close."

"It's ok. You just hang in there. I'll figure out a way to get us out of here."

"Sure you will," the demon said.

The Indian had returned to his feet and he picked his toma-hawk up from where the demon had thrown it. The Indian approached more cautiously now, and the demon turned to face him. Todd's father took advantage of the fact to move closer to his son, trying to keep between him and the demon.

The Indian didn't look so impressive now that his war paint and headdress were gone. Now he was dressed in jeans and a T shirt. Even the tomahawk had become a jagged stone now. But, still, the Indian was defiant, brave, and bold as he stood up to the monster.

"I curse thee and kill thee in the name of the God!" he said, and charged the demon with the sharp stone.

The demon opened its arms wide and laughed as the Indian ran into him and plunged the stone full into its chest. The weapon broke in two and fell to the sand where the demon squashed it under its feet, burying it deeply in the loose sand. It pushed the Indian away with one hand, as if brushing off a fly.

"Your God can't hurt me here," he said. "We are in my world now. I make the rules here."

The Indian went sprawling on the ground and the demon followed him down, punching him and kicking him in the head and face. Todd's father charged forward and pulled the monster off of the Indian. Then it turned on him.

Todd couldn't watch and stay helpless. He ran to his father's side and began pummeling the demon with his fists.

The monster picked him up and held him before its face, grinning.

"Have you already forgotten your lesson, boy?" it asked.

The last thing Todd remembered was its fist heading straight for his face.

-3-

For the third time in a half hour, Pastor Mark tried to explain again that Erik and Dovecrest had gone through a portal in the altar to destroy the demon and rescue Todd and Vickie. And for the third time in a half hour Captain Burns shook his head in disbelief.

"People don't just go through rocks and into other worlds," he said.

"Well, they did."

"Then why can't any of my men get through?"

"It's not that simple," Mark said. "You have to say the right things...."

The captain just shook his head again. He paced back and forth in front of the altar, stopping once to pound on it with his fist.

"That thing's solid as a rock," he said. "Pardon the expression. There's no way anyone's going to go through it."

Mark sighed. "So you're willing to believe that a demon has run amok in western Rhode Island, destroying a town and killing over forty of your men and maiming a couple dozen more, but you're not willing to believe that it escaped through a portal to another world? That, Captain, doesn't make sense."

"I never said I believed this was a demon."

"Then what is it?"

"I don't know. An alien force, maybe. It could be anything.

But I don't believe that this rock is a gateway to.... Where'd you say it led?"

"To hell," Mark said. "It leads to hell."

"There's no such thing as hell. That's a fairy tale you preachers make up to keep people from misbehaving."

Mark shook his head in frustration. "Well if that's what it is, it doesn't seem to be working very well, does it?"

The soldier stopped for a moment and laughed. "Yeah, you got me there," he said. "No, I guess the threat of hell hasn't stopped many people from misbehaving. Not lately, anyhow."

"I'm glad you find that amusing," Mark said. "But I'm telling you that my friends have gone through that portal and are in hell—or wherever it is that demon has gone. I can't allow you to destroy that altar stone until they come back."

"I'm afraid, Pastor, that you don't have the authority to tell me what I can and cannot destroy. Whatever that thing is, it poses a threat to national security and it disappeared into that rock. I don't know how, but it did. It might have gone back to its own world, or maybe it's become part of the rock. I don't know and, frankly, I don't care. All I'm concerned with is keeping it from coming back here. And I think a thousand pounds of explosives should do just that. No problem."

Mark stopped and looked at the ground. Maybe he was going about this the wrong way. He didn't want to get into an ego contest with this soldier. He was just a humble pastor and sure to lose.

"Ok, Captain," he said. "I understand that you want to close that thing up forever. So do I. They left me here to stop that thing in case it tries to come back out."

"You're going to stop it."

Mark sighed again and tried to remain patient. The soldier didn't know or understand what had happened here. And he didn't have the time or the energy to teach theology right now.

"Yes. I know the right words to drive it back in. That's how we drove it away the first time."

The soldier rolled his eyes, as if to say "yeah, right."

"The point is," Mark continued, "That there are some very good people in there and they're going to need a way out. If you destroy that stone they'll be trapped forever."

"I have to destroy it. I have my orders."

"Ok. But do you have to destroy it now? Can't you give us some time?"

He thought for a moment and looked at his watch. "It's midnight now," he said. "It would be better to set up the charges in daylight. I can justify that. You have until seven a.m. Then we start setting charges. When they're done, we detonate."

"Thank you, Captain. I suspect that if they're not back by morning, they won't be coming back."

-4-

Erik knew he was in trouble now. Dovecrest was down and probably unconscious; his son had been knocked out and pitched into the sand. And now the demon was coming for him. It turned and faced him and glared at him with hatred in its eyes.

The thing didn't look so menacing in human form. But it had one distinct advantage: it couldn't be killed. Then again, they were in hell. Were they already dead? He looked past the demon at Dovecrest. Most of his face had been smashed in, yet the Indian was still alive, slowly sitting up and holding his injuries. Maybe he couldn't be killed here either, Erik thought. Or maybe if he were, his body would just return to earth. There was no way to know.

The demon took a step forward and Erik backed up a step to keep the distance between them. Even as a human, this thing was powerful. It hadn't taken on the shape of just any human. This wasn't your typical computer programmer or historian. This man would have made a formidable human, a bodybuilder or a linebacker or, judging from the way it fought, a boxer or a soldier.

And here he was, an English teacher who had taken a year

of Martial Arts while in College so very long ago. He didn't even no where to begin the fight. If the sharp rock didn't hurt the thing, what could he be expected to do without any weapon?

The monster rushed at him with fists flying. Somehow Erik managed to duck under the assault and slip behind him.

"Just come and get it and I'll make it easy on you," the demon said. "There's nowhere to run."

Erik had to admit that the landscape held no possibilities for escape, but something about him just refused to give up. He turned and kicked the demon in the side. It was like kicking a cement wall and only made his foot hurt.

The demon laughed. "No, I don't think that will do," it said. "And your Bible and your God can't help you here. This is my domain. And you came here of your own free will. You belong to me now."

"I don't obey you," Erik said. "None of us obey you."

"Oh, you will! Make no mistake about that."

Then it stepped forward and leveled its fist at him. Erik tried to dodge the blow, but the demon was quicker. It felt like a hammer had crashed into the side of his skull as he staggered backwards. Then he felt his head go light as the blood drained away and his feet collapsed under him. He felt himself land on the loose sand and then darkness came down like the curtain on the final act.

CHAPTER TWENTY-EIGHT

-1-

Erik woke up to a blinding headache. He sat up and tried to get his bearings, but everything seemed to be moving, as if he were on one of those thrill rides that toss you upside down and around in circles until everything becomes a blur. His stomach felt like he was on a thrill ride, too, as it jumped up and down as if on a trampoline.

"Just relax." It was Dovecrest's voice. He felt the Indian's hand on his shoulder. "You've taken quite a whack to the head. We both have. Just close your eyes for a minute and let it come back slowly."

"Where's Vickie and Todd?"

"I don't know," Dovecrest replied. "I guess it took them again."

Erik felt all of his hope disappear once again. He opened his eyes and waited for the world to stop spinning. Eventually, it did.

He found himself sitting in the middle of a sand pit that was perhaps fifty feet deep and about the size of an average living room. There were no rock outcroppings, no stairs or ladder—no way out short of scaling up the soft sand walls.

"I already tried it," Dovecrest said, anticipating his question. "There's nothing to hold on to. The sand just slides out from underneath your feet. We can't climb out of here."

"So it's left us here to die?"

"That's the real hell of it," Dovecrest said. "Pardon the pun. We won't die."

"What do you mean?"

"Think about it for a minute. When was the last time you ate? Or drank?"

"I don't remember. It must have been hours."

"Are you hungry? Thirsty?"

"No. Not the least. But I should be. I should be, shouldn't I?"

Dovecrest nodded. "We should be hungry. We should be thirsty. We should be tired. Look at my face. I should be dead."

Sure enough, the Indian's skull was cracked and broken. The injury should at least have landed him in intensive care, if not the morgue. But here he was standing there talking like it was nothing more than a scratch.

"You see, we can't die. We're already in the world of the dead. That means we're either already dead, or else we can't die, not as long as we're here, anyway."

"So that's why the demon didn't kill us."

"Exactly. We are as immortal as it is—at least while we're here."

"So now all we have to do is get out of this sand trap and find the demon again. Only we still don't know how to stop him. And why did it keep Vickie and Todd? What's it got in mind for them?"

"I don't know. But we'd better figure a way out of here if we expect to find out."

Erik sat in the middle of the pit and pondered the problem.

"Give me a boost," he said.

Dovecrest knelt down and he stood on the Indian's shoulders at the edge of the pit. He was still nowhere near high enough to escape. He reached out to grab what edge there was, but it just collapsed. There was nothing to hold onto. It just crumbled away at his touch.

"This isn't going to work," he said. Then he climbed down from the Indian's shoulders.

"Maybe we could make a rope out of our clothes," Dovecrest

suggested.

"Maybe. But I don't think we have enough to make a rope that long. And we'd have nothing to hook it on to at the top."

"You're right. I'm grasping at straws."

"Yeah, me too," Erik said. "I don't suppose we could dig ourselves out."

Dovecrest forced a laugh. "I think we're already as far down as we want to go."

"I'd hate to think what's down deeper than hell."

"Wait a minute," Dovecrest said. "Suppose we don't dig down, but dig up."

"Dig up. What do you mean?"

"When you stood on my shoulders and dug at the side, what happened?"

"I got sand all over you."

"Exactly. And that sand fell to the bottom of the pit. If we dig at the sides, it'll fill in the bottom. Eventually, we can fill in the hole enough to be able to climb out."

Erik thought for a minute. "It might work. But it'll take forever, won't it?"

"I don't know. But do you have anything else to do to pass the time?"

Erik shook his head. "Unfortunately, I don't. Let's get started."

-2-

Todd found himself lying on an open stretch of sand next to his mother, who was breathing furiously and fighting back the pains of her labor. He opened his eyes and looked around. The demon sat nearby, as if waiting. Todd couldn't imagine what it was waiting for, unless it was for the baby to be born. Maybe he had something in mind for the baby.

"Where's Dad?" he asked.

"I have taken care of the intruders," the demon said. "They

won't be bothering us any more."

He looked at his mother, then back at the demon. "What are you going to do with us?"

"Oh, I have plans for you. I have plans for you all. Don't you worry. You and I will be going back to where you came from. We will have a great time together."

"And my Mom?"

"That depends on how well you cooperate," the demon said. "Right now it could go either way."

Todd thought for a moment. It looked like the thing had killed his dad. But he didn't have the energy to think about that now. That would come in time, but right now he had to think of his Mom. His mom and the new baby.

"Ok," he said. "What do you want me to do?"

"Ah, that is so much better. We can work together, you and I. First, I want you to stay with your mother and don't try anything foolish. Don't try to run away or fight me. There's nowhere to run and, as you can see, you can't defeat me."

Todd could see the logic in that. "Ok," he said.

"Your mother is going to have her baby very soon. I need you to help her."

"I'll try," he said. "But I don't know what to do."

"It's ok, Honey," his mother said. "I'm ok. Everything's going to be all right."

But his mother didn't look all right. She was pale and gray-looking. His hands were clammy and she was having great trouble breathing.

"Mom, remember how they told you to breathe?"

"Yeah, Todd. I do."

"Well you're not breathing that way, Mom. It's not sounding the same. You're gasping for air. You're not breathing it."

"Ok, Todd. You've got to help me. You know how Dad would count along with me when I practiced?"

"Yeah."

"Well you've got to do that now too."

"Ok."

"And one other thing. When the baby comes, I'm going to need you to help take her out."

"Mom, I can't deliver a baby. Why can't he do it?"

"Todd, do you really want a demon delivering your little sister? You don't want that, do you?"

"But I don't know what to do."

"Have faith. You will know what to do. Just do your best."

Her breathing started again, erratically this time too.

"Slow down, Mom," he said. "Just listen to me and follow along."

He breathed the way he'd seen his mother doing when she was practicing, and his dad had been helping. He had listened to these breathing lessons for the last three months until he literally knew them by heart. His Mom and Dad had practiced them in the next room, and he'd thought it was fun to listen in at first. After awhile, though, it had become boring. Todd had learned it better that either of his parents and had used it on himself late at night when he was having trouble sleeping. It was ironic that he was so good at this and his parents were the ones who took the lessons.

His mother looked at him and forced a smile through her pain and he saw that she was watching him. Already her breathing was getting stronger.

-3-

Erik had never worked so hard in his life. His body couldn't die here in this place, but that didn't mean it couldn't feel pain. He had Dovecrest scratched and dug at the sand around the pit for what seemed like hours. All they had to use were their bare hands. The sand scraped painfully and lodged under their nails until their fingers bled.

"This is not any fun." Erik said. "What I wouldn't give for a shovel."

"I'd settle for a teaspoon," the Indian replied.

Still, they appeared to be making progress. The hole slowly filled in around them, allowing them to stand on the new sand as it fell in. Just a little more and Erik knew he would be able to stand on Dovecrest's back and reach the edge of the pit. Then he could push in more sand from the top with his feet until he could reach in and pull his friend out.

"What time do you think it is?" Erik asked.

"I don't think this place has time. Though if we were still back home I'd guess it would be the middle of the night."

"My watch stopped working when we got here."

"There'd be no way to keep time here anyway. There's no sun. No moon or stars either."

Time did seem to stand still here, he thought. It was never light or dark—everything was simply black and illuminated by an unchanging reddish glow. He wondered if that was how the mythology of the black and red colors of evil came about.

"No days of the week here," Erik said. "No Mondays. That's probably the only good thing about this place."

"Definitely the only thing. If I never see another grain of sand in my life it will be too soon."

"I don't think I'll ever be able to go to the beach again."

They continued the small talk for some time, mostly to keep their minds off their misery.

"So," Erik asked, "How do—or did—your people view heaven and hell?"

Dovecrest laughed. "That's a very complicated question. I don't know if I have a simple answer."

"There is no simple answer to anything, is there? That's why God made the world so complex. So we'd have things to worry about."

"In that respect, the world of my people probably is simpler than your world. My people—and most of the tribes of this land—never thought of themselves as powerful people, as conquerors. My people were simple. They lived off the land and prayed very simple prayers. For a good harvest. For a mild winter. For plentiful shell fishing. For health and fertility. We consider ourselves to be humble, pitiful people whose lives depend upon the creator's mercy and bounty."

"That sounds like a very Christian way of life."

"That depends. I know of your history. Your crusaders thought of themselves as Christians."

"Good point. But Christ preached humility. The meek shall inherit the earth."

"Yes. And so they shall."

"So what is your concept of hell?"

"Since my people are God's people, they would not go to hell."

"Yet you believe in demons."

"Yes, demons spawned by the evil one." Dovecrest laughed. "Do you know: the greatest demon that the tribes spoke of most was the white man. The 'white devil'."

"I guess I can understand that."

"No, you probably can't understand that. But I appreciate the attempt."

The Indian was right. He had no idea what it must have been like. He felt suddenly ashamed of himself and of his race. Even if he hadn't been personally involved, he was ashamed of what had happened just as a fellow member of the human race.

They were getting very close now. As they dug and filled in the hole, the outer rim widened, making the angle less steep. Erik figured that they'd soon be able to crawl their way out.

"Looks like we're almost free of this pit," he said. "What's our plan once we get out?"

Dovecrest stopped digging and looked at him directly. "My friend," he said. "I have absolutely no idea."

-4-

The demon sat back on its haunches and watched, fascinated by this whole birthing process. The ritual it had begun had been interrupted by the two intruders, but that was no matter. It could finish the ritual later, as soon as the baby was born. It wouldn't work to complete it until the victim was ready, so it would be better to wait. This baby didn't look like it was in any great hurry to be born. Actually, given the details of where it was about to begin its life, the decision to come late was a rather good one for the baby's sake.

The baby would sure have a quick entry and exit from the world. It would take its innocence immediately, before it had the chance to become corrupted by earthly sin. Taking a blameless, innocent soul was always a victory, and he felt about to be victorious now. The blood of an innocent was sure to sharpen any spell and take it to the limits. The trouble was, there weren't many innocents left in the world. His colleagues on the sin team had been victims of their own success. Now the pure material, needed for only the most powerful spells, was very scarce, almost extinct.

But this one would do very nicely. It might even bring her up to the altar stone itself and kill her. It could do it right here, of course, but something about returning to the original scene just seemed so damned poetic.

He wasn't an expert on human births by any means, but this one seemed to be going particularly slow. And he was getting impatient. He could remove the child forcibly—but that would end the innocence. But if something was wrong and the baby killed her mother, that would destroy the innocence as well. He'd just have to be patient and watch very closely, he thought. It wouldn't be unlike the mother to try to trick him again. Of course she was probably in too much pain and under too much stress to even think of a plan, let alone use it. But still, something told him not to ever trust this woman.

He watched as the woman screamed in pain and tried to control her agony with some sort of regular breathing method, which her son was coaxing her through. It was almost comical. He wondered why these people feared hell at all—there seemed to already be so much pain and suffering on the earth that there really didn't need to be a hell, in its humble opinion. No, take that back, it thought. Humility was definitely not one of its trademarks. And neither was patience, for that matter.

Fortunately, fascination was one of his strong suits, and he had to admit he was fascinated by this birth concept. He'd seen and had taken part in the end of countless numbers of lives. But this was the first time in all of these millennia that he had ever seen a new life being born. This was something different, worthy of study.

No, he wouldn't rip the infant from the womb, though he was quite capable of doing so. Instead he would wait this thing out and see how it went. He expected that as an added bonus, she'd learn about suffering as well. The mother would surely suffer when her newborn was killed. She might be able to keep it together until she learned that the demon was going to steal her son's body, and that she would have to take him home and care for him as her own child.

That moment would show what she was made of. She might react in any of a few different ways. She might just blank the entire incident from her mind and pretend her son was normal, and that none of this had happened. She might refuse to accept the boy as her son, or try to put up a fight, in which case he'd simply kill her and be done with it. Or she might just lose her mind, which might make for an interesting scenario of its own.

It really didn't matter how she reacted. It would all work out the way the demon wanted it to. It would be able to inhabit the body of this boy for as long as it wanted, and return to the earth. When it became tired of being human, it could return to its demonic form again and pick up exactly where it had left off. Now that the meddlers were permanently trapped here in hell's waiting room, it had nothing left to worry about.

Now all it had to do was wait for the baby to be born. And from the looks of it, the wait wouldn't be long.

CHAPTER TWENTY-NINE

-1-

The last of the sand finally collapsed enough to where Erik and Johnny Dovecrest could crawl out of the sand pit and back to the surface of this strange world. Erik got to his feet and helped pull his friend up. Then, suddenly, he jumped back as he noticed that the place was very different from the way it was when he was unconscious. There were people everywhere.

"What's happened?" he asked.

Dovecrest shrugged. "I'm not sure why, but I think we can see them all now."

"See them all? Who?"

"The damned. The souls of all those who were sent to hell."

"Oh my God...," Erik said.

They were everywhere, looking pathetic and empty and completely without hope. He could hear them now, too, as they moaned and wailed. There were hundreds of them, no, thousands of them, stretching off as far as they eye could see. There were young and old, men, women, and children, in all sizes and shapes and from all races and cultures. They weren't people, really, but were shades, ghost-like and yet human at the same time. They were all dressed in their burial clothes, which had rotted away to rags on their bodies, and now hung from them like moldy laundry.

They did not seem to be aware of one another as they ceaselessly wandered, searching, it seemed, for something.

Then, all at once they stopped and turned towards Erik and Dovecrest. The two men looked at one another, and with sudden realization he knew what had happened. The shades couldn't see each other, but they could see them. In a single moment of realization, Erik understood. He could tell that Dovecrest did, too, and sudden terror flooded his soul.

All of these damned souls were searching for someone, for *anyone* in this place of utter desolation and aloneness. There must be billions of them here, and they couldn't see one another. They'd been alone since they died—some of them had been here for thousands of years. All of them damned, from serial killers, rapists, murderers, and child molesters, right down to liars, cheats, and unbelievers. They were all here, searching for someone to interact with. And now suddenly Erik and Dovecrest had appeared, as if out of nowhere.

"We are so screwed," Erik said softly.

It took a moment for the scene to register, but when it did the hundreds of damned souls nearest to them reacted as one. Erik could see their faces lighting up. They thought it was merely a vision, at first, a mirage. But then he could see the realization dawning on their faces.

There were three of them closest to him, an old woman, a middle aged-man, and a teenaged boy. They stepped forward, coming towards him, and leading a swarm of hundreds more that followed. They held their hands out to him and began to touch him, grope him. He staggered backwards, but more were surrounding him now. He looked over at Dovecrest and saw that he, too, was being overrun. The voices were everywhere, almost blending into one.

"Help me!" the teenager screamed. "Mom, please help me."

"Betty, is it you? Is it you at last?"

"Oh, Harold, hold me!"

They all thought he was their loved one. And they all wanted a part of him. They swarmed like an army of ants, knocking him down, climbing on him. Their bodies melded into one another, and still they weren't aware of the shade next to them, the shade that had actually melted into them....

So this was how the demon had really imprisoned them, Erik thought. He'd trapped them within a mountain of damned souls. He'd buried them in a sea of ruined, lost souls who were searching for something that he couldn't give them....

"Leave me alone!" he screamed. "I'm not your mother! I'm not your wife!"

But still they came, an endless tide that overwhelmed him, suffocated him with their needs. He could hear their thoughts, feel their despair. Their misery was infinite; their wretchedness was endless. And he knew he was now doomed to endure their agony and despair forever.

"This isn't fair!" he screamed. "I wasn't sent here! I'm not one of you! I don't belong here!"

Their need suffocated him as more and more of them came, like vultures to a rotting carcass. They buried him so he couldn't see. He felt like he couldn't breathe, and he desperately gasped for air that didn't even exist in this nocturnal place. His mind, his body, and his soul were crushed beneath them. Even as their mass was without weight, their need was so very heavy. Their voices were deafening. Their smell was stifling. They grabbed him touched him, squeezed them against their formless bodies.

He felt like Jesus must have felt when the crowds of deformed and sick and diseased had come to him, swarming upon him to heal them.

"Dear, sweet Lord, help me!" he screamed. "I can't heal them!"

-2-

The demon knew his prisoners had escaped their sand trap when the hordes of doomed souls stopped their aimless wandering and all turned in one direction, like a massive herd of animals all driven to one central point. There were billions of them. Surely those meddlers now faced the ultimate hell. This was worse than if they had been damned themselves, it thought. To be overrun by the needs of a billion lost souls.

The sand pit had been a diversion. They thought they had escaped, but in reality they had gone from bad to worse. The sand pit was for its amusement, really. It was designed so they'd be able to dig out rather quickly. It would give them hope. Giving hope in the hopeless place was the most fun thing to do. The portal actually did say "Abandon Hope All Ye Who Enter Here," but no one took the oath seriously. If they had, they would be better off. But in reality they had been given their chance and had not accepted it. So now they were consumed with false hope for things that were never going to change. They'd led their lives the wrong way, but somehow they thought that God would show up one day and say, "Ooops, I made a mistake about you, Jack the Ripper. You don't belong down here at all. You're a good man, just ridding the streets of those evil women. You need to be upstairs with me. Besides, I understand you're a great cook and do extraordinary things with kidneys."

No, God didn't make mistakes. If you were doomed to be down here, it was for a reason, a very good reason, and you knew damned well what it was. There would be no stay of execution here. No slap in the wrist and just don't do it again. You had a whole lifetime to make things right and you couldn't be bothered. Even after you did, you had a chance to plead your case. No one did. They just didn't think hell was real. They'd be sent off to some summer camp to play.

But the shock of hell was all too real. Still, most of them kept their hope, which was ironic about the sign, for they really needed to abandon it. Hope just did not exist in this place. Their search for something that was completely lacking made their existence all the more unbearable.

It was a very cruel joke. But this one belonged to the creator. This time God was having the last laugh.

"What's so funny?" Todd said. He'd been watching the demon closely. Very closely.

"Don't worry, son, you're going to get to know me like the

back of your hand in no time flat. We'll be best buddies, you and I. We will be a force to be reckoned with."

"I don't want to have anything to do with you," he sneered, "All I want to do is get my Mom out of this terrible place and then to never see you or hear from you again. Isn't that simple?"

"You have a well-developed mind for one so young. Unfortunately, you don't understand the one cardinal point of this whole game."

"And that point is?"

The demon laughed. "The point is that I'm the demon and you're not. That means I have the power and you don't. In other words, I call shots and you don't. I give the rules and you follow. I'm the brains and you're the body."

"And if I don't follow the rules?"

The demon laughed. "You ask some very interesting questions. Let me help you to understand. Suppose for a moment that I had an itch on my face just above my left eye. What would I do?"

"You'd scratch it."

"That's right. I'd scratch it. I would do that by commanding my hand to come up to my face and scratch. And my hand would obey."

"Yeah."

"Would the hand not obey?"

"Only if it couldn't. Like if it were paralyzed or something."

"But if it could, it would. The hand doesn't concern itself with good or bad, right or wrong. The mind does that, does the thinking and the evaluation and the moral thing. The mind decides it's ok and the brain just does it. It doesn't have a mind, a conscience of its own. It just does what it's told."

"So what's this got to do with me and you? You're not a mind and I'm not a hand."

"Ah, not yet. But we will be. We will become very close. Inseparable. You'll be like the hand and will be able to have all the fun. And I'll be the mind and will tell the hand what to do. It'll be easy and it'll be fun. You won't have to worry about that right and wrong nonsense they fill you up with. You can let me decide that for you.

The boy stopped and looked at him for a long moment. "You've really got this demon thing all figured our, haven't you?"

"Well, I've had a lot of years to practice."

"You forgot just one thing, though. Why would I want to help somebody who killed my Dad?"

The demon laughed. "No, son, you've got it all wrong. You won't have any choice but to serve me. You'll be part of me, like the hand and I'll be the brain. If the brain tells the hand to make a fist, it really doesn't have any options not to, don't you see? You'll become my little puppet, and I'll make you do whatever I want you to do. Play your cards right and you might even enjoy it. Many of them do."

"What if I hate it?"

"You'll get over it. And if you don't, too bad. But you'll obey because I'll control the nerves."

"I think I just want to go home," Todd said. "I just want things to be back the way they used to be."

"Well, you will be going back home soon enough, though I don't think things will ever be the way they used to be. But you'll get used to it in time. You'll enjoy being the most powerful kid on the block. You'll be able to do things you couldn't do before."

Todd just shook his head. All of that might be ok. He wasn't sure and there was something about it that made him want to wet his pants. But even if it did turn out cool, he'd still rather have his father back.

-3-

Johnny Dovecrest was overwhelmed by the weight of the doomed souls that smothered him from all directions. There were hundreds of them already, with thousands and thousands more on the way. They stank of death, decay, sin, and evil.

Their wants pressed horribly upon his soul. They demanded the love and intimacy they had been denied for so long, and they thought that he was their loved one. It was more than he could bear. Especially for a man who had grieved for his own family for almost 300 years.

But at least they were not here. They were with the Creator. And now he would be trapped here forever, never to be with them again.

He knelt on the ground and wept bitterly, for himself and for all of these miserable, wretched souls. But mostly he wept for himself.

His entire life had been dedicated to watching for the demon and protecting his tribe from it. He had not chosen this task. It had been thrust upon him. He hadn't wanted it. He hadn't wanted the long life that went along with it. He would have been content to die with his family and move on to a better world. He'd done his job, led a good life, believed in the Creator, and still, after all that, he found himself in hell, overwhelmed by countless damned souls who all wanted a part of him.

"Go away!" he screamed. "Leave me alone!"

He struggled and flailed and tried to escape, but they held him down, not by the weight of their shapeless bodies, but by the weight of their needs. Their desperation was crushing. Dovecrest just wanted to die, but not even that option was possible.

"This isn't right!" he screamed. "I'm not supposed to be here. Dear God, help me! I'm not supposed to be here!"

-4-

Erik closed his eyes and curled into a fetal position on the black sand. He put his arms over his head and drew his knees to his chest. But he couldn't blank out the awful sounds of the pitiful, wretched souls who crushed down against him. They were suffocating and smothering him so badly that he couldn't think, couldn't feel, couldn't breathe. Hundreds of millions of plaintive wailings mixed together as one awful cry, with only bits and pieces even recognizable.

"Mary! At last! I've found you!"

"Billy! It's me...."

"Mommy, where are you?"

And so it went. It was the weight of a hundred million souls upon him.

He was just about to give himself over to the desperate despair when it happened. They all stopped and froze where they were, as if time itself had been suspended. The voices stopped, and there was only silence.

Erik became aware of a gradual lighting; the brick red glow slowly turned orange, and then yellow. The shades dissolved around him, backing away from him as if he had become some fearful, frightening creature.

Erik noticed that the light wasn't coming from around him, but from *inside* him, as if he himself had been illuminated from within. He could feel the radiance warming and refreshing him. He felt rejuvenated, as if he had taken a cool, refreshing shower on a hot summer's day, and had been given a magical potion of energy and life.

To the damned souls around him, though, it was as if he had become poisoned. They retreated from him now, holding their hands and arms over their eyes in distaste and terror. He could no longer hear them—their voices had become mute to him—but he could see their lips moving as they cried out in fear and loathing. Whatever he had become was hateful to them.

He slowly crawled to his knees and looked over at his friend, Johnny Dovecrest. The Indian had also become transformed. His whole body was lit up, as if he had a strong fire burning inside him. The effect reminded Erik of paintings he had seen of angels, where the artist had somehow embodied them with a magical, mystical glow.

The doomed souls were moving away from Dovecrest as well, slowly backing away and holding out their hands as if to ward him off. The swarm had stopped completely and was now moving away from them both. It backed up against itself like a traffic jam as the shades melded into one another, and then slowly, almost with a delayed reaction, turned back the way they had come.

Dovecrest, too, had crawled to his knees and he met Erik's gaze. A small, smile parted his lips, and Erik smiled in return. The two men sat and watched as the doomed hordes moved away. They could still see the damned souls, but could no longer hear them, or feel their anguish. And they no longer attracted the damned, but repelled them.

"What happened?" Erik said, finally.

Dovecrest stood up slowly and shook himself off. "I'm not sure," he said. "But I think our prayers were heard."

"Heard and answered."

"Yes. Heard and answered."

Erik got to his feet and looked around. The masses of the damned ignored them completely now, as if they had never existed. Erik took a step towards one of them, an old man who must have died recently, since his rags were not as rotted. The soul of the man backed away in disgust.

Erik noticed that the glow of light was fading away now, and both he and his friend were returning to normal. But the feeling of refreshment remained. They had experienced just a drop of heaven here in this hellish place, and it was enough to rejuvenate their spirits, at least for the moment. Neither man knew if it would be enough to sustain them for the rest of the battle. But it was obvious that they had not been destined for this place, and, whatever happened, their fate would not mean staying here for all of eternity. Whatever they had to face, it couldn't be worse than this, Erik thought.

"Come on," Dovecrest said. "I have a demon to destroy."

"And I have a family to rescue."

CHAPTER THIRTY

-1-

Todd could tell something had happened, but he didn't know exactly what. He knew the demon knew it, too, because it became angry and agitated and swore under its breath. Todd knew that whatever had happened must be good if the demon didn't like it. Still, he had no idea what had to be done next.

His mother was in bad shape now. Her pains were more regular.

"The baby's coming soon," she told him. "Very soon. Just stay and help me, Todd."

"It's ok, Mom," he said. "I'm not going anywhere. You'll be fine."

"Hey, you'll be the only kid on the block to have delivered a baby," she said. "Won't you have a story to tell your baby sister!"

Todd forced a laugh. "Yeah, she'll owe me big time!"

"She sure will. We'll both owe you big time. I'll tell you what, when we get out of here we're going out for a huge ice cream sundae."

"I want chocolate chip ice cream with whipped cream and cherries," Todd said, playing along with his Mom.

"And I want strawberry. With whipped cream and nuts."

His mother's face winced in pain and she struggled not to cry out.

"I think she's coming, Todd," she said. "You know what to do?"

He nodded. She had told him what to expect and what he had to do. He thought it was gross and disgusting, but he couldn't let that stop him. When the baby's head came out he was supposed to hold it steady and help guide it out by pulling, but not too hard, as his mother pushed. He knew about cutting the chord, and had found a sharp stone for this purpose. And he knew about getting air into the baby's lungs if she didn't cry. The only thing he didn't know was what the demon was going to do next.

He looked at the monster from the corner of his eyes. It didn't actually look like a monster anymore. It appeared as a normal man. But he knew better. He'd seen it transform and he knew what it really was. Even now, he wondered what it was up to as it drew shapes in the sand and chanted foreign-sounding words. He knew nothing good could come of that. He'd never seen anything like that in the normal world.

He turned back to look at his mother. Her face was scrunched up in pain. He knelt down between her legs and waited. He'd never seen his mother naked before, and it made him very uncomfortable. He just wanted this whole thing to be over. He wasn't a doctor and he didn't know how to deliver a baby. What if something went wrong? What if it got stuck.

Todd blinked hard to hold back the tears. And suppose the baby was born ok, and things went right. What then? The demon wasn't going to just let them all go, just like that. It had something horrible planned for them. And Todd was afraid he would be the one to come out the worst.

He'd seen that awful head growing from the thing's shoulder earlier. Would he end up like that? He knew he'd rather die than become a monster like that. He thought if it came to that choice he'd figure out a way to kill himself. He'd keep that sharpened stone just in case he needed it for more than just cutting his sister's chord when she was born. He might have to use it on himself.

Then his mother clenched her teeth and reared up, and a pool of liquid flowed from her and onto the sand. She'd told him this would happen, but it grossed him out anyway and he wished he could be sick. But he swallowed hard and didn't let on that it bothered him. He had to be strong now. They were in enough trouble without him caving in and being a baby.

"It's ok, Mom," he said. "I'm here. We're going to be ok."

She forced a smile and wiped away a tear.

Todd took another look at the demon. The monster was totally absorbed in whatever it was doing now. Todd wished the baby would hurry up and be born before this thing finished whatever weird plans it had cooked up.

-2-

Erik knew he had to find his wife and son, but he had no idea where to go next. This entire world had been designed with one thing in mind—to be completely and totally monotonous, featureless, and uninteresting. The black sand went on for as far as the eye could see, broken only by obsidian rocky outcroppings that became tedious in and of themselves. The sky—or whatever it was—was completely black and starless. Erik suspected it was more a ceiling than a sky. He had the dreadful image of being trapped underground in an infinite cave on a planet that made Jupiter look like a speck in the universe.

There was no sun or moon to point out time or direction. Only a red glow to the edges of the horizon in all directions. It shed enough light to see by, bathing everything in a hellish red tint, but did not throw enough light to give even the impression of daylight. It was like a perpetual sunset in all directions, but an ugly black-red monotone sunset not broken up by atmosphere or clouds.

The doomed souls still wandered around the place, but their movement was aimless and pathetic, and Erik tried not to look at them. He was still sickened by their presence, and didn't think he'd ever forget their horrible touch upon him. They would be no help. He was just thankful that they now shied away from him as if he were poison.

He looked at Dovecrest and shrugged. "So where do we begin?"

Dovecrest looked carefully in every direction. He seemed to study the horizon, searching for clues. He knelt down and put his ear to the sand. He seemed so intent, so focused. But after a few moments, he stood up and shook his head.

"Nothing," he said. "I'm not even sure they're still here."

"Where else would they be?"

"I don't know. But this place is endless. I don't even know where to begin."

Erik shook his head. "We have to do something. We can't just give up."

"It won't do any good to just go off wandering without knowing where we're going," Dovecrest said.

Erik nodded. "But what else can we do?"

"Unless you can make some connection with your wife...or your son...."

Erik thought for a moment. It seemed impossible, but why not? Everything that had happened to him during the past week was impossible by all scientific standards. If people could raise demons and go through a portal to the waiting room of hell, why couldn't he establish a psychic connection with his own wife or son?

"What the hell?" he said. "No pun intended."

He had read a little bit about meditation, and, though he was certainly no expert, he had learned how to relax and train his thoughts when he was searching for ideas in his writing. And Dovecrest had taught him how to find the altar stone. He sat down on the sand and squirmed around until he had dug himself a comfortable seat. Then he pulled his feet into his thighs, closed his eyes, and covered them with his hands. He heard Dovecrest sit down across from him, but there were no other distractions to bother him. There was no sounds of traffic, or even nature— no birds, no wind.... Not even a breeze. It was perfectly silent.

He tried to empty his mind of everything. The stillness helped, but it was difficult not to think. So much had happened.

His mind had been ripped raw, his nerves pulled and prodded and tortured beyond what he could bear. He'd gone from earth to hell to heaven and now back to hell in just a few short hours—if he could even measure things by earthly time. It might have been minutes—or days, for all he knew. Time just didn't make sense anymore. For that matter, nothing made sense.

He tried to stop the wheels from spinning in his head. But all he could think about was his family, and what he would do if he found them. They had no plan, no idea.... The frontal attack had failed miserably. Even if he could rescue his family he had no way of escaping. He wondered if Vickie was even strong enough to be moved. Had she delivered the baby yet? Was the child all right? What had happened to Todd? They could all have been killed by now, for all he knew, and all of this might be for nothing.

"Stop worrying and relax."

It was Dovecrest's voice, almost as if the Indian had been reading his thoughts. Erik opened his eyes and looked at him. Dovecrest had been watching him. The two men smiled.

"Ok. Let me try this again."

This time Erik stretched out on the sand as if he were at the beach, putting his arms up over his eyes to block out the eerie, red glow. He took a deep breath, then exhaled slowly. He paced his breathing and concentrated on letting his body go loose, beginning with his feet and working upwards. He listened to the sound of his breathing as he relaxed his legs, then his hips, then his chest. He imagined a purple dot in the sky and concentrated all of his efforts of seeing it and experiencing it.

His mind went blank. Then he saw an image of his son. It came suddenly, unbidden, suddenly snapping into focus like a photograph. He saw the boy squatting in the black sand of this awful place, looking very worried and concerned. Erik knew he was seeing things as they really were when he noticed the demon standing beside Todd, its back towards the boy as it drew in the sand and seemed to be chanting. Erik knew that Todd was looking at his mother, and that Vickie was just about to give birth.

Suddenly Todd's eyes widened, and Erik could see his gasp.

"Dad!" he heard him whisper. "Are you dead?"

Erik channeled his thoughts to comfort the boy. "Shhh. I'm not dead. I'm still here. I'm coming for you. Just don't let it know you know."

Todd forced a smile, and then the picture faded, slowly, as if at the end of a scene in a movie. Erik was suddenly aware of where the boy was. Every muscle in his body was tense and tightened up like a guitar string. He felt sweat pouring down his face.

"Erik...Erik.... Are you all right?"

Dovecrest was calling to him. He opened his eyes slowly.

"Yeah. I'm fine," he said. "They're still alive. And I know where they are."

-3-

Todd tried not to show his feelings as the vision of his father passed. It had been so real, as if it had been happening right there in front of him. Dad was alive! He knew it. He had seen him. Had heard him. And he was coming for them. He even knew where they were.

He tried to keep his feelings quiet, though. He knew the demon could tap into people's thoughts and feelings, and he didn't want to give anything away. Surprise might be his Dad's only advantage and he didn't want to take that away. It was all they had going for them right now.

He looked at his mother and wondered if she knew, if she had seen Dad, too. Her face was all twisted in pain, though, and her eyes were closed. She gritted her teeth and seemed to be straining as she tried to push the baby out.

"She's coming, Todd," she said, her voice barely above a whisper. "You know what to do."

"Ok, Mom," he said. He tried to sound confident but his

insides were torn up with fear. If only this baby could wait a little while longer, until his Dad could get here. Dad would know what to do.

But it wasn't meant to be that way. He saw a blackness appear, and realized it was the top of the baby's head. She had thick, black hair, a fact that both surprised and fascinated him. He'd thought babies had no hair. But this one seemed to have a full head of it.

He put his hands down and her head pushed forward into his grasp.

"Hold her head, Todd," his mother said. "Don't let her drop."

Todd held her head firmly. He found that he didn't have to pull her; his mother's pushing was enough. She was wet and sticky, covered in blood and mucus, not at all clean and neat like the babies he'd seen on television. He pulled her slowly away, and quickly cut the chord like his mother had told him. A gush over afterbirth followed and the baby began to cry.

Todd was surprised at how quick the birth itself had been. It was weird, because it had taken so long to get to that part, and then it was over.

His mother tried to sit up.

"Can I see her?" she asked.

Todd crawled around her and placed the baby in her arms. She took her and carefully cradled her.

That was when Todd saw the demon coming closer.

"Ah, what have we here?" it said. "Just what we've all been waiting for. I'm afraid I'm going to have to take that."

"No! You can't have my baby!" his Mom screamed.

The demon reached forward. His Mom scuttled back, trying to get away.

"No!" she screamed.

The demon moved towards her, arms outstretched as she held the baby away. Todd could see the outcome as clear as if it had already happened. The demon would kill the baby as part of some weird ritual that it did to get more power. He could see it all before it even happened. And he knew what had to be done.

Without even thinking, he grabbed the baby from his mother's arms and darted away from the demon. He knew it would buy just a few moments, at best, but his body just reacted from instinct. This was his baby sister. He couldn't let this thing take her. He put his head down and ran for the horizon, using every bit of speed he could get. He didn't look back, didn't even think about what would happen next.

-4-

Erik knew where he had to go as clearly as if he had a compass in his head. Not that a compass would have done any good in this place that had no directions. But his path was marked clear and straight.

He and Dovecrest had set off immediately once Erik knew where to go.

"I don't think they're very far away," he said. "The demon is still there. Do we have a plan yet?"

"Find them," Dovecrest said. "And then see what happens."

"I'm really not comfortable with 'see what happens'," Erik replied.

"Neither am I. But do you have a better idea?"

Erik had to admit that he had no idea. Still, he couldn't hide his frustration.

"Didn't your legends give any idea about what we do once we find it?"

"It never went that far," Dovecrest said. "I'm afraid we're writing the instruction manual."

"That's a comforting thought."

"This is a comforting place."

Erik forced a laugh and tried not to betray the terror that was eating away at him. It was ridiculous—to have come so far and still not know what to do. If the thing didn't have Vickie and Todd he would have just turned around and gone back home. Although come to think of it, he didn't know how to do that, either.

He knew it wasn't much farther. They had to pick up the pace.

Then he felt an odd tightening in his chest; he stopped and dropped to his knees. He suddenly couldn't breathe, couldn't continue. He wondered if he were having a heart attack.

"What's wrong?" Dovecrest was at his side.

"I...I don't know...I think something's...happened."

He closed his eyes and relaxed his breathing. That's when he felt Todd's presence close to him and he knew something had gone terribly wrong. He could hear Todd calling out to him over the vast sands, calling that he needed him, that they needed him. He felt three spirits calling to him now, not just Todd, but Vickie as well. Somehow, she knew he was near. And a third one, someone he didn't know....

The baby. The baby had been born, and even though he didn't know her, he could feel her presence calling out to him as well.

They were in serious trouble, and although he didn't know how to save them, he and Dovecrest were their only hope. And he knew that there was more at stake than just his wife and children. If the demon succeeded here, he knew it would return to the earth again to cause more doom and misery. He couldn't let that happen. But most of all, he couldn't let his family be taken.

Erik swallowed hard and straightened up. "Come on!" he said. "This thing is coming to a head right now!"

CHAPTER THIRTY-ONE

-1-

The demon had never been so furious in its life. It was wrath in the flesh, and now its own wrath was stronger than it had ever been, all because of this brat who had bested him once again. But it wouldn't last. This one would pay. He would wish that he had never, ever clashed with the demon called Wrath.

First the brat had gotten away from the altar stone when he'd hit the rock with his foolish little hammer. And now he had stolen the baby away from it just when it was about to pluck its prize and hold it inside hell's hottest flames until it was scorched alive. It couldn't believe the kid had the nerve, the audacity to cross it like this.

At first it had been too surprised and shocked to even react, and had simply stood there and watched the boy run away with the baby. The mother had been screaming as if she were the one being tortured, and the boy had just reacted, so quickly that even it didn't know what he was going to do.

He was most angry that he had timed the spell so perfectly, so it would work best when the baby was first born, only seconds old. Now he'd have to redo the whole thing, and it wouldn't be as effective—or as much fun. The newborn had already lost so much of her innocence. That pure innocence—that was what it had longed to destroy most of all, in a long, terrifying and agonizing torture of its own devising. It would have been so perfect....

Staying in human form had been a mistake. That's why the boy had challenged it. If it had still been made of fiery lava, or of rock-hard stone, then the boy wouldn't have dared do anything but comply. It had let its guard down. He had seen it as a fellow human being, mortal and weak, not as the powerful supernatural being that it was. That was going to change. It would not let the boy be fooled into thinking that he could win.

It also knew that the boy's father and the meddling ancient had escaped and were on their way. The hordes of doomed souls had stopped their swarm towards the pair and were now going about their regular routine of restless misery. It wasn't sure how they had escaped, but it wouldn't help them. If they found him before he'd completed his plans, he would destroy them. If not, they were of no consequence; once he made his return, he would trap them here in hell where they could wait with the damned until judgment day.

It looked into the distance and could still see the boy running away. He wouldn't get very far. It looked at the mother, who was huddled in a ball crying so hard that she shook all over. It felt no pity, only loathing. Only contempt and disgust. It sneered at the woman and turned away. She had reason enough to cry. And very soon, she'd have even more reason to weep.

The demon closed its eyes and slowly began to transform once again. First it had been fire. Then it had been rock. Now, for something different. It thought for a moment.

"And there were stings in their tails," it said out loud.

Yes, stings in its tail. What a perfect, exquisite creature to inhabit this desolate, empty world. A perfect, cold-blooded, terrifying creature.

Even as it imagined the shape, the transformation began. A hard black shell, as hard as when it had been formed of stone. Razor-sharp pincers to tear and ruin flesh. Multiple legs that could scuttle along the sand. A tail with a sting of fire, a sting that would paralyze the nerves and the body, keeping the mind—and the pain receptors—intact. It was perfect, with one small modification: a human head between its shoulders so it could hear and see and speak. A human head on a giant scorpion. The dichotomy alone would inspire terror and repugnance. Just the sight of this monstrosity would be enough to stop the boy—and the meddling pair who were coming for him.

Sure enough, the woman saw what it had become and was screaming, shielding her eyes with her arms.

"Don't worry, my dear," it said. "I'm not going to eat you. At least not yet!"

Then it scuttled off in pursuit of her obnoxious brat and his newborn sister.

-2-

Erik saw the boy up ahead and began to run. He recognized Todd immediately, of course. His son was holding something close to his chest, which slowed his running, but it looked like what he lacked in technique he more than made up for in adrenaline. It was difficult to run in the sand, but Erik now had some adrenaline of his own. Todd was carrying his newborn baby.

He wondered what had happened to Vickie, but somehow he felt reassured that she was all right. Weak, hurt, and terrified, but otherwise ok. He heard Dovecrest running just behind him, and was filled with awe for the old man's stamina. He was a good ally.

"Dad!" Todd's call carried across the open space.

"I'm coming!" Erik replied, closing the distance quickly.

They met in a heap at the half-way point as they both collapsed on the sand. Erik hugged his son, and then his daughter. He took a moment to hold her up so he could look into her face.

"She's beautiful," he said.

"Actually, she's kind of a mess," Todd said. "I didn't know babies were so gross."

Erik forced a laugh and showed the baby to Dovecrest.

"I think she's beautiful too," the Indian said.

"The demon was gonna kill her but I stole her away. I wasn't gonna let it have her."

"Todd...." Erik couldn't even begin to say what was on his mind. This young boy had shown so much courage and tenacity. He'd risked his life to try to save his mother, and had even delivered his baby sister. He'd stood up to this demon and rescued his baby sister.... No, words couldn't come close.

"You're a very brave man," Dovecrest said.

"I'm not a man," Todd said. "I'm still a boy."

"No," Dovecrest corrected. "You are a man."

Todd shrugged. "It made the demon mad. I know he's coming after me. He wants the baby. He wants to do bad things to her."

"I know," Erik said. "And we're going to stop it."

Todd looked at his father for a moment. "Mom's ok, at least for now. I don't know what it'll do to her later, though."

"We're not going to let it hurt Mom, or the baby, or you."

"Good. What do you want me to do?"

"You are going to look after your baby sister," Erik said, and handed the infant back to his son. "Do you know how to hold her?"

"Hey, I've done ok so far, haven't I?"

"Yes. Yes, you have. Just make sure you support her head."

"She'll be ok, Dad. Trust me."

Erik nodded. Then he stood up beside Dovecrest and looked in the direction Todd had come. Sure enough, something was coming towards them, but it didn't look like anything he had ever seen before.

"It may have taken on a new shape," Dovecrest said. "Or maybe this is something different."

"No, it's Wrath. I can tell. Let's go meet it."

"I'm ready," Dovecrest said, and they both took a step forward. Todd followed with the baby.

"Todd, you wait here," Erik said.

"No way, Dad. I'm coming. Besides, if you don't kill it, it's gonna find me anyway. You don't really think I can get away on my own, do you?"

"I don't know what to think anymore. I really don't."

The boy shrugged. "Good. Then I'm coming. Don't worry. I'll stay out of the way, just so I can keep the baby away from that thing."

Once the monster spotted them and saw they were coming towards it, it stopped and waited. Apparently, it wasn't in any hurry now that the baby had been born.

"I think I screwed up its plans," Todd said. "It's gonna be mad."

Erik quickly saw that it wasn't shaped anything like a man any more. This thing really was a monster, a scorpion the size of a horse but with a completely human face and head where the scorpion eyes and mouth should have been. The thing had a thick, hard shell of deepest black that shined with an eerie red glow from the light. Its pincers were the size of his writing desk. They clacked open and closed menacingly and could easily cleave a man in two. Its legs twitched in anticipation and its stinger, the size of a knitting needle, was poised and ready.

But as terrifying and repugnant as the arachnid body was, the human face was even worse. Vaguely reminiscent of the cult leader that the demon had taken over, this creature had long, tangled brown hair, brown eyes with thick brows, a long, sharp nose, and a grin that was so horrible it defied description. The thing stopped and stared at them, mostly allowing them to stare at it, Erik suspected, so that they might have the opportunity to completely experience the full effect of its horrible new shape.

Whatever terror it was supposed to inspire certainly worked. Erik felt his insides turn to jelly. It was as if the thing knew that his worst fear was spiders and scorpions. Especially large ones with stingers. He swallowed hard and tried to look relaxed. But he realized he was failing miserably. His body trembled despite his best efforts to control it, and he knew if he spoke his voice would be cracked and weak. His mouth was so dry that he couldn't even swallow.

He looked over at Dovecrest and realized the Indian was probably just as afraid as he was. He wasn't sure if that were a comforting thought or not. While it made him feel better about himself, he wished that one of them would be able to look this thing in the eyes with defiance.

Then, horribly, the thing spoke. Its voice was so incongruous with its shape that Erik didn't even hear what it said at first. He'd expected the thing to sound like a monster. But instead the voice was smooth and female, like the voice of a Hollywood starlet trying out for a sexy role.

"Ah, what a quaint reunion," it said. "It's so nice to see you all here together at last."

Erik just gaped at the monster, speechless.

"Oh, I see my voice doesn't match my form," it said. "How silly of me. Hold on while I change into something more comfortable. Maybe you'll like this better...."

The demon's face dissolved into a smoky mist and Erik wondered if it was going to shed the scorpion shape. No such luck, though. The massive terrifying body remained firm, but the face slowly metamorphosised into the face of a female. He could just see the edges at first, as the long, silken blond hair appeared and framed a delicate face. The mist dissipated and the transformation was complete: gorgeous blue eyes like swimming pools to drown in, sensuous lips, a small, perfect nose, and silky, delicate skin designed to make a man melt. All this on the body of a stinging, pinching arachnid.

"Is that more to your liking?" it said. Then it stretched out one of its jointed, exoskeleton limbs. "All the guys say I have great legs. Don't you agree?"

Erik threw up suddenly and fiercely, which only made the monster laugh. "Come here and give me a kiss," it said. "I'll make you forget all of your troubles."

Erik knelt down and wiped his face with a handkerchief. "Why don't you just let us go," he said. "Haven't you caused us enough grief?"

The monster laughed. "I just want to be a part of your happy family," it said. "Come, let's go join your wife. Then we can have a real reunion. Or would you rather I just kill you now and get it over with?"

The thing turned and scuttled off a few feet in the direction from where it had come, then turned and looked back at Erik again. The contrast revolted him: it was the face of the most beautiful, most exquisite woman he had even seen pasted onto the body of a hideous invertebrate monster. He almost threw up again. When the thing had been a grotesque-looking male, it had been bad enough. But this beautiful female transposed onto this body—it was just more than he could stand.

Still, he had no choice than to follow along. His wife was waiting for him. And to Erik, she was the most beautiful, perfect creature in existence. He'd do anything to save her—even be devoured by this awful thing, if that's what it took.

Everyone was looking at him: the demon, Todd, Dovecrest... even the baby seemed to be watching to see what he'd do. He wanted to run and hide. He'd rather die than get any closer to this thing. But he couldn't just think about himself. Whatever happened, he suspected it would all be determined very soon, and would end either one way or the other. There wasn't any use putting off the inevitable. Todd was right. There was no place left to run.

"Come on," he said. "Let's get this thing over with."

They all turned and followed the demon back to where it had left Vickie.

-3-

Todd didn't think he could be any more shocked until he saw the demon appear as a scorpion, and then change his face into that of a woman. As much as he was repelled by the thing, he was also fascinated, and he couldn't really explain why. The woman was so beautiful that he made his head spin. But then when he looked at the hard, scaly body with pincers and a sting, it made him cringe just at the thought of being anywhere near it.

He knew this was the worst shape it had taken on yet. When it was a mass of burning lava it had been frightening—but instinctively people stayed away from fire and knew what it was. When it had taken on the rock shape it had been little more than a beast, almost like something out of a comic book or a bad horror movie. And as a man it hadn't been anything, really, except a very bad person. Todd knew there were enough of them running around in the real world, so this was nothing new. He'd been taught to watch out for and avoid bad people all of his life.

But this was different. The body was so hideous. But the face was so beautiful—and so human. It almost looked friendly, affectionate, welcoming. He knew it was still the demon, of course, but this was...different. He was afraid that if the thing had completely transformed into a woman he would have just followed after it like a lovesick puppy and done whatever it wanted just to be near it.

But he couldn't let himself think that way, and he was grateful that the monster still looked like a monster to remind him of what it really was.

He cradled his baby sister close to his chest and followed his Dad and the Indian, staying just behind them in case the demon should turn and launch an attack. He didn't even fear for himself much anymore—he'd almost become immune to shock and pain and the fear of death—but he didn't want anything to happen to this tiny, innocent baby that he had helped to bring into the world.

He followed along, knowing that whatever was about to happen would occur very soon, and one way or another, this thing would be over. He just hoped that whatever happened to him was final, one way or the other. He was willing to face death, if that were his fate. Or go back to the world and try to pick up his life.

He did not want to be the host body for this terrible demon, even if it did have a gorgeous face and beautiful blonde hair and blue eyes. He would rather die than face that. Because as beautiful as that face was on the outside, he had seen the ugliness, the hideousness of what lie within. Sharing his body with that thing would mean living with this revolting presence constantly, eating, sleeping, and being with it always until it grew tired of him and cast him off for something else. Anything, even death, was better than that.

He still had that sharp stone in his pocket and would use it on himself if he needed to—though he wasn't even sure he could die while he was still in this world. But he'd keep it, just the same, in case the need arose. He knew that killing yourself was wrong—but he suspected it would be ok if you were doing it to save yourself, and others, from a demon like this one.

He looked ahead at his father and could sense his Dad's fear. He knew his Dad was deathly afraid of spiders and scorpions and anything like that. It was as if the demon had sensed what would be most unpleasant. Todd wondered if he were the strongest one of the three right now; the thought that he might be terrified him more than the demon even.

Then his Dad looked back at him, smiled, and flashed him the thumbs up sign. Maybe they'd be ok after all, he thought

He grinned back at his Dad and, holding the baby carefully, returned the thumbs up sign.

CHAPTER THIRTY-TWO

-1-

Erik saw Vickie sprawled out on the sand looking miserable and helpless. As soon as he saw her his heart melted and he began to run, skirting around the demon and hurrying to her side. She was weeping uncontrollably as he knelt beside her and took her in his arms.

"It's ok, Sweetheart. It's going to be ok."

"Oh, Erik," she sobbed. "I love you so much."

"I love you. I love you so very deeply."

"The baby...."

"Todd has her." Erik held her up so she could see Todd and the baby, and Johnny Dovecrest. "We're all here."

"Even that thing," she sneered. "It tried to take our baby."

"I know, Vic. I know."

The demon clicked its pincers together as it watched them. Its human head was tilted slightly to the side as it scrutinized them, as if it were trying to understand what was happening. Love was a foreign thing to its world. Its entire existence was based upon hatred, anger, fear, and wrath. Love was repugnant to it, and that was why it had been banished to this other world, far away from any kind of companionship or compassion or caring. It belonged here, not on the earth where it could infect others with its hate. There was already enough rage and hate in the world of men. The earth certainly didn't need any more.

"So what are you going to do with us?" Erik asked. "What

comes next?"

The demon laughed, still in that silky-sweet feminine voice that didn't sound right coming from a monster.

"That all depends," it said. "They have something I want. And I am going to have it. You can try and stop me. Or not. That is your choice."

Dovecrest stepped forward and addressed the creature in a confident voice. "What is it you want?"

"I'm tired of being here. I've had a taste of the earth and I enjoyed what I found. I want more."

"Why?"

"Because I'm not supposed to be there. And because now I can be there."

"So you're going to go back to the earth and create more destruction? I can't let you do that."

"I'm afraid you don't really have any choice about what I do. But this time I'd like to go back in a different form. As a human. As a child. I could be more...subtle...about the things I did."

"As a child?" Dovecrest said.

"No one would even know I was anything but an innocent little boy," it said smoothly. "Or perhaps a baby girl. I could take either one of them."

Vickie screamed. "I won't let you take my children! Either of them!"

"I will take one of them. If you don't cooperate, I'll take both of them."

"No. Please don't take my children. Take me. But please don't take my kids."

"Ah, life is so unfair," the demon said. "I had planned to kill you and your meddling friends, then sacrifice one child to take the other. But I'm prepared to offer you a chance to sacrifice yourself and save one of the children."

"Sacrifice myself?" Erik said. "You're going to kill me anyway. What's the difference?"

The demon laughed softly. "You don't understand. I don't want your life. I want your soul. I can sacrifice the baby, who knows no better, and take her innocent soul. That would be best, would be the most satisfying, since the rest of you are already corrupt. Or I could take another soul. One of you."

"And end up...here in this place...forever?" Dovecrest said.

"Not forever. This is just a stopping point, really. Eventually you'd be sent directly to hell, which is much worse than this."

Erik looked around and shuddered. He could still see the shadows of the doomed souls wandering aimlessly, searching for someone or something they would never find. This world truly was devoid of all love, of all feeling except endless despair.

"No takers, I see. Then I will have the baby."

The monster stepped towards Todd, who turned away, shielding the baby behind him.

"No! Take me!" Vickie screamed. She jumped up and ran towards the demon.

Erik grabbed her from behind to stop her.

"I'll go," he said.

"No, I'm her mother!"

Erik held her tightly in his arms. "I can't let you do that," he said. "I'll be the sacrifice."

"I could take you both," the demon said. "Unless you want to fight about it."

"Hey, what about me!" Todd said. "I don't want to be part of that thing!"

The demon acted so quickly that Erik didn't even realize what had happened until it was done. The thing's deadly stinger flashed out like a whip, shooting past him and across the twenty-foot space to where Todd was standing. Erik couldn't believe a thing so huge could move so quickly.

The sting caught him in the back of left shoulder as he turned away from it, still shielding the baby. Then it was back where it had begun in a millisecond, as if nothing had happened.

Vickie gasped and Erik held his breath as Todd turned around, looked at demon and then at them in wide-eyed surprise, and then dropped to his knees. He knelt there for a moment in shocked amazement, and then fell to his side, still cradling the baby.

<h2 style="text-align:center">-2-</h2>

Dovecrest couldn't believe the demon had killed the boy He stood there like a wooden soldier looking at Todd, completely paralyzed by shock and horror. He never imagined the thing could be so deadly so quickly. It had assumed it would take its time with them, maybe giving them an opportunity to act, or at least fight back. He suddenly felt so totally and completely hopeless that he didn't know what to do. All he could do was watch.

Vickie pulled away from her husband and ran to the boy's side, taking the baby from his arms.

"You killed him!" she screamed. "You killed my son!"

The demon laughed. "Actually, he's not dead—yet. He's merely paralyzed. He can see and hear everything that's going on—although, I will say that the pain of the venom is excruciating."

"Why?" Dovecrest asked.

"He'll be fine—once I take over his body. Until then he'll be in agony. But he will be silent and won't cause any more trouble. Besides, once I take over he'll be so glad to be rid of the pain that he'll welcome me. I know what pain is like, believe me. He'll do anything to make it stop."

"How long does he have?" Erik said.

"He has until eternity," the demon said matter-of-factly. "He won't die unless I let him."

Dovecrest looked at his friends and saw the agony on their faces. Erik was torn apart with grief. He walked over to his wife and took their baby in his arms. He whispered something to the baby and then to his wife. She began to sob violently and grabbed onto him, pulling him close.

"Oh, Erik, please, please, do something. I can't do this

anymore."

Erik hugged her hard, and whispered some comforting words. Then he stepped toward the demon.

"I'm ready. Take me and let's get this over with," he said.

-3-

The sun had come up and Mark paced up and down beside the huge altar stone. Soldiers were already setting the charges, stringing the wire and preparing the detonator. They'd be finished in a half an hour—maybe less. Then the captain would give the order to blow the altar stone to pieces and his friends would be trapped in whatever world they had been taken into.

He had spent the night in prayer, begging, pleading with God to intercede on his behalf.

"Please, God," he said again softly. "I ask not for myself but for your people who have served you so well."

But for some reason, God was strangely silent on this morning and he suspected it was already too late.

The captain came and stood next to him. Captain MacKensie, his nametag read, and Mark knew he was a good man. But he had a job to do.

"It's not looking good, Pastor."

"No, Captain, it's not looking good."

"I wish there was something I could do. I'd even send people in there if I knew how."

"Do you have any idea what's happened here?" Mark said.

The soldier looked down at the ground for a long moment. He was middle-aged and grim-looking, with hard eyes.

"Pastor, I've seen a lot of things in my years. A lot of suffering. I've served in some bad places and have seen some bad things. Terrible things. But I've never seen anything like what happened here.

"I'm a God-fearing man myself. I suppose you have to be in my line of work. You never know when you'd going to meet your maker. I don't claim to understand any of this. But I did some praying of my own last night. I never believed in spooks and demons and such nonsense. But now, in the light of day, I'm thinking maybe I don't know much about anything anymore."

"What about your theory about aliens?"

"Aliens, demons...one is as far-fetched as another. All I know is that rock is truly a bad thing, and I'm going to make sure no more bad comes from it."

Mark nodded. "I understand, Captain."

-4-

Erik held his hands out to his sides and stepped slowly towards the demon. He had to sacrifice himself. There was no other way. There was nothing else he could do. He'd seen this monster in action, and there was simply no way to fight against it. His options had run out.

He turned and looked at Vickie one last time and smiled. Somehow, he managed to keep his composure, though he was dying inside. Everything he had worked for, everything he had believed in was coming to an end. He was about to exile himself forever to hell.

Hell wasn't a fairy tale from a book of Bible stories anymore. He'd been there—was still there—and had experienced all of its agony and despair. He had felt the anguish of the swarms of doomed, damned souls, and he was about to become a permanent part of their number. He was about to forsake everything— his life, his family, even his eternal salvation. And he was about to do it by his own choice. Willingly.

Vickie tried to smile back at him but she couldn't and he had to turn away. He couldn't bear to see her cry anymore.

"Ok, what's the deal here?" he asked. "I submit to the sacrifice and then what?"

"You give up your soul to the Dark One and I take your son."

"And my wife? And my friend?" He pointed towards

Dovecrest. "You take them back and let them live their lives in peace?"

"They won't remember that any of this happened," it said. "They'll be brought back and as far as they know, you were killed destroying me, and Todd is a normal boy."

"All right, then. I agree. Let's get it on. What do you want me to do?"

The demon grinned. "You must stand here," it said, pointing to a spot in the sand with its right pincer. "Just stand there for a moment. I'll do the rest."

The monster extended its claws to either side to make room for Erik to move forward. He stepped in between the thing's deadly pincers, knowing full well that the monster could tear him in half at any moment if it wanted to. Then again, he'd seen what it did to Todd from twenty feet away, so what did it matter how close he was.

"Just look at my face," the thing said. "It'll be more pleasant that way."

Erik swallowed hard and looked into the creature's blue eyes. The face that looked back at him was stunningly beautiful, and he tried to forget about the body that housed it. The eyes were bright and feminine, and they looked at him with sensual delight.

"Just look at me and pretend I'm real," the face said in a sexy, seductive voice. "I can be your dream woman."

Erik looked into her eyes and saw only her face. He tried to relax and lose himself in her sensuous gaze as she slowly and methodically began to recite the words of the spell that would keep him here in this world forever. The woman was beautiful—the demon certainly recognized what would appeal to a man. But as much as he tried to concentrate on those cool, blue eyes, his mind kept seeing them as green. The blond hair kept turning red, and he just couldn't get Vickie's beautiful features out of his mind.

He longed to turn back and look at her again, but dared not. He did not know how he would bear existence without her.

He could tell from the tone and speed of the demon's chants that the time was coming to an end. Then the demon was silent, looking at him intently.

"Swear that you willingly give up your immortal soul to the Dark One," it said. "Do it now."

Erik swallowed hard. His mouth was so dry he didn't know if he would even be able to speak. He opened his lips to mouth the words.

Then, just before he could speak, he suddenly heard an animal-like shout from behind him and felt arms grabbing at his shoulders, pulling him down. He fell backward and on his side. A pincer reached for him but missed its mark and snapped on dead air.

He hit the ground and rolled onto his side just in time to see Johnny Dovecrest charge into the demon's embrace, carrying a sharp obsidian stone. He plunged the stone into the demon's eye and shouted at the top of his lings.

"I sacrifice my soul for these good people in the name of Christ who died for our sins!"

The demon's eye disintegrated into a mass of blood and pulp and it staggered backward in shock. It looked at them with its remaining eye full of hate and rage as Dovecrest merely stood there in the place between its claws and waited. The monster drooled and raged, but nothing happened. Erik rolled clear of the demon and rushed to Vickie, Todd, and the baby, who were watching in horror.

"I gave him my stone," Todd said. "He told me he needed it."

Erik nodded. "That was a good thing," he said. "A very good thing."

"Damn you!" the demon screamed, and then it began to dissolve and transform once again.

"It can't take him," Erik said. "It can't take his soul."

Then the demon lashed out in uncontrolled wrath, grabbing Dovecrest in its huge claw.

"You can kill me!" the Indian said. "But you can't have me!"

The Indian seemed to be covered in a yellow glow, like Erik

had seen before when they'd escaped from the crush of the doomed souls.

The demon's face was ugly now, one eye missing and oozing and the entire face contorted in rage. It screamed a piercing cry of agony, and then snapped its claw shut, cutting Dovecrest in half at the waist. The monster dropped the body to the ground and curled up on itself, still transforming, growing solid once again.

Erik held his family close as they watched, transfixed in horror. The thing formed once again, this time in a grotesque parody of a being. The thing was about four feet tall and bloated like a toad, with warts and ugly red splotches on its dry brown skin. Its eyes were yellow and glutinous, and it had grotesque-looking horns on its head. Erik thought the effect was almost comical as he saw the demon for what it really was.

The thing suddenly looked terrified and weak.

"You have no more power, here or anywhere," Erik said. "In the name of Christ, be gone."

The thing's eyes went wide and glazed over. Then fire began to consume it, beginning at its feet and working its way up. It burned away to nothing, from the bottom up, until only the bloated head remained, perched on a pyre of flame. The monster screamed once, and then exploded in a meteor shower of red and white sparks. When the smoke cleared, it was gone. All that remained were a few ashes that slowly floated to the ground, where they quickly blended away into the black sand.

Erik watched in stunned silence. The monster was gone. But Dovecrest's torn body still lay on the ground, shrouded in a yellow glow. Then the glow brightened, giving him an angelic appearance. Although cleaved, his body appeared pieced together, and the Indian stood and looked at his friends. His smile was huge and genuine and he seemed totally free from pain.

"Follow your instincts to escape," he said. "God will show you the way." Then his body shot off like a lightening bolt and was gone.

"Did he go to heaven?" Todd asked.

"Yes," Erik replied. "He's with his family now."

"And so aren't we."

"Right. Now I think we have to get the hell out of here. Pardon the pun."

Follow your instincts, Dovecrest had said. The Lord would show the way. Erik took a moment to look around in every direction, scanning the horizon for a sign, any sign at all. There seemed to be nothing. The same old plain monotonous landscape.

Strangely enough, the baby saw it first and begin pointing. Todd called to his father and showed him. Erik didn't think babies could respond so quickly, but this one was definitely pointing to a single bright star that had appeared in the horizon.

"Look, it's like the star or Bethlehem," Todd said.

Erik nodded. Something told them they needed to leave while the getting was good.

"Are you up to walking?" Erik asked Vickie.

"I'll try."

"Are you up to being carried then?"

Before she could answer he had carefully picked her up and slung her over his shoulder.

"Come on," he said. "It'll be like following the yellow brick road in the Wizard of Oz."

"It's not actually a road, Dad."

"No, but it'll give us a roadway. Hurry!"

They passed the empty stretches quickly now—even here in hell it seemed to take less time to go home than what it did to get there, he thought. They made it back to the entranceway, and then into the huge funnel leading back to where they had come from. Vickie was getting heavy and difficult to carry up the incline, but he knew she was so weak that she'd hold them behind and he had a strong feeling that their window of opportunity was quickly closing.

Climbing up the funnel was more difficult that coming down. Not only was the climb steep, but Erik carried his wife and Todd carried his baby sister. They were running on sheer adrenaline now, pumped up with the knowledge that they might actually be able to escape this ordeal after all. His arms were aching, his lungs were burning and he didn't know what would happen next when he got to the top.

Slowly, he climbed up over the lip to the spot where they had entered originally. He looked in every direction. Solid rock walls surrounded him on all sides, circling the pit and even covering the top. It seemed that, once again, they were trapped with nowhere to go. He placed Vickie carefully down on the rocky ground and sighed.

"There just doesn't seem to be a way out of this mess," he said.

"It's ok, Dad. Just wait. Something will happen."

He nodded. "I guess we have to have faith." And he put his arms around Vickie. He knew she was so weak and needed a doctor, but there was nothing else to do but hold her.

"Look, Dad. Something's happening."

Erik looked up. Sure enough, of the walls had began to glow in a soft, yellow light. It became progressively brighter and took on the form of a portal, almost. The light intensified more, until it almost hurt the eyes with its radiance.

"What is it?" Vickie asked.

Erik stood up and took a step forward, but the light burned too brightly, like a welding torch and he had to step back.

"It's the Indian," Todd said.

Johnny Dovecrest stepped to the edge of the doorway and smiled. He was young now, and beside him was his wife and his children. They were all young and happy as they embraced.

"It's ok now," Dovecrest said. His voice was very far off, as if coming from a long way off. But the words were crystal clear.

Then a small cat walked out between the Indian's feet and meowed softly. Dovecrest bent down and picked the creature up and stroked it gently on the ears.

"Faith!" Todd said. "Faith is in heaven too."

Dovecrest nodded and spoke again, but he was too far away

now to hear and already the white images were dissolving. Just before he went he pointed to the opposite wall.

"Hurry, there are people on the other side waiting for you," he said, and then he was gone.

Erik turned and looked to where the Indian had pointed. Another door had opened up. This one was more mundane—it was simply an oblong opening cut into the rock. Erik looked through it and saw the morning sky.

"It's the altar," he said. "From the other side. Hurry up. We've got to get through quickly before it closes."

The opening felt like a magnetic force that was repelling them rather than attracting them.

"It's trying to keep us in," he said. "We can't let it. Todd, hold the baby tight."

Erik dragged his son to the edge of the opening and forcibly pushed. The opening pushed back for a moment, and then something seemed to pop, and he and the baby slipped through. He picked up Vickie in his arms and walked deliberately towards it. It was like walking into hurricane force winds, but he closed his eyes and walked on, determined.

"Did you see a glimpse of heaven?" Vickie asked softly.

"Yeah," he said. "Just a tiny corner. It was beautiful."

"Yes. It was," she said.

Then they were outside, standing on the top of the altar stone surrounded by a hundred soldiers with rifles leveled at them.

Pastor Mark walked forward and hugged them both. "Boy, am I glad to see you," he said.

"And I am glad to see you," Erik said. "It is so good to be home."

EPILOGUE
AUGUST 2003

Erik watched as the backhoe dumped the last of the fill into the yellow dump truck. The altar had been blown into a million pieces by the military, and now it was all being gathered up, collected, and shipped somewhere. Erik didn't know where, but he hoped it was somewhere safe. Knowing the military, it would wind up in a government lab somewhere where it would never be seen or heard of again. If you wanted to really lose something, he thought, just put it in a government file.

July had been the worst month of his life. His home had been turned into a battlefield. He'd lost his cat, and now had no desire for a new one. He'd lost his new friend, Johnny Dovecrest, whom he would have liked to have spent more time with. He had seen his wife and son tortured, and had endured the worst despair and torment that hell could possible dish out this side of judgment day. He'd seen more death, destruction, and anguish in just one short month than most people would see in two lifetimes.

He just hoped and prayed that it was over and that he could pull his life back together.

There had been some positive things, though. His daughter, Faith, was doing well. They hadn't intended naming her that, but somehow it seemed appropriate for what had happened. Faith the cat was in heaven, so it was time for a little more Faith on earth.

He had been to hell and back, but he'd also caught a glimpse of heaven, just a tiny, miniscule corner, but it had been enough. He knew that's where he belonged and where he wanted to be. He'd tried to explain the things he'd seen to Pastor Mark, but the words just wouldn't come. He couldn't describe the glow or the peace or the joy that had emanated through. Finally, he had given up trying.

"They have cats there," he said finally, as if that could capture it all. Mark was more of a dog lover, though, so Erik didn't think he would ever really understand until he went there for himself.

Erik smiled and waved at the truck driver as he backed up and pulled away. They'd planned to level this site completely and turn it into a nature walk and a bird sanctuary. This would be a small picnic site, a peaceful contrast to what it had stood for in the past. Erik didn't think he'd use it himself, but it would be nice to have other families come here and help mend the ground of this place.

Erik turned away and began the short walk home. Vickie and Todd and Faith were waiting for him. They were going to take a short vacation north, to the mountains in New Hampshire. After that, maybe he'd think about his next book.

ABOUT THE AUTHOR

JAMES ARTHUR ANDERSON currently teaches writing and literature at Johnson & Wales University's North Miami Campus at the rank of Professor. He holds a Ph.D. from the University of Rhode Island, where he specialized in horror and science fiction, and the work of H. P. Lovecraft. He is also an Adjunct Professor at Florida Memorial University, where he teaches creative writing and advanced literature.

His science fiction and fantasy stories have appeared in a number of magazines and anthologies, including *Horrors!: 365 Scary Stories*; *Weird Tales 4*; *Swords Against Darkness V*; *Fantasy Tales*, and others. He has also published poetry, nonfiction, and scholarly pieces, including *Out of the Shadows: A Structuralist Approach to Understanding the Fiction of H.P. Lovecraft*, also from The Borgo Press.

Dr. Anderson lives in South Florida with his wife Lynn, three spoiled cats, and two spoiled horses. In his free time he can be found target shooting at the Hollywood Rifle and Pistol Club, or riding his Paso Fino *Ilucion* ("Lucy") at Southwest Ranches Equestrian Club.